Susanna Gregory was a police officer in Leeds before taking up an academic career. She has served as an environmental consultant during seventeen field seasons in the polar regions, and has taught comparative anatomy and biological anthropology.

She is the creator of the Matthew Bartholomew series of mysteries set in medieval Cambridge as well as the Thomas Chaloner adventures in Restoration London, and now lives in Wales with her husband, who is also a writer.

Also by Susanna Gregory

# SUSANNA GREGORY

## The Executioner of St Paul's

sphere

SPHERE

First published in Great Britain in 2016 by Sphere
This paperback edition published in 2017 by Sphere

1 3 5 7 9 10 8 6 4 2

A CIP catalogue record for this book
is available from the British Library.

ISBN 978-0-7515-5284-3

Typeset in Baskerville MT by Palimpsest Book Production Limited,
Falkirk, Stirlingshire
Printed and bound in Great Britain by Clays Ltd, St Ives plc

Papers used by Sphere are from well-managed forests
and other responsible sources.

Sphere
An imprint of
Little, Brown Book Group
Carmelite House
50 Victoria Embankment
London EC4Y 0DZ

An Hachette UK Company
www.hachette.co.uk

www.littlebrown.co.uk

*For Pete Pritchard and Alan (Dick) Pritchard–*
*much loved and much missed*

Chaloner's London

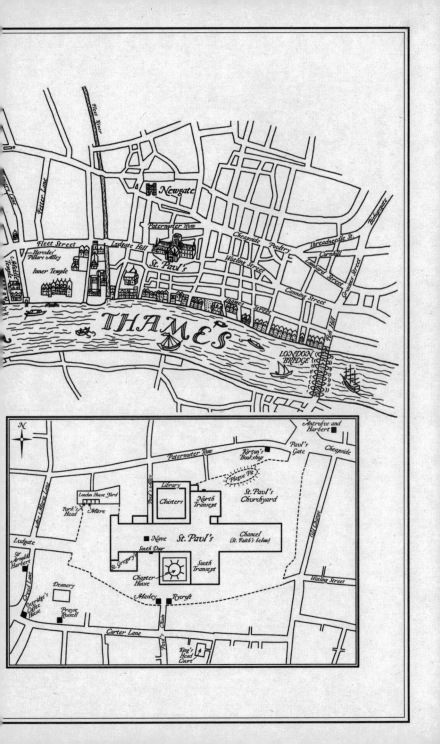

# Prologue

Sir Arnold Harbert hated Inigo Jones with a passion that verged on the fanatical. He did not care that the man was hailed as the greatest architect of his age, or that he was a favourite of the King. As far as Harbert was concerned Jones was the Devil Incarnate, put on Earth for the sole purpose of defiling all that was beautiful and holy.

St Paul's Cathedral was a magnificent building, but it cost a fortune to maintain, and time had taken its toll. There were cracks in its roof, its stonework was crumbling, and several walls were at angles never intended by its medieval builders. However, it was only when a lump of ceiling dropped on the high altar one Sunday that the Dean and Chapter finally accepted that something needed to be done. Their response had been to hire Inigo Jones.

Unfortunately, Jones's idea of sympathetic restoration was to slap Italianate façades over the crumbling sections, which jarred horribly with the Gothic elegance of the originals. Harbert had been appalled. He lived on Creed Lane, and it was difficult to ignore the 'improvements' when they were visible from all his windows. He objected vociferously, and most Londoners thought he was right. The King, on the other hand, declared that Jones had done a wonderful job, and urged him to continue.

Buoyed up by the royal encouragement, Jones next turned his attention to the cathedral's unstable west end, which he decided was in need of an enormous Classical portico. But there was a problem: the ancient parish church of St Gregory, which huddled against the cathedral's south-west corner like a child at its mother's skirts, was in the way. He was not about to let a lowly church interfere with his grand designs, so he began to tear it down. Outraged, its congregation took their grievances to Parliament, and the high-handed architect was ordered to put everything back as he had found it.

But by then war was in the air, and the King and his government were more interested in fighting each other than in repairing ancient monuments. St Gregory's was rebuilt and the portico hastily completed, but funds dried up for the rest of the cathedral. Harbert heaved a sigh of relief – his beloved St Paul's was safe again. Unfortunately, he had reckoned without Canon Robert Kerchier.

Kerchier was determined that Jones should finish what he had started, so he recruited a group of wealthy and influential individuals to bring it about – they jokingly called themselves the Agents of God. Harbert snorted his disgust. Agents of the Devil, more like, given that they aimed to destroy all that was old and venerable. He clenched his fists in impotent fury when he thought about the canon's smug face and irritating smile. How dare he inflict his passion for innovation on England's best-loved church!

Harbert pondered the Agents as he walked home one evening, feet crunching on the frost that had formed since dusk. They were an exclusive set, sworn to secrecy, but he knew the identities of a few. For a start, there were the Hall brothers, three selfishly ambitious vicars determined to rise high in the Church – which they might, if they made names for themselves by helping to 'save' St Paul's. Then there were Canons Stone and Owen, both too dim-witted to see the harm they were doing by supporting Jones's nasty schemes. And finally – the bitterest blow – there was Harbert's estranged brother Matthew, who had joined the Agents because he was young and stupid.

As Harbert crossed the churchyard, he saw some of the Agents walking to the cathedral for Evensong. Anger flared within him, and he fingered the sword at his side. How he would love to use it on them! Unfortunately, he was no warrior, and if he did whip out his blade to strike them down, he was more likely to hurt himself.

They were talking in low voices, but fell silent when they saw him. He wondered how they could bear to squander their money on Jones's nonsense, or why they trusted Kerchier to look after their donations, for that matter – the portly canon was devious and ruthless, and Harbert would not have trusted him with a penny.

Kerchier smirked as he passed, which made Harbert grind his teeth and tighten his grip on the sword. He could not slash them to pieces there and then, perhaps, but there would be other opportunities, and he was willing to wait – to strike them down one by one, carefully, neatly and secretly.

Filled with dark thoughts, Harbert stalked away into the night.

'I cannot abide that man,' said Kerchier, once he was sure the testy knight was out of earshot. 'He wants us stuck in the past for ever, clinging to silly traditions like sheep. Now is the time for reform, and we should seize new concepts with open hands.'

'I know what *I* should like to seize with open hands,' sniggered Canon Stone, stopping to ogle a young woman who was hurrying past, her head down against the icy wind.

'Not her, if you have an ounce of sense,' remarked Francis, the eldest of the Hall brothers. He was a dour man with a cap of neat black hair. 'That is Pamela Ball, one of the Seekers who has recently moved into London House Yard.'

'Seekers?' asked Stone, frowning. The civil wars had spawned such a profusion of new religious sects that it was difficult to keep track of them all. 'Is that the violently anti-clerical one, with members who will only pray in silence?'

Francis nodded. 'Although she will not stay silent if she sees you leering. She has a mouth like a trumpet, and will bray her indignation to the world – accusations that will be difficult to deny given your past . . . indiscretions.'

Hastily, Stone began walking again. 'I was only looking. If ladies do not want to be admired, they should stay indoors, where men cannot see them.'

Before Kerchier could tell him that such an attitude was hardly proper for a man of the Church, the middle Hall changed the subject. His name was William, and he was clever with finances – so clever that most Agents thought their money should be given to him to manage. William fully agreed, but Kerchier stubbornly refused to hand it over.

'It was an unwillingness to change that set Parliament against the King,' he declared. 'If His Majesty had been ready to make a few concessions, our fellow countrymen would not now be slaughtering each other.'

No one dared reply, as it was dangerous to voice that sort of opinion in a public place – the night was dark, and the cathedral cast deep shadows for eavesdroppers to lurk. Then the clerics reached the door, where Francis began to wrestle with the latch. Dust showered from the lintel as he did so, reminding them all of the building's parlous state.

'Our cathedral is more unstable than ever now that the parishioners of St Gregory's are digging themselves a crypt,' said Stone. He nodded towards the tiny parish church, which stood a few feet to his left. 'I appreciate that they need somewhere to bury their dead, but did they *have* to delve directly under our foundations?'

'Go on without me,' instructed Kerchier, as the door sprang open and his cronies began to file into the cathedral. 'I have a little business to attend in St Gregory's first.'

'If it is begging its vergers to dig in another direction, do not waste your time,' advised Stone. 'They will refuse. They have not yet forgiven us for letting Jones pull the place down, despite the fact that we have been forced to put it back up again.'

'Damn them!' spat William. 'Jones was right to demolish it, because his portico looked much nicer when there was no nasty St Gregory's to spoil its beautiful symmetry.'

A sly expression suffused Kerchier's face. 'Poor St Gregory's. It has never been very stable, and its vergers have done it a grave disservice by burrowing beneath it. It will probably collapse of its own accord soon. These things have a way of happening, as I am sure you know.'

'How do you—' began William, but his colleagues bundled him away before he could finish the question. It was another conversation that should only be held in private.

Kerchier waited until the door had closed behind them, then continued alone. He heard a peculiar slithering noise as he walked, but assumed it was a rat or a dog – nothing to concern him. However, when he reached St Gregory's he heard it again. He stopped and glanced around uneasily, but there was nothing to see, and the only sound was distant singing as Evensong began in St Paul's.

He shook himself irritably. It was easy to become anxious in these unsettled times, with King and Parliament forcing everyone to take sides – brother against brother, father against son. It was a wicked war, and he was appalled that so much money was being squandered on guns and troops, when it could have been used to rebuild St Paul's.

He entered St Gregory's, immediately aware of the scent of wet plaster and new wood. He grimaced angrily. What a waste of resources, and all because a few small-minded men were afraid of progress! Well, they were going to be in for a shock soon, because he had a plan that would see him triumph over the fools who clung to the past – a plan that would put London at the very forefront of all that was enlightened, modern and exciting.

\*

6

The following day, Kerchier did not appear for Morning Prayer. His friends were puzzled, but assumed that he was away raising money for their bulging coffers, a task that was taking ever more of his time. However, when he failed to attend Evensong as well, they grew uneasy, especially when it emerged that no one had seen him since he had gone into St Gregory's the previous night.

'What about the Agents' fund?' asked William worriedly, the only one brash enough to voice what they were all really thinking. 'Where does he keep it?'

No one knew. A quick search was made of Kerchier's house, and when that failed to locate the enormous sum they had amassed for Jones's reconstruction, they embarked on a hunt that saw floorboards torn up and holes hacked in the walls. But it was all to no avail: the hoard was nowhere to be found.

As days turned into weeks, and there was still no sign of Kerchier or the money, even his most steadfast friends were forced to concede that both had gone permanently.

'It is time we accepted that he is not coming back,' declared William at a meeting of cathedral staff some six months later. 'We cannot keep his post – his canonical stall – open indefinitely.'

'No, not indefinitely,' agreed the dean. 'But for thirty years. Only then can we appoint a replacement. The statutes are quite clear on that point.'

'The statutes!' spat William. Canons earned good livings, and he was tired of scraping by on a vicar's stipend. 'A set of outmoded laws that should have been abolished years ago.'

'They were written by wiser men than us,' said the dean with quiet dignity. 'So we shall abide by what they decree. No one will be nominated to Kerchier's stall until the full three decades have passed. Or that we have incontrovertible evidence that he is dead.'

'All this clinging to hoary customs is stupid,' hissed William to his brothers when the meeting was over and they were alone. 'St Paul's belongs to the future, not the past. It belongs to *us*.'

*Tunbridge Wells, September 1665*

Not for the first time since his appointment ten months earlier, William Sancroft wished he had never accepted the post of Dean of St Paul's. His canons were fractious and opinionated, his cathedral was falling to pieces, and to top it all, there was plague in the city. It had started with two or three cases in April, but was now claiming thousands of lives a week. Sancroft knew he should have stayed in London to comfort the sick and dying, but he was not brave enough. He had nominated a deputy and fled.

He stared at the letter in his hand. It was unsigned, but he knew who had sent it – years of teaching crafty undergraduates at the University of Oxford had made him adept at identifying handwriting. However, it was not the anonymous nature of the missive that bothered him. It was the content, which detailed a worrisome discovery.

But what could he do? He had no desire to return to London and investigate the matter himself, and he was not so craven as to ask someone else to do it for him. Yet nor could he do nothing, as ignoring the issue would make him look weak and indecisive. He half-wished the informant had kept his nasty news to himself, although he supposed he should be grateful that at least someone had taken the trouble to keep him informed.

8

'What is wrong, old friend?' asked the Earl of Clarendon kindly. He had come to Tunbridge Wells for the healing waters, and the two men had been enjoying a glass of claret together when the post had arrived.

'A body,' replied Sancroft unhappily. 'Found in a place where it should not have been. Duty dictates that I should return to the city and resolve the situation, but there were more than six thousand plague-deaths last week . . .'

'I heard,' said the Earl, and shuddered. 'Is it a matter you could delegate to Spymaster Williamson? He has investigated unwelcome corpses in the past.'

Sancroft sighed. 'Unfortunately, he is with the King in Oxford, and has no more intention of braving London than I do.'

The Earl considered for a moment. 'One of my gentleman ushers is good at solving mysteries, and he is usually discreet. Would you like to borrow him?'

Sancroft smiled his appreciation for the offer. 'It is good of you, but I cannot send a healthy man to that place of death. My conscience would never allow it.'

'Nonsense,' countered the Earl briskly. 'Chaloner will be delighted to help.'

Sancroft stared at him, moral objections receding fast as he realised that a solution to his problems might be to hand – and at no risk to himself. 'Will he?'

'Of course! He loves a challenge, and will jump at the chance to show off his talents. And do not worry about his safety – we shall give him plenty of medicine to ward off infection. London Treacle is said to be the best, although *sal mirabilis* is cheaper.'

Sancroft ignored the niggling voice at the back of his head that told him neither remedy worked – if they did, the plague would not have claimed so many victims. He became businesslike before the Earl could change his mind – which he well might, as there was a very real possibility that the retainer could die, and good staff did not grow on trees.

'In that case, summon him while I prepare the necessary paperwork,' he said crisply, reaching his pen.

'What paperwork?' asked the Earl, puzzled.

'A pass to get him through the city gates – you can no longer stroll in and out as you please, you know – and a writ authorising him to ask questions on my behalf. Assuming he is willing to approach strangers, of course – strangers who might have the plague.'

The Earl shivered again. 'This dreadful pestilence has spread to Colchester and Salisbury now. I blame General Monck and Mayor Lawrence, personally. They were told to make sure that did not happen – to keep the sickness in London, so that the rest of us would be spared.'

'It must be like trying to caulk a sieve,' said Sancroft, shaking his head at the enormity of the task. 'And I admire their courage. They are brave men, and I cannot find it in myself to criticise or condemn their efforts.'

'Did I tell you that Christopher Wren is also in Oxford with the King?' asked the Earl, disliking the censure implicit in Sancroft's remark, and so changing the subject before they quarrelled. It was too hot for an argument, and he was comfortable in his friend's airy parlour. 'They both want to tear down your cathedral and build another. Do you mind?'

Sancroft shrugged. 'They may do as they please. I have no strong feelings one way or the other, although my canons' opinions are deeply divided.'

'They squabble in Chapter meetings?' probed the Earl, who loved ecclesiastical gossip.

'Incessantly,' sighed Sancroft. 'Will you send for your man now? If he leaves today, he could be in London by Thursday. All I hope is that we are not sending him to his death.'

# Chapter 1

London was a city of ghosts. Gone was its habitual hubbub of bustle and noise, and in its place was an oppressive silence, broken only by the bells that tolled for the dead. The wharves that should have been thick with ships were empty, and even the mighty Thames seemed subdued, its flow reduced to a fraction of its normal size by weeks of drought.

Thomas Chaloner, spy to the Earl of Clarendon, reined in at the Southwark end of London Bridge. He was used to seeing it crammed with carts, coaches, horses and pedestrians, all vying for space and yelling their displeasure when there was not enough of it. That morning, the only living things were two pigeons, which stood preening in the middle of what had been one of the country's most hectic thoroughfares.

It was still early – not yet seven o'clock – but the day was already scorching, the sun beating down remorselessly from a cloudless blue sky. It had been hot in Tunbridge Wells, too, but cooling breezes had wafted in from the

13

surrounding fields, carrying with them the clean scent of ripe crops. Here, the air was still, dusty and foul, full of the stink of death and uncollected rubbish.

A fortified gatehouse stood at the entrance to the bridge, presenting a wall of solid oak and stone to would-be travellers. Above it were spikes bearing the heads of traitors, so that a forest of skulls grinned down as Chaloner pressed his heels into his horse's sides and began to ride forward. He had the uncomfortable sense that they were laughing at him for the folly on which he was about to embark.

'What do you want?' came a suspicious voice from one of the gun loops.

'I have business in the city,' Chaloner called back.

He watched as the left-hand door was pulled ajar to reveal two guards. One wore a scarf over his face to ward off infection, while the other had donned a plague mask with a long 'beak'. They were not alone – he sensed unseen eyes watching from various vantage points, and had no doubt that their owners had muskets primed and ready.

'You cannot pass,' the scarfed man declared, although he peered at the letter Chaloner handed him – the one Dean Sancroft had written two days before, appointing Chaloner as his official envoy. 'The only thing that lies over this bridge is death.'

'And the poor,' added the second, his voice muffled through the mask. 'The rich fled weeks ago, and the only folk left now are those with nowhere else to go.'

'Return home,' urged the first, firmly but kindly. 'Only drunks, fools or madmen cross the river these days.'

'Or those with orders to follow,' said Chaloner, nodding to the missive.

The fellow handed it back with a shrug that expressed exactly what he thought of such stupidity. 'As you wish. However, if you live long enough to want to leave again, make sure that you have enough money to buy a Certificate of Health.'

'A Certificate of Health?' queried Chaloner.

'A document signed by a priest and a physician, stating that you are free of the sickness,' explained the second. 'Because you will not be allowed out without one. And they are expensive. *Very* expensive.'

'So is food,' put in the first grimly. 'It is in short supply over there, because no one wants to trade with a disease-ravaged city, and who can blame them? Even coins soaked in vinegar may not be safe, and farmers are unwilling to risk it.'

The gate was pulled open just wide enough to let Chaloner pass, after which it was slammed shut again, setting up a hollow boom that reverberated through the abandoned buildings beyond. The horse shied, and Chaloner leaned forward to pat its neck reassuringly, although the truth was that he was also unsettled. The bridge was eerie without the rattle of wheels, hoofs and feet, and he could not even hear the comfortingly familiar roar of water thundering through the arches below, as the river was too sluggish to make a noise.

When he reached the other end of the bridge, unseen hands unfastened a second gate to let him pass, although there was no acknowledgement of his shouted thanks. He rode on, up Fish Street Hill, dismayed to see that weeds had grown between the cobblestones because there was not enough traffic to keep them clear. When he reached the junction with Thames Street, he stopped for a moment to take stock of his surroundings.

Wooden houses with tiled roofs stood all around him, many with stark red crosses painted on their doors. Looming over them all was the lofty bulk of St Paul's Cathedral, strong, massive and timeless, although there were cracks in its central tower and patches of moss on its roof. Yet despite the unnerving stillness, there was still life in the city. Shadows flickered as people scurried in the smaller streets, faces prudently covered, and there was even a hackney carriage touting for business outside All Hallows the Great.

A little further on, Chaloner saw a dozen folk queuing outside a fishmongery, the sign above which read *Godfrey Wildbore, Purveyor of Fyne Fisshe, Fresh, Dryed and Salted*. The fishmonger looked uncannily like the animal that shared his name: he had an unusually hairy face, a snoutish nose, and dark, glittering eyes.

'But I do not know when my next delivery might be,' he was declaring, half helpless and half defensive. 'Fishermen refuse to trade with me. I show them my Certificate of Health, to prove I am free of the plague, but they are too frightened to come near my—'

'Candles!' came an excited yell from up the road. 'A penny each!'

It was criminally expensive for so basic a commodity, but Wildbore's customers raced away to investigate regardless, leaving the fishmonger alone with his empty marble slabs. He shuffled disconsolately back inside his shop, and closed the door.

Chaloner rode on, wishing Sancroft had chosen someone else to do his dirty work, because he did not feel easy in this strange, sullen, unfamiliar London. Of course, he doubted it had been the dean's idea to send him there – he suspected he had the Earl to thank for that.

His relationship with his employer was ambiguous. On the one hand, the Earl was proud of Chaloner's investigative skills, and never missed an opportunity to show them off to his friends. On the other, Chaloner had backed the 'wrong' side during the civil wars – he had fought for Parliament and then worked for Cromwell's intelligence services – which the Earl could not bring himself to forget or forgive. As a result, Chaloner was regularly given assignments that were demeaning, peculiar or sometimes downright dangerous.

He had an unpleasant feeling that Sancroft's mission was going to fall into the last category, because the dean had been suspiciously reluctant to answer basic questions – such as why the discovery of a body in St Gregory's Church should have so alarmed him, and who had written to tell him about it. It was frustrating, as Chaloner knew he would find out anyway, and Sancroft's cooperation would have saved time – which *was* of the essence, because Chaloner was determined not to spend one minute longer than necessary in the hot, reeking, filthy pit of disease that was currently London.

A short while later, Chaloner stood in St Gregory's undercroft, staring at a skeleton. The bones were black, dry and dusty, and although no expert on such matters, he could tell that their owner had been dead for a very long time. He glanced questioningly at the vicar, Ralph Masley, a skinny, bald man with asymmetrical eyes – one black, one blue – who had only reluctantly dragged himself from his paper-laden desk to conduct him to the 'body'.

'This particular vault should have been empty,' explained Masley. 'It was built for Sir Arnold Harbert, you see, on the understanding that he alone would occupy it when he died. But when the verger opened it up at dawn on Sunday . . .'

Chaloner did some quick calculations. It was Thursday morning now, which meant the skeleton had been found exactly four days before. 'When did Harbert die?'

'Saturday. But my verger says that whoever these bones belong to must have died at least twenty years ago, because that is when this particular pit was last open.'

Chaloner looked around him. He and Masley were in a huge, cool cellar with a barrel-vaulted ceiling and a bewildering number of interlinking aisles. Its walls were brick, and its floor made of paved slabs, which could be lifted up to provide burial spaces beneath. Coffins of various sizes and states of decay were stacked in recesses along the walls.

Sir Arnold Harbert's marble-lined vault had pride of place beneath the chancel. It comprised a large rectangular hole, ten feet deep, eight feet wide and twelve feet long. The skeleton lay at the bottom, an untidy sprawl of bones, partly covered by cloth.

'Do you know of anyone who went missing twenty years ago?' asked Chaloner.

'I have only been in post for six months,' replied Masley. 'But I assume they belong to a drunken pauper, who fell in before the hole was sealed. I recommend we put Harbert's coffin on top of him and say no more about it. Then I shall be spared a lot of inconvenience and you can go back to the safety of Tunbridge Wells.'

'We cannot,' said Chaloner, although the offer was seriously tempting. 'Dean Sancroft wants to know who he is and how he came to be here.'

Masley's eyebrows shot up. 'He expects you to unearth

that after all this time? How? By communing with the dead?'

'With the living, preferably. There must be someone left who can enlighten me.'

'Twenty years is a long time,' harrumphed Masley. 'And even if there are witnesses who can oblige, they will not be in the city – they will have fled, to escape the plague. Sancroft's demands are unreasonable.'

Chaloner was inclined to agree. 'Harbert,' he said, indicating the fancy casket that stood behind them. 'How did *he* die? Plague?'

'Wounds,' replied Masley, pursing his lips disapprovingly. 'He fought a fellow named Tam Denton, and that was the end of him. It was wicked to throw away his life so recklessly when everyone else is struggling to survive. Myself included.'

'You are brave to have stayed,' said Chaloner, aware that many clerics had been among the first to go.

'I am,' agreed Masley loftily, then grimaced. 'Although the truth is that I have no choice. St Gregory's is a plum appointment, and there are vicars galore who itch to leap into my pulpit. Well, they will wait in vain, because I am not abandoning the job that took me so long to win.'

'Unless you die of plague,' muttered Chaloner, although too low for the man to hear.

'Who was the interfering busybody who blabbed to the dean about these bones, by the way? An official investigation is a nuisance for a busy man like me – I have seven funerals today alone. And as my clerk is dead, I have his duties to perform, as well as my own.'

'The letter was anonymous.'

'The coward! Meanwhile, his tattling creates extra

work for me, and puts you in danger. Why is Sancroft interested in a few mouldering bones anyway? Surely a single, ancient corpse cannot matter when we are burying hundreds of new ones every day?'

'It makes no sense,' acknowledged Chaloner. 'But perhaps all will become clear once I learn more about the victim.'

'*If* you learn more about the victim. I told you – I doubt there is anyone left who can answer questions, and you will almost certainly return to Tunbridge Wells empty-handed. Assuming you do not die of disease first, of course.'

'If I did, Sancroft would just appoint a replacement.' Chaloner was under no illusion that he was indispensable. 'Has the skeleton been moved since it was discovered?'

Masley glared at him. 'Of course not! Who has time to meddle with old bones? What you see now is exactly what my verger found on Sunday. I just wish we had dumped Harbert on top of them at the time. Then you and I would not be having this conversation.'

'So why didn't you?'

'Because the verger gossiped about the discovery to his friends, and then the whole parish was awash with the news – which is why everything must now go through official channels. And I am sure you can imagine how time-consuming *that* will be!'

Chaloner knew enough of Restoration bureaucracy to guess. 'Are you sure there is no one left who can talk to me? The sooner I learn what Sancroft wants to know, the sooner I will be gone from under your feet.'

Masley was silent for a moment, thinking. 'I suppose Canon Owen might help, if he is sober. Shall I fetch him?'

*

Once Masley had gone, Chaloner explored the crypt on his own. According to Sancroft, it had been dug because Inigo Jones – the cantankerous architect in charge of repairing St Paul's before the wars – had thoughtlessly built over St Gregory's graveyard, leaving the parishioners with nowhere to bury their dead. In revenge, they had started to dig themselves an undercroft – one that just happened to run directly beneath the cathedral's already precarious foundations. Outmanoeuvred, the Dean and Chapter had hastily conceded defeat, and had donated a patch of land for them to use as a cemetery instead. The excavating had stopped, and church and cathedral had settled into an uneasy truce.

The crypt really was huge, thought Chaloner, as he wandered through its myriad chambers and aisles with a lamp. The silence was absolute, and he had an uncomfortable sense of the great, crushing weight of the cathedral above his head. It was disconcerting, and he was seized by a sudden urge to bolt.

To take his mind off it, he stopped to admire an unusually elaborate tomb, which stood near the steps that provided the crypt's only access. It was much older than its surroundings, so he supposed it had been dismantled and rebuilt there. When he read its inscription, he understood why: it was the final resting place of the scandalous Countess of Devonshire, famous for her extramarital affairs. He supposed the Puritans had stuck her down there, out of sight and mind, lest her exuberant monument reminded people of all the fun she had had in her unashamedly merry life.

When he had finished prowling, and Masley had still not returned, Chaloner went to look at the skeleton again.

A ladder leaned against a nearby wall, so he lowered it into the pit and climbed down.

The bones were mostly covered by a dark cloak, with a skull poking from under the top of it and a pair of feet – still wearing shoes – sticking out of the bottom. All were surprisingly well preserved, which he attributed to the crypt's cold, dry air. There was still hair on the skull, and desiccated skin adhered to the face and ankles. He lifted the material to see that the body lay on its side, with one arm caught beneath it and its legs askew.

He inspected the clothes first, amazed that they should be in such good condition – and grateful for it, as it would make identification just that little bit easier. There was a round black cap of the kind worn by clerics, while the breeches, shirt and cloak also suggested that the victim had been in holy orders. Astonishingly, there was a political broadsheet folded up in one pocket, and although it fell apart as Chaloner unfurled it, he was still able to make out most of the words. Perhaps most important for his purposes was that it had a date – the first day of March, 1645.

Then he turned his attention to the bones themselves. Several indentations on the back of the skull were indicative of blows to the head. Their location was such that they could not have been self-inflicted, while the position of the body made it unlikely that the damage had occurred during its descent into the vault. There was only one other possibility: someone had come up behind the victim and hit him multiple times – which meant that Dean Sancroft was right to order an investigation into what had happened.

Not long after, Masley arrived with a man in his mid fifties, who had probably once been handsome, but who had allowed himself to go to seed with drink and high living, so that his face was sallow, his eyes were bloodshot and his hands shook. He wore clothes that marked him as a cathedral canon – garments similar to those on the skeleton. Masley introduced him as Richard Owen, before turning to hurry away again.

'Close the door behind you when you leave,' he called over his shoulder when he reached the door. 'If you need me, I shall be working at home.'

And then he was gone.

'I have not dared look,' said Owen without preamble, red-rimmed eyes fixed on Chaloner, who was still inside the vault. 'I know it is cowardly, but . . . Is it him?'

'Is it whom?' asked Chaloner.

'Robert Kerchier.' Owen wrung his hands in agitation. 'The canon who disappeared twenty years ago, and whose fate has remained a mystery ever since. He was last seen – by me and several friends – entering this very church.'

'Do you remember what he was wearing?'

'What we all wear – black cloak, breeches and cap, and a plain white shirt. But perhaps more useful for the purposes of identification is that he was missing two fingers on his left hand.'

'An accident?' Chaloner crouched by the bones and inspected them closely.

'Gunpowder,' replied Owen, and when the spy glanced up in surprise, added, 'Kerchier disappeared during the civil wars.'

'He was a combatant?'

'No, but that did not keep him – or any of us – safe from danger. I once suffered a very nasty bruise when someone lobbed a *Book of Common Prayer* at me.'

As sinews and leathery skin still held the hand together,

23

it was easy to determine that two fingers had indeed gone. The skeleton was Kerchier without question. While Owen turned away to compose himself after hearing the news, Chaloner wrapped the bones in the cloak and carried them up the ladder.

'You say Kerchier vanished after coming to visit St Gregory's?' Chaloner asked, laying them carefully on the floor. 'Two decades ago?'

Owen nodded unhappily. 'On the first day of March – the Feast of St David, which I remember because I am Welsh. The year was the same as the one in which poor Archbishop Laud was beheaded.'

Chaloner glanced at the broadsheet he had taken from Kerchier's pocket. The date was the same, which was encouraging. Perhaps the case would not be so difficult to solve after all, given that he already had the victim's name, a probable cause of death, and the time when it was likely to have happened.

'Did no one look down here for him? Sancroft told me that this crypt was a work in progress two decades ago, so it should have been an obvious place to search.'

'Of course we did,' replied Owen shortly, dabbing at his eyes. 'However, we did not lever the lids off the vaults. Why would we? None of us had any reason to believe that Kerchier was dead.'

'No?' fished Chaloner. 'Why not?'

'Because of the money – a great chest of it – which had been raised for rebuilding the cathedral. Kerchier looked after it for us, and when he disappeared, so did it.' Owen stepped forward to peer hopefully into the vault. 'I do not suppose it was down there as well, was it?'

'As far as I know, there was just the skeleton.'

Owen sighed, his eyes distant as he reflected on the past. 'Kerchier vanishing with the money was a tremendous scandal, causing a massive uproar and much avid speculation, which is why I recall it so vividly and why others will, too. We fended off the accusations for a while, but eventually even his friends assumed that he had made off with it.'

'Including you?'

Owen hung his head. 'Yes, God forgive me. But he was innocent all along! It is obvious now what happened – thieves killed him for the money.'

'Who else knew about the chest?'

Owen shrugged. 'All of London. It was no secret.'

'Do you have any suspects for the crime?'

'Yes – three hundred thousand of them, which is how many people were living in the city at the time. We are talking about a *lot* of cash here, Chaloner – a sum beyond the wildest dreams of avarice, which would pose a tempting target to even the most virtuous of men.'

'So you think that whoever killed Kerchier also stole the chest?'

'It stands to reason, given that they both vanished on the same night.'

'It is not possible that someone else witnessed the murder, then hurried to take advantage of the fact that the money was left unguarded? Two culprits, rather than one?'

'I suppose so,' acknowledged Owen. 'And Kerchier did have lots of enemies. He was a controversial figure, who thought the cathedral should be demolished and something more worthy built in its place. Naturally, not everyone agreed.'

Then nothing had changed, thought Chaloner wryly.

25

Some folk still itched to replace the old cathedral with something new and different. Personally, he liked it the way it was, and was appalled by the designs for its replacement. The most recent involved a dome instead of the mighty central tower, and a lot of Italianate cupolas, which he thought would look very peculiar in the midst of a medieval city.

'*Everyone* has opinions about what should be done,' Owen went on. 'Even you, I imagine. It boils down to one question: should we repair a crumbling ruin, a project that may not succeed and that will cost a fortune; or should we knock it down and start again, an option that may ultimately be cheaper?'

'Both schemes have their merits,' hedged Chaloner, not about to reveal what he really thought to a man he did not know.

'Well, I sided with Kerchier,' said Owen. 'I still do. St Paul's was on the verge of collapse then, and the intervening years have only made it worse. It will fall about our ears unless we do something soon.'

'Where did Sir Arnold Harbert stand?'

'Oh, he hated Kerchier with a passion,' replied Owen promptly, then gaped as the implications of his reply dawned on him. 'Did *he* kill Kerchier and put him down here, knowing the truth would remain concealed until it could no longer hurt him?'

'It would make sense, but I did not know either man, so what do you think?'

Owen considered carefully. 'It is possible. Yet Harbert was such a feeble fellow, and I find it hard to see him as a coldly calculating murderer.'

'Feeble? I understood he was killed in a fight.'

'He was,' acknowledged Owen. 'Which astonished all

26

those who knew him. He was quarrelsome certainly, and an opinionated ass, but he had never been violent before.'

'Was Kerchier involved in any other contentious schemes?'

'No – the cathedral was his life, and he did not have the time or the inclination to involve himself in anything else. His murder will be connected to his plans for it – or the money he had amassed to see them through. You can be sure of that.'

'Then I shall need a list of all the people who were touched by his machinations,' said Chaloner. 'Supporters and opponents, living and dead.'

'My word!' gulped Owen, daunted. 'That is a tall order! Two decades is a long time, and while I recall his disappearance clearly, my memories of other events are hazy . . .'

'Is there no one who can help you? You did say that the Kerchier affair was a great scandal at the time – so great that it will be indelibly etched in many minds.'

'True,' conceded Owen. 'But it will take some serious pondering, even so. Come to the Deanery tomorrow morning. I will try to have it ready by then.'

'Thank you. Did Kerchier have a family? Or any particular friends?'

'Just us, his cathedral colleagues.'

'I want to speak to the verger who opened the vault. Do you know him?'

'His name is Gaundy and he lives near the Poultry. Interviewing him is a good idea, actually, because *he* built this crypt – he was once a mason, and his father was verger here before him. He knows it better than anyone. But before you go, tell me who wrote to the dean. There was no need to bother Sancroft with this matter.'

27

'The letter was unsigned.'

Owen's expression hardened. 'Only sly rogues hide behind anonymity.'

Chaloner raised his eyebrows. 'You think Sancroft should be left in the dark about a canon who was murdered and stuffed in someone else's tomb?'

'Sancroft!' spat Owen. 'What does he care? He will not even say whether he favours a new cathedral or repairing the old one. And where is he now? Leading us in our hour of need? No! He appointed a deputy and fled to the safety of the countryside. He did not even come to see these bones for himself, but sent you instead.'

'Is he the only cathedral official to have left the city?'

'I am sorry to say that twenty-four of our thirty canons followed his cowardly example, and so did most of the staff. Tillison – Sancroft's deputy – is forced to make do with five canons, two vicars and Bing, who copies music for the choir. Or he did, when we had one.'

'You stayed on here out of duty?' Chaloner tried not to sound sceptical.

'And because I do not want decisions about the cathedral's future made in my absence,' admitted Owen. 'As I said, everyone has opinions about St Paul's, and when better to act on them then when most of its officials are hiding from the plague?'

The cathedral occupied a large swathe of land known as St Paul's Churchyard, which it shared with two cloisters, a library, the Deanery, a school, various halls and service rooms, and houses for its clerics. It was bordered by Paternoster Row in the north, Carter Lane in the south, Old Change in the east, and Creed and Ave Maria lanes in the west.

28

The area had once been much bigger, but bits had been parcelled off to developers over the years, usually to raise quick cash for emergency repairs. Other sections had been built over by tradesmen, who had set up shop illegally, but who paid a percentage of their profits to the Dean and Chapter in lieu of rent. Most of these premises were now abandoned, either because their owners were dead or because they had nothing left to sell.

But it was the northern part of the precinct that held the sorriest sight – the enormous plague pit. It was a vast oblong, wide enough for four corpses to lie head to toe, and long enough for a hundred side by side. It had been dug very deep, as attested by the towering mound of excavated earth that stood to one side, but the dead were so numerous that it was close to overflowing. The foul reek of death was in the air, and fat flies were in such profusion that their buzzing was louder than the tolling bells. Masked workmen toiled around its edges, while dead-carts came and went in a never-ending procession, emptying their grim cargoes before trundling off to collect more.

Chaloner was glad to step through Paul's Gate – one of the churchyard's eight entrances – and out on to Cheapside. Cheapside was one of the city's widest and busiest thoroughfares, but there was barely a soul on it that morning. It was also devoid of cats and dogs, because the authorities, in their desperation, had decreed that these were responsible for spreading the plague. They had been slaughtered in their thousands, and in their place were rats, so bold that they scuttled openly along roads that had once thronged with people.

As he walked, Chaloner thought about Kerchier,

although more to take his mind off the city's torment than because he had much to ponder. How long would Owen's list of 'suspects' be? He hoped it would not name every person in London at the time of the murder, as then the crime would likely never be solved. Of course, even if Owen was sensible about who to include, it was possible that Kerchier's killer might be dead himself by now.

It was a pity, he thought, that the Earl of Clarendon had been visiting Sancroft when the news had arrived. It was the sort of investigation that should have been passed to Spymaster Williamson. Of course, Williamson had not lingered long in the city once the disease had taken hold. He had hastily decanted to Kent and then Oxford, where he devoted all his time to gathering intelligence on the Dutch, with whom the country was currently at war. Chaloner imagined he was delighted that Holland posed such imminent danger, as it allowed him to claim he was too busy to help London deal with the plague.

Chaloner reached the Poultry, where business had at least a semblance of normality, albeit on a small scale. Squawks, clucks and honks filled the air, along with the hot stench of soiled straw and droppings. Tightly packed cages were stacked in the sun, an act of thoughtless cruelty that both angered and sickened Chaloner, while in nearby Scalding Alley, hissing boilers were going full pelt to remove feathers and entrails.

Beyond this was the market proper, where trade had always been brisk and noisy. There was a different atmosphere there that day, though. At first, he assumed it was simple fear of the plague – most folk kept their faces covered, and any coins that did change hands were carefully dunked in vinegar first. Next, he decided that the problem lay in the fact that there was very little for sale, which resulted in wildly inflated prices and a lot of understandable resentment. However, he finally realised that the real source of the unease could be attributed to several rough men who wore green ribbons tied around their arms.

At first, these men just watched, although from vantage points that made their presence very obvious, and more than one anxious glance was cast in their direction. Then they began to mingle, which caused consternation among sellers and buyers alike. One vendor was marched behind his stall, emerging a few minutes later minus his purse and with blood dripping from his nose.

Chaloner was disgusted but not surprised. Crises like the plague were always a boon to profiteers, who leapt to capitalise on the misery of others. It was unscrupulous and dishonest, and he could only suppose that those in authority had more serious problems to manage than the selfish antics of criminals.

He reached the end of the market and was just deliberating how best to locate the verger's house when he saw that a small crowd had gathered outside a mansion just north of Cornhill. The house was quietly elegant, and boasted an ornate façade with a first-floor balcony. It was the home of the current Lord Mayor of London, Sir John Lawrence, who could be seen stepping on to his veranda in a way that suggested he was about to make a speech. Intrigued, Chaloner went to hear what he had to say.

The King had not abandoned his capital without some thought of how his subjects were to be governed during

31

his absence, and he had appointed two men to rule in his name. General Monck had been given the metropolis, while Lawrence had the city. Their remit was twofold: to ensure the sick did not leave London to infect other places; and to implement the 'plague measures' that would contain and then eradicate the outbreak.

Lawrence had been elected mayor the previous September, although Chaloner was sure he wished he had picked a better time to stand. He was a tall, handsome man in his forties, whose burgundy-coloured clothes were rich without being showy. He was known for condemning the excesses of Court – for which most Londoners loved him – and had supported Parliament during the wars. He had made his fortune as a merchant, and was one of the richest men in the country.

Standing next to him was George Monck, who had played a major role in restoring the monarchy after the collapse of the Commonwealth. In return, the King had created him Duke of Albemarle and claimed to love him like a father. He was a large, florid-faced Scot with a warrior's bearing, who was known for blunt speaking – which everyone knew was a tactful way of saying that he was rude, opinionated and abrasive.

'Monck is right,' Lawrence was assuring his listeners earnestly. 'These street fires *are* necessary, because without them, the plague will overwhelm us.'

'*Will* overwhelm us?' drawled a cathedral canon, who eschewed the current fashion for wigs and wore his short black hair uncovered. Chaloner overheard someone mutter that his name was William Hall. 'It *has* overwhelmed us, and we die like flies. Last week's Mortality Bill was more than sixty-five hundred – the highest yet.'

'It will grow higher still without the fires,' growled

Monck unpleasantly. 'So you should thank God that I command soldiers who are brave enough to light them. If it was up to me, I would let you all die, which would serve you right for being an ungrateful horde.'

A startled murmur of indignation rippled through the crowd.

'He jests,' said Lawrence hastily, shooting Monck a warning glance. 'Now, I appreciate that lots of thick smoke will be uncomfortable in the heat, but our plague measures *are* working. They—'

'They are not!' cried a crook-backed apprentice. 'Nothing you do makes any difference – locking the sick inside their houses, washing the roads with lime, closing the theatres, banning large gatherings of people . . .'

'Of course they have made a difference,' countered Lawrence, all sincere passion. 'You standing there proves it.'

'It does?' asked the lad warily.

'You are alive, are you not? You are not lying dead in a pit?'

'Clearly not. But—'

'You are here because we have all united against a common enemy,' Lawrence went on ardently. 'Noble Londoners will not be defeated by a mere disease. Will we?'

'No!' cried one or two folk, while Chaloner noted that several more stood a little taller or nodded agreement. The mayor knew exactly how to win them to his side – unlike Monck, who oozed contempt. Lawrence continued to encourage and cajole, until most of his listeners were in a more receptive mood, then gestured to a man in the street below.

'I bought more copies of *The Plague's Approved Physitian*,

33

and my secretary Cary will give one free of charge to anyone who will read it and act on its very sensible advice.'

'Which is more than they deserve,' muttered Monck, although he had a naturally loud voice and his hostile words carried. 'You should save your money, Lawrence, and—'

'The book outlines all the precautions you can take in your own homes,' Lawrence went on, quickly cutting across him. 'Such as taking *sal mirabilis* before going out, and wearing masks.'

'And if I see any more copies thrown on the ground and trampled on,' put in Monck darkly, 'I shall ferret out the culprits and hang—'

'Hang plague-repelling herbs around their necks,' put in Lawrence loudly and firmly. 'Herbs like alehoof, scabious and tormentil.'

While he expanded on his list of worthy botanicals, his secretary moved among the crowd, handing out pamphlets. Cary was a compact, wiry fellow of about forty. He had gingery grey hair, a short beard and skin that looked as though he spent too much time outdoors. He could have smiled at the folk who accepted the books, but he scowled instead, giving Chaloner the impression that he was one of those people who enjoyed being in a perpetually bad temper.

Chaloner took the copy that Cary shoved ungraciously into his hands, and flicked through it while Lawrence continued to woo the crowd with honeyed words.

The treatise was not very long, although it had an impressively full title: *The Plague's Approved Physitian, Shewing the Naturall Causes of the Infection of the Ayre, and of the Plague. With divers Observations to Bee Used, Preserving from the Plague, and Signes to Know the Infected Therewith. Also Many True and Approved Medicines for the Perfect Cure Thereof. Chiefly a Godly and Penitent Prayer Unto Almighty God, for Our Preservation, and Deliverance Therefrom.*

It told him nothing new, and merely reiterated the advice that had been trotted out when the outbreak had first started – to smoke as often as possible, to hang a dead toad around the neck at the first hint of fever, to light a dish of brimstone every night, and to buy a decent lucky charm. And if all that failed, pray.

'The pestilence is the Quakers' fault,' the apprentice yelled suddenly, a comment that drew nods from those who heard it, including Monck. 'They insist on visiting each other when they are infected, and they will only be buried in pits of their own choosing. They are a menace.'

'They are, and I should like to hang them all,' stated Monck matter-of-factly. 'But there are too many of them.'

'Just you try it, you miserable Scotch dog!' bawled a woman whose clothes suggested she was a member of that beleaguered sect, although her feisty response was at odds with their creed of gentle passivity. 'God will strike you down and good riddance!'

'The Lord is more likely to kill *you*,' retorted Monck, nettled. 'Because if everyone was a good Anglican, there would be no plague.'

This particular opinion achieved what Lawrence could not: raising Monck in the crowd's estimation. There was a cheer from the conformist majority, and the woman prudently made herself scarce. It seemed the antagonism was over – until the apprentice spoke out again.

'So what about food?' he demanded. 'There has been no bread for a week now.'

'Or ale,' called someone else. 'We are reduced to drinking water. Or worse yet milk.'

There followed a chorus of complaints detailing the disgraceful lack of flour, meat, cheese, butter, vegetables, candles, coffee, soap and a host of other items that were once freely available.

'Either take control of the markets or I am going shopping in Chelsey and damn the consequences,' declared the apprentice challengingly. He pulled a document from his pocket – a tawdry thing on cheap paper. 'I can do it – I have a Certificate of Health here, signed by a physician and a priest.'

But Canon William Hall had something to say about that. He happened to be standing near the lad, and Chaloner saw him do a double-take before snatching the document away.

'You are not Samuel Pepys,' he declared, crumpling it into a ball and tossing it on the ground, much to the apprentice's dismay. 'You need a *valid* permit if you intend to leave.'

'You do,' agreed Monck, eyes flashing dangerously. 'And anyone presenting forgeries to my soldiers will be strung up.'

There was a growl of outrage at this remark, while Chaloner thought that Monck used the threat of execution rather too freely. At that point, Lawrence sprang up on to the rail that surrounded his balcony, where he balanced rather precariously. The yelling faltered into astonished silence, as people gazed at the unusual sight of a wealthy merchant bouncing about like a monkey.

'Good people of London,' he cried, raising his hands in appeal. 'No more fighting talk, I beg you. We all want the same thing: to survive this visitation without passing it to others. So let us work together to see it done.'

By the time he had finished explaining how, everyone had calmed down again, and when they eventually began to disperse, it was peacefully. Monck turned on his heel and stamped inside the house, appearing moments later on the street, where his horse and a gaggle of soldiers were waiting. He was chewing tobacco, and when he saw the opinionated apprentice, he spat a stream of brown juice that hit the lad squarely between the eyes.

A number of paupers lingered after the bulk of the horde had gone, and Lawrence's secretary began dispensing alms. He greeted most by name, and as he seemed to know so many locals, Chaloner went to ask him where Gaundy lived.

'The verger of St Gregory's?' asked Cary suspiciously. 'Why? Has he been shirking his duties again?' He shook his head. 'Yet I do not blame him – it cannot be pleasant to dig graves all day. He was once a master mason, but was forced to become a verger after the Restoration – the price of supporting the Commonwealth.'

Chaloner knew all about the perils of having chosen the 'wrong' side in the wars. 'It can he hard,' he said ruefully.

'For some,' acknowledged Cary, then gave a smug smile. 'But not for me. I was fortunate enough to fall in with Lawrence, and it all worked out rather well.'

'You fought for Parliament?' asked Chaloner, envying him for being employed by a man who shared his politics.

'With Cromwell himself,' replied Cary with undisguised pride. 'Much to my family's consternation. My uncle was Valentine Cary, you see, and I was named after him.'

'Oh,' said Chaloner, then felt compelled to ask, 'Who is Valentine Cary?'

Cary was clearly offended. 'How can you not know that? He was once Dean of St Paul's, and is buried in the cathedral. He was a loyal servant of the Crown, hence my family's shock when I rode off with Cromwell.' He looked Chaloner up and down critically. 'But what about you? You do not appear to be old enough to have fought, but some families sent boys to war.'

Chaloner had indeed been hauled from his studies to join the New Model Army, and had almost lost his life, aged fifteen, at the Battle of Naseby, when a cannon had exploded next to him. However, he was not in the habit of discussing his past with strangers, so he merely smiled and explained why he wanted to speak to Gaundy. After all, there was no harm in the Lord Mayor's staff knowing about an investigation in their city.

'Then I pity you,' said Cary when Chaloner had finished. 'The crime will be impossible to solve after all these years. Sancroft cannot care about your welfare or he would not have let you come.'

'The same might be said of you and Lawrence,' retorted Chaloner, nettled by the man's presumption. 'You have just spent an hour moving through a crowd on his behalf, and any one of them might have the plague.'

'They might,' acknowledged Cary stiffly. 'But I know my duty – which is to serve him and his family, and repay them for the trust and kindness they have shown me all these years. Have you met his wife yet? Abigail is a very remarkable person.'

There was something in his voice that made Chaloner glance sharply at him, noting the wistful gleam in his eyes and how his glance kept straying to the balcony, presumably in the hope of catching a glimpse of the lady in question.

'I have not yet had the pleasure.'

Cary's expression was oddly dreamy. 'I am sure your paths will cross soon, because she is as bold and noble as her husband in her efforts to help the city.'

'Does she tend the sick?' asked Chaloner, knowing that some women had undertaken that dangerous work as an act of Christian charity.

'She and Lawrence do not enter plague houses – on my advice,' said Cary, a little defensively. 'But they walk through the streets without masks, so that folk can see them. If anyone can save London in her hour of need, it is Abigail and John Lawrence.'

'And Monck, presumably.'

Cary snorted to express his opinion of that notion. 'He protects buildings – White Hall, Westminster Palace, the exchanges, the Bridge. He cares nothing for people, and I suspect that he wishes we would all die, so that the plague will burn itself out.'

Chaloner nodded down the road, where a lout with a green arm-ribbon had grabbed a woman and was muttering in her ear; she looked terrified. 'Then Londoners are besieged from all sides – Monck from without, and profiteers from within.'

Cary winced. 'We do our best to stamp out such practices, but as soon as we crush one rogue, two more appear in his place. All we can do is provide the poor with money to buy what they need to survive – and bide our time to punish the racketeers.'

Gaundy's cottage was in Bell Court, a tiny yard fringed by half a dozen small but neat cottages, none of which were marred by the dreaded red crosses. Chaloner's knock was answered by a man of middle years with a sad, weatherworn face and powerful hands. He had long, greasy grey hair and a straggly beard, and he smelled of sweat.

'Have you got a certificate?' he demanded, before Chaloner could speak.

Chaloner frowned. 'You mean a Certificate of Health?'

'What other kind is there? Here is mine, signed yesterday by Dean Sancroft and Mr Wiseman, Surgeon to the Person. And you cannot get higher authorities than those.'

'Perhaps not,' said Chaloner. 'But Sancroft is in Tunbridge Wells and Wiseman is in Oxford. Your paper is a forgery, and I have just been listening to General Monck's thoughts on those.'

Gaundy shot him an unpleasant look. 'What do you want with me?'

'To ask about the discovery you made in St Gregory's crypt.'

'I suppose the dean sent you,' said Gaundy sourly. 'You had better come in then, although I shall have to have a nip of London Treacle first, lest you carry the disease.'

He pulled a flask from his pocket and took several substantial swallows before leading the way into his house, muttering about the inconvenience of visits from Sancroft's envoys when he was busy entertaining.

His guests – three of them – sat at a table in a small parlour. Only one was familiar to Chaloner: Godfrey Wildbore, the fishmonger who had had no wares to sell earlier. Sheets of paper covered in numbers were strewn across the table in front of them. To the uninitiated, they looked like the jottings of a deranged mathematician, but Chaloner recognised them for what they were.

Recent developments in bell-hanging allowed ringers to control exactly when their clappers struck, which meant that bells could be sounded in a specific order, rather than clanged randomly, as in the past. There were hundreds of different patterns – or 'cross-changes' – that could be rung, and ringers took great pride in the number they had mastered. Chaloner had learned the art in his early teens, and associated it with the happy, carefree time before the civil wars had turned his world upside down.

'Plain Bob,' he said, picking up the nearest page.

'You are a ringer?' asked Wildbore keenly. 'That is good news! Too many of us have died, and we are in desperate need of replacements.'

'They died because they stayed to do their duty,' said Gaundy grimly, 'and did not flee like cowards. Of course, some of us have no choice but to remain. I can hardly look after St Gregory's from Greenwich or Deptford.'

'And I cannot abandon my shop,' sighed Wildbore. 'I may have no fish to sell, but my stall is worth a pretty penny, and if I uproot and leave, I shall have nothing.'

Gaundy made some introductions. Wildbore was St Gregory's 'ringing master' – the man in charge – while the others were his band. One was a bookseller named William Kirton, an angular fellow with bushy white eyebrows. The other was Tam Denton, Keeper of Fish in St James's Park, who had a small body topped by a large head, lots of tiny pointed teeth and a glassy stare. Idly, Chaloner wondered if he had started to look like a perch before or after he had embarked on his chosen career.

'Are you the Tam Denton who killed Sir Arnold Harbert?' he asked, wondering how anyone, but especially a knight, could have been defeated by such a puny specimen.

41

Denton fixed him with a cool stare. 'We had a disagreement, but we both left in one piece. I do not know how Harbert died, but it had nothing to do with me.'

'Pemper and his cronies,' spat Wildbore. 'The cathedral ringers. *They* spread that slanderous lie about you stabbing him.'

'They are jealous of our superior talent,' explained Kirton to Chaloner. 'So they avenged themselves by inventing nasty stories. You should ignore them.'

'You will see what we mean when you hear the racket they make,' said Wildbore loftily. 'Compared to *our* tuneful cross-changes. Indeed, we would perform for you now, but we are one ringer short – the fifth and last member of our band is out tolling for the dead, which is a full-time business these days.'

'It is, but better that than digging graves all day,' put in Gaundy morosely. 'Which is all *I* do from dawn to dusk.'

Chaloner glanced out of the window. The sun's position told him it was nearing noon.

'We hired a deputy to manage the graveyard side of things yesterday,' explained Wildbore quickly. 'Entrusting the digging to someone else will leave Gaundy free to ring for the dead – something that is ultimately far more important.'

Chaloner was not so sure about that, feeling that most folk would rather their loved ones were committed to the ground in silence than left to rot above it while the verger enjoyed himself with cross-changes.

'And it will spare me the distress of discovering that some tombs are illicitly occupied,' put in Gaundy with a sniff. 'It was a nasty shock to find a corpse in Harbert's vault, I can tell you! It was meant to be empty.'

'I understand you are the mason who built it,' said Chaloner.

'I am.' There was a sudden gleam of pride in Gaundy's eyes. 'I lined it with two contrasting shades of limestone. Very pretty. Did you notice?'

Chaloner had not, but he nodded anyway. 'Did you make the slab that sealed it, too?'

Gaundy frowned as he struggled with his memory. 'I must have done, although I do not recall setting it in place. Maybe my father did it. Unfortunately, he has been in his own grave these last ten years, so we cannot ask whether he checked for bodies first. However, the crypt is very dark, and we vergers have to buy our own candles . . .'

'And the old man did love his ale,' put in Denton. 'As do you, Gaundy.'

Chaloner imagined the scene: a drunken verger in a poorly lit undercroft, carelessly lowering a slab without bothering to make sure the vault was empty first. Had the killer known his victim would go unnoticed down there? Or had it just been a stroke of luck?

'I do enjoy a tipple,' acknowledged Gaundy. 'It is why I learned bell-ringing – for the free drink that comes after every service. But do not judge my poor old sire too harshly, Denton. Those were turbulent days.'

'Because of the wars?' asked Chaloner.

'Because Inigo Jones was at large,' replied Gaundy darkly. 'A devil in human form. You must have heard how he pulled down our church, and it took an order from Parliament to get him to put it back up again.'

'His antics meant that we could not ring for a *whole year*,' put in Wildbore, bristling with remembered outrage. 'We had to use the cathedral bells instead.'

43

'Terrible, terrible times,' sighed Kirton. 'I should not like to live through those again.'

'When was the crypt last used for a burial?' asked Chaloner.

'Oh, years ago,' replied Gaundy. 'Everyone prefers the cemetery, well away from the tainting influences of the Countess of Devonshire. It is a pity she was put down there actually, as the crypt would be a lovely place to spend eternity. I did most of the brickwork myself, and I used only the best quality slabs for the floor.'

'Harbert always claimed that *he* did not mind the Countess,' put in Denton. 'Of course, he had prepaid for his vault, and was determined to go in it regardless of who else was in the vicinity.'

'We have identified the bones as belonging to one Canon Robert Kerchier,' Chaloner told them before they could range too far from the subject he wanted to discuss. 'Do you remember him?'

'Well, well!' breathed Gaundy, wide eyed. 'So that is where the old rogue went. No wonder he was never found.'

'Was he the one who vanished with all that money?' asked Wildbore.

Gaundy nodded, and gave a sudden grimace of disappointment. 'But it was not in the vault with him – I would have noticed. I wonder what he did with it then.'

'Perhaps nothing,' said Chaloner. 'Because it appears that he was murdered.'

'Murdered?' echoed Denton, fishy eyes wide with astonishment. 'You mean someone killed him and *stole* his hoard?'

'If so, I hope you do not expect to find out who,' said Gaundy, before Chaloner could reply. 'Because I remember Kerchier very well – he had so many enemies that unearthing the culprit will be nigh on impossible, especially after all this time.'

Chaloner wondered how many more people were going to tell him that his investigation was doomed, and experienced a sudden urge to prove them wrong. After all, he had his professional pride, and he had cracked 'unsolvable' mysteries in the past.

'Enemies who took exception to the fact that he wanted to demolish the cathedral,' mused Kirton. 'It is all coming back to me now.'

'Well, the cathedral *should* be demolished,' averred Denton. 'It should have a fine peal of bells, but its central tower is useless – too weak to bear the weight. All it has are those tinny items in the north-west turret – objects that do not deserve to be called bells.'

'There was a rumour that Kerchier tried to blow it up once,' said Kirton suddenly. 'Lord! I had forgotten all about it until now. The story was that he decided to blast it to Kingdom come, so that we would have no choice but to build a new one. But his barrels failed to ignite, and when he went to find out why, it cost him two fingers.'

'What nonsense!' declared Denton. 'How could a clergyman acquire enough powder to destroy a place that size? You cannot go out and buy it from the nearest grocer, and its sale has always been strictly controlled.'

'However, Kerchier *was* missing two fingers,' put in Chaloner. 'And Canon Owen told me that gunpowder was to blame.'

'Perhaps it was, but that does not mean he lost them trying to blow up St Paul's,' retorted Denton.

'Of course, Kerchier disliked bells,' said Gaundy, somewhat irrelevantly. 'I shall never forget how he moaned about the noise. I recall telling him several times that if he did not like it, then he should not have become a clergyman.'

Wildbore and Kirton also knew people who did not like their campanological efforts, and began to list them in indignant voices. It went on for some time, during which Denton managed to slip out without Chaloner noticing. The spy was thoughtful. Why was the Keeper of Fish so sure that the tale about Kerchier's fingers was untrue? And what was the real truth about his quarrel with Harbert? He supposed he would have to track him down and ask.

He also wanted to see what more Kirton could tell him about the tale of Kerchier and the gunpowder, but each time he raised the subject, Wildbore and Gaundy contrived to change it back to bells. Eventually, Chaloner took his leave, knowing that the only way to interview the bookseller would be by cornering him alone.

Once outside, he took up station in a shady doorway and settled down to wait.

# Chapter 2

As morning gave way to afternoon, the heat intensified. Chaloner was on the verge of abandoning his vigil and retiring to an inn for a cool ale when Gaundy's door opened and the three ringers emerged. Gaundy and Wildbore turned towards Thames Street, while Kirton went west. Chaloner followed the bookseller, and contrived to 'bump into' him near St Mary le Bow. Kirton said his shop was in St Paul's Churchyard, and agreed amiably when Chaloner suggested they walk that way together.

'It grieves me to see London in such a state,' Kirton sighed, as he threaded through a series of empty alleys, where dandelions defied the drought to sprout in a thick carpet under their feet. 'I fear the city may never recover.'

'There cannot be many booksellers who elected to stay here,' remarked Chaloner. 'Yet you did.'

'Like Wildbore, my shop is all I have, and I hate the notion of abandoning it to thieves. Of course, it would be a bold felon who raided it now – it is right next to the plague pit.'

'That cannot be good for trade.'

'What trade?' said Kirton bitterly. 'I have sold one volume since June. One! Butler's *Hudibras* to Samuel Pepys the navy clerk, who is also obliged to remain in the city, although he has wisely removed his wife to Woolwich.'

He led the way down a lane so narrow that they were obliged to walk sideways to pass along it, and Chaloner, who was stockier, feared he might get stuck. But he managed to squeeze through, and they emerged on Watling Street, with the cathedral looming ahead of them. Every shop was closed, although a few people milled around outside one, pleading with its owner to sell them the vegetables they knew he had stockpiled within. The man who appeared at an upstairs window to order them away wore a green arm-ribbon.

'What else can you tell me about Kerchier?' asked Chaloner. 'Other than the tale about him losing his fingers to gunpowder?'

'Nothing really – it all happened too long ago. If you must persist with what will almost certainly transpire to be a waste of time – and a dangerous one, into the bargain – then speak to the canons. They were his colleagues, whereas I just sold him the occasional tome.'

'I have spoken to Richard Owen. He is preparing me a list of suspects.'

'Then treat it with caution,' advised Kirton shortly. 'Because he will include all his enemies and none of his friends.'

'Owen has enemies?' fished Chaloner.

Kirton stopped walking to consider. 'Perhaps "enemies" is too strong a word. Like Kerchier did, he wants to demolish the current cathedral and replace it with a new one, preferably something designed by Christopher Wren.

In this, he is opposed by the Maurice Men, who think it should be restored.'

'Morris Men?' Visions of whirling folk dancers filled Chaloner's mind, and he wondered why they should concern themselves with the cathedral's fate. In his experience, they tended to be more interested in good ale and each other's wives.

'Named after Bishop Maurice, who laid the foundations for the present building in the Conqueror's reign. Owen's list will contain lots of Maurice Men but no one who thinks that Wren should be allowed a free rein.'

'Which of the two sides do you believe is right?'

Kirton looked to where the cathedral rose majestically from the huddle of houses around its feet. 'I cannot imagine London without it, yet new cracks appear on a daily basis. I am not sure it *can* be fixed now – we have neglected and abused it for too long.'

'Did Kerchier ever talk to you about it?'

'As I recall, he talked to *everyone* about it. Anyone who would listen.'

'What was your impression of him?'

'Heavens – you are testing my memory today! It all happened so long ago . . .'

'Please try,' urged Chaloner. 'It is important.'

Twin lines creased the spot between Kirton's eyes as he struggled to remember. It was some time before he spoke.

'He was determined and ruthless,' he said eventually, 'and had he lived, I have no doubt that we would now be looking at a very different building. The civil wars were raging, but he would have found a way for Inigo Jones to implement his schemes.'

'Which were to repair the cathedral,' Chaloner reminded him. 'Not to rebuild it.'

'Yes and no. Jones pronounced some parts beyond salvation, and aimed to pull them down. There would have been very little of the original left in the end.'

'Did you like Kerchier?'

There was another long silence as Kirton pondered the question. 'I recall thinking him too single-minded to be pleasant company.'

'Do you remember any interactions between him and Harbert?'

Kirton laughed suddenly. 'Now that I can answer, because they loathed each other and were always arguing. However, I doubt Harbert is your killer – he was all bluster and no substance, even then. He was also indiscreet, and if he *had* mustered the courage to kill, he could never have kept it to himself. He would have blurted it out.'

'I see.' Owen had also thought that Harbert was unlikely to be the culprit, but Chaloner was not ready to discount the knight just yet – at least, not until he knew a lot more about him.

'You will never solve the case,' predicted Kirton, regarding the Knight soberly. 'Too many people have passed away since then – half the canons, the dean, St Gregory's vicar and its verger . . .'

'Yes – Masley told me that he has only been in post for a few months.'

'Masley!' spat Kirton in disgust. 'A man who skulks indoors while his parishioners sicken and die. Every time I pass his house, he is sitting in his parlour, writing.'

'His clerk is dead. I imagine he is record-keeping.'

Kirton lowered his voice conspiratorially. 'Between you

and me, I suspect he is penning an account of his plague experiences, a book that will make him rich when the disease loosens its grip and the ghouls who fled want to know what they missed.'

'It might make you rich as well, if you sell it,' Chaloner pointed out.

'I would not demean myself,' declared Kirton haughtily, and changed the subject. 'Where are you staying tonight? If you have any sense and have booked accommodation outside the city, remember to leave before sunset. Monck's soldiers refuse to let anyone out after dark, even those with Certificates of Health.'

Chaloner lived in Covent Garden, but his landlord – his friend Richard Wiseman, Surgeon to the King – had written to tell him that the house was currently under quarantine because someone had died there. Thus he would have to find an inn, preferably one near St Paul's, so as to be more convenient for his investigation. He asked Kirton to recommend one.

'Why insist on risking your life for an unsolvable mystery?' asked the bookseller, shaking his head in incomprehension. 'Go back to Sancroft, and tell him the task he set you is impossible.'

'Not yet,' said Chaloner, wondering whether Kirton's determination to see him gone warranted *his* inclusion on any list of suspects.

'Then may God protect you,' said the bookseller flatly. 'But if you will not listen to good advice, then try the Mitre in London House Yard. Its beds are fairly clean, and the landlord could do with the business. Shall I take you there? It is not too far out of my way.'

Chaloner thanked him, aiming to interrogate him en route, but Kirton talked non-stop about the book trade and skilfully avoided any questions Chaloner did manage to interject. Then they reached St Paul's Churchyard, where the pile of bodies awaiting burial was twice as high as it had been earlier.

'Come this way,' said Kirton, grabbing Chaloner's arm and pulling him to the left. 'It takes longer, but only fools skirt the pit in the afternoons.'

'When I was last here, the plague dead were only buried at night.'

Kirton winced. 'That practice was abandoned weeks ago, when there were more victims than the hours of darkness could accommodate. The pits operate continually now – they must, or the dead would outnumber the living. It is a sorry business.'

As Kirton led the way around the south side of the cathedral, the hairs on the back of Chaloner's neck began to rise. He had been a spy long enough not to ignore the innate sense that told him he was being watched, so he looked around covertly. At his side, Kirton had segued from the city's burial strategies to the rising cost of food.

'A penny loaf now costs threepence, and Wildbore has had no fish to sell for weeks. Mayor Lawrence will have a riot on his hands unless he does something soon, because it is becoming all but impossible to survive. I can scarce afford to feed myself, let alone my apprentice, who accuses me of letting him starve.'

Chaloner listened with half an ear as he tried to identify the source of his unease. Then he saw it: a man slouched in a nearby doorway. The fellow wore a hooded cloak that was ridiculous for so sultry a day, and his face was unusually swarthy, as if he hailed from warmer climes. Greece, perhaps. He ducked into the cathedral when he saw he had been spotted, but Chaloner did not follow – it was too hot for a chase.

Kirton's tirade stopped abruptly when they rounded a buttress and found themselves walking towards five men. The quintet had been enjoying a lively conversation, but fell silent when they saw Kirton, and made a point of altering their course to avoid him, noses in the air. As they went, one sneaked a glance behind him, to ensure that the snub had been noticed; he smirked his satisfaction when he saw that it had.

'The cathedral ringers,' explained Kirton between gritted teeth. 'Our most deadly adversaries. They are going to chime for Evensong. The old one with the bandy legs is their leader, Robert Pemper, who thinks he is better than us, because he has been practising the art for fifty years. But he cannot dodge to save his life.'

A dodge was when two ringers sounded their bells before and after each other twice in succession, which could make for a pretty tune. However, it was not many moments before Chaloner realised that Pemper's band was not very good at it. The cross-changes began well enough, with each ringer chiming his bell evenly, but they quickly degenerated into a clanging mess. Chaloner winced: even he could do better, and he was sadly out of practice.

Yet the racket served its purpose, as people began to converge on the cathedral for evening prayers. Some came from the Deanery, clad in the robes that marked them as canons, vicars or minor officials, including the cleric who had been in the crowd outside Lawrence's house earlier. He was accompanied by two men who looked so much like him that they could only be his brothers.

'Francis, William and John Hall,' supplied Kirton, when he saw where Chaloner was looking. 'The older two are canons, but the youngest is still waiting for a stall. *He* will be glad that Kerchier has been found, because it means there is now a vacancy – the post could not be filled as long as there was a chance that Kerchier was still alive, you see.'

'Who is next to William?' asked Chaloner.

'The elderly fellow with white hair? That is John Tillison, Sancroft's deputy – old, wise, and neutral in the dispute between those who want the cathedral demolished and those who want it repaired.'

'And there is Owen,' said Chaloner, seeing the thin, dissipated face near the back of the procession.

'The fat man with him is Ben Stone,' added Kirton. 'Infamous for his lechery. See the way he ogles that woman who stands by the door? And on his way to worship, too! All of them knew Kerchier. Will you go now to quiz them about him?'

Chaloner shook his head. Evensong was about to begin, and he did not want the discussion cut short by them agitating to attend their devotions. He would tackle them in a more leisurely fashion the following day, preferably when armed with Owen's list.

He and Kirton were just passing the entrance to the road called Paul's Chain, when someone shot out of the house on the corner like a cannonball. It was a pleasant-faced man with blue eyes, who was wigless and in shirtsleeves. There was a vivid red smear down his front and a smudge of yellow on his nose. He seemed familiar, although Chaloner was not sure why. He was followed

54

by a loud bang, after which smoke billowed through the door in a great brown ball.

'Too much turpentine,' he murmured, brushing himself down.

'Are you preparing a new batch of London Treacle, Rycroft?' asked Kirton affably. 'Good! My last bottle is almost empty. Of course, I cannot afford more than a dribble . . .'

'Speak to the canons about it,' replied Rycroft, rather defensively. 'I only make the stuff – I do not set the price. However, it *is* the best plague preventive money can buy, even if I do say so myself. Much better than *sal mirabilis*.'

'Not if it causes explosions,' retorted Chaloner. Sancroft had furnished him with a pint of London Treacle before he had left, along with an equal amount of *sal mirabilis*, although he had so far taken neither. And nor would he if they contained turpentine.

'That was not an explosion – it was a pop.' Rycroft glanced down at his shirt. 'Damn! My sister will be livid when she sees this. It is the third one I have ruined this week. Unless you can save me by recommending a good laundress?'

'All the ones I know are dead,' said Kirton soberly. 'And besides, that looks like beetroot to me, which means you are doomed.'

'I suppose I am,' sighed Rycroft, then grinned. 'But beetroot does impart a lovely rich colour to my medicine, and people tell me that it greatly improves the flavour.'

If beetroot was the ingredient that rendered the concoction palatable, Chaloner could only assume that it must taste foul indeed. While he pondered the matter, Kirton made some introductions.

'This is Captain Matt Rycroft – the alchemist chosen

by the cathedral as the sole and exclusive manufacturer of London Treacle,' he said, but could not resist a dig. 'Which is not as popular as *sal mirabilis*, because it is so damnably expensive.'

'It is expensive because I use only the finest ingredients,' countered Rycroft shortly. '*And* the canons bless it before it is sold. *Sal mirabilis*, on the other hand, is brewed by unlicensed practitioners whose sole objective is profit.'

'It also smells of worms,' put in Kirton, and changed the subject before anyone could argue. 'Chaloner is here to find out who killed Kerchier. Do you remember him, Rycroft? He vanished, along with all the money he had raised for mending the cathedral.'

'Of course I remember,' said Rycroft keenly, rubbing his nose and smearing the yellow smudge across one cheek. 'It was a dreadful scandal and speculation was rife for years after. His enemies claimed he had stolen the cash, while his friends brayed that he had not.'

'Which enemies?' asked Chaloner innocently.

'Those who wanted the cathedral renovated, rather than knocked down and rebuilt,' replied Rycroft. 'The so-called Maurice Men, who were led by Canon Henchman.'

'Who still *are* led by Canon Henchman,' put in Kirton.

'Of course, the Maurice Men were not the only ones Kerchier annoyed,' Rycroft went on, eyes gleaming as he allowed his memory free rein. 'He founded a semi-secret society called the Agents of God, the aim of which was to fund Inigo Jones. It attracted a lot of wealthy and powerful men, but he was fussy about who he let join – he insulted a lot of folk by refusing to admit them.'

'I had forgotten that,' said Kirton. 'Now you mention

it, I recall thinking at the time that it was rash to offend such influential personages. Perhaps one of them dispatched him then.'

'Well, none were men *I* would want to aggravate,' averred Rycroft, 'and I have met more than my share of terrifying villains. Of course, none are worse than the rogues I fought during the Second Battle of Newbury.'

And with that remark, the alchemist's face snapped into place in Chaloner's mind. That particular encounter had been a bloody affair, when two armies had hammered at each other for a whole day, resulting in no or little gain for either. It had ended with a Royalist retreat, although few Parliamentarians had considered it a victory. Chaloner's unit had become hopelessly scattered, and at one point he had found himself fighting a bitter hand-to-hand duel with a single enemy – Rycroft.

The alchemist had been younger, of course, but the blue eyes were unchanged. He and Chaloner had slashed and swiped at each other for what had seemed like an age, until Rycroft had slipped in mud. Chaloner could have killed him then, but he had hesitated, enabling his opponent to scramble away and disappear into the swirling smoke.

Chaloner blinked and the memory faded. However, there was no spark of recognition in Rycroft's face, which he supposed was not surprising – Chaloner had been fourteen, and there was little of the rosy-cheeked boy left in the seasoned warrior of thirty-five. He asked Kirton for directions to the Mitre and walked the rest of the way alone.

The Mitre was a substantial tavern with several large public rooms and an air of gracious hospitality. The plague outbreak meant that no one had stayed there for weeks, and its owner, Will Paget, was so startled when Chaloner asked for a bed that for several moments all he did was gape. Then he pulled himself together, and the spy was offered a handsome room with a fine view of the churchyard, although thankfully one that did not include the pit.

'It is the best chamber we have,' said Paget, wringing his hands obsequiously while his wife fussed around with soft feather pillows, lavender-scented blankets and warm water for washing. 'Will you be staying long?'

The last was asked so hopefully that Chaloner did not have the heart to say that he intended to finish his work and leave London as soon as possible. He mumbled something vague, after which Paget insisted on providing him with a meal.

'Chicken,' the landlord said, pointing out of the window to where several hens scratched contentedly in the dust. They were pretty creatures with shiny brown feathers and sharp orange eyes. 'Although it may take a while to prepare, given that they are still . . . raw.'

'No,' said Chaloner quickly, the horrors of the Poultry still fresh in his mind. He liked birds, and had never much enjoyed eating them. 'Not chicken.'

Paget's wife did her best, but it quickly became apparent that even reputable establishments like the Mitre were struggling to buy basic victuals. The bread was made from flour bulked out with wood shavings, the cheese was ripe enough to strip paint, and the apples were soft and wormy. These were followed by two boiled eggs and a 'pastry' filled with an unidentifiable yellow paste. The eggs were the only palatable items.

While he ate, Chaloner read the latest government

newsbook – *The Newes*, which was published on Thursdays. Since the plague, the editor had moved his operation to Oxford, on the pretext that he needed to be near the King. As a result, there was plenty of overseas news and Court gossip, but nothing about London.

The main story was a grovelling account of His Majesty's recent foray to Hull, ostensibly to inspect that port's defences, although it seemed that there had been a lot more carousing than inspecting. Then there was a report that the King of Sweden's sister was dead, a snippet that would hold little interest for most Englishmen, while Portsmouth sent a gloating report that *it* was free of the plague.

There was, however, a marked rise in advertisements for potions that claimed to cure the disease, including the Countess of Kent's powder, Bayhurst's Lozenges, Mr Burnebies' Pestilential Powder and Dr Cocke's Blistering Plaister. The editor evidently had opinions about these, and it seemed there were only two remedies that were worthy of consideration in his eyes. As a result, they were given much larger print and more prominent positions on the page than their rivals.

The first was *sal mirabilis* – or miraculous salts – which had been developed to 'relieve those in case of extremity'. It claimed to cure even the most hopeless cases, and could be bought all over the city, including most taverns, and was very reasonably priced.

The second was London Treacle, more expensive and so only available to those with plenty of money:

```
London Treacle, an excellent and approved
remedie for the Removing or Preventing of
the Plague; being also of singular virtue
```

against the Megrim, swimmings in the head,
all Fainting and Convulsion Fits; very good
likewise against Worms and Sudden Death;
and manie times more Superiore than *sal
mirabilis*. London Treacle is blessed by the
Right Reverend Gentlemen of God at St Paul's,
and is to be had in the North Transeptt. Made
by Matt. Rycroft, alchemical physitian.

Idly, Chaloner wondered if either was effective, or if desperate souls were wasting their rapidly dwindling funds on potions that made no difference one way or the other.

'Kirton dropped in a moment ago,' reported Paget, setting a bowl of raisins on the table; they were old and hard, like gravel. 'To check that you are comfortably settled. He says you are here to find out who killed old Canon Kerchier. Well, do not waste your time.'

'No?' Chaloner was getting used to receiving this advice. 'Why not?'

'Because I recall him *very* well, and he was a rogue who wanted to destroy our lovely cathedral. Indeed, he might have succeeded had he lived – he had a silver tongue and coaxed many powerful men to his side. He invited me to join his nasty cabal, but I refused.'

'What did he say to that? Do you remember?'

'I most certainly do! He was livid, and called me a damned fool, but I told *him* that he was the fool for plotting to destroy God's best-loved house. That shut him up.'

'I see,' said Chaloner, sure such a petty exchange would not stick in anyone's mind for two decades, and suspecting that Paget had just made it up.

Paget turned to gaze at the cathedral through the window. 'St Paul's represents all that is grand and good about our city, and I do not want it changed into "something better". It has been with us for hundreds of years, so who are we to knock it about to suit ourselves?'

'It is full of cracks,' said Chaloner, playing devil's advocate. 'It will collapse of its own accord if we leave it alone for much longer.'

'Not if we shore it up with buttresses,' argued Paget. 'And I do not mean ugly great things like the ones Inigo Jones inflicted on us. I mean *proper* buttresses, like they have in Westminster Abbey – ones that look as if they belong there.'

'That will be expensive,' said Chaloner, 'and perhaps ultimately a waste of money.'

But Paget did not listen, and embarked on a diatribe about the men who aimed to finish what Kerchier had started. 'The Hall brothers and Owen are the worst,' he fumed. 'They want a new cathedral so that they can be buried in its chancel when they die – the present one is full, you see. They are selfish, greedy men.'

'They were Kerchier's supporters?' fished Chaloner, wondering if this meant they could be eliminated as suspects for his murder.

'His friends, although they probably argued with him, too – he was a quarrelsome soul who could aggravate a saint. I hope our music will not disturb you tonight, by the way. I know it is forbidden for people to gather together while the pestilence rages, but we must have some enjoyment, or we may as well go and jump in the plague pit right now.'

'Music?' asked Chaloner keenly. It was his greatest love, and the thing that kept him sane during his dangerous and chaotic life. It calmed him when he was fraught, cheered him when he was sad, and the joy he derived from playing often allowed him the clarity of thought needed to solve difficult problems.

'A few trusted friends who sing.' Paget swelled with pride. 'They include Mayor and Abigail Lawrence, their nine daughters, officials from the cathedral, a smattering of merchants and General Monck. Oh, and Secretary Cary, although I am afraid he has no voice at all, and he only comes because he likes goggling at Abigail.'

'Does Monck sing?' asked Chaloner, unable to imagine what manner of sound would emerge from that rough and crusty old warrior.

'He warbles along, if he knows the tune,' hedged Paget diplomatically, and turned the subject back to Cary. 'He is Lawrence's right-hand man. Cambridge-trained, no less. Lawrence says he is indispensable.'

'Tell me about the music,' ordered Chaloner, more interested in that than the secretary's credentials. It had been weeks since he had heard so much as a note.

Paget smiled. 'Singing in parts – madrigals, popular songs and sacred pieces. We offer a wide variety. Why? Are you thinking of joining us?'

'Oh, yes,' replied Chaloner.

People began to arrive an hour later, congregating in a pleasantly appointed room at the back of the inn – grandly named the Musick Hall – which had been designed with acoustics in mind. Paget handed out sheets of lyrics.

'We only ever sing,' he informed Chaloner. 'Because instruments are more likely to summon up the pestilence than unaccompanied voices.'

Chaloner blinked his astonishment at this claim. 'Are they?'

Paget nodded earnestly. 'They set up vibrations that attract deadly miasmas. It is a scientific fact. However, there are no vibrations with singing, so we are safe.'

'Oh,' said Chaloner, thinking he had heard some outlandish theories in his time, but this one took the prize by a considerable margin. 'I had better not send for my viol then.'

'Heavens, no!' cried Paget. 'You would have us all dead in a week. Keep your viol in a dark room, and do not touch it until all danger of infection is past. Of course, no harm will befall you if you confine your bowing to Sundays.'

Before Chaloner could ask how he had reached this particular conclusion, Paget bustled away to greet Lawrence. The mayor was even more imposing close up than he had been on his balcony, resplendent in a rich burgundy gown and matching hat. His hair was short and he wore no wig, so he looked a good deal more comfortable than most others in the gathering, whose devotion to fashion saw them sweating heavily under false hair and frills.

He was followed by his wife Abigail, a plump woman with frothing ginger hair. She had chosen to wear a pink dress with a close-fitting bodice, which was an unfortunate decision for someone her shape, size and colouring. Chaloner could not begin to imagine what it was about her that had won Secretary Cary's passionate devotion.

In her wake waddled nine fat girls, tallest at the front, and the shortest – a child of four or five – bringing up the rear. All were miniature copies of their mother, and

Chaloner was put in mind of a hen with chicks as they filed in, hands clasped demurely in front of them.

On their heels was another woman, who wore the kind of gown that was popular with courtesans. It was so low-cut as to be indecent, and sewn with tiny jewels that flashed in the lamplight. A jaunty face-patch adorned one cheek, and she was slathered in face paints which, as the Musick Hall was hot, immediately began to melt.

'That is Mrs Driver,' whispered Paget, coming to gossip. 'Lawrence's mistress. I wonder he has time for one, what with producing all those girls, but there you are.'

'Abigail does not object to her?' asked Chaloner, amused.

'Oh, very much, but Lawrence refuses to give her up. Well, who can blame him? Just look at that magnificent bosom!'

'And what does *Mr* Driver have to say about this arrangement?'

'He has been in his grave these last ten years. After his death, she had a choice: take over his pig-slaughtering business or find a wealthy lover. She chose the latter, and set her sights on Lawrence.'

As if she sensed she was the subject of discussion, Mrs Driver sashayed across the room towards them, moving in a way that ensured she snagged the attention of every man present. She snagged Abigail's, too, although her gaze was rather less appreciative.

'I have been practising some ballads for tonight,' she informed Paget with a sultry smile. 'Ones that will lighten the sombre atmosphere after your dull old madrigals.'

'I hope they are not lewd, like they were the last time,'

said Paget anxiously, 'when Abigail called you a vulgar strumpet. Surely you have not forgotten?'

Something unpleasant flashed in Mrs Driver's eyes, but she flapped a scented and heavily be-ringed hand in a dismissive gesture. 'I do not care about the opinion of that old trout. And you *will* like my songs, Mr Paget. I promise.'

'Oh, Lord!' groaned Paget as she undulated away. 'What can I do to stop her? And why must she insist on coming, when she knows that Abigail would rather she stayed away?'

Chaloner was spared from responding by the arrival of the three clerical brothers from the cathedral, who bustled in importantly and claimed everyone's attention by telling them about trouble at Evensong.

'Over London Treacle,' explained Francis Hall, the eldest, largest and spottiest of the trio. 'Folk interrupted the rite to shout that it is too costly.'

'And that we do not produce enough of it,' added William, the middle sibling. 'Rycroft must work faster or we shall have a riot. Of course, I do not blame folk for complaining about the shortage. The alternative is to take *sal mirabilis*, which is next to useless.'

'It is,' agreed John, the youngest, smallest and most clear-complexioned. 'Anyone with a cook-pot can throw a few ingredients together and call them *sal mirabilis*. London Treacle, on the other hand, is produced by *one* man and sold from *one* place: St Paul's.'

'People say it is too dear, but quality costs,' William went on. 'And only fools baulk at paying for something that will protect them from a dreadful death.'

From the murmur of assent that rippled around the room, Chaloner surmised that most of those present put

65

their faith in London Treacle, no doubt reasoning that because it was expensive, it must therefore be effective. By contrast, *sal mirabilis* was for paupers who could not afford anything better.

'And the mortality figures prove that London Treacle is the best,' declared Francis. 'The plague pits are full of *sal mirabilis*-quaffing commoners, while people of quality, who use London Treacle, are rarely infected.'

Chaloner was tempted to point out that very few 'people of quality' remained in the city, so it was small wonder that the statistics were skewed in their favour. But no spy liked to draw attention to himself, so he held his tongue and went to stand by the door instead, hoping for a breath of fresh air – there was a widely held belief that deadly miasmas rose at night, so all the tavern's windows were tightly closed and the room was stuffy.

He glanced into the dark yard outside, and saw Cary there, with a gaggle of loutish men. When the secretary had finished with them, he came to talk to Chaloner, although he took up a position that allowed him to watch Abigail at the same time, and Chaloner had the sense that a good part of his mind was on what he could see, rather than a dull interaction with the dean's envoy.

'I hired these fellows to escort Abigail and Lawrence home when the singing is over,' he said, apparently feeling that he needed to explain why he was associating with such ruffians. 'Keeping them safe is important.'

'I am sure it is,' murmured Chaloner.

Cary tore his eyes away from the object of his desire, and his expression turned furtive, as if he had just realised that his tongue had betrayed him. 'The Lawrences are essential to the city's continued existence,' he declared defensively. 'No one else is strong enough or sufficiently charismatic to step into their shoes.'

From what little he had seen of the mayor – and of plague-infested London – Chaloner suspected that was true, at least. 'Have there been many attempts on his life? Or hers?'

Cary scowled. 'Yes, and two were because of stupid musical soirées, like this one. It is illegal to gather in groups of more than three or four, you see, and Londoners object to Lawrence and Abigail doing something that they are not permitted to enjoy themselves.'

'Perhaps these Londoners have a point.'

Cary's glower deepened, resenting the criticism of his idols. 'Lawrence and Abigail need some relaxation or the strain will turn their wits. I just wish they would choose to do something other than caterwaul with the likes of Paget.'

Chaloner felt he could come to dislike Cary. 'And what does Abigail do for the city, exactly? Other than be married to the mayor?'

'She does lots – more than anyone appreciates,' declared Cary sharply. 'She is a saint, always looking to the city's needs.'

Chaloner was about to tell him that this reply had not really answered the question when there was a flurry of activity in the street – a clatter of horses' hoofs, followed by a good deal of unnecessary swearing. It was General Monck.

'He told me that he would put in an appearance tonight,' said Cary, regarding the new arrival with open contempt, 'although only when he heard that Mrs Driver was coming, too. He likes her.'

'The feeling seems to be reciprocated,' remarked

Chaloner, as the lady in question swept forward to drape herself over the crusty old warrior, winning herself a craggy smile.

Abigail watched her husband's immediate dismay with a satisfied smirk, so that Chaloner guessed exactly who had told Monck about Mrs Driver's plans for the evening. What a tangle, he thought in amusement: Cary besotted with Abigail; Lawrence and Monck lusting after Mrs Driver; and Mrs Driver flirting with any man who caught her eye.

'Yet I suppose we should be glad that Monck deigned to come,' said Cary, giving Chaloner his full attention when Abigail moved and was lost from view. 'Lawrence will use it to reiterate the many difficulties we face – food shortages, spiralling costs, a frightened populace, rampant profiteers, a growing trade in forged Certificates of Health . . .'

'I heard about the Certificates of Health. Does it mean that infected people are able to *buy* their way out of London?'

The scowl returned to Cary's face. 'Yes, and it is a serious problem – one we must stamp out fast. The plague has already spread to other towns, and I am sure these false documents are responsible. We need Monck to add his voice to ours in demanding more help from the government – more money and more soldiers to implement our plague measures. He has a thousand men, it is true, but they are not nearly enough.'

He gave a brief but surprisingly insightful review of the situation that made Chaloner understand exactly why Lawrence was prepared to overlook his secretary's brazen and inappropriate infatuation with Abigail. Cary was quick and clever, and would doubtless be a great asset in a crisis – grumpiness and lust notwithstanding. Chaloner complimented him on his analysis, which drew a brief smile of pleasure.

'My Cambridge education,' Cary explained proudly. 'It taught me how to think, and I owe a great deal to my tutors at Sydney Sussex.'

Chaloner recalled his own time at the University, when thinking had been actively discouraged on the grounds that the dons disliked being challenged on precepts they considered inviolable. But before he could ask which particular masters had taken this innovative approach to teaching, Cary had segued to the subject to fish.

'We had a lovely range of specimens back in July,' he griped. 'Beasts of all shapes and sizes, but now we are lucky to see a skinny trout. Fishermen will not bring their wares to the city, and there is nothing left in the river. And speaking of fishing, how are your enquiries into Kerchier coming along? Do you have any suspects yet?'

'Owen will give me a list tomorrow, but I have a feeling that most people on it will either be dead themselves, or will have fled to the country.'

'Not necessarily. Kerchier's most vocal antagonist was Richard Henchman, and he is still here. So is Ben Stone, who changed sides after Kerchier's disappearance – he went from saying that the cathedral should be destroyed to braying that it should be preserved.'

Chaloner regarded him sceptically. 'You seem very sure of your facts, but Kerchier died twenty years ago. How can you be certain about who did what after all this time?'

Cary eyed him haughtily. 'Because God blessed me with an excellent memory and my Cambridge tutors taught me how to use it – which is why Lawrence deems me so useful, of course. But you interrupted before I had finished my list. You should also include Master Bing, the cathedral's music copyist, who is . . . well, you will see when you meet him.'

Chaloner made a mental note of the names. 'Anyone else?'

'Oh, lots of folk, but I imagine Owen will name those for you.' Cary shot him an unexpectedly sympathetic glance. 'I thought *I* had a difficult job, but it is a piece of cake compared to yours.'

It was not an encouraging thing to hear.

Usually at such gatherings, victuals were provided – a venison pastry, perhaps, or a pie with beef and oysters. However, all that was on offer at the Mitre were the rock-hard raisins that Chaloner had declined earlier, which no one touched except Lawrence's portly daughters. There were, however, several dishes of prettily coloured pebbles and a painting of a fruit-bowl, which he supposed were meant to make up for the lack of real comestibles.

'It is not Paget's fault,' came a soft voice from behind him. It was Rycroft the alchemist, resplendent in a smart grey long-coat and a shirt with lace, although a pink stain on one cuff suggested that he had worn the outfit to work at some point. 'Food is in such short supply that no one can afford to share what they manage to snag.'

He began to describe the difficulty in acquiring some of the ingredients in London Treacle, but he had not been holding forth for long before someone else joined them. It was Mrs Driver, who had tired of Monck and was looking for more lively companions. Up close, she was not pretty – her lips were too big, her chin too small, while her bulging bust made her oddly top heavy. A few moments in her company revealed that she was no great intellectual either, and Chaloner wondered yet again what Lawrence and Monck – and Rycroft, who had suddenly turned tongue-tied and gauche under her sultry gaze – saw in her.

'I have lots of food,' she informed them huskily. 'Mayor Lawrence will not let *me* starve. And if you two gentlemen ever visit, I shall give you each a slice of fat ham.'

'Really?' asked Rycroft wide-eyed. 'I have not tasted that in weeks.'

'Then come home with me tonight,' she purred. 'You may have the meat in exchange for a pot of your best London Treacle – which is the one thing that Lawrence fails to provide. He only dispenses *sal mirabilis*.'

She tapped him coyly with her fan, and swayed away. Rycroft watched her go admiringly, but then shook his head.

'It is a tempting offer, but if I went, I would probably run into Monck. I am no stranger to battle, but I am not such a fool as to challenge a man with a thousand warriors at his back.'

'Very wise,' said Chaloner.

'Monck only came here tonight to meet her,' Rycroft went on disapprovingly. 'He cares nothing for music, and it is common knowledge that the only tunes he likes are the kind he can march to. He rarely leaves his quarters in Westminster Palace these days, lest he catches the plague, so it is very unusual to see him out in the city. The coward!'

'Do you play?' asked Chaloner, not about to engage in a disparaging discussion about one of the King's favourite barons. People were arrested for that sort of thing.

'The viol, although not as well as I should like. You are a violist as well – I can tell by the calluses on your fingers.'

The marks in question were barely visible, and Chaloner was disconcerted that he should have been inspected quite so closely. Why would the alchemist have done such a thing? Was he simply observant, or did he have a reason for learning all he could about the man who aimed to solve Kerchier's murder? Chaloner was about to see if he could find out when Monck stormed up to them.

'Where is that whore?' he demanded curtly. 'I saw her here a moment ago. She promised me a romp – and I want it now, so I can leave before all the yowling begins.'

'You do not like singing?' Chaloner struggled to mask his distaste for the man.

'No,' replied Monck shortly, pulling a plug of tobacco from his pocket and shoving it into his mouth. 'It is a waste of time. Now where is that harlot? Can you see her?'

'She is talking to Lawrence,' replied Rycroft, and then sighed ruefully. 'Perhaps she is offering *him* a slice of fat ham.'

'Is that what she calls it?' growled Monck. 'Well, he had better not get his piece before I get mine. And the moment we finish, I shall go home. It is too dangerous to be out after dark – the time when plague-infected people leave their sickbeds for a breath of fresh air.'

'My London Treacle will protect you,' said Rycroft confidently. 'It contains more than sixty separate ingredients, including roots, leaves, oils, seeds and minerals.'

'It is not as good as chewing tobacco,' averred Monck. 'Staying away from Quakers helps, too.' He turned to regard Chaloner through small, suspicious eyes. 'Paget tells me that you are here to solve a murder. Is it true?'

'Yes – on Dean Sancroft's behalf.'

'Then you are a fool and he is a greater one,' said the general unpleasantly. 'What can one murder matter now, when thousands die every week?'

'But this victim was a cathedral canon,' said Rycroft, before Chaloner could reply for himself. 'Robert Kerchier, who vanished two decades ago with a lot of money that did not belong to him.'

'Kerchier, Kerchier,' mused the general, rubbing his chin thoughtfully. 'The name is familiar. Hah! I have it. He is the cleric who once begged me for a barrel of gunpowder. I refused, but he must have got one from elsewhere, because the next time I saw him, he had lost two fingers. I recall laughing my head off.'

'Did he say why he wanted it?' asked Chaloner, his repugnance for Monck deepening.

'I do, actually. It is embedded in my mind because it was one of only five times in my life that I felt compelled to make a joke. He said he needed it to clear a blocked sewer, but I told him to hire some paupers instead – they do not explode and they are cheaper.'

'The joke being?' asked Chaloner coolly, when Monck guffawed at his own wit.

Taking him at his word, Monck opened his mouth to explain, but then his eye lit on Mrs Driver. 'Hah! There she is! You will have to wait until we next meet to hear my views on paupers and drains.'

He ploughed through the gathering towards her, and she allowed him to tow her outside. Lawrence's jaw tightened in annoyance, although Abigail smirked her satisfaction. Then Paget announced that the entertainment was about to begin. Mrs Driver was back before everyone had taken their seats, but without Monck. The general, it seemed, had taken what he had been promised, and had escaped to the safety of his Westminster bolthole.

For two glorious hours, Chaloner was transported to another world as Paget's guests took it in turns to sing. The pleasure lasted until Mrs Driver was allowed to contribute, at which point the occasion took a distinct nosedive. Abigail assumed an expression of haughty disdain as her rival warbled a medley of increasingly bawdy tavern songs, although her husband remained stoutly impassive. Paget stepped forward hastily when Mrs Driver began the infamous broadside ballad named 'The Butcher's Daughter'.

'You have entertained us royally,' he gushed, 'but time is passing and I think we must end. We shall finish with a little Melvill – my favourite, "Hey ho, to the Greenwood".'

It was a safe choice, as everyone knew it, and the entire gathering joined in. Mrs Driver pouted sulkily through the first verse, but perked up when Lawrence contrived to stand next to her for the second. Then Paget declared the evening over, and his guests began to take their leave. Chaloner was about to retire himself when Lawrence approached, his wife and daughters in tow. Cary was with them, his eyes fixed unblinkingly on the object of his desire.

'Cary tells me that you are here to investigate the murder of Canon Kerchier,' said the mayor pleasantly. 'I remember him vaguely, although I confess I was probably one of those who thought he had absconded with the money. If so, it seems I misjudged him.'

'*I* always maintained that he would never steal from his cathedral,' declared Abigail importantly. 'He was not that sort of person. And unlike my husband, *I* remember Kerchier *very* well – I am not a person to forget a high-ranking cleric.'

She seemed blissfully unaware of Cary's adoring gaze, although Chaloner suspected it had not escaped Lawrence's notice – the mayor was clearly an astute man. Again, Chaloner could only conclude that Cary's usefulness earned him a certain degree of leeway, although Chaloner would not have appreciated another man ogling any wife of *his* so brazenly, and admired Lawrence's forbearance.

'Then what can you tell me about him?' probed Chaloner, although instinct told him to treat her claims with caution, as she was clearly one of those people who would rather invent something than admit her ignorance.

'He was a man who knew his own mind,' she began grandly. 'Ethical and determined, and he would rather have died than betray a principle. I said at the time that someone had done him harm. It was obvious.'

Having had her say, she sailed away, her offspring waddling at her heels. Chaloner watched them go, wondering how the slim, darkly handsome Lawrence had managed to sire nine fat ginger girls. Surely one of them should have taken after him? He stole a glance at Cary, who was also red-headed, but quickly dismissed that notion. Abigail thought far too much of herself to entertain a mere secretary, especially one who was not particularly attractive and who always seemed to be glaring.

'I doubt it *was* obvious,' said Lawrence, once she was out of earshot, 'or his friends would have spent more time looking for him. As far as I recall, even they eventually came to assume the worst.'

'I agree,' said Cary, all his attention on the discussion now that Abigail was not there to distract him. 'Kerchier used sly tactics to get that money – he put undue pressure on local merchants, he denounced those who refused, and he made dubious deals in return for donations. When he and the cash disappeared, it all made sense as far as I was concerned – he had not cared who he upset, because he knew he would not be around to endure it for very long.'

'An assumption that was in error,' remarked Lawrence, 'given that the poor man has been mouldering in someone else's grave all these years. So, Chaloner, not only do you have a murderer to catch, but a thief, too – a rogue who made off with money intended for the cathedral. I am sure Sancroft will be anxious to have it back.'

'I imagine the culprit will have spent it by now,' said Cary, startled. 'He would have to be a very restrained individual to resist its lure for two decades.'

'Well, try,' Lawrence ordered Chaloner. 'And if we can be of assistance, just ask. You may need our help, as the city is dangerous at the moment – and not just from disease. It is almost impossible to keep order and crime is rife. Theft, profiteering, burglary, unlawful killing . . . it always happens when supplies dwindle.'

Chaloner recalled Monck's words – that one murder paled into insignificance when compared to what else was happening in the city. Perhaps he was right. What *did* one life matter amid so much agony? But no killer should get away with his crime, and maybe identifying Kerchier's would make a difference – a small spark of justice at a time when nothing seemed fair.

'I once knew another Thomas Chaloner,' said Lawrence suddenly. He smiled, an expression that lightened his features and made him look boyish. 'The regicide. Was he kin?'

'My uncle,' replied Chaloner with an inward sigh, wishing he could deny it. It was difficult enough to be an ex-Parliamentarian soldier and a Commonwealth spy, but to own a kinsman who had signed the old king's death warrant made matters far worse.

'He was a character,' mused Lawrence wryly.

'He was,' agreed Chaloner, aware that being 'a character' was usually a euphemism for some very unattractive traits. His uncle's had been myriad, although there were plenty who had loved him for his lively wit and devotion to high living.

'You look like him,' Lawrence went on, which was not something Chaloner was pleased to hear – his kinsman had been seedy in his later years, with drink-ravaged features and thinning hair. 'Are you sure he was not your father?'

'Quite sure,' said Chaloner shortly, thinking the question impertinent. 'My mother knew the difference between her husband and a brother-by-marriage.'

Lawrence laughed, an openly amused guffaw that was infectious enough to make others turn towards him and smile. 'I like a man with a sense of humour – and one who can sing into the bargain. Are you in the market for a wife? I have nine lovely daughters, and I should like one of them to wed a baritone.'

'I am afraid not.' Chaloner had been married twice, but had lost both wives to the plague; he was not about to take a third lest it happened again. 'But perhaps Mrs Driver can suggest some alternatives.'

Lawrence chortled again. 'She already has, but her choices are unsuitable. She is a magnificent lady, but wholly lacking in refinement.'

'To say the least,' muttered Cary, although too low for Lawrence to hear. Clearly, the secretary failed to understand why his employer should dally with a vulgar courtesan when he was married to the elegant and deeply desirable Abigail.

At that moment, a messenger arrived, a rough, unshaven rogue with scarred knuckles. He shoved a note into Lawrence's hand without a word, and slouched away.

'From our man in the Green Dragon tavern,' said Lawrence to Cary, scanning it quickly. 'George Antrobus and Matthew Harbert have been causing trouble again.'

'Harbert?' pounced Chaloner. 'Is he kin to Sir Arnold Harbert?'

'His brother,' supplied Cary. 'Although they were estranged, and had not spoken in years.' He turned back to Lawrence with a frown. 'What kind of trouble?'

'More of the same – telling people that they will die if they stay in London. I am sick of repairing the damage they do with their foolish tongues.' Lawrence turned to Chaloner. 'It is cruel, because people *cannot* leave. First, because they might spread the disease, and second, because there is nothing for them in the country – the villages do not want them and they are likely to be shot.'

'Or they will starve in the woods,' put in Cary. 'You may not believe it when you see the plague pits and the empty markets, but their best chance of survival *is* to stay put.'

If that were true, then Chaloner pitied London.

In bed a little later, Chaloner reflected on his day, feeling he had made reasonable progress with his enquiries. He shifted restlessly. The room was hot and airless, even though the window was open. He closed his eyes, but a rustle made him open them again. At first, he assumed there was a bird in the ivy that coated the wall outside, but then he heard the very distinct sound of human breathing. He rose and padded stealthily into the shadows: if the burglar expected an easy score, he was going to be in for a surprise.

Chaloner was so sure that his nocturnal visitor was an opportunistic thief that he was wholly unprepared for what happened next. There was a flash followed by an almighty bang, and he had the vivid sense of a bullet punching into the pillow where his head had been, although it was far too dark to see any such thing.

He raced for the window and saw someone scrambling down the wall outside. He started to follow, but a second ball cracked into the sill, narrowly missing his hand – the culprit had an accomplice in the garden. The first gunman glanced up in alarm, and there was just enough moonlight for Chaloner to see his face – thin and with a stubbly beard. He wore a ribbon around one arm, and although Chaloner could not tell its colour, he suspected it was green.

Knowing he would be a sitting duck if he clambered down the ivy, Chaloner ran for the stairs instead, but the garden was empty by the time he reached it, and the back gate was ajar. He listened intently for footsteps, but there was only silence. The gunmen had escaped.

He returned to the tavern, where Paget and his family cowered under a table, wailing their terror. Chaloner assured them that the danger was over, although most of his mind was mulling over what had just happened. He was able to deduce three things.

First, he was the Mitre's only guest, so the bullet had definitely been intended for him. Second, no attempt had been made to steal, so the purpose of the exercise had been to kill. And third, the attack meant that there *was* something to discover about Kerchier and the missing money, and that someone was determined to stop it from coming to light. Perversely, he was pleased: it meant the culprit was still alive and active, and thus could still be caught.

# Chapter 3

Chaloner slept well once he had been provided with a bedchamber that was not quite so easily accessible from the outside, and woke as the first glimmers of dawn painted the night sky. He flung open the window and leaned out, breathing in deeply of what should have been clean morning air. Instead, it was hot, dry, dusty and reeked of death. It was unusual for high summer to last so long, and he wondered if the doom-mongers were right to say that the unseasonable heat was a sign of more calamities to come.

Water for washing had been left outside his door, although it was warm, tinged with brown and did little to refresh him. He scrubbed lethargically at the stubble on his chin with a pumice stone, then stared at himself in the mirror.

He had a pleasant but unremarkable face, grey eyes and thick brown hair. He was neither tall nor short, fat nor thin, although the past few weeks in Oxford and Tunbridge Wells had taken their toll around his middle – he was unused to quite so many sumptuous meals. When he came to dress, the waistband on his blue breeches was tighter than it had been a month before, and he was obliged to use the looser notch on his belt.

He donned a clean shirt with the barest minimum of lace, white stockings and short boots, but it was too hot for a coat, so he opted for a sleeveless doublet instead. It was drab attire, and nothing he could have worn at Court, but it was good enough for investigating murder in a plague-infested city.

He trotted down the stairs and entered the tavern's main room, where a jug of breakfast ale had been left on the table. He poured some and took it into the garden, to drink while he examined the ivy for clues that might help him identify the gunmen. All he found was a green ribbon, which had fallen off during the culprit's scramble to escape.

He was about to go back inside when he heard the hens squawking inside their coop. As Paget was nowhere to be seen, he let them out, which prompted a sudden memory of his very happy childhood in Buckinghamshire, when he had taken it upon himself to tend the family poultry. It had been a time of love, laughter and music-filled evenings, before the civil wars had broken out and turned his world upside down.

He sat on a bench to finish his ale, and the chickens followed, scratching in the dust around his feet. He rarely sat in deliberate idleness, but he did it that morning, relishing the touch of the rising sun on his skin, the chatter of happy hens, and the sweet scent of the herbs from the garden. Then Paget appeared.

'No,' said Chaloner sharply, when the landlord made to shoo the birds away, resentful that his brief moment of peace was at an end. 'Leave them be.'

'They will go to the Poultry today,' Paget said, flopping

so heavily on the bench that the chickens scattered anyway. 'We only had two eggs this week, so we shall sell this lot and buy some better ones.'

Chaloner recalled the horrors of Scalding Alley. 'Please do not.'

Paget eyed him lugubriously. 'You would have me waste good corn on useless birds?'

'I will buy them. Just keep them here until I leave.'

Paget's eyebrows shot up in astonishment, and Chaloner was irked with himself. What was he going to do with a flock of hens? Take them back to Tunbridge Wells and keep them in his room? But the offer had been made and he was loath to retract it.

'Very well,' said Paget, although he continued to eye his guest askance. 'But only if you agree not to decant to another inn. I know you were shot at here last night, but it was not our fault – it was yours, for probing dark matters.'

Chaloner nodded acceptance of the terms, then held up the ribbon he had found. 'One of the gunmen wore this around his arm.'

Paget's expression hardened. 'Mims! They have grown bolder since the plague because the forces of law and order do not have the resources to stop them. Have you heard of the Mims? They are mostly felons from the slums – the rookeries.'

'I know of the Hectors and the King of Cheapside – professional criminals, who unite to transform themselves into a formidable force.'

'The Mims are more of the same, although they are less organised and have no particular leader. They will do anything for money, though, including murder. Your investigation must have someone seriously worried.'

'It would seem so,' agreed Chaloner, supposing he would have to corner a few green-armed louts and find out which of them had been paid to kill him – and by whom.

Paget stood to leave. 'Are you sure about these birds? I can get you some much better ones. Of course, the choice is not what it was before the plague . . .'

'I want these,' stated Chaloner firmly, knowing it was an act of reckless eccentricity, but disinclined to care. 'There is a walled vegetable garden in Clarendon House. I will take them there when I have time.'

'A vegetable garden!' sighed Paget. 'They will be better fed than me. I cannot recall the last time I had fresh produce. All we get these days is countrymen's leftovers.'

'Then someone should negotiate a better arrangement with the farmers.'

'How, when none of them will risk talking to us? Besides, Monck's soldiers will not let us out without a Certificate of Health, and at a shilling apiece, they are too costly to waste on futile missions. And do not suggest *sneaking* out – we would be caught.'

Chaloner thought about the size of London – not just the city, but the suburbs and outlying villages as well. 'Monck cannot possibly control every road and field.'

'Well, he does,' retorted Paget. 'And the villages help. They have trainbands, which patrol with muskets, and strangers are either shot or driven back. It is a wicked state of affairs. How I long for a juicy pear or a crisp lettuce! And I cannot recall when I last ate fish.'

'There must be some in the river.'

'All gone. A few weeks ago, there were fish of all shapes and sizes, but not now. Perhaps Monck means to eradicate the plague by starving us all to death. I did hear a rumour to that effect yesterday. I am not sure which fate would be worse.'

Back in the Mitre's main room, Chaloner ate an odd breakfast of coddled egg, gravy and apples. Bells tolled almost continually for the dead, and he was glad that all his friends had left the city. The best of them was John Thurloe, his old Spymaster, who was currently in Oxfordshire enjoying a family wedding. The others were Surgeon Wiseman and Temperance North, who had followed the Court to Oxford, and Captain Lester, who was fighting the Dutch at sea.

He wrote a brief message to Sancroft, outlining what he had learned so far, and was just setting out for the General Post Office when his nostrils were assailed by the scent of roasting beans. It came from the Turk's Head Coffee House, which was next door. Feeling that a dose of the beverage might help to sharpen his wits for the day ahead, he entered.

There were dozens of coffee houses in London, and the Turk's Head was no different from the rest. It comprised a single room that reeked of burned beans and tobacco smoke, with long tables where patrons could sit to debate politics, religion and other contentious subjects. Normally, it would have been abuzz with news and lively chatter, but that day, no one sat next to anyone else, and its few patrons eyed each other warily.

'What news?' asked the owner nervously, voicing the traditional greeting of such places. His name was John Hayes, a small man with sorrowful eyes. 'But please do not tell us that the plague has reached the Midlands, because we already know.'

'Personally, I blame the Quakers,' growled a man

whose cloak covered him from head to toe, which must have been uncomfortable in the heat. 'They claim that God sent the plague to test their faith, but if they were decent folk He would not have needed to bother, and the rest of us would have been spared.'

It was convoluted logic, but the other patrons nodded fervent agreement. Chaloner had seen it all before: there always had to be a scapegoat when disaster befell a city.

Hayes poured Chaloner a dish of coffee, then offered sugar that had been nipped from a loaf with pincers. Chaloner declined. The sugar trade was a cruel one, and he wanted no part of it. However, while his moral stance made no difference to the slaves on the plantations, it did make drinking Hayes' coffee a deeply unpleasant experience. It was unusually bitter, suggesting that either the beans had been reused or that something else had been added. He swallowed it without pleasure and left quickly.

He reached Post House Yard, where the duty clerk – who wore a mask so that nothing could be seen of his face – warned that the missive might take some time to reach its destination, as the post-boys were reluctant to handle mail from the city. Chaloner wondered if the clerk would even bother to hand it over to them, or if the letter would be left in a sack somewhere, and conveniently forgotten.

Outside again, Chaloner glanced up at the sun and judged the hour to be about eight o'clock. It was time to visit the Deanery and collect Owen's list of suspects.

He was just passing St Thomas's Church on Knightrider Street when its bell began to toll. Two coffins were being lowered into a hole that did not look deep enough to take them, leading him to suppose that other caskets were already in there.

He could see into the porch from the road, and spotted some familiar faces – Wildbore and his fellow ringers, chatting to the congregation. The scrap of conversation he heard before the door was closed told him that they were discussing flight from the city – the mourners were terrified of joining their kinsfolk in the grave, so the ringers were recommending that they buy Certificates of Health and leave at once. Chaloner wondered how many of them were already infected, and would bear the disease away with them if they followed the advice.

He had not taken many more steps before he sensed eyes on him. He whipped around fast, and saw the same man who had watched him the previous day – the one who looked Greek. He started to walk towards him, but the fellow was too far away to catch, and had vanished long before Chaloner reached the door where he had been standing.

Chaloner turned west again. Dead-carts rumbled past, toting their teetering loads to the pits. Monck's soldiers patrolled in wary packs, ready to implement the city's plague laws – breaking up illegal gatherings of people, shutting up infected houses, lighting fires to fumigate 'pestered' places, and overseeing the cleansing of streets. All wore bird-head masks and long leather coats to protect themselves.

By contrast, Mayor Lawrence strode along with his face uncovered, readily identifiable in his trademark burgundy coat. He exuded confidence and energy as he called cheery greetings and words of encouragement to passers-by. Cary was at his side, and when Lawrence stopped to chat to a trio of street-sweepers, who were patently delighted to have been noticed by so important a person, the secretary came to talk to Chaloner. His idea of a friendly greeting was a curt nod, so that Chaloner wondered if he was even capable of cracking a smile – other than at Abigail Lawrence, of course.

'Paget sent us a message earlier,' he said, clearly not a man for exchanging morning pleasantries before getting down to business. 'Someone tried to kill you. Is it true?'

Chaloner nodded. 'Two Mims were hired to do the honours. Fortunately for me, the room was dark, so they shot the pillow instead.'

'Mims?' asked Cary sharply, and nodded across the road, where a pair of green-ribboned men strutted. 'You mean louts like them?'

'Yes – although my attackers were younger and smaller.'

Cary shook his head in disgust. 'All felons have grown brazen since the outbreak began, but only the Mims sport their badges as an open challenge to our authority. They know we do not have the wherewithal to stop them, you see.'

'Shall we escort those two down an alley, and see if they know which of their fellows offer an assassination service?' suggested Chaloner. 'Because the culprits were almost certainly hired by Kerchier's killer – no one else can object to me investigating his murder.'

'I suppose we could,' said Cary. He sounded unenthusiastic, so Chaloner was caught off guard when the secretary turned to hare after the two men at once. He had grabbed the larger of the pair and shoved him into a doorway almost before Chaloner realised what he was doing.

Unfortunately, it did not take long to determine that the felonious duo knew nothing to help, and Chaloner indicated that they could go. They scuttled away in relief, although one turned to make an obscene gesture the moment he felt he was far enough away to be safe.

'I did not really expect answers,' muttered Cary, 'but it would have been nice.'

Chaloner agreed. 'Although Landlord Paget told me that the Mims are a loose affiliation of petty criminals, rather than a structured gang, and as they have no real leader, few will know what their cronies do.'

'He is right,' said Cary. 'But it was worth a try.' Then he rummaged in the bag he carried over his shoulder, and produced a handgun and a pouch of ammunition. 'As your life seems to be in danger, you had better borrow these. We cannot have you killed in our city – not only would it would be bad for morale, but Dean Sancroft would be vexed with us.'

Chaloner disliked firearms. They were noisy, unpredictable and cumbersome to carry. 'No, thank you,' he began. 'It—'

'Do not be a fool,' interrupted Cary shortly, shoving the gun at him rather roughly. 'Even if you are disinclined to use it, the sight of a dag may make an assassin think twice.'

Chaloner supposed that was true. He took it and shoved it in his pocket.

The Deanery was a great palace of a building, lit by huge mullioned windows and bristling with chimneys. Chaloner opened a thick wooden door and stepped inside. A hand-bell on a table had been placed for those wishing to attract attention, so he gave it a shake. No one came, so he did it again, wondering if the porter had abandoned his post for safer pastures. Or perhaps his name was on Owen's list, so he had disappeared before he could be asked any awkward questions.

Chaloner looked around him while he waited. The hall was sumptuous, a stark contrast to the cathedral with its peeling paint and crumbling plaster. Its walls were touched with gilt, and there were paintings of famous churchmen by Cooper and Lely. The one given pride of place above a huge marble fireplace was Archbishop Laud, beheaded twenty years ago for making the Church too powerful.

'*WHAT?*' came a shriek, so shrill and unexpected that Chaloner almost jumped out of his skin. He turned quickly, hand on his sword, and was greeted by a curious sight.

The man who had yelled was tall, thin and had the wildest eyes Chaloner had ever seen. A closer inspection revealed that they had been ringed with black dye. His hair appeared to have been cut with a knife, because his scalp was visible in some places, while in others his grey locks were several inches long. He was wearing clerical coat and breeches, but looked as though he might have escaped from Bedlam.

'State your business,' he hollered, and began to dance in a little circle, feet drumming on the floor. 'Business, business, business.'

'I am here to see Canon Owen,' Chaloner explained cautiously, tensed and ready to defend himself should the man attack. 'And John Tillison, if he is available.'

'Tillison, Tillison, Tillison,' the man chanted, accompanying the words with agitated flaps of his hand. 'Do you have the plague or are you safe?'

'Safe,' replied Chaloner firmly. 'Or I would not have come.'

'You are not a Quaker then? They visit the sick, and afterwards they stroll among the healthy, buying bread and meat from the markets.'

'No, I am not a Quaker,' said Chaloner, resisting the urge to add that few folk were likely to stroll around the markets these days, because there was virtually nothing to buy.

'You have not told me your name. Shall I tell you mine instead? It is Stephen Bing. Bing Bing, Bing. I am a musician.'

'*Stephen* Bing?' blurted Chaloner in dismay. 'Not the violist?'

Bing mimicked playing the viola da gamba with his hands. 'I bow, I pound the organ, I copy music for the cathedral. Copy, copy, copy.'

Chaloner experienced a sharp stab of sadness. Stephen Bing was a legend among violists, and Chaloner had long harboured a desire to meet him. There were so many questions he would have liked to ask, but he seriously doubted he would have any meaningful answers from the gibbering specimen who grinned and hopped in front of him.

'I do not copy music now, of course,' Bing went on in his oddly sing-song voice. 'Because no one wants it. Except for funerals. Do you play at funerals?'

'No,' replied Chaloner. 'Why are you still in the city? You could be safely in Oxford with the Court.' Where one more lunatic would make scant difference, he thought acidly.

'I am a minor canon, so my place is here,' explained Bing earnestly. 'Besides which, Sancroft told me to keep his people safe, and I must do as I am bid. I have five canons to look after, plus Deputy Tillison and two vicars. The rest have all flown away, away, away.'

'I heard,' said Chaloner. 'Is Owen here now? Will you take me to him?'

'He is with Tillison – Tillison the old, Tillison the bold.'

'Good. Then I can speak to them both at the same time. Where are they?'

'The cathedral is full of the dying,' whispered Bing. 'And the churchyard is full of the dead. Masked death – he will have them all in the end.'

'Not all,' said Chaloner, wondering what had caused Bing to lose his reason. Had it happened before the plague broke out, or was it staying in a disease-ravaged city that had done the damage? 'Some of us will survive.'

'You are here for Kerchier,' said Bing, and suddenly his mad eyes locked unblinkingly on Chaloner's. 'Owen told me that you would come. I knew Kerchier. He wanted to pull down the cathedral and build a new one – something that even Inigo Jones hoped to avoid. Kerchier did not like Gothic things, you see.'

'Do *you* like Gothic things?' asked Chaloner, although he hoped Bing would not transpire to be the killer. It would be a terrible waste of an amazing talent.

'I do,' nodded Bing. 'But they crumble and tumble. Everything does. It is a fact.'

'I suppose it is,' said Chaloner. 'Do you—'

'Owen is waiting,' interrupted the violist sharply. 'Stop babbling and come with me.'

The room to which Chaloner was conducted should have been magnificent, but it had recently been decorated with hand-painted wallpaper, which was a poor choice for an old building with damp problems. Several sheets were peeling at the edges, some had come off completely and lay on the floor, while the dye had run on the rest, making a terrible mess. There was also a musty smell, and Chaloner wondered if it emanated from the decaying wallpaper or the very ancient man who sat at the table in the middle of the room.

'Tillison, Tillison, Tillison,' sang Bing, jumping from foot to foot and pointing at him. 'The man who the dean left here to die. We were *all* left here to die, but the plague will not get me. Oh, no! I shall eat a toad, and it will pass me by.'

Tillison was well into his nineties, with a skull-like visage, a hunched body and a few strands of wispy white hair – he looked far older close up than when Chaloner had seen him across the churchyard the previous day. Yet there was something about him that commanded respect, and Chaloner reminded himself that Sancroft would not have left his cathedral in the hands of an ineffectual deputy.

'Thank you, Bing,' said the old man kindly. 'Return to your post now. We do not want others to come knocking while you are away – they might think we have fled, and it is important for Londoners to know that we are here if they need us.'

'God's eyes are always open,' declared Bing, and pirouetted three times before dancing back the way he had come.

Tillison was not alone, as seven other clerics were with him – five canons and two vicars. Chaloner's arrival had interrupted a meeting. Owen stood and began to make introductions, although Kirton the bookseller had identified most of them the day before. Chaloner studied each in turn as they came to exchange bows with him.

The three Hall brothers were identical, except in size and complexion. Francis the eldest was the biggest and most pimpled, John the youngest was the smallest and least spotted, while William was somewhere in between. Chaloner recalled what Kirton had told him: that the older two were canons, but John was a vicar, still waiting for the post that would provide him with a princely living.

Meanwhile, Richard Henchman could not have been anything but a cleric. He was a pink-faced person in his sixties, with silky white hair, watery blue eyes and a pious smile. Owen added gushingly that he was brother to the Bishop of London, while Chaloner recalled that he had been identified as one of Kerchier's enemies – the leader of the Maurice Men, who wanted to preserve the old St Paul's. He was also the cathedral's treasurer.

Next was Thomas Cartwright, young, handsome and athletically built. Like John Hall, he was only a vicar, but it quickly became apparent that he did not intend to stay one for long, and was determined to bring himself to the attention of anyone who mattered. He evidently thought Dean Sancroft's envoy was such a person, because he monopolised the conversation for several minutes, much to his seniors' irritation.

By contrast, Ben Stone barely bothered to look at Chaloner. He was grossly corpulent, and had thick red lips, like bloated worms. Kirton had mentioned an inappropriate fondness for women, and Chaloner found himself thinking that they would have to be willing partners, because the bulky canon was not built for the chase. He remembered what Cary had said about Stone – that he had originally supported Kerchier's plans for the cathedral, but had turned against them when man and money had vanished.

'We are all who remain in the cathedral,' said Tillison, when Owen had finished. 'We eight and Bing.'

'I am eager to do *my* duty,' declared John nobly. '*I* am no coward, thinking only of my own safety.'

'And he would like that to be borne in mind when the hunt begins for Kerchier's successor,' put in Cartwright nastily.

'Courage *should* be rewarded,' declared John, unruffled. 'And St Paul's needs men who do not shirk their responsibilities.'

'But not ones who remind us of it every time we meet,' Cartwright shot back.

'The next occupant of Kerchier's stall will be chosen by the dean and the treasurer – which means Sancroft and me,' said Henchman. He winked encouragingly at Cartwright. 'And I know who *I* want.'

The young vicar glowed, while John's face grew dark with anger.

'I shall have a say in the matter, too, Henchman,' warned William coolly, laying a soothing hand on his brother's arm. 'On the grounds that I am also a treasurer – I hold the funds raised to rebuild the cathedral, which represents a far larger sum than the measly amounts entrusted to you.'

'You should pass that money to me,' said Henchman sharply. 'You have no right to hoard it when we are in desperate need of cash for emergency repairs.'

'Our donors gave that money for *rebuilding* St Paul's, not for shoring up a teetering ruin,' retorted William. 'So it stays with me.'

'How much is in the fund exactly?' asked Tillison. He smiled sweetly. 'I have asked you several times, William, and you always promise to let me know, but it must slip your mind because I have been in the dark ever since Sancroft appointed me as his deputy.'

'I cannot tell you *exactly*,' hedged William. 'Because it changes on a daily basis as public-spirited citizens come to me with contributions. However, I can tell you that it has almost reached the level it was at when Kerchier disappeared.'

'When Kerchier *stole* it, you mean,' sneered Henchman.

'He never did!' cried Owen. 'And his murder proves it. Some vile thief killed him and made off with the fortune he had amassed so painstakingly.'

While they argued, Chaloner noted that Owen and the Hall brothers were on one side of the table, while Stone, Cartwright and Henchman were on the other, as if battle lines had been drawn, with the neutral Tillison in between. The Halls and Owen began to list the advantages of a nice new building, while the three Maurice Men argued the case for keeping the old one. Tillison made no effort to mediate, and only sat and listened.

'We have prepared your list, Chaloner,' Owen said, eventually realising that it was unwise to squabble in front of a man who was there to investigate murder. 'Tillison and I drew up a preliminary draft last night, and my colleagues here honed it this morning.'

In other words, thought Chaloner in disgust, everyone had been given an opportunity to eliminate those names he did not want included, and to add others for spite or mischief. But Tillison read his mind and shook his head.

'It is an honest effort, Mr Chaloner. It even includes me, although you will appreciate that I was elderly even then, so in no condition to dispatch my younger colleagues.'

'It will waste your time,' stated Francis sullenly. 'They have included everyone who had even the remotest connection with Kerchier, although it is patently obvious that the guilty party will not be a cleric.'

That claim sparked another row, and this time Tillison

joined in. While they bickered, Chaloner picked up the list, which comprised two pages of close-packed writing. On it were at least two hundred names, although some had *requiescat in pace* next to them. He was surprised to note that it included most of the eight men who sat around the table – Kirton was wrong to predict that it would include only Maurice Men. One name was notable by its absence, though.

'Where were you when Kerchier was killed, Cartwright?' he asked, speaking loudly to make himself heard.

'In a cot, probably,' came the jocular reply. 'I was a babe-in-arms at the time, and therefore innocent of theft and murder.'

'We are *all* innocent,' snapped Francis. 'As I said, no cleric made an end of Kerchier.'

'I appreciate that twenty years is a long time,' began Chaloner. 'But can any of you recall where you were the night he vanished?'

'I can,' said Francis immediately. 'I spent it ministering to my flock. I was a vicar at the time, and far too busy to murder colleagues.'

'As I recall, Kerchier was last seen shortly before Evensong,' said the corpulent Stone. 'And he was first missed at Morning Prayer the next day. How can you possibly know where you were every minute of that night?'

It was a good point, but Francis had an answer. 'Because his disappearance made it memorable – just like everyone knows exactly where they were when the old King was beheaded. I recall that night as though it was yesterday, and I was with needy parishioners every moment of it. But what about you? Where were you when the crime took place?'

Stone smirked. 'I never left the cathedral. After Evensong, I was approached by a certain young lady, and we spent the night in ways that I recall fondly even after all these years. Of course, she is dead of the plague now, so you cannot ask her to verify it.'

'I went home to my bed,' put in Owen. 'It is a night I have replayed in my mind on countless occasions, so, like Francis, I remember it well. Unfortunately, I cannot prove it, because I was alone.'

'Well, I have no idea what I did,' shrugged Henchman apologetically. 'Attended Evensong, probably, but after that . . . I am afraid it is simply too long ago.'

'The same is true for me,' admitted Tillison. 'But it was during the wars, when I did little else but try to keep the cathedral's plate from greedy soldiers. I imagine I was thus engaged that night, but I cannot say for certain.'

Chaloner supposed he should be grateful that Tillison and Henchman were prepared to be truthful, rather than fabricating some tale that they thought would see them exonerated. Yet how was he supposed to solve a case where memories were dim, false or non-existent? It made him realise again the enormity of the task he was facing.

'That leaves you two,' said Cartwright, looking at the younger Halls.

'Like Francis, we remember it well,' declared William. 'We left the cathedral after Evensong and walked home together. We talked for a while, then retired to our respective beds.'

Chaloner was not sure he believed that such a mundane evening should have stuck in their minds so clearly after two decades. Nor was Cartwright.

'That is not much of an alibi,' he remarked snidely.

'Perhaps not,' said John haughtily. 'But it happens to be the truth. Besides, why would we harm Kerchier? He agreed with us that St Paul's is not worth saving. He was on our side.'

'He was, and our cause suffered a grievous blow when he disappeared,' agreed Owen. 'We would be worshipping in a glorious basilica by now, if some rogue had not taken his life. *He* would not have allowed progress to be thwarted by foolish traditionalism.'

'There is nothing foolish about preserving our heritage,' declared Henchman hotly. 'And most Londoners agree. They love St Paul's, and do not want it replaced by some hideous modern monstrosity. It would be an act of unmitigated barbarism.'

'Quite right,' put in Cartwright. 'I may be young, but I appreciate the importance of maintaining what is ancient and solid.'

'But the cathedral is *not* solid,' argued Owen. 'That is the problem. Especially the south transept – one good gale will see it tumble down.'

'A gale,' sighed Francis. 'Now *that* I would welcome. This heat is unbearable, and a storm would cool things down. I thought I was going to expire when I went to Rycroft's house to collect the London Treacle last night.'

'The next batch is ready?' asked Tillison eagerly. 'Good! There is nothing left of the last lot – not a drop. Whose turn is it to bless the stuff?'

'Mine,' said Henchman. 'But are you sure it is safe to be near it? I heard blasts when I passed Rycroft's lair the other day, and you should have seen the state of his shirt.'

'Of course it is safe,' replied Francis irritably. 'I take a dose of it myself each day – which I would not do if it was dangerous.'

'Well, I put *my* trust in Bayhurst's Lozenges,' averred Stone, and to prove it, he took one from a packet and popped it in his mouth.

'I hope you do not do that in public,' said William warningly. 'Declaring a preference for another remedy undermines ours and sets a bad example.'

'I do not care,' replied Stone. 'My life is worth more than pennies in our coffers, and I have never liked London Treacle. It tastes of turpentine.'

The Halls took exception to that remark, but before they could quarrel afresh, Tillison declared the meeting adjourned. There was a collective scraping of chairs as the clerics rose, followed by a concerted dash for the door. Chaloner watched them go, wondering if their desire to escape the room stemmed from an eagerness to be away from the acrimonious atmosphere or to avoid being asked more questions about Kerchier.

'It is the heat,' said Tillison when the clatter of hastily departing footsteps had faded. 'It makes us all more irritable than is our wont. Shall we talk more in the cloisters, Mr Chaloner? There is usually a nice breeze at this time of day.'

St Paul's was in the unusual position of having two cloisters. One adjoined the south transept and was mostly filled by the chapter house; the other abutted the north transept, and was overlooked by the library. Tillison chose the latter. Most of the vegetation in the middle had been burned a crispy brown by the sun, while the fountain in the centre, which should have provided a restful tinkle of water, was dry and crusty with algae.

Tillison chose a bench in full sunlight, and settled himself down with a sigh of contentment. 'It is most pleasant out here,' he murmured. 'I do love a warm day.'

It was not pleasant at all, and Chaloner felt himself wilt. There was no 'nice breeze' either, and the cloisters' design and location meant there probably never would be. Had Tillison chosen an uncomfortable spot deliberately, to ensure a short interrogation? Chaloner determined that if so, the ploy would not work, even if it meant him being broiled alive.

'The list,' he began, sitting next to Tillison and pulling the pages from his pocket. The bench was stone and burned his legs through his breeches. 'Perhaps you will tell me why some of these names are on it. They are nearly all men . . .'

'And one woman,' said Tillison, closing his eyes and tilting his face skywards. 'Namely Pamela Ball, who also hated Kerchier.'

'Why did she hate him?'

'Because he detested nonconformists, and she has been a religious dissenter ever since she was old enough to speak.' Tillison opened one wry eye. 'She was a Quaker last week, but flits from sect to sect like a butterfly, so she may have adopted another one by now.'

'And Kerchier challenged her views?'

'As often as he could, Mr Chaloner. I remember clearly how easy he found it to tie her in logical knots – and how he derived a good deal of delight from the exercise.'

'So he was an unkind man?'

'On occasion, although she does contrive to bring out the worst in people. Kerchier jibed her about her hypocrisy, too. For example, when she was a True Leveller, she urged her followers to give away all their property, but parted with none of her own. She was – and is – a very avaricious lady.'

101

'Were their exchanges acrimonious enough to make her want to kill him?'

Tillison chuckled. 'She probably wants to kill most of the folk she meets. She is very passionate, as you will see when you meet her. She lives in King's Head Court with her husband Jasper. I pity him. He is a decent soul, and I cannot imagine what madness prompted him to propose marriage. She has made his life a living misery.'

'If she is the kind of person to kill priests for taunting her, then the chances are that she has claimed other victims, too. Are you aware of any other unsolved murders in the area?'

'No, I am not. Of course, we did not know that Kerchier *had* been murdered until yesterday, when you announced it.'

Chaloner squinted at the pages in his hand, narrowing his eyes against the sun's bright glare. 'I have met the first nine men here – you, Henchman, Bing, Cartwright, the Hall brothers, Owen and Stone.'

Tillison smiled. 'We are not the culprits obviously, but you did say that you wanted a *complete* list of those who were touched by Kerchier's plans – supporters and opponents.'

'What did *you* think of him?'

Tillison was silent for a while, and when he spoke, it was in a whisper, although the cloisters were deserted and there was no possibility of being overheard.

'I considered him a dreadful man, and so did everyone else on that list, with the possible exception of Owen and the Halls. He was dogmatic, sly, overbearing and convinced of his own rectitude.'

'I see,' said Chaloner, grateful for Tillison's honesty, but alarmed to hear that the victim had possessed a character that was unlikely to have made him popular. 'Now tell me about Canon Stone. I understand he supported the cathedral's destruction when Kerchier was alive, but defected to the other side when Kerchier vanished.'

'To the Maurice Men, yes. You see, Kerchier had persuaded Stone to donate a lot of money to "the cause", and when it later appeared that Kerchier had stolen it all . . . well, Stone felt betrayed. Changing stances was his way of expressing this hurt.'

'I do not suppose any of these suspects had a sudden windfall after Kerchier vanished, did they?'

'No one on that list is stupid, Mr Chaloner. They are all aware that flaunting a lot of unexplained cash would invite awkward questions. Even Pamela.'

It was a good point, so Chaloner moved to another subject. 'What do you know about the accident in which Kerchier lost his fingers?'

'Now *that* I do recall. He just appeared one day with his hand swathed in bandages. He refused to say what had happened, which gave rise to all manner of speculation, including that he had been playing with explosives – which was nonsense, of course. This was during the wars, when the King and Parliament hoarded every grain of powder with a view to blowing each other up.'

'He asked General Monck for a barrel.'

'I know – it was that which started the gossip. But Monck did not have one to spare.'

Chaloner turned his attention back to the list. 'I have also met Kirton, Gaundy, Wildbore and Denton – they are bell-ringers.'

'St Gregory's bell-ringers,' nodded Tillison. 'The next five men, starting with Robert Pemper, are the cathedral's.

As you have been told, Kerchier was last seen just before Evensong – which is a time when all of them would have been in the vicinity.'

'If you were a betting man, which of these names would you choose as the culprit?'

Tillison smiled serenely. 'Anyone who is not a cleric, Mr Chaloner. Start your enquiries with them, and do not waste your time by investigating us.'

Chaloner nodded, although it was not advice he planned to follow. 'Is there anything else I should know about Kerchier, other than that he wanted to demolish St Paul's, taunted nonconformists, was mysterious about how he injured his hand, and made enemies by dint of his unattractive personality?'

Tillison winced. 'He had his virtues, too – he wanted a new cathedral because he felt London deserved it. He revelled in Inigo Jones's innovations, especially the portico.'

As far as Chaloner was concerned, the one good thing to have come from the wars was that they had put an end to Jones's antics. The portico, tacked on to the cathedral's west end with a complete disregard for architectural harmony, was a frightful affair, and he considered it no less than an act of wilful vandalism.

'Really?' he asked.

'Oh, yes! He thought it was magnificent.'

'Was he in his right wits?'

Tillison chuckled. 'Each to his own, Mr Chaloner. Have you seen Christopher Wren's latest proposal, by the way?' He stood abruptly, and the sweat that beaded his face told Chaloner that the bench had grown too hot even for him. 'Come, I shall show you. We have a model in the library.'

Chaloner had seen it before, when it had . been displayed in White Hall, but had no objection to spending longer in Tillison's company. He still had plenty more questions to put.

# Chapter 4

The library was an attractive building, with windows that allowed enough light inside for reading, but not so much as to damage the books. It smelled of dust and old paper, and was silent except for the occasional rustle as someone turned a page. It had a high barrel-vaulted roof, and the books were stored in cases of oak so ancient that the wood was almost black, lending the place an air of solid venerability.

As Inigo Jones had died some years before, the Dean and Chapter had appointed a new set of Commissioners to devise options for the cathedral's future. One was the thirty-four-year old Christopher Wren, who believed the great church was beyond saving and should be demolished. His idea of what should replace it stood in an alcove at the far end of the library – a scale replica on a purpose-built table.

'God's teeth!' muttered Chaloner, appalled all over again. Wren's design comprised a marble mausoleum dominated by a vast dome, which was wholly alien to all that was London. Like a peacock in a pigeon shed, he thought, eyeing it in distaste.

'It is a masterpiece,' came Owen's voice from behind, and Chaloner turned to see that others had followed them there – Owen himself, Henchman, Stone and the Halls. 'Look at those elegant lines. Beautiful!'

Owen was unhealthily pale and his hands were unsteady. His breath carried the sickly scent of wine, and Chaloner wondered if he was drunk – which would certainly explain his peculiar taste in ecclesiastical architecture. His opinion was not shared by the pink-faced Henchman, however.

'It is not beautiful at all,' the treasurer declared angrily. 'It is a cruel joke. Wren must really hate London to have devised such a monstrosity.'

'He does not hate our city,' cried Owen, stung. 'He loves it with all his heart.'

'Does he?' demanded Henchman. 'Then why is he not here, helping us fight the plague? Instead he skulks in Oxford, currying favour with the King in a sly effort to see his vile schemes implemented.'

'He is not *skulking* in Oxford,' countered Owen crossly. 'It is where he lives – he works at the University. It is not his fault that the Court chose to settle in that particular city. It is coincidence.'

'Perhaps the plague will follow him there and take his life,' muttered Henchman darkly. 'Because the Almighty cannot want this thing built in His name.'

'Then let us pray for Wren's deliverance,' said Tillison serenely, cutting across the retort Owen began to make. 'And for our own. I find prayer more efficacious than London Treacle if you want the truth. I know we sell the remedy in our cathedral, but I would far sooner put my trust in the Lord.'

'I admire your faith, Tillison,' said Francis coolly. 'But

most of the corpses in the plague pits prayed – and took *sal mirabilis* – but neither did them any good. London Treacle, on the other hand, saves lives.'

'I beg to differ,' said the corpulent Stone. 'London Treacle might do wonders for the cathedral's coffers, but Bayhurst's Lozenges are better for our health.'

He took a whole handful from his packet and tossed them into his mouth. Chaloner was not sure what Bayhurst put in them, but the stench that immediately pervaded the little room made him wonder if the formula was safe.

'You are a fool,' said Owen contemptuously. 'London Treacle has sixty different ingredients *and* it is endorsed by the Society of Alchemical Physitians. Bayhurst's Lozenges only have seven, while God only knows what rubbish is tossed into *sal mirabilis*. It stands to reason that our treacle is the best.'

Tillison cut the spat short by telling Chaloner what the cathedral was doing to help London in its hour of need, which snagged the clerics' attention. However, it was not long before they were at loggerheads again.

'No!' snapped Henchman, after William had claimed with pride that St Paul's would remain open to Londoners no matter how fiercely the disease raged. 'How many more times must I say it? We must close until the danger is past. It is irresponsible to provide a venue for people to gather. Besides, just think of the money we could save on candles and lay staff salaries if there were no people tramping through the place.'

'Spoken like a true miser,' said William in distaste. 'We cannot shut up shop, Henchman. People *need* the comfort we provide.'

At that point, the cathedral bells began to clang, and Chaloner was again reminded that Pemper and his band were terrible ringers. Their efforts were not helped by the bells themselves, which were about as tuneful as flower pots.

'The new peal will hang in here,' said Francis, pointing to the model's north-west tower. 'It is high time we had a better one.'

'Our old bells have been calling the faithful to prayer for centuries,' flashed Henchman, offended. 'So they are an institution, and it is not for us to melt them down. Besides, *God* likes them. If He did not, He would have made His opinion known.'

'He *did* make it known,' retorted Owen. 'Eighty-four years ago, when He set fire to the spire and sent it crashing through the nave roof. But still we procrastinate.'

'Of course we procrastinate!' snarled Henchman, and waved a pink hand at the model. 'When *that* is what you intend to put in its place.'

'It is splendid,' countered Owen stubbornly. 'Bright, clean and modern.'

The debate raged back and forth, but Chaloner was learning nothing he did not already know, so he took his leave, unwilling to waste time listening to another quarrel. Only Stone noticed him slipping out. The plump canon hastened to follow, and Chaloner supposed it was to make sure he left the cathedral's property, and did not go snooping around on his own.

'Lord, I am glad to be outside,' the canon declared, pulling uncomfortably at his collar. 'It was sweltering in there. It must be all the hot air being vented – on both sides.'

'Speaking of sides, I hear that you have supported both at one time or another.'

'Tillison!' spat Stone. 'What a gossip he is. He doubt-less claimed that I was vexed with Kerchier for stealing the money that I donated to the cause. But he is wrong. I *never* believed Kerchier filched it. However, when Kerchier disappeared, it was the Halls who took over . . .'

'You dislike them?'

'Let us just say that they are not of his calibre.'

He nodded a brisk farewell, then waddled to the lane called Paul's Alley, which ran between the cathedral and Paternoster Row. Chaloner followed at a discreet distance, and smiled when Stone, after looking around to ensure he was not being watched, ducked into a doorway where he was greeted with a very passionate embrace from Mrs Driver, who proclaimed in strident tones that she was *delighted* to see him, but would he be so kind as to honour his promise and buy her that emerald necklace now?

She certainly knew how to look after herself, thought Chaloner wryly, watching the pair hurry away, arm in arm. There could not be many courtesans who were in demand by mayors, generals and high-ranking clerics.

Chaloner entered the cathedral, intending to find a quiet spot where he could sit and study Owen's list. It was cool after the heat outside, and he stood for a moment, awed as always by the sheer scale of the place. The nave and chancel combined to make one of the largest buildings in the world – the rose window behind the high altar was enormous, yet looked no larger than a porthole when viewed from the westernmost end.

Huge pillars soared upwards, supporting three tiers of arches, each lit by windows. Light flooded in through brilliantly coloured glass, which shed bright patterns on the creamy flagstone floor below. The chancel boasted two Saxon shrines, although these had suffered from the attentions of Puritan iconoclasts – both effigies were missing faces, hands and feet.

Because of its immense size, the cathedral was in the way when people wanted to cross the city, so for centuries it had been used as a shortcut. Over time, tradesmen had set up in its aisles, aiming to make the most of the teeming hordes that traipsed past. Officially, they were supposed to sell religious goods – books, candles and pilgrim souvenirs – but few observed this particular stricture, so a wide range of secular goods was available as well.

That day, however, most booths were closed, their owners either dead or gone to the country, and Chaloner had never known the cathedral to be so empty or so quiet. It was also strangely devoid of cats and dogs, and he was unimpressed to note that a family of rats had taken up residence in what had once been a bookstall. Above his head, birds flitted in the slanting sunlight – sparrows, pigeons, swifts, martins and finches.

Yet despite its grandeur, it was clear that St Paul's was in trouble. Its lofty ceiling was crazed with cracks, and several piers listed at an angle that was far from natural. The south transept was the most badly affected – its floor was littered with rubble from recent collapses, and ropes were strung between the pillars, hung with notices that warned people to stay out.

Dominating the south transept was an ornate tomb, and Chaloner took his life in his hands to step over the rope and scramble across the debris to inspect it. The Latin inscription on the side told him that that it was the final resting place of Dean Valentine Cary – Secretary Cary's uncle. It had been a glorious affair, a riot of reds, greens and yellows, with an effigy on top, slathered in gold leaf. The Puritans had been at that as well, and had slashed at it with an axe until it was all but destroyed.

'Did you know that is the most expensive monument ever to be built in here?'

Chaloner jumped at the voice so close behind him, and whipped around fast. It was Matt Rycroft, and Chaloner was all admiration for the alchemist's stealth, as there were not many who could creep up on him undetected, especially over a floor that was strewn with things that crunched and cracked. The knife he always carried in his sleeve had automatically slipped into his hand, and he hastened to put it away before it was seen.

'Is it?' he asked.

Rycroft nodded. 'It was started when the dean was still alive and cost him every penny he owned. Then fanatics came along during the Commonwealth and smashed it all to pieces.'

'His children did not repair it?'

Rycroft laughed. 'No – they were furious that he bought himself a fine mausoleum but left nothing to them. Yet I understand why he did it. He was the illegitimate son of a lord, and was always conscious of his lower status. The tomb was his way of telling the world that he had achieved high office despite the disadvantages of his birth.'

'His tomb will not be making that point for much longer if the Hall brothers have their way – it will be demolished, along with everything else in here.'

'Perhaps, but my money is on the Maurice Men winning that war. Henchman's brother is the Bishop of London, and *he* does not want this place pulled down. But why are you in here, Chaloner? Can you not see that it is dangerous?'

Chaloner waved the list. 'I wanted somewhere quiet to think about my investigation.'

He saw the alchemist try to read what was written there, which prompted him to fold the pages up and put them away.

'Then let me find you somewhere safer. The Lady Chapel is usually empty. You can do your quiet thinking there.'

Chaloner followed him over the crossing and into a beautiful little oratory in the north-west corner, near the bell tower. Rycroft murmured a farewell and was gone, gliding away as soundlessly as he had arrived. Chaloner watched him go, wondering why an alchemist should have perfected such a stealthy tread.

Chaloner spent a long time in the chapel, poring over Owen's list. Fortunately, it was not as formidable as he had first feared, because he could dismiss anyone who was dead. Once they had been crossed off, he was left with a hundred and forty-seven 'suspects'. He had already met the cathedral men and the bell-ringers, while two more had been mentioned in discussions: the rabid nonconformist Pamela Ball, and Matthew Harbert, brother of the knight whose tomb Kerchier had occupied for the last twenty years.

The remaining names meant nothing to him, but each would have to be explored, so he supposed he had better make a start. He was just aiming for the south door when the bells started up again, clanging so vigorously that dust fell from the ceiling.

The ringing chamber was on the ground floor, and he glanced through the door to see Pemper and his band hauling away for all they were worth. Their efforts were accompanied by a lot of flying ropes, cursing and grunting, while Pemper barked bad-tempered commands which ensured that no one much enjoyed the exercise.

As he watched, the hair on the back of his neck rose, and he turned to see Bing, whose black-rimmed eyes were fixed unblinkingly on him from across the nave. As the mad violist was on Owen's list, Chaloner beckoned him over.

'I did not kill Kerchier,' declared Bing immediately. 'I am no executioner. But I was with him the night he disappeared. Oh, yes. I remember that as clear as glass.'

'Will you tell me what happened?'

'It was just before Evensong,' replied Bing, and the crazed look eased slightly. 'We were walking to the cathedral together – Tillison, Owen, the Halls, Stone, Henchman, me and several others who are dead now. We reached the south door, but Kerchier wanted to visit St Gregory's first and wandered off on his own. That was the last we ever saw of him.'

'Did you and your companions stay for the whole service? No one left at any point?'

'Oh, now that I cannot say. It was dark in here, because the wars had deprived us of candles and it was too long ago to recall such tiny details. But I remember Kerchier heading to St Gregory's well enough.'

'Why did he go? Was he meeting someone there?'

'Yes – holes and cracks and fissures.' Bing sang the words, then lowered his voice. 'Inigo Jones pulled St Gregory's down, but the parishioners complained to Parliament, so he had to put it back up again. He was angry, but Kerchier was angrier and told him to skimp.'

Chaloner struggled to understand what he was being told. 'In the hope that St Gregory's would be condemned and demolished anyway?'

Bing laughed and clapped his hands. 'You have it! You have it! Kerchier's exact words to us that night were: "It has never been very stable, and its vergers have done it a grave disservice by burrowing beneath it. It will probably collapse of its own accord soon. These things have a way of happening, as I am sure you know."'

He began to caper in tight little circles, robes flying, so Chaloner caught his arm and pushed him against a pillar, to keep him still. As Bing stared back, there was a flash of something hard and calculating in his eyes that made Chaloner wonder if he was as mad as he wanted everyone to think.

'And how is it that you can remember Kerchier's exact words, when you have just confessed that it was too long ago to recall tiny details?' he asked suspiciously.

'Because I do,' retorted Bing, struggling to free himself. 'Believe me or not. I do not care. Oh, no, I don't.'

'So Kerchier expected St Gregory's to fall down?' Chaloner tightened his grip on the wriggling violist. 'Please, Bing. This is important.'

'He did, but St Gregory's is still here, and so are we are all – except Kerchier.' Bing managed to pull away, and began to dance again. 'Stone, Stone, Stone. He will talk about Kerchier. Oh, yes, he will. John Upton might have talked, too – about Kerchier *and* Harbert.'

'Who is John Upton?'

'A stationer who will sing no more. He loved *sal mirabilis*, but the salts were not miraculous enough. Stone plans to visit the devil tonight, but you will not find him, because he does not wish to be found. Stone loves the devil.'

And with that, the violist winked, grinned and loped away.

*

As Pemper and his band were on Owen's list, too, Chaloner decided it was as good a time as any to corner them. He entered the ringing chamber to find Pemper berating his team for their uneven striking – the timing between dongs – although Chaloner thought that Pemper himself had been the worst offender. Pemper's temper frayed even further when he discovered that his cronies had finished all the free ale that was provided as a perk of the job.

'It is the second time this month,' he snarled. 'So you are all fined a penny. No, do not argue, Flower! *I* am ringing master, and I have the right to punish you as I see fit – it is in our set of rules.'

'*Your* set of rules,' countered Flower resentfully. All five were elderly, but he was by far the oldest. He was totally bereft of hair and teeth, and was obliged to cling to a bell rope for support. 'The ones you wrote and implemented, even though we voted against them.'

Pemper had no answer to this, but then he spotted Chaloner in the doorway, which absolved him of the need to think of one.

'What do *you* want?' he demanded. 'If it is to join our band, the answer is no. We do not welcome outsiders into our fraternity. Especially ones who know Kirton. I saw you with that villainous rogue yesterday, so do not deny it.'

'That is Dean Sancroft's man,' said Flower, speaking as though Chaloner was not there. 'Vicar Masley told me about him – he is here to find out what happened to Canon Kerchier.'

'That sly old rogue!' spat Pemper venomously. 'I am *glad* he has been dead all these years, because it made me sick to think of him enjoying all that money he stole. So what happened to it? Come on, man. Speak up.'

'It was not with his body,' replied Chaloner. 'Perhaps his killer took it.'

'Well, do not look at me,' declared Pemper belligerently. 'Do you think I would still be selling coal if I had filched a fortune? No, indeed! I would have bought a tobacco plantation in New England, and made myself richer still.'

'I would have become a dancing master,' said Flower, rather wistfully. 'I know all the right steps, and no one is lighter on his feet than me.'

'And *I* would keep goats,' interposed one of the others. 'They are lovely—'

'Kerchier,' interrupted Chaloner, before they could veer too far from the subject at hand. 'Do you remember the day he went missing?'

'I remember we rang for Evensong,' replied a man with long grey hair that almost reached his waist. 'Unfortunately, the rest is a blur, but I imagine we had some ale, attended the service and went home. We usually do.'

'You do not remember, because you are old,' declared Pemper scornfully. 'But there is nothing wrong with *my* memory. The events of that night are as clear as a bell in my mind.'

'And?' asked Chaloner, not sure whether to believe him. Pemper was the kind of man to put besting his cronies above telling the truth.

'And we did what he said,' replied Pemper, nodding at his long-haired crony. 'Rang, drank, prayed and went home. However, Kerchier was not in the cathedral when we left – I would have noticed.'

'Would you?' asked Chaloner warily. 'Why?'

'Because I always watched him when he was about,' replied Pemper darkly. 'I did not trust him with our bells, see.'

117

'He was the sort of man to steal clappers,' elaborated Flower. 'Or damage ropes. He never actually tried, as far as I know, but it was obvious that he wanted to.'

'Because he did not appreciate good ringing,' explained Pemper. 'And he wanted us silenced. He hated bells.'

'Do you know why he went to St Gregory's?' asked Chaloner, feeling *he* might be tempted to indulge in sabotage, too, if he was obliged to listen to the paltry efforts of Pemper and his band day in and day out.

'The only time he spoke to us was to criticise our striking.' Pemper bristled. 'Do you know what he once said? That none of us was fit to handle a bell and we should let St Gregory's ringers take over our duties. He had the audacity to claim that they are better.'

'That must have annoyed you,' fished Chaloner.

'Oh, it did,' agreed Pemper. 'I felt like walloping him over the head with a clapper and— Oh, no!' He glared at Chaloner. 'You will not catch *me* out with your sly questions. I might have *felt* like braining the old bastard, but I would never have actually done it.'

'None of us would,' averred Flower, while the others nodded vigorous agreement. 'We would not have sullied our hands with his nasty old blood.'

'The plague take whoever wrote to Dean Sancroft about those bones!' spat Pemper. 'Gaundy should have deposited Harbert on top of them and kept his mouth shut. No one cares about Kerchier now, and you have no business interrogating us.'

'Interrogate Wildbore and his band instead,' put in Flower spitefully. 'They are the kind of men to murder canons and keep quiet about it, not us. Is that not so, lads?'

'It is,' chorused the others, leaving the long-haired

118

ringer to finish with, 'We hate them and we hate their bells.'

'Now go away,' ordered Pemper, beginning to tug on his rope. 'Evensong will start soon, and we have work to do. Do not come back. We have no more to say to you.'

By the time Chaloner left St Paul's, the sun was setting in a fiery ball that turned the ancient stones red. People heading for Evensong muttered that it was the colour of blood, and thus a bad omen, although Chaloner thought it was just the end of another hot day. He had exited by the south door – the one next to St Gregory's – so he stood for a moment, thinking about Kerchier. It was here, just before the evening service, that the canon had last been seen alive. Other than by his killer, of course.

Then, as now, the bells had been ringing. Had Pemper and his band then gone outside to drink their ale and spotted Kerchier alone? It would have been easy to knock a vocal critic over the head, and St Gregory's newly dug crypt was an obvious place to hide a body. They could have dropped it in Harbert's freshly created vault, after which Gaundy's drunken father had sealed it up without noticing that something was amiss.

But what about the missing money? Chaloner was fairly sure the cathedral ringers had not taken it – if they had, they would have spent it recklessly, which would have seen them caught. So had someone else witnessed them killing Kerchier, and taken advantage of the situation by burgling his house?

No answers came, but Pemper and his cronies certainly warranted further investigation, and Chaloner determined to snag each of them alone, to see what they

119

might blurt when they did not have each other for moral support.

He returned to the Mitre, where he fed his new chickens a few handfuls of grain before shutting them away for the night. Afterwards, he prowled through the darkening streets, to make himself more familiar with the area. He knew the cathedral well, but now he explored the alleys and squares that surrounded it – London House Yard, where the Mitre and the Turk's Head Coffee House were located; Paternoster Row, with its myriad bookshops, now all closed; and the handsome mansions on Carter Lane that housed the cathedral's precentor, chancellor and treasurer.

Eventually, he reached Paul's Chain. Rycroft's windows were shuttered, although a gleam under one showed that a lantern was lit within. Chaloner glanced around. No one was watching, so he tiptoed towards it and put his eye to the gap. However, it was not the alchemist labouring over the pots on the table, but Francis Hall. Chaloner supposed it was his turn to recite the prayers that rendered London Treacle more efficacious.

Directly opposite Rycroft's home was St Gregory's vicarage. Its windows were open in the hope of catching a breeze, and Masley sat within, working at a document-piled desk by lamplight. He happened to glance up as Chaloner passed, and waved to indicate that he wanted a word. As he stood, someone else entered the room, collected a sheaf of papers and walked out again. There was a fleeing moment when Chaloner thought it was Kirton the bookseller, but although both men had the same angular build, the fellow in Masley's house lacked the bushy white eyebrows.

'Put them in the box with the others, Joshua,' Masley

called after the man, then approached Chaloner. 'You did well to identify those bones within hours of your arrival. No wonder Sancroft hired you. Yet I confess I am astonished: it never occurred to me for a moment that they might belong to Canon Kerchier.'

'No?'

Masley shrugged. 'He vanished so long before I came to the city that he simply did not cross my mind. All I know about him – other than the fact that he disappeared with a lot of the cathedral's money – is that he wanted to knock poor St Gregory's down. I still have parishioners who think the devil came along and dragged him down to hell.'

'Satan did not creep up behind him, hit him over the head, and hide his body in someone else's tomb. That was the work of a person.'

'True,' sighed Masley, and rolled his eyes. 'And the murder means that now I shall have to resanctify the crypt – a chore I could do without, given that I am so busy.'

Chaloner recalled what Kirton had suspected. 'Are you writing a book?'

'If only I had the time for such leisure! No, my parish clerk is dead of the plague, so it falls to me to keep records of all those who perish.'

Chaloner was puzzled. 'Surely it cannot be that arduous? It is just a case of entering names in a ledger.'

'We do things properly at St Gregory's,' replied Masley haughtily, 'which entails writing a full report for every corpse I bury. There will be a lot of confusion when the crisis is over, and I want to avoid unnecessary distress when people come looking for their loved ones. Verger Gaundy helps, when he is not tolling bells.'

'I spoke to him about Kerchier, but he told me little of use.'

'No surprise there. You will not solve this crime, Chaloner, and if you have any sense, you will concede defeat and leave before you catch the plague.'

Chaloner had now lost count of the people who wanted him to give up and go home, but the more he was told that he would fail, the more determined he was to prove them wrong. He bade Masley goodnight and continued down Paul's Chain, where a flicker of movement at the entrance to an alley caught his attention. The fellow melted quickly into the darkness, although not before Chaloner had glimpsed a dark, foreign face and a mass of blue-black curls. It was the Greek again.

Chaloner started to run after him, but then stopped. It was madness to give chase. First, the alley was squalid and likely to be full of plague-stricken hovels. And second, it might be a trap to lure him to a secluded spot where an assassin could complete what had been started the previous night. He returned to the Mitre, aware now that it had been reckless to venture abroad for no good reason.

There was no music at the inn that evening, but Paget did have one other customer: a man in full plague costume, who sat hunched over a flagon of ale – although Chaloner was not sure how he expected to drink it with a mask buckled around his head. Chaloner sat at the opposite end of the room, and was surprised when Paget brought him a jug of wine that he had not ordered.

'From him,' the landlord said, indicating the man with a nod of his head before lowering his voice. 'But I do not know him, so you might want to be cautious, given what happened last night. Shall we feed some to your hens, and see what happens?'

Chaloner eyed him coldly. 'No, but you can pour a cup for my benefactor and ask him to join me in a toast to the King's health.'

Paget went to oblige, but the moment the request was made, the man leapt up and bolted for the door. Chaloner set off in pursuit, but it was pitch black outside, and there were no hammering footfalls to indicate which way his quarry had gone. Reminding himself yet again that haring around London in the dark was not a good idea, he returned to Paget.

'Look at this!' the landlord hissed, showing him the inside of the jug, which was scored with tiny pits. 'I poured it away when he darted off, and I swear it smoked when it went down the drain. It was poisoned!'

Chaloner was more offended than concerned. Did the culprit really think he would accept wine from a stranger who was suspiciously determined to keep his face hidden? Still, he thought as he retired to bed – one in the attic this time, which would be impossible to reach from outside – at least the 'attack' had reminded him that he needed to stay on his guard.

# Chapter 5

The next day was Saturday. Chaloner rose early and dressed in clothes that had been washed and pressed to within an inch of their life – one of Paget's daughters was a laundress and was so desperate for business that there was not an item in Chaloner's saddlebag that had been spared her vigorous attentions. He fed and watered his hens, and was rewarded with three brown eggs, which Mrs Paget boiled for him. He took them into the garden to eat, thinking about the day ahead, while the birds jumped on the bench next to him and preened.

He pulled Owen's list from his pocket and studied it again. Paget had asked to see it the previous evening, and had been able to eliminate another thirty-one names – people who had moved away over the years, including a family of twelve who had gone to make new lives for themselves in the Province of New York.

Even so, he was still left with a hundred and sixteen 'suspects'. All would have to be interviewed, which represented no mean task. The plague would not help, given that folk were naturally suspicious of strangers, and persuading them to talk to him would not be easy. Of course, the killer had to be in the city *now* – if he had fled to avoid the disease, he would not have been in a position to hire Mims – so the list would be shorter still once anyone who was currently away had been eliminated.

For no particular reason, Chaloner decided to see Pamela Ball first. Owen and his friends had thoughtfully included any addresses they happened to know, and had written that she lived in King's Head Court.

He stood, brushed eggshell from his shirt, and went in search of Paget's children, whom he paid handsomely to tend his chickens for as long as he and they were in residence at the Mitre – to feed them, repel would-be predators of both two- and four-legged varieties, and to shut them away at night and let them out in the mornings, should he be too busy. The boys accepted the commission eagerly, although it was clear they thought him short of a few wits for the trouble he was taking over his new acquisitions.

When he was satisfied that they understood their responsibilities, Chaloner aimed for the gate, aware of the reassuring weight of the sword at his side and Cary's dag in his pocket. The Mims would not find it easy to best him in a fair fight.

He started to walk south, but his attention was caught by what he first thought was a religious procession making its way across St Paul's Churchyard, but that transpired to be Abigail Lawrence and her daughters. All ten wore identical grey cloaks and held pomanders to their noses. Their ginger hair was bundled into turbans – a fashion that was thought by some to prevent deadly plague miasmas from taking root in the head.

'We are going to pray for an end to the pestilence,' Abigail informed him in a loud, self-important voice. 'As

125

we do every Saturday, Monday and Thursday. No one can say that *we* do not do our duty for the city.'

Cary certainly would not, thought Chaloner wryly, recalling how the secretary liked to extol her virtues.

'There is to be a special service on Wednesday evening,' put in one of the younger girls brightly. 'Where we shall beg God even harder to deliver our city from the sickness.'

'All London will be there,' elaborated Abigail, 'and the canons plan to put on a splendid show, to prove to everyone that the Lord has not abandoned us. I hope you will attend, Mr Chaloner.'

Chaloner pondered the wisdom of holding such an event. Surely it was irresponsible to encourage large crowds to assemble while an infectious disease raged? Of course, while the government forbade anyone from going to sporting events, playhouses, large funerals or family gatherings, folk were still expected to attend church. The rationale was that God would never allow the devout to catch something nasty in one of His houses.

'We invited Mrs Driver to join us in our prayers today,' said a girl from the upper middle section of the line. She sniffed her disdain. 'Although I doubt she will bother to put in an appearance.'

'She will not,' predicted Abigail archly. 'There is not a selfless bone in that . . . that *person's* body.'

A murmur of agreement from her brood said that this was true. But Chaloner was more interested in the past than the future, and while Abigail was not on Owen's list, she was certainly fierce enough to kill, not to mention sufficiently strong to lug corpses about.

'Were you in London when Canon Kerchier went missing?' he asked.

He was not surprised when her answer came promptly

and decisively. Abigail Lawrence was not a woman to think too deeply before she opened her mouth.

'My husband and I were visiting kin in Kent at the time, and we only heard the tale of his vanishing when we came home. However, as I told you last night, I never believed that Kerchier took the lost money. He *lived* for the prospect of a St Paul's remodelled to his own specifications, and would never have done anything to jeopardise that dream.'

'We take London Treacle,' announced the smallest child, in the random manner often favoured by very young children. 'One dose in the morning and another at night.'

'It is the only remedy that works,' averred Abigail, regarding the girl fondly. 'Do you have some, Mr Chaloner? If not, I shall send you a pot, gratis. Do not use *sal mirabilis* – it will do you no good at all, and it smells of worms.'

'Father gives *sal mirabilis* to Mrs Driver,' piped up the middle child.

'Yes,' said Abigail smugly. 'I know.'

'He gave her this as well,' said the eldest. She produced a piece of paper with a grin that was all wicked innocence. 'It accidentally fell out of her reticule, but I keep forgetting to give it back.'

'A Certificate of Health,' mused Abigail, taking it from her with a triumphant gleam in her eye. It was a tatty document on paper so cheap that the fibres used in its production had not been properly de-coloured, rendering it a mucky grey-brown. 'Hah! She has been braying for weeks that she will never abandon "her" city, but I knew her nerve would fail in the end. So she wants to leave, does she?'

127

'But she cannot – not without that,' said the girl with a vindictive smirk.

'Whores are well paid, Rachel,' said Abigail, all dignified distaste as she handed it back. 'She can afford to buy another. And I want her gone, so do not steal it next time.'

'How easy is it to get a certificate?' asked Chaloner, supposing he would have to acquire one himself when his enquiries were complete – assuming he did not catch the plague in the interim, of course.

'Not easy at all,' replied Abigail. 'It must be signed by a cleric *and* a doctor, but most of those have fled. Even if you do find two professional men willing to oblige, it costs the Earth – they can charge whatever they like, in the knowledge that they have you over a barrel. Of course, it is not just certificates that are in short supply these days.'

'Food is scarce, too,' put in Rachel.

'Which is heinous,' said Abigail, pursing her lips in disapproval. 'Victuals *are* being sent to the city, but they are stolen before they can be fairly distributed – by rogues who sell them at criminally high prices. If *I* catch the villains, I shall give them a piece of my mind.'

She stalked away with her offspring in tow, leaving Chaloner thinking that it was a bold felon indeed who would risk incurring the wrath of Abigail Lawrence.

King's Head Court had once been a very fashionable place to live. The tavern for which it was named was a large Elizabethan affair of black and white timber, while the houses around it were brick-built and had slate roofs. It had been popular with wealthy clerics and merchants, but when these had left the noxious atmosphere of the city for the newer, cleaner developments to the north, King's Head Court had slipped into decline.

The tavern still clung to the vestiges of respectability, but the surrounding houses were shabby, and the cobbles in the yard were hidden by a layer of dirt. Two body-shaped bundles lay outside one home, although there was no red cross on the door to warn of the plague within. Chaloner could only assume that the authorities were so overwhelmed by the number of cases that they had stopped bothering to mark some pestered places. Or that King's Head Court had escaped notice because of its secluded location – at the end of a tiny alley, which led off a little-used lane.

The bodies had been very carelessly wrapped, and an arm spilled from one – an arm sporting a green ribbon. Common sense warned Chaloner to keep his distance, but his curiosity was piqued. He drew his sword and used it to poke the blanket away from one corpse's face. It was unfamiliar, so he repeated the exercise with the second, exposing the thin cheeks and straggly beard of the gunman who had put a bullet in his pillow.

Cautiously, Chaloner investigated further. There were no plague tokens, but that meant nothing – sometimes, victims died too quickly for visible symptoms to appear. He looked for signs of violence, but detected nothing obvious. However, both men had a line of white froth on their lips. Had the plague caused it, or was it evidence of poison? After all, it was a peculiar coincidence that they should die quite so soon after trying to kill him. Or was it? Perhaps Pamela Ball would be able to throw some light on the matter.

He was just debating which house might be hers, when the sound of singing drifted from the building outside

129

which he stood. It was a hymn popular with the more fervent species of nonconformist, and he recalled Tillison saying that Pamela was currently a Quaker.

The window was open, and he looked through it to see a dozen women and one man, all kneeling on the floor. They were being led by a tiny person with shiny black hair and a clean white apron. She held herself erect, and oozed the kind of confidence that indicated she thought a very great deal of herself, and that all of it was good. Chaloner had seen her before – outside Lawrence's mansion, where she had bellowed a furious retort to Monck's disparaging remarks about Quakers, calling him a 'miserable Scotch dog'.

Next to her was a woman of roughly the same age – nearer forty than thirty – whose hair was tucked demurely into a cloth cap, although a spark in her green eyes suggested a sense of fun. She wore a black shawl around her shoulders, a garment that had recently become indicative of widowhood. The sole man in the gathering was a handsome, grey-haired fellow with kind eyes. He sang, but without enthusiasm, giving the impression that he wished he was somewhere else.

Then the small woman saw Chaloner. Her dark eyes flashed as she leapt to her feet and stormed towards him. Her reaction startled the others, and their singing faltered into silence.

'We meet in accordance with the Declaration of Breda,' she snarled. 'The agreement the King made with us, his people, before we let him have his throne back. It promised religious toleration – and we intend to have it!'

'I see,' said Chaloner, wondering if she thought him some kind of halfwit, who could not recall the treaty that

His Majesty had signed on the eve of his Restoration. 'I need to speak to Pamela Ball. Is she here?'

'I am she.' The little woman pulled herself up to her full height, which was several inches lower than his shoulder. 'What do you want? I am doing *important* work here – far more vital than anything that can occupy *your* time.'

'Is that so?' Chaloner felt he could quickly come to dislike Pamela Ball.

'What is the matter?' The woman with the green eyes had come to stand by her side, where they were soon joined by the man.

'This fellow wants to speak to me, Ester,' explained Pamela haughtily. 'But he had better say his piece fast, because I am too valuable to be kept standing around. I am a *nurse*.'

Chaloner was not sure how those two statements went together, as nurses had a poor reputation in the city. They tended to be old women with a fondness for drink, famed for letting their charges die from neglect or through incompetence.

'We know,' said Ester tiredly, while the man rolled his eyes. Pamela saw him.

'Do not make faces behind *my* back, Jasper Ball! Now go to the kitchen and warm some broth for our sisters. Well? What are you waiting for?'

'He has deliveries to make, Pamela,' said Ester quietly, raising a hand to prevent Jasper from obliging. 'There are families all over London waiting for their London Treacle. Indeed, he should not have spared the time to come to this meeting, because—'

'He will do what *I* say or there will be trouble,' interrupted Pamela dangerously. 'I thought he had good

131

prospects when I agreed to be his wife, but it transpires that he is nothing but an errand boy for an alchemist.'

She spoke with such rank contempt that Jasper flushed with shame. Then she pointed an imperious finger towards the kitchen, and he scurried away with his head down. Ester opened her mouth to object, but Pamela cut across her.

'Well?' she demanded of Chaloner. 'What do you want?'

'Yes, how may we help you?' asked Ester, far more pleasantly, so that Chaloner wished he was interviewing her instead. 'Would you like to join our community?'

'I came to ask about Canon Kerchier,' he replied, suspecting that new recruits would not come along very often if Pamela Ball was left in charge. 'You may have heard that his body was found recently, and that he had been murdered.'

Pamela smirked nastily. 'He got what he deserved. He accused me – *me*, Pamela Ball! – of arrogance and inconstancy. He disapproved of my religious views, but I showed him what was what when I stopped being a Muggletonian and became a Seeker. Or was it a Fifth Monarchist? Regardless, it wiped the smile off his face.'

Chaloner blinked, amazed that she should have enrolled in quite so many radical sects, when most folk found that one was as much as they could manage. And such controversial ones, too: Fifth Monarchists thought that King Jesus was poised to take up residence in White Hall; Seekers believed that all organised religion was corrupt; while Muggletonians were hostile to philosophical reason and cursed anyone who disagreed with them.

'And now you are a Quaker,' he remarked wonderingly.

'Yes, I am! The society was foundering before I joined it, but now it flourishes.'

Chaloner doubted her membership had done it any favours, but her claims were irrelevant to his investigation, so he hastened to ask his questions and leave. He had no wish to spend any longer than necessary with the opinionated Pamela Ball.

'I have been charged to find Kerchier's killer and bring him to justice. Do you know anything that might help?'

'On whose authority?' demanded Pamela. 'Because I only recognise God's.'

'Just answer the question,' advised Ester. 'It will be a lot quicker in the end.'

'But I have nothing to tell him,' declared Pamela, putting her small chin in the air and eyeing Chaloner defiantly. 'Kerchier's disappearance had nothing to do with me.'

'But you remember when it happened?' pressed Chaloner.

'Of course. The cathedral staff made such a to-do about it that you might have been forgiven for thinking that the world was about to end – such weeping and wailing. The fuss meant the incident is deeply engraved in my mind.'

'So what were you doing that particular evening?'

I was busy, although I danced for joy the next day when I heard he was missing. And with all that money, too! It proved that I was right all along – he was corrupt and greedy.'

'Busy doing what?'

'Praying for an end to the civil wars,' she replied, rather too glibly for Chaloner's liking. 'And for a rich husband. However, God's attention must have been wandering that night, because the wars dragged on and I was sent the pathetic Jasper to marry.'

133

'Was anyone with you?'

'Yes,' replied Pamela, and her chin went up again. 'The Almighty and *all* His saints. However, I had no hand in Kerchier's death. You should ask his devious colleagues about that, because they are lying if they tell you that they loved him.'

'Which devious colleagues specifically?'

'All of them: Owen, the Halls, Henchman, Tillison, Mad Bing, those stupid bell-ringers. But start with Stone. I cannot abide that lecherous oaf, and I always did think he knew more about Kerchier and the missing money than he admitted.'

'What gave you that impression?'

'I cannot recall now – it was two decades ago. Perhaps it was something to do with that nasty old cathedral, which should be knocked down before it falls on top of someone. Stone agreed once, but now he thinks it should stay. You should press him on his sudden change of mind, and see where it takes you.'

And with that, she turned on her heel and flounced away. Chaloner considered going after her to question her further, but sensed that pressing so stubborn and arrogant a witness would be a waste of his time. He bowed politely to Ester, and went on his way.

Although still early, the day was excruciatingly hot. There was scarcely a breath of wind, and the dung and rubbish that usually formed a soft carpet on London's streets had been baked so hard that pedestrians' feet kicked up small clouds of dust as they went. Some was being produced by Jasper Bell, who had evidently completed his duties in the kitchen and was hurrying back to his place of work.

'You might want to tell your wife to cooperate,' said Chaloner coolly. 'Or she will find herself in serious trouble.'

'It is more than my life is worth to "tell" Pamela anything,' retorted Jasper shortly. 'A few moments in her company should have told you that.' Then hope flared in his eyes. 'What sort of serious trouble?'

'The murder of Canon Kerchier twenty years ago. Were you in London then?'

Jasper's name was not on Owen's list, but that did not mean he should be overlooked.

'I have no idea. Can you recall what *you* were doing two decades ago?'

'I might, if the date coincided with some significant event,' replied Chaloner. 'Like the disappearance of a high-ranking cleric and a great chest of money.'

'Yes, but that was not significant to *me*. I might remember more if you could put it in context – tell me what else was happening in the world at that time.'

Chaloner struggled with his own memory, but the only noteworthy events that he could recall pertained to the wars. 'It would have been the same year as the Battle of Naseby and the sieges of Bristol and Chester.'

Jasper eyed him lugubriously. 'I am, and I have always been, a Royalist – I tend to expunge momentous Parliamentarian victories from my mind. Is that the best you can do?'

Chaloner recalled the portrait he had seen hanging in the Deanery. 'Then what about the beheading of Archbishop Laud? That was a few weeks before Kerchier—'

'Yes!' exclaimed Jasper. 'Now that wicked deed I *do* recall, so if you are talking about that year then I *can* answer your question. I was in York. My mother died that summer, and I nursed her from January to June.'

'Did Pamela go with you?'

'No, she stayed here, doing her religious work.'

'So you cannot confirm her claims or give her an alibi?'

'I am afraid not. However, I do remember old Kerchier fairly well. Would you like me to tell you what I remember about him?'

Chaloner was irked, thinking Jasper could have mentioned this sooner. 'Yes, please.'

'Well, his friends will tell you that he was a saint, and his enemies will say that he was a dangerous radical, but neither is true. He was just a man with a man's failings. He had a vicious tongue though, which made him unpopular in some quarters.'

'Including your own?'

'More my wife's – I had no strong feelings about him one way or the other.'

'How did you come to know him?'

'In my capacity as a deliverer of medicine. I work for Matt Rycroft now, but back then, my employer was Mr Bayhurst. Kerchier liked his digestive lozenges, which I took to his house twice a week. He invited me in for an ale on occasion, allowing us to talk. Or rather, for him to talk and me to listen.'

'What did he talk about?'

'St Paul's mostly; it was his driving passion. I recall several diatribes about his colleagues, not just those he deemed to be his enemies, but his friends as well – Owen, the Hall brothers and Stone. I vaguely recall that there were disputes over tactics.'

'Tactics?'

'For rebuilding the cathedral. For example, Kerchier encouraged Inigo Jones to demolish St Gregory's, which lost their faction much popular support. Stone in particular was vexed. And I suspect that if Kerchier had lived, St Gregory's would have "accidentally" collapsed entirely, which would have given rise to even more bad feeling.'

'He confided all this to you?' asked Chaloner sceptically.

'Oh, it was not a confession – it was a tirade directed at an available pair of ears.'

'Do you think Pamela was really praying that night?'

'I was not here, so I cannot say. However, I can tell you that she was a Seeker back then, not a Fifth Monarchist. Not that it matters, I suppose. Both are radical sects with controversial ideas.'

'So are Quakers, yet you seem to be one.'

'Only because she would skin me alive if I refused to enrol.'

Chaloner was torn between sympathy and the opinion that Jasper should learn to stand up for himself. 'Do you have any theories about who might have killed Kerchier?'

Jasper pondered the question carefully. 'Well, you should not overlook St Gregory's parishioners. I suspect they knew exactly who told Inigo Jones to pull down their church.'

He began to name some, and when he had finished, Chaloner's list had expanded from a hundred and sixteen to a hundred and thirty-two.

'And now I must go,' said Jasper. 'Because Ester is right: folk need their London Treacle, and I should not keep them waiting.'

'Before you leave, there were two bodies outside your house. Who were they?'

'Plague victims – John and Robert Edwards, who were taken ill in the King's Head. Of course, they were Mims, so it is hard to mourn them too deeply. Nasty fellows, Mims.'

'Were they King's Head regulars?'

Jasper shrugged. 'I never set foot in the place, so I cannot tell you. Pamela does, though – she goes to bully its patrons into joining whatever sect she happens to favour at the time. Ask her about the boys.'

'Has she ever hired Mims to do her bidding?'

Jasper's smile was wry. 'I would not have thought so, because "hiring" suggests parting with money, and she would rather keep that for herself. She would rather keep my earnings for herself as well, and is always vexed when I share them with the poor.'

'Money,' sighed Chaloner. It had been a source of friction in his own marriage, too, and although he thought a little less of Jasper for sharing sensitive marital information with a stranger, he did understand the aggravation generated by having a spouse with different financial views. 'It is more trouble than it is worth.'

'She wants my wages to fund her "good works", but I refuse to give them to her. Rycroft helps – he pays me when he knows she is not watching.'

'That is considerate of him.'

'Very, but you should expect no less – he is a decent man. But I *must* go – the sick are waiting. If you want to quiz me further, you will have to come back later.'

The rest of the day was spent working through the list, and Chaloner was glad when none of the other interviews transpired to be as trying as the one with Pamela Ball. This was mostly thanks to some unexpected but welcome assistance.

'Borrow Val,' offered Mayor Lawrence, when Chaloner happened to meet him and his secretary near the Turk's Head Coffee House.

'Me?' blurted Cary, clearly none too pleased by the notion. 'But I—'

'Who better?' interrupted Lawrence, and smiled at Chaloner. 'He knows the city like the back of his hand, and he carries my authority.'

'You can spare him?' asked Chaloner cautiously, not sure he wanted help from someone who was making it blatantly obvious that he felt he could be more profitably employed elsewhere.

'Not really, but it will tell everyone that we take murder seriously, and you catching the culprit may boost morale. God knows, we need it.'

'We do,' acknowledged Cary stiffly. 'But—'

'Just help him, Val,' said Lawrence impatiently, and then shot him a meaningful glance. 'It will do us no harm to be in Dean Sancroft's good books. He is an honourable man, who will want to repay the favour – and you never know when the services of a powerful churchman might come in useful.'

'I suppose not,' conceded Cary reluctantly.

'But you may only have him for the rest of today,' said Lawrence to Chaloner. 'I shall want him back tomorrow, so use him well.'

'Sorry,' said Chaloner, when the mayor had gone and he was left alone with a very resentful helpmeet. 'I can manage alone if you are busy.'

'I cannot ignore a direct order from Lawrence,' said Cary sulkily, snatching the list from Chaloner and scowling at it, as though it was responsible for the ruination of the day's plans. Then he turned the glare on

Chaloner. 'Well, come on then. What are you waiting for?'

Chaloner was pleasantly surprised when it transpired that not only was Cary good at persuading folk to answer questions, but he also knew where many of the folk on the list lived. Together they made excellent progress, and were able to eliminate any number of suspects. These included most of the cathedral ringers, who had not attended Evensong after their duties in the belfry as they had claimed, but had engaged in a drunken brawl with rivals from Westminster Abbey – gaol records showed they had spent the night in Newgate and thus had a rock-solid alibi. Pemper had not been with them, though, which perhaps explained his reluctance to cooperate with Chaloner the previous day.

'Marmaduke Almond,' said Cary, reading the next entry on the list. He grimaced. 'What a ridiculous name! His parents should be ashamed of themselves. However, we can eliminate him – he has been dead for years.'

'Are you sure?' asked Chaloner.

'He committed suicide. He was a tanner's apprentice, and the letter he left for his mother said he could stand such filthy work no longer. And who can blame him? I should not like to be employed in such a noxious trade either.'

'No,' agreed Chaloner, although it occurred to him that being involved in espionage was sometimes not much better.

At the Three Bibles tavern, they were able to delete fifty-four men in a single stroke – members of a large choir that had been singing in Rochester on the night of the murder, and who had written evidence to prove it.

As it was safer with Cary at his side, Chaloner also used the opportunity to corner a few Mims and demand the names of any would-be assassins. Unfortunately, it transpired that they all had aspirations in that direction, which perhaps explained the amateur bungling – most had unreasonably high opinions of their abilities. One casually offered three victims for the price of two, while another agreed to shoot the King for a barrel of ale.

By nightfall, Chaloner's list had been reduced to just sixteen names: nine cathedral men, Pamela Ball, Harbert's brother Matthew, four ringers from St Gregory's and Pemper. He was delighted, feeling the enquiry was far more manageable than it had seemed that morning, although he was bone weary, and his feet ached from trudging along dusty streets all day. Meanwhile, Cary was limping and he was tetchier than ever, although he rallied when he saw a familiar figure in the distance, lit by ten bobbing lanterns.

'Abigail,' he breathed, eyes fixed adoringly on the spectacle. 'Delivering medicine to the poor. She is such a fine lady.'

Chaloner was tempted to tell him that lusting after his employer's wife was likely to see him out of a job, but the secretary's romantic fantasies were none of his concern, so he held his tongue. Then Cary gripped his arm suddenly, hard enough to hurt, and his face turned black with anger.

'Look!' he snarled. 'Thieves, in the very act of stockpiling the city's food!'

Chaloner followed his stabbing finger to a small, scruffy warehouse. Three carts stood outside it, and several men were in the process of unloading sacks and lugging them within. Even in the dim light of their single lamp, ribbons were visible on their arms. One barked a warning when he saw they had been spotted, after which the door was slammed shut and the empty carts clattered away at top speed.

'We are unlikely to catch those,' remarked Chaloner, watching them vanish around the corner. 'But we can lay hold of whoever is still inside. Perhaps a few judicial hangings will remind folk that profiteering is illegal.'

'No one will be inside,' predicted Cary bitterly. 'They are not stupid, to linger now that they have been seen. So, do you want to guard the food or go for help? One of us must stay, because the hoard will disappear if we leave it unattended, even for a moment.'

Chaloner offered to stay, and when Cary had gone, he stared at the building thoughtfully. He hated to stand by impotently while the thieves escaped to steal again – and he did not share Cary's conviction that the culprits would abandon what looked to be a substantial hoard. He climbed through a window, aiming to nab them himself. He could then hold them at gunpoint until Cary returned. But the secretary knew his city and its felons, and Chaloner entered to find the Mims gone and the warehouse deserted, just as Cary had foretold.

The secretary appeared a few moments later with half a dozen soldiers in tow, and was clearly unimpressed to discover that Chaloner had gone in alone.

'That was reckless,' he growled. 'And selfish. What would we have told Dean Sancroft if you had been killed? You heard Lawrence say how we need his good auspices – which we will not get if his envoy is dispatched in our city.'

'You told me no one would be inside,' shrugged Chaloner. 'So how could there be any danger?'

Cary scowled, unappeased. 'You should have waited for . . .' But he trailed off when he saw what the felons had abandoned, and his dour face lit with a grin of delight. 'Apples, salt beef, candles, beans! Abigail will be overjoyed.'

'So will the poor, presumably,' remarked Chaloner. He hastened on when Cary fixed him with an unfriendly glare. 'Did you recognise any of the culprits?'

'A couple, but I know neither their names nor where they live.'

'But if you have seen them before, it means they are local, so it should not be too difficult to—'

'Not difficult, no,' interrupted Cary shortly. 'But impossible, nonetheless. We have our hands full with the plague measures – we do not have the resources to hunt down felons as well.' His scowl deepened. 'However, the plague will relinquish its hold eventually, and when it does, these rogues will pay for their greed. I swear it on my uncle's grave.'

'Your uncle the dean?' asked Chaloner, aiming to placate the secretary by showing an interest in his family. He did not want to spar with a man who had been so helpful. 'I saw his tomb yesterday. It must have been splendid before the iconoclasts got at it.'

Cary's expression softened. 'It was. But I wish he was buried somewhere other than the south transept. It is the most unstable part of the whole cathedral, and I live in fear that the rest of it will be destroyed at any moment.'

Chaloner took his leave and began to trudge towards the Mitre, aware that he needed to be on his guard now that it was dark and he was alone. Even so, he still stopped off at St Gregory's Church when he saw the door was open, recalling what Bing and Jasper had told him: that Kerchier might have arranged for it to fall down 'accidentally' if someone had not killed him first.

It was dim inside, although there was enough light for him to see that the newer parts were of a much lower standard than the rest, so it would not be long before there were problems with damp and leaks. Did it mean that Inigo Jones and Kerchier *had* conspired to make inferior repairs, in the hope that the place would tumble around its parishioners' ears?

He was about to leave when he saw a shadow – the shape suggested the largest Hall brother – near the entrance to the crypt. He crept forward, only to find that door was closed, although he could hear someone padding down the stairs beyond.

He picked the lock and followed. There was a brief flicker of light near the Countess of Devonshire, but by the time he had groped his way towards it, no one was there. The air around it reeked of urine, and he frowned his bemusement. Had the canon gone down there to relieve himself? Surely not!

He recalled from his last visit that there was a lamp in an alcove at the bottom of the steps, so he lit it and began to explore. But although he searched the undercroft from top to bottom, there was no sign of Francis or anyone else. Had the canon doubled back and sneaked out unseen? It would not be difficult – the crypt was huge – full of pillars and interconnecting aisles. But why would Francis do such a thing? And why had he shut himself inside in the first place? Chaloner supposed he would have to ask him in the morning. He doused the lamp, and was just re-securing the door when he heard someone sneak up behind him.

'Lord!' gulped Rycroft, gripping the Bible he carried as though it was a weapon. 'I thought you were a ghost come to haunt us. Kerchier's perhaps, released from its borrowed tomb at last. I was about to see if I could exorcise you by reading a bit of holy scripture.'

Chaloner regarded him askance. 'You, a man of science, believes in ghosts?'

'These are dark times, Chaloner. Who knows what evil has been awakened as Death stalks our streets? My mind remains open.'

It was superstitious claptrap, but his words still sent a shiver down Chaloner's spine. 'What are you doing here?' he demanded, curt because he disliked being unnerved.

'Praying,' came the glib reply. 'Unlike you, who appears to have broken into the crypt – a place that no sane man should want to venture into in the dark. Especially alone.'

'I thought I saw someone go down there.'

'Did you find him?' Rycroft promptly backed away when Chaloner shook his head. 'Then I am not staying here a minute longer. I shall come back in the morning, when it is light and I can see exactly what lurks in the shadows. Good night, Chaloner.'

Chaloner joined the Paget family for a bowl of stew when he reached the Mitre. The children provided him with a blow-by-blow account of his chickens' activities that day, to prove they had earned their pay, while Mrs Paget interrupted constantly to assure him that the stew was poison-free. She could be certain, because she had not left the pot unattended for a moment, and as she devoured considerably more of it than anyone else, Chaloner was willing to believe her. The kitchen was very dark, so he could see little of what was in his bowl, which was perhaps just as well, he thought, as he wrestled with a lump of gristle that stubbornly refused to yield to his teeth.

Afterwards, he was restless, and although it was madness to venture out again, he went anyway. He kept to the shadows, listening to the sounds of the night, and thinking how different they were than a few months ago.

Then, he would have heard laughter and lively conversation emanating from taverns, and the rattle of wheels or hoofs on cobbles as people attended playhouses, music halls and noisy parties. Now, the silence was almost deafening, punctured only by the occasional cry of pain or despair, the squeak of a rat, or the sinister rumble of the dead-carts.

He spied on the homes of several of his remaining suspects, peering through windows to see Tillison dozing by a fire, Owen pacing back and forth agitatedly, and Henchman reading. Stone's house was in darkness, but Pemper's was brightly lit – he was treating two fellow ringers to an odd meal of seed-cake and radishes.

Chaloner spent the longest time outside Bing's cottage, though, where he listened to one of the finest violas da gamba he had ever heard. In Bing's hands it sang, although he seemed to take scant pleasure from the exercise, and his rendition of Dowland's 'Flow my Teares' was so painfully desolate that Chaloner felt a lump rise at the back of his throat.

Francis and John Hall were next door, labelling a batch of London Treacle. William was there, too, but left after a few moments. Chaloner trailed him all the way to Rycroft's house, where a very fierce quarrel ensued between canon and alchemist. He did his best to eavesdrop, but they were apparently cognisant of the fact that sounds travelled at night, because both kept their voices too low for him to hear.

In the house opposite, Masley was working at his desk, although he stopped to stretch when Gaundy appeared. Wordlessly, the verger removed a handful of documents from a pile and left again. Chaloner followed him to the Poultry, where the remaining ringers from

St Gregory's were waiting. Wildbore had brought ale, and the band settled down to an in-depth and fractious discussion about which cross-changes should be rung for the next service.

Bored, Chaloner left them to it, and walked to King's Head Court, where Jasper was in his kitchen, relaxing on a bench with a cup of wine in one hand and an onion in the other – Chaloner supposed it was one way to ensure that Pamela would not want to kiss him. The woman herself was in her parlour, leading a noisy prayer meeting that must have been very annoying for her neighbours. Several members of the congregation wore green arm-ribbons.

Ester was in the next cottage but one, sewing by candlelight; clearly, her devotion to Quakerism did not extend to bawling late-night demands at the Almighty. Eventually, she yawned, stood and pulled off her cap to release a cascade of shiny chestnut hair. Chaloner left when she began to brush it; he was a spy, not a voyeur.

He reached Carter Lane just as the watchmen were calling ten o'clock, aware of the nagging loneliness that had been with him ever since his wife Hannah had died in June. Was it wrong to hanker after female company when he was not many weeks a widower? He was so engrossed in his morose thoughts that he forgot to keep to the shadows, and cursed his reckless stupidity when someone in full plague costume stepped out to intercept him.

'You should not be out here alone, Tom. Not at this time of night.'

It took a moment to place the voice, because it was not one Chaloner had expected to hear – not in disease-ridden London.

'Nor should you,' he replied, struggling to regain his equanimity before John Thurloe could see his astonishment – he hated to appear flustered in front of a man whose good opinion was important to him. 'You should be with your family in Oxfordshire.'

Thurloe had been Cromwell's Secretary of State and Spymaster General, and had recruited Chaloner as one of his intelligencers. He had declined a post with the Restoration government, and now passed his days quietly, dividing them between his estates in the country and Lincoln's Inn. He sighed wheezily through his mask.

'You are right. The city is no place for a man with a delicate constitution.'

'Were you following me?' Chaloner was ready to be horrified if so. Thurloe had been an excellent spymaster, but his practical skills were poor, and if Chaloner had not noticed *him* lumbering along behind, then he was losing his touch and it was time he retired.

'No, but Paget told me that you had gone out, so I decided to wait here, in the hope that you would happen past. But I can barely breathe in this outfit. Come to my lodgings. We have much to discuss.'

Thurloe had taken rooms in a house at the western end of Carter Lane, a neat, respectable place taxed on eleven hearths. He opened the front door with a key, explaining that the property belonged to his friend Prayse Russell.

'The physician,' he added. 'You have probably heard of him. He is famous for his work on veins.'

Chaloner pondered the unmistakably Puritan name. 'Is he a radical?'

'A Quaker, which is why he has remained in the city

when most other *medici* have fled. He believes in helping those in need.'

'Then should you be staying with him?' asked Chaloner, aware of the ex-Spymaster's fear of disease in general and the plague in particular.

'Fortunately, he confines himself to dispensing remedies, and never makes house calls to the sick. I shall be safe enough.'

'I have been told that Quakers like to pray at the bedsides of their stricken brethren, then saunter outside to mingle with the healthy.'

'Some do,' conceded Thurloe, 'but Prayse does not. And it is very convenient living with a physician, as free consultations are included in the rent.'

'Rent?' echoed Chaloner. 'I thought you said you were friends.'

'He uses the money to buy medicine for the poor, so it is a mutually acceptable arrangement. I cannot live in Lincoln's Inn, because it is closed, so I am glad to have found a clean and convenient alternative, while Prayse has additional funds for a good cause.'

He opened the door to a gracious parlour that smelled of the miasma-repelling herbs that were piled on the mantelpiece. The walls were hung with tasteful paintings, and there were three shelves of books, although Chaloner's interest in them evaporated when a glance showed they were all religious tracts of the kind written by the more fervent type of fanatic.

'So?' he asked, helping the ex-Spymaster to unbuckle the straps that fixed the mask to his head. 'What dark business requires you to wear such a disguise?'

Thurloe tugged it off and took a gulp of fresh air. 'This is not a disguise, Tom – it is armour against the pestilence. Indeed, I am astonished that you should venture out without some. Or have you discovered a reliable preventative?'

He was a slightly built man of forty-nine, with blue eyes and brown hair. Despite his claims to be delicate – and a reckless habit of downing all manner of potions that promised to make him feel young again – he was as strong as an ox. After all, Cromwell would not have appointed a weakling as his sole Secretary of State, and it was often said that the Commonwealth would not have survived for as long as it had without Thurloe at its helm.

'According to Surgeon Wiseman, there is no such thing,' said Chaloner. 'He thinks the only way to stay safe is to keep at least thirty miles between you and the nearest victim.'

'Unfortunately, that is not always practical.' Thurloe struggled out of the cloak that covered him from head to toe; it was immensely thick, and he emerged hot and sweating. 'I had no choice but to come here – family honour is at stake.'

Thurloe was the acknowledged head of an enormous brood of relatives, all of whom he loved and considered to be under his personal protection. He took great pride in the fact that the Thurloe name was honoured and respected wherever it went, and he was willing to go to extraordinary lengths to keep it that way.

'It involves my wife's favourite sister – Ursula – who recently found herself a new husband,' Thurloe went on. 'A young stationer by the name of John Upton.'

'Bing mentioned a stationer called John Upton,' mused Chaloner. 'He told me to talk to him about Kerchier's murder. Of course, Bing does seem to have lost his reason . . .'

He outlined the task he had been set by Sancroft, along with all he had learned to date. The ex-Spymaster listened without interruption until he had finished.

'And Bing told you to speak to Upton about this canon's murder?' he murmured unhappily. 'That is worrisome.'

'Is it?' asked Chaloner curiously. 'Why?'

'Suffice to say that I was alarmed when I learned that Upton and Ursula were to marry – he did not seem like the sort of man who could make her happy. Despite my reservations, they were joined ten days ago at my estate in Great Milton.'

'You mentioned a family wedding in your last letter to me,' recalled Chaloner. 'It was Ursula and Upton's?'

Thurloe inclined his head. 'The same afternoon, a message arrived, summoning Upton back here on urgent business.'

'Did he show you this message?'

Thurloe gave a faint smile. 'No, but I read it anyway – I have not lost all the habits I acquired when I was Spymaster General. Unfortunately, it told me nothing other than that the sender wanted him to return to London with all possible haste.'

'Was the letter signed?'

'It was not, which alone was enough to raise my suspicions. Then, a few days later, another missive came telling us that he was dead.'

Chaloner recalled Bing's words: that Upton would sing no more, and that *sal mirabilis* had not protected him. They made sense now. 'Dead of the plague?'

'Yes, according to the letter. However, all my instincts clamoured at me that something was amiss, so I decided to look into the matter, lest it transpired to be something to harm the family. And I was right to be wary, because

Upton did not die of the plague – he died from a blow to the head.'

'How do you know? Did you see the body?'

'Yes, with Prayse. He told me the location of the wound makes an accident unlikely, while Upton could not have hit himself in such a place. In other words, he was murdered.'

'Who wrote the second letter? Someone who can provide more information about what happened to Upton?'

'Unfortunately not. The body was taken to a church by a masked "friend", and the vicar was ordered to bury it at once. Luckily, the vicar – a former spy of mine – had the courage to look inside the coffin first. He recognised Upton as Ursula's new husband, and wrote to tell me so. But he knows no more than I have told you.'

'*Did* Upton have friends in the city?'

'Probably – he lived here until the plague drove him out – although I know nothing about them. But real friends would have notified his widow in person, do you not think?'

Chaloner nodded. 'What kind of man was Upton?'

'I disliked him on sight. Oh, he was personable enough, and he professed to be in love, but there was something *sly* about him, and I feared at once that he would be trouble. Of course, I did not think it would happen within hours of his marriage . . .'

'So why did you allow the wedding to go ahead?'

'I am not a tyrant, Thomas, and Ursula is ten years my senior. If she wants to wed a pretty boy of twenty-six, then it is not for me to stop her.'

'Twenty-six?' Chaloner raised his eyebrows. 'Then she

is old enough to be his mother! Did he woo her for money? I recall her first marriage left her very wealthy.'

'He claimed not, but I did not believe him. All I hope is that whatever devious business led to his murder does not reflect badly on the rest of us. You understand my worry, Tom – you know better than most the damage that a rogue kinsman can inflict.'

Chaloner did: the antics of his regicide uncle regularly came back to haunt him. 'So why did Bing suggest asking Upton about Kerchier? Upton was too young to have known a canon who died twenty years ago – at least, in any meaningful way.'

'He is,' agreed Thurloe, 'but he did brag about the cathedral being one of his biggest customers. I assumed he was trying to impress me by claiming ties to a respectable institution, but perhaps there is a rather different – and perhaps sinister – association that we need to explore.'

'I wonder if it is significant that both he and Kerchier died from blows to the head.'

'Or that Kerchier's bones were found last Sunday, which is the same day that Upton was killed. It may be coincidence, but I suggest we reserve judgement until we know more about it.' Thurloe frowned thoughtfully. 'Did you say that Kerchier was in the vault intended for Sir Arnold Harbert?'

Chaloner nodded. 'Why?'

'Harbert was a "person of interest" during the Commonwealth, because he was violently opposed to any kind of change and was outspoken about the plans for a new cathedral. He had a brother – Matthew – although all I can tell you about him is that he did nothing to warrant attention.'

'The older Harbert is said to have been killed in a

153

fight with the royal Keeper of Fish. Denton denies it, and he does not seem like a brawler, so I am not sure what to think.'

'The Keeper of Fish,' echoed Thurloe disapprovingly. 'There was no such post in Cromwell's day. Foreign ambassadors tried to present him with exotic creatures, but it was a practice we discouraged on account of its cruelty.'

'Lots of people are angry that Sancroft was told about the skeleton,' Chaloner went on, his mind following a different track entirely. 'They feel that one death is irrelevant in the face of so many, and want me to forget it.'

'Which would suit the killer, of course. But he is going to be disappointed, because I suggest that you and I work together to find him.'

'You will not be too busy protecting your family from whatever Upton was about?'

'It will be my first priority, naturally, but our investigations seem to be converging, so it makes sense to pool our resources. Besides, Bing – whether insane or not – must have had some reason to suggest Upton as a source of information about Kerchier's murder.'

It had been several weeks since Chaloner and Thurloe had last met, and both had news to exchange, so it was nearly midnight before Chaloner finally stood to leave. He was just reaching for the door when it opened and a man entered.

The fellow who strode in was an anachronism in his black sugar-loaf hat and austere Puritan clothes – attire that had been popular during the Commonwealth, but that few dared sport in Restoration London. His features were pinched and sour, and he looked as though he would rather die than laugh. Thurloe introduced him as Prayse Russell.

'You will catch the plague walking around like that,' he declared, looking Chaloner up and down appraisingly. 'So borrow a scarf to cover your face and make sure your boots are tightly fastened – to prevent deadly miasmas from running up your breeches. And remove your hat.'

'My hat?' asked Chaloner warily, accepting the scarf that Thurloe immediately pressed into his hands.

'Fancy Cavalier headpieces are attractive to plague-bearing vapours,' the physician replied with considerable conviction. 'Whereas plain, modest ones are not.'

'How can they tell?' asked Chaloner doubtfully.

'They just can. Trust me. I am a physician.'

'You were out very late tonight, Prayse,' remarked Thurloe pleasantly.

'I have been at prayer,' explained the *medicus* piously. 'Which is all I can do for those who cannot afford London Treacle. Did I tell you that it is the only remedy that works?'

'You did.' Thurloe patted his pocket, where a bottle of it nestled. 'But *sal mirabilis* is more popular, because it is cheaper and can be bought from places other than the cathedral. St Paul's is a long way to go if you live in Charing Cross or Whitechapel.'

'Perhaps, but it is worth the trek, because those who take *sal mirabilis* might as well drink milk for all the good it does. *Their* only hope is my prayers.'

'It is good of you to take the trouble,' said Thurloe warmly, although Chaloner imagined most folk would prefer a free pot of London Treacle – it was clear from his house that Prayse was wealthy, and so could afford to be generous.

155

'I heard a worrisome rumour this evening,' reported Prayse. 'Namely that Londoners feel we *medici* are not doing enough to help them, and plan to leave the city en masse. I hope it is untrue, because we do not want other places to suffer as we are doing.'

'No,' agreed Thurloe, concerned. 'You had better tell Lawrence and Monck about this tale, so they can put an end to it before it does any harm. We all know how quickly rumours can gain a momentum of their own and turn fiction into fact.'

'We do,' acknowledged Prayse gravely. 'I shall write to them at once then.'

He turned and marched away without another word. Chaloner bade Thurloe goodnight, tied the scarf over his face and headed for the Mitre, glad it was not far. He reached the tavern's door, but some sixth sense warned him not to enter. He kept walking until he turned the corner, then peered back to see two men with arm ribbons lurking in the shadows. He had no doubt that they were lying in wait for him, but Thurloe's scarf had rendered him anonymous.

As he watched, another pedestrian approached, one who wore a wide-brimmed hat similar to the one that Chaloner had stuffed in his pocket on Prayse's recommendation. The Mims were on the fellow in a flash. Both wielded cudgels, and as Chaloner had no desire for an innocent to be bludgeoned on his account, he raced to the rescue. He disabled the smaller of the pair with a savage slash to the arm, then grabbed the other around the neck before the fellow realised what was happening. Wailing in pain, the wounded Mim fled.

'Who are you?' Chaloner demanded of his frantically struggling captive.

'Tommy Suger,' bleated the terrified Mim. 'From Pissing Alley. But we meant no harm, sir – we were just told to scare him off.'

'Scare who off?'

'A man called Chaloner, who lodges here. We were ordered to make him leave the city. Please let me go, sir. I am just a poor man trying to earn an honest penny.'

It was not a very honest penny as far as Chaloner was concerned. 'Who sent you?'

'Someone in plague gear,' came the unhelpful reply. 'I never saw his face.'

'It was definitely a man?' asked Chaloner, thinking of Pamela. 'How big was he?'

'I could not tell – he was sitting down. And you know what those masks are like, sir. You can hardly understand a word, let alone recognise a voice.'

'If you try to ambush me again, Tommy Suger,' whispered Chaloner in a voice that was low and soft with menace, 'I will kill you.'

It was a hollow threat, as he had better things to do than dispatch petty felons, but Suger whimpered his fear. Chaloner released him, and Suger raced away as though the devil was on his tail. Meanwhile, his victim was unsteady with shock, so Chaloner helped him to his feet and then into the Mitre to sit down and recover. He would have offered a restorative cup of wine, but Paget did not have any.

'Who were they?' the man gulped. 'Did you see their faces?'

'No,' lied Chaloner, lighting a lamp from the embers of the fire. 'Did they hurt you?'

'Only my pride.'

The lantern flared into life, and Chaloner was astonished

to see it was Mayor Lawrence who sat struggling to regain his composure.

'You should not be out alone at this time of night,' he chided. 'Cary thinks London will not survive this crisis without you.'

'I know he does,' said Lawrence, and blanched in sudden mortification. 'Lord! I carry a sword *and* a dagger, but it never occurred to me to defend myself with either when push came to shove. I hope I can rely on your discretion, Chaloner – I should not like it put about that I am quite so easily bested.'

'Of course. Are you here to see Paget?'

'No, I arranged to meet Val here, to discuss our most recent findings.'

'Findings about what?'

'About the city's mood. We trawl the taverns and coffee houses in disguise most nights, listening to murmurs of discontent – if we know what makes people unhappy, we can address their grievances before there is trouble. It is the only viable way to govern the city, given our limited resources.'

'Yes, but it is the sort of thing trusted agents should be doing. Not the mayor.'

Lawrence shot him a rueful smile. 'I agree, but my only "trusted agent" is Val. The others are too frightened of catching the plague, which is understandable, although disappointing.' He sighed unhappily. 'And they are not the only ones who have proved unreliable. Mrs Driver . . .'

'She spies for you, too?'

Lawrence laughed without humour. 'She has many skills, but that would not be one of them. No, I arranged to meet her for an hour of relaxation, but she was out.

158

I have a bad feeling that she has fled, despite her promises to stay here and support me.'

Chaloner recalled the certificate that his daughter had filched, and could only suppose that Mrs Driver had bought a replacement. Then the door opened and Cary walked in.

'What happened?' he demanded in horror, seeing his employer's rumpled appearance.

'Footpads,' explained Lawrence. 'But Chaloner saw them off.'

'They were waiting for me, I am afraid,' explained Chaloner apologetically. 'Two men with ribbons on their sleeves.'

Cary glared, ready to be angry. 'The same pair who shot at you the other night?'

'No, they are dead. Have you heard of Pamela Ball?'

'Oh, yes,' replied Lawrence wearily. 'Why did that woman have to choose *now* to become a Quaker – a sect that takes particular delight in flouting our plague measures?'

'What does Mrs Ball have to do with the Mims, Chaloner?' asked Cary suspiciously. 'Or are you suggesting that *she* hired them?'

'Well, she is on Owen's list of suspects,' replied Chaloner. 'Moreover, the gunmen's bodies were outside her house yesterday and Mims attended her prayer meeting today.'

'My word!' breathed Lawrence, wide-eyed. 'Will you arrest her? Do you need to borrow a few soldiers to back you up? I would not risk doing it alone if I were you. She may be small, but she is deadly.'

'I cannot arrest her – not until I have solid proof of wrongdoing,' said Chaloner. 'But I will speak to her again

159

tomorrow, and see what a few threats can shake loose.'

Lawrence nodded his approval, then turned to his secretary. 'What did you learn from the taverns tonight, Val? Anything new?'

'Not really,' replied the secretary, sounding disgusted that he had wasted his time. 'People are hungry, and want to leave the city to forage for themselves. We should double the guards on the gates, because there is talk of a mass exodus next week.'

'We can barely afford their regular hours, so paying for overtime is impossible,' objected Lawrence, and then grimaced. 'But you are right, of course – we dare not risk losing control of the gates, as we might never get it back again. And none of us want infected folk travelling to other towns and cities.'

'Do you know anything about the death of a man named John Upton?' asked Chaloner, somewhat out of the blue.

'The stationer?' asked Cary. 'Only that he died of the plague about a week ago.'

'Actually, he was hit over the head,' said Chaloner, and then added for no particular reason, 'Murdered – in an identical way to Kerchier, in fact.'

Cary regarded him as though he were insane. 'Surely you cannot think there is a link between the two? Their deaths are decades apart, and Upton was too young to have known Kerchier.'

'I agree with Val,' said Lawrence. 'The Uptons did not begin trading in the city until after the wars – by which time Kerchier had been missing for five years.'

At that moment, two soldiers arrived, so Cary ordered them to escort Lawrence home. The mayor went gratefully, clearly exhausted and longing for his bed.

'He does far more than Monck,' said Cary, watching them go. 'He works all day and half the night, whereas the general does nothing but sit in Westminster and chew tobacco.'

'Monck helped to address that crowd in Cornhill on Wednesday. I saw him.'

'He made inflammatory remarks,' corrected Cary shortly. 'I would suggest that Lawrence take control of the city *and* the metropolis, and dispense with that foul-mouthed Scot altogether, but that would be too heavy a burden, even for him.'

'Perhaps Abigail would help,' remarked Chaloner, a little mischievously.

'Abigail!' sighed Cary, his eyes moist with longing. Then he seemed to recollect himself, because he cleared his throat and went on briskly. 'It would be far too dangerous a task for a woman, even one as bold and skilful as she.'

'Perhaps Monck thinks it is too dangerous for him, as well.'

'No doubt he does, and we are fortunate that Lawrence is no cowering fool. He is the best of men, and no one else could have steered London through this crisis – not the King and his monkeys, not my uncle the dean, and probably not even Cromwell himself. If London survives, it will be because of John Lawrence.'

'And Abigail,' put in Chaloner wickedly.

'Of course and Abigail,' nodded Cary earnestly. 'That goes without saying.'

# Chapter 6

Chaloner slept well for what remained of the night, but was woken the following morning by an ungodly clanging. He was out of the bed with his sword in his hand before he realised that it was only the cathedral bells, calling the faithful to the first of the Sunday services.

He lay back down again, and his mind immediately filled with his investigation. He now had Thurloe to help him gather information, although it was no longer just Kerchier's death that had to be explored. He also wanted to find out exactly how Harbert had died, given that the knight's death had led to the discovery of Kerchier's bones, while he was sure that Thurloe would appreciate him asking questions about Upton.

He frowned thoughtfully. *Was* there a connection between the ex-Spymaster's new kinsman and a canon who had died twenty years ago? It did not sound very likely, and yet there was no getting away from the fact that Kerchier had been found – in Harbert's vault – on the same day that Upton had been killed, or that Bing thought Upton might have 'sung' about Harbert and Kerchier had he not been dead himself.

Staring up at the ceiling, Chaloner reviewed what he had to do that day. First, visit Pamela again, and conduct a more vigorous interrogation – her 'alibi' for Kerchier's death was unconvincing, and he disliked the fact that she associated with Mims. Second, learn more about Harbert by questioning his family and servants. And third, talk to Canon Stone, as Bing, Pamela and Jasper Ball had suggested.

As it was Sunday, he donned smarter clothes than usual – a crisp white shirt with extra lace, green breeches and a black long-coat, although it did not take many moments in the garden before he shrugged out of the coat. It was too hot for anything other than shirtsleeves.

He let his hens out, then joined Paget for another curious breakfast, this time of salted herring, lettuce and honey. The landlord was in a pensive mood, harping back to the days, not long before, when his Musick Hall had been packed out every evening, drawing audiences from all across the city.

'It was busiest when Canon Stone was singing, because he is the best counter-tenor in London, and folk travelled miles to hear him. Unfortunately, I saw him leaving yesterday in a coach. He said he would not be gone for long, but I do not believe him. The coward!'

Chaloner doubted it was happenstance that had caused the fat canon to flee just as Kerchier's murder was being investigated, which meant the man knew something important about the matter. He sighed irritably, not relishing the prospect of setting off in pursuit when the weather was so hot.

'Where has he gone?' he asked, hoping it was not to the other side of the country.

'He did not say, but his colleagues will know. Perhaps

163

he wanted to be away before the general exodus later this week. Have you heard about that? I might go myself, because life here is no fun any more. Oh, I almost forgot – there is a letter for you.'

It was from Sancroft, but contained nothing other than a plea for Chaloner to do his best to solve the mystery of the bones, as the cathedral could not afford to be sullied by damaging rumours. It ended with the kindly recommendation that he stay away from drains, which were well-known sources of contagion.

It was too early to visit suspects, and there was no point in deliberately aggravating a prickly woman like Pamela Ball, so Chaloner walked to the cathedral in the hope that Morning Prayer would be accompanied by some decent music. Unfortunately, the choir was down to three boys and two men, none of whom had voices of note.

He headed for the door, and his route took him past the south transept. Pemper and his band were there, lounging by Dean Cary's tomb and wiping the sweat from their brows after their exertions in the ringing chamber. They were sharing a jug of ale, and clearly hoped that using a part of the building that was notoriously unstable would grant them some privacy.

'Stay back,' ordered Flower, a little indignantly when he saw Chaloner. 'This ceiling is ripe for collapse, and you do not want to be standing beneath it when it goes.'

'And you do?' asked Chaloner pointedly.

'God will protect us,' declared Pemper, 'because we have just rung Paradox, which is His favourite set of cross-changes – one that is wholly beyond the skills of Wildbore and his miserable crew. Did you hear my three-four dodges? The striking was perfect.'

Chaloner had not thought so, but he nodded politely. He wondered how to get Pemper alone, sure the man would not answer questions honestly while his cronies were listening.

'Wildbore's men are rubbish because they never practice,' declared the man with the long grey hair. 'They just ring in St Gregory's on Sundays.'

'That is not true,' countered Pemper, startled. 'They are always out in the city, chiming for the dead. You cannot go anywhere without bumping into the rogues.'

'But *they* do not do the tolling,' argued Flower. 'They stand around chatting to their friends, while that young fellow – I forget his name – does all the work. It is— *Ow!*'

A pigeon had flapped from one rafter to another, dislodging a shower of dust. Among it was a thumbnail-sized piece of stone, which had hurt when it had struck his head.

'Perhaps your Paradox was not to God's pleasing after all,' remarked Chaloner, unable to help himself.

Pemper glared. 'I suppose you think you could do better. Well, you are wrong, because we are the best ringers in the city. Now, come along, men. We need to take Communion.'

Chaloner trailed them to the nave, but Pemper took a place at the very front of the queue of congregants, where he would be impossible to extricate without a fuss. As Chaloner was unwilling to linger until the rite had finished, he supposed he would have to wait for another opportunity to corner the haughty ringing master alone.

It was a swelteringly unpleasant walk to Pamela's house, even though it was not far. The weather seemed hotter and more airless than ever, and Chaloner dreaded to imagine what it would be like that afternoon, when the sun was at its zenith.

He arrived at King's Head Court to find it body-free – he had half expected to see the failed ambushers from the previous night. Pamela's parlour window was open, which allowed him to look through it and see her addressing another large gathering of people. A few were Mims, but most were not, and included, he noted with pleasure, Ester.

'Mayor Lawrence cannot stop us,' Pamela was informing them defiantly. 'If we want to visit the sick and go to the market afterwards, then that is *our* business, not his. God sent this plague to test our faith, and if we put our trust in Him, no harm will befall us.'

'But we heard that your Jasper is sick,' called a woman from near the back; she sounded frightened. 'He was fit and well yesterday, but now he lies on his deathbed. Is it true? Because if so, it means that your faith is not—'

'Jasper is weak,' interrupted Pamela shortly. 'And he fell by the wayside. But we are stronger and— What do *you* want?'

She had seen Chaloner at the window.

'To talk to you,' he replied, and glanced pointedly at the Mims in her audience. 'Especially about your association with felons.'

Scowling, Pamela bustled towards him. One or two of her flock craned forward to hear what she and Chaloner had to say to each other, but she drove them back with a basilisk glower. The rest evidently knew better than to try the patience of so prickly a character, so stayed where they were.

'My Mims are lost souls looking for salvation,' she hissed, eyes flashing dangerously. 'Which is why I became a Quaker – to save folk like them. Now go away. I am too busy to answer your stupid questions.'

'Are they grateful enough to do you favours?' asked Chaloner evenly. 'Such as acting to ensure that there is never an investigation into Kerchier's murder?'

Pamela's expression hardened. 'In other words, you have been attacked, and you are here to accuse me of it.'

'How do you know I was attacked?' pounced Chaloner.

Pamela did not flinch. 'Because some Mims have been known to undertake such commissions in the past. But not on my account, and you cannot prove otherwise.'

'I saw two bodies lying outside your house the last time I was here. Mims, who—'

'The plague is a terrible thing,' she interrupted shortly. 'The Edwards boys were full of life one night, but dead by the next morning. God rest their souls.'

Chaloner could tell this particular discussion was going nowhere, so he turned to another matter. 'How well did you know Sir Arnold Harbert?'

Pamela glowered. 'I despised him! I had to give him a piece of my mind on several occasions, when he accused me – *me*, Pamela Ball! – of being inconstant, just because I am fussy about religion. I cannot recall whether I was a Fifth Monarchist or an Anabaptist at the time, but my personal creed was none of his affair regardless.'

'What about John Upton the stationer?' asked Chaloner. 'Did you know him?'

'Another imbecile, all foolish grins and limp hand-shakes. Now, if there is nothing else, let me get back to the important business of proselytising. Unless you want to buy some *sal mirabilis*? I happen to have a spare bottle.'

'From your Mims?' asked Chaloner in distaste. 'Who

167

snap up the supplies meant for everyone and sell them at grossly inflated prices?'

'From Mayor Lawrence,' she countered, 'who buys it with his own money and distributes it to the poor and needy – folk such as myself. I acquired an extra bottle or two, and you may have one for sixpence.'

Chaloner saw she had learned well from her criminal associates. Or had they learned from her? 'It is contrary to the Quaker creed to acquire selfish amounts of medicine and hawk it at extortionate prices. What do your co-religionists think of your profiteering?'

She bristled anew. 'Selling goods at current market rates is *not* profiteering. Besides, I am in the process of making our movement more pragmatic, so its other members will not be in a position to criticise me for much longer. And if they baulk at my improvements, I shall throw them over and enrol in another sect instead.'

'They will be devastated, I am sure,' murmured Chaloner. 'Have you thought any more about the day that Kerchier—'

'No,' she interrupted curtly. 'I have been too busy. Now go away.'

The shutter was slammed in his face before he could stop her. He gazed reflectively at the upstairs windows for a moment, but then turned to leave – breaking in when her house was full of Mims was not the best idea. He would return later, when she was alone.

Chaloner's next task was to visit Harbert's home, but he had only just reached Carter Lane when hurrying footsteps snagged his attention. He turned, and his stomach did a curious flip when he saw Ester, one curl escaping from her bonnet in a way that was distinctly alluring.

She was wearing a simple dress that hinted at the pleasing curves of her body, and she was smiling apologetically. She was, he thought appreciatively, a very attractive lady.

'I am sorry if Pamela offended you back there,' she said, falling into step at his side. 'All I can say is that her bark is usually worse than her bite.'

'I am not sure her husband would agree.'

Ester winced. 'Poor Jasper may not be in a position to agree or disagree with anything for much longer. He has the plague.'

'Are you sure? He was healthy yesterday.'

'It strikes its victims very fast, as I am sure you know. Besides, Pamela diagnosed it, and she is a nurse.'

'Pamela did?' asked Chaloner uneasily, thinking about the froth on the lips of the two dead Mims. Had Pamela poisoned them, then turned her murderous attentions on the husband she so obviously despised, lest he revealed something that she would rather kept quiet about the murder of Kerchier? And what better time to do it, than when so many bodies were being shoved in the ground with no questions asked? He decided to return to King's Head Court at once, and find out what really ailed the hapless Jasper.

'I suppose she will sit with him this morning,' he fished, aiming to ascertain if he would need to devise a ploy to get Pamela and her Mims out of the way first.

Ester's expression was wry. 'She encourages us to visit the sick, in defiance of the government's plague measures, but she does not do it herself. She says she is too important to take the risk. But Jasper is a good man, and if God spares anyone, it will be him. He gives nearly all his wages to the poor, which is why she has grown to resent him.'

Chaloner raised his eyebrows. 'I thought you and she were friends.'

'Neighbours,' corrected Ester. 'And fellow Quakers, although it will not be long before she tires of us, and turns to another organisation in her hunt for inner peace.'

As she was being helpful, Chaloner decided to ask her a few more questions. 'There were Mims in Pamela's congregation. Does she ever hire them to work for her?'

Ester laughed, showing strong white teeth. '*Hire*, no – she never pays for anything. She might bully them into doing what she wants, though. Why do you ask?'

'Because Kerchier's killer is using Mims in an attempt to stall my investigation. Perhaps you could encourage her to cooperate with me – before I assume that her mulishness is a sign of a guilty conscience and order her arrest.'

'I will try,' said Ether without enthusiasm. 'Although she does not usually listen to advice, no matter how sensible.'

'A lot of money disappeared when Kerchier died,' Chaloner went on, 'and several people – you among them – have told me that Pamela is a hoarder. Could she have taken it?'

'She might, I suppose. It would certainly explain the fortune she has amassed for herself. I asked her where it came from once, and she told me that she had earned it doing God's work – which left me none the wiser.'

'Where does she keep it?' asked Chaloner, thinking that if it contained one item that could be traced to Kerchier, the case would be solved.

'I do not know, although she claims it is not in her house. I warn her that such a deep love of lucre is at odds with our religious principles, but she is disinclined

170

to accept any opinions that are different to her own. But this is where our paths part. Good day to you.'

Chaloner watched until Ester was out of sight, admiring the jaunty swing of her hips, then returned to King's Head Court. The prayer meeting had ended, and the last of the congregation were being bundled unceremoniously out through the door. Moments later, Pamela herself emerged, the Mims trailing after her. Ester was right: Pamela had no intention of nursing her ailing husband. She strutted across the yard and was gone.

Chaloner waited a moment, to make sure she did not return, then aimed for the back of the house, where it was simplicity itself to pick the lock on the kitchen door and step inside. The place was silent, and smelled of the stew that was simmering over the hearth. A glance into the larder showed it was bursting with edible luxuries, ranging from cheese and smoked meats, to candied fruits and cakes. He could only suppose that a well-stocked pantry was a perk of fraternising with the men who controlled the black market.

It was not only food that Pamela had amassed, he noted. She also had two crates of *sal mirabilis* – small pots with labels stating that each contained a single daily dose – and one of London Treacle, with a certificate attached to say that it had been blessed by Canon William Hall. Clearly, Pamela was taking no chances with her personal safety.

He made for the stairs, aware of a flutter of unease in his stomach. What if Jasper did have the plague? The man's job was delivering medicine to the sick, so it was entirely possible that one of them had infected him. With that in mind, Chaloner was not sure what it was that kept him climbing upwards until he reached the first-floor landing.

There were three bedrooms. The largest was a grand affair containing a lot of feminine paraphernalia and nothing of Jasper's, while the second was full of dresses. Chaloner pushed open the door to the smallest – more cupboard than chamber – and found Jasper writhing on the bed. The windows were closed, so it was hot, dark and stank of vomit. Watered wine had been left, but too far away for the patient to reach, and an empty pot of *sal mirabilis* lay on its side on the floor.

Chaloner flung open the shutters, but declined to give Jasper the wine. Not only was there a dead fly floating in it, but it smelled sour from sitting around too long in a stuffy room. He tossed it out of the window, and fetched a fresh jug from Pamela's personal supplies downstairs. Then he helped Jasper to sip some, uncomfortably reminded of the times he had done the same for his first wife, when she had been dying of the plague in Holland. He pushed the memory away impatiently. It was no time to be maudlin.

'*He* has been,' babbled Jasper. 'He wanted Pamela, but he found me. She cheated him.'

'Easy,' said Chaloner gently. 'Rest now.'

'I know nothing, but it has destroyed me anyway,' muttered Jasper, clutching Chaloner's wrist. His eyes were fever bright, so Chaloner doubted he knew what he was saying. 'I have swallowed a dragon and it will devour me from within.'

Then he closed his eyes, and his breathing grew even with sleep. Chaloner pulled his hand free and lifted the sheet. There were no plague tokens that he could see – no swellings, rashes or lumps – but there was a trace of froth on his lips, which was similar to the foam that he had seen on the Edwards boys. Was it just a symptom of a complex disease that affected its victims in so many different ways, or an indication of something more insidious? He examined the cup that had contained the sour wine, but could see nothing amiss with it.

He was still pondering the matter when the door opened and two elderly women stepped in. They wore the plain clothes that marked them as Quakers, and immediately set about changing the sheets and fanning the patient's face.

'We will look after him now,' said one kindly. 'Do not worry.'

'Is it plague?' asked Chaloner, moving away with relief. He had not wanted to leave Jasper alone, yet it was hardly his place to act as nursemaid to a man he barely knew.

'Of course. What else could it be?'

'I do not suppose you know where Pamela keeps her money, do you?' asked Chaloner, disinclined to share his suspicions with strangers.

The women exchanged a startled glance. 'No one does,' replied the first. 'It is a secret she keeps to herself, and not even Jasper is in her confidence.'

'But you may look for it, if you like,' added the other, and grinned conspiratorially. 'Although we have one condition: that if you find it, you give us half. Then we can hire a ship and take our brethren to live in New England – London is no place for Quakers.'

Chaloner took them at their word, but it did not take him long to establish that Pamela's money was not in the house. He stared out of the window. Had she buried it in the garden? If so, he would never find it, because the plot was far too large to excavate on his own. He

173

made his farewells to two very disappointed ladies, and tiptoed out.

Slowly, because it was too hot for haste, Chaloner trudged to Harbert's mansion, but no one answered his knock. He went to the back of the house, and peered through a window. The remains of a hasty breakfast sat on the kitchen table, which told him that someone was still in residence, but that whoever it was had gone out, probably to church. He could have broken in, but there was no point when there was no one to talk to him, so he decided to try again later.

Frustrated at being thwarted at every turn, he headed back to the cathedral, to ask Stone's colleagues where the canon might have gone – they should be free now that Morning Prayer was over.

He saw a flicker of movement out of the corner of his eye as he went – the Greek was watching him again. He pretended not to notice, but he had had enough of his foreign shadow, so he turned down a narrow alley with the intention of doubling back and laying hold of him. Unfortunately, something in his demeanour must have alerted the fellow, because there was no sign of him by the time he returned.

Sighing irritably, Chaloner resumed his journey up Paul's Chain. He glanced into Masley's house as he passed. The parlour was empty, and an open copy of *Fourty sermons by the Right Reverend Father in God, Ralph Brownrig, late Bishop of Exceter* suggested that St Gregory's parishioners would have second-hand offerings from the pulpit that day.

As usual, Masley's table was piled high with papers, testament to the dreadful toll the plague was taking on his flock. Then Chaloner saw that the room was not empty after all, because Kirton was kneeling on the floor, sorting documents into piles. Chaloner frowned. No, not Kirton, but the man that he had mistaken for the bookseller the last time he had seen him – similar, but without the bushy white eyebrows.

He was about to walk on when he was assailed by the rank stench of sulphur. It came from Rycroft's house opposite, along with a lot of yellow smoke – the making of London Treacle stopped for no man, even on a Sunday. Chaloner knocked on the door and entered, coughing as fumes caught at the back of his throat.

'Put a mask on,' instructed Rycroft, who was clad in protective clothing from head to toe. 'Or state your business and leave. This stage of production is a tad noxious.'

'Jasper Ball,' said Chaloner, covering his mouth and nose with his sleeve. He did not want to don one of the masks hanging on the back of the door, lest the last user had had the plague. 'Your delivery man. He is very ill and—'

'He was not "very ill" when I visited him last night,' interrupted Rycroft sharply. 'It was just a mild fever.'

'Well, it is not mild now. And—'

'Then this can wait,' said Rycroft, snatching a cauldron off the fire and setting it on a trivet to cool. 'Hand me a bottle of London Treacle from the shelf behind you. I suspect Jasper has given his own allowance away – he has always been recklessly generous.'

The alchemist exchanged his remedy-making gear for a plague costume, and was gone in a flash, leaving Chaloner alone in a room that was filled with a swirling yellow smog. Absently, Chaloner glanced at the jars that sat in serried rows on the shelves around the walls, and then looked again. Belladonna, monkshood, hemlock, mandrake. Rycroft had enough poison to kill half of London!

'What are you doing here?' came a sharp voice from the door. 'Where is Rycroft?'

It took a moment for Chaloner to recognise William Hall, as the man was wearing a mask – the same style as the ones hanging on the door, only newer and cleaner.

'Gone to visit Jasper,' explained Chaloner, 'who is unwell.'

'The plague?' asked William softly. 'Then I shall pray for him. But you should not be in here without protective clothing. These fumes are dangerous.'

Chaloner was certainly aware of an unpleasant burning at the back of his throat, and was more than happy to step into the street, where the air was cleaner. William followed, but then began to close the door – with him on the inside of Rycroft's house.

'You are staying?' asked Chaloner, surprised.

'To bless the next batch of London Treacle,' explained William. 'People will expect to buy some later today, and we do not like to disappoint.'

'I need to talk to Canon Stone,' said Chaloner. 'Where is he?'

'In the cathedral, of course. It is Sunday – our busiest day of the week.'

'I was told that he left the city last night. He was seen in a carriage.'

'*What?*' William was plainly shocked. 'But we are struggling to manage as it is, and we cannot afford to lose another pair of hands. I hope you are wrong.'

'Are you sure Rycroft will not mind you being in his workshop unaccompanied?' asked Chaloner, as the door began to close again. 'Alchemists do not usually appreciate laymen among their wares. Is that why you quarrelled with him yesterday?'

'We quarrelled because he is always haring off on business of his own,' replied William shortly. 'Secret business, which he refuses to divulge. It takes him away from what he *should* be doing – namely making London Treacle. I imagine it is why he is not here now, when he promised he would be.'

'I have learned a lot about Kerchier since I arrived,' lied Chaloner, turning abruptly to another subject in an effort to disconcert. 'You might have approved of his plans for a new cathedral, but that does not mean you liked him.'

'No, it does not,' agreed William. 'But I did. His dedication and fervour were an inspiration to me, and his disappearance was London's loss.'

'Because he was so passionate a crusader?'

'And because he was a friend. He had his failings, but who does not? Besides, they were outweighed by his many virtues. Now I have work to do. Please excuse me.'

William shut the door with a brisk and very final snap.

No one was in the Deanery when Chaloner called, and a servant informed him rather curtly that everyone was in the cathedral, as was right for a Sunday morning. Chaloner traipsed there tiredly, grateful to enter its cool shade after the ruthless glare of the sun, where he discovered that the next of the day's services was about to begin.

'Ah, Tom,' came a muffled voice. It was Thurloe in full plague costume. 'You are here for Holy Communion. Good. We shall sit together.'

The ex-Spymaster was a very devout man, unlike Chaloner, who was of the opinion that religion was generally more trouble than it was worth. However, Chaloner had no wish to be branded a dissenter, so he kept such radical thoughts to himself, and meekly attended church each week, like any good Anglican.

They found a pew just as the clerics were processing in from the Chapter House, all hot and uncomfortable in their thick vestments. They were not the only ones to suffer: many of the congregation had taken precautions against the plague, most of which involved masks or scarves. Two fainted from lack of air, an entire family had to be escorted out for water, and a girl vomited all over her brother as a result of inhaling the strong herbs in her pomander.

The rite was an uninspired affair. The celebrants were John Hall and Owen, who were apparently of the opinion that the sooner they finished the better. Owen's sermon did no more than remind everyone to pray for an end to the outbreak, while John omitted most of the intercessions in the interests of brevity. It was over in record time and the congregation left in relief, many dashing for the doors while Owen was still intoning his final blessing.

'There,' said Thurloe, nodding his satisfaction, although Chaloner felt vaguely cheated. 'Now we are spiritually refreshed. But I have received reports from several old friends since we last met, and we need to discuss them somewhere quiet.'

Even though he was no longer a spymaster, he still had an enormous network of contacts, and it was no surprise that they had been set to work on his behalf.

'Prayse's house?' asked Chaloner, suggesting it because

he knew he would be offered a cold drink there. 'You must want to remove that heavy cloak.'

'No, here will do,' came the disappointing reply. 'We shall use St Faith's. Follow me.'

Thurloe led the way past the south transept, now devoid of unfriendly bell-ringers, to the crossing, where a flight of steps dipped beneath the chancel. They led to an undercroft, where the parish church of St Faith had been located ever since the cathedral had appropriated the land on which the original chapel had stood. It comprised a low, vaulted room supported by squat piers, and was a dark, gloomy place, unadorned except for an elaborately carved wooden tomb belonging to a former rector named Jonathan Brown.

'No one comes down here now,' said Thurloe, unbuckling his mask in anticipation of privacy. 'Its congregation left the city at the first sign of plague and—'

He trailed off because someone *was* using it. Val Cary knelt at the altar rail, head bowed in prayer. The secretary started in alarm at the intrusion, and Thurloe began to back away, hands raised in apology. Cary clambered to his feet.

'I should be going anyway,' he said, although with poor grace. 'My uncle loved this chapel, so I often visit when I feel the need for solitude. But it was only ever a matter of time before it was rediscovered and the hordes invaded again.'

'I am glad to meet you, as it happens,' said Thurloe, manfully resisting the urge to point out that he and Chaloner hardly represented a horde, and that the chapel was large enough to accommodate them all. 'Lawrence asked me to listen for rumours, so I have. The most serious is that there will be a gathering of discontented

179

people on Wednesday – three days hence. They aim to protest against the paucity of food and the profiteers who control it.'

'We already know that,' said Cary ungraciously. 'And we will beg the farmers to give us more, but we can do nothing about the Mims. It is difficult to crush an organisation with no real leader – the moment we close down one scheme, two more spring up in its place.'

'Regardless, you must be *seen* to take action,' argued Thurloe, 'even if it does no good. I recommend arresting anyone who flaunts a green arm-ribbon. That will show Londoners that you do not countenance felons strutting about unchallenged.'

'How?' asked Cary crossly. 'We do not have enough men to tackle Mims *and* implement the measures needed to stamp out the plague.'

'Then hire more.'

'With what? The city's coffers have been empty for weeks, and Lawrence and Abigail have all but beggared themselves to pay for what is needed out of their own pockets. So have I. None of us have any money left to give.'

'Borrow from the banks,' shrugged Thurloe, his bemused expression suggesting that he would not have allowed a lack of funds to hinder *him* from taking control of the situation.

'They refuse to accommodate us because—'

'Then *make* them,' interrupted Thurloe sharply. 'It is in their interests to have the city back to normal, so present it as an investment in their future.'

'We can try,' conceded Cary resentfully. 'But they—'

'All it requires is a firm hand. You need to show your mettle in other ways, too, because Londoners are beginning to resent being held prisoner in their own city. They want to come and go as they please, and there is talk of a mass departure – which is the second rumour I have to report. Such an episode *must* be stopped.'

'Yes, we know that as well,' Cary snapped, nettled. 'And Monck has readied his artillery in anticipation. There will be a bloodbath if folk do try to break out, so let us hope they have more sense than to attempt it.'

'Take a leaf from Cromwell's book, and detain the people who sit in taverns and coffee houses fomenting unrest,' advised Thurloe. 'There is much to be learned from the tactics of a military dictatorship.'

'Right,' said Cary, eyeing him warily and clearly wondering if this was a stab at humour. Chaloner knew it was not. 'Although it is like fighting the hydra – you chop off one head, but another just grows back somewhere else.'

When he had gone, Thurloe asked Chaloner for an update on his enquiries, although that did not take long, as the spy had little to report.

'So what have *you* learned?' Chaloner asked when he had finished. 'The nature of the business that dragged Upton back to London on his wedding day?'

'Unfortunately not, although my contacts have sent me a great deal of information about his customers. I am afraid to say that most are not men with whom I would care to associate. Perhaps I *should* have prevented him from marrying Ursula.'

'What about the cathedral? Have you discovered any more about his ties with that?'

Thurloe nodded. 'He sold its clerks paper, apparently. Also, something was overheard by the maid at the inn where he was staying – that he planned to visit

181

a bookseller in St Paul's Churchyard. The area used to be full of them, but most are closed now.'

'Then it should not be too difficult to determine which one he met. I will look later – after I have tracked down Stone.'

'I want to believe that Upton came here for innocent reasons,' Thurloe went on unhappily. 'But all my instincts tell me that he did not, and I have learned to trust those.'

They fell to discussing the prospect of an uncontrolled exodus, which both feared was all but an inevitability, given that the forces of law and order seemed powerless to prevent it. Then Chaloner heard a sound. He turned quickly, and saw Francis Hall standing by Rector Brown's tomb, although he had not seen him arrive.

'Has he been listening to us?' he whispered uneasily.

'He might have tried,' Thurloe murmured back, 'but he did not succeed – our voices were too low. So much for me thinking that this chapel is always empty.'

Chaloner started towards Francis, to ask if he knew where Stone had gone, but the canon was already halfway up the stairs, and by the time Chaloner reached the top, he had disappeared into the forest of pillars along the cathedral's nave.

'I really do need to speak to Stone,' he said to Thurloe, looking around for Francis in some irritation. 'Even if it means leaving the city to find him.'

'I will set some of my people to ask after his whereabouts if you do not track him down today,' promised Thurloe, and then winced. 'I spoke to Bing, by the way, but I failed to decide if he is a genuine lunatic or if he feigns madness to avoid awkward questions. He is impressive – there are not many who can flummox me.'

\*

The first port of call, once Chaloner left the cathedral, was the Deanery. Thurloe offered to accompany him, and they arrived to find three of the cathedral's senior officials enjoying refreshments after their arduous devotional duties. Tillison picked at a plate of soused herring, looking wearier and older than he had the previous day. Cartwright sat next to him, fresh-faced and handsome, eating a frugal meal of bread and fruit, while the pink-cheeked Henchman grumbled about the poor quality of the bacon he was devouring.

'John!' exclaimed Tillison warmly when Thurloe removed his mask to reveal his face. 'You should not be here, old friend. Two members of the congregation were carried out in a swoon during today's service – plague, most likely.'

'Or fear of it,' put in Cartwright with all the scorn of a youth who had never seriously contemplated his own mortality. 'People see every sniff and snuffle as a portent of doom, and lose hope altogether at the first sign of a fever.'

'Who can blame them?' muttered Henchman. 'I am frightened myself.'

'I was sorry to hear about your new brother-in-law, John,' said Tillison kindly. 'The plague is nothing if not even-handed – it takes the young and vigorous just as readily as the old and infirm.'

He shot a pointed glance at Cartwright, but it was water off a duck's back.

'Upton did not die of the sickness,' said Thurloe. 'He was hit on the head – murdered.'

All three clerics gazed at him in shock.

'Then I am sorry to hear it,' said Tillison eventually. 'Deeply sorry. There is enough death in the city without violence adding to the tally.'

'Did you know Upton well?' asked Chaloner.

'Not really, but we buy our paper from him,' replied Tillison. 'Or we did. We have not needed him for months, as we do not have enough working staff to run down our stocks.'

'Did you see him when he arrived in the city a few days ago?' asked Thurloe.

'I did not, but Bing mentioned his visit,' said Tillison. 'It was unusual, you see – no other wealthy merchant has returned. Not while the death toll still rises.'

'So he came to the cathedral?' probed Thurloe.

'Yes – to see Owen. Or so Bing told me. I assume it was to discuss the purchase of more supplies, although I cannot be sure. You will have to ask Owen about it.'

Thurloe continued to press them with questions, but prised loose nothing of interest. Chaloner listened carefully, disgusted when he was wholly unable to tell if Tillison, Cartwright and Henchman were truly ignorant or just very clever dissemblers.

'Will you tell me about Kerchier's last day?' asked Thurloe, eventually turning to another subject. 'I appreciate that it is none of my affair, but he was an old friend, and I have often wondered what became of the poor man.'

It was a lie, but Tillison and Henchman obligingly recounted every detail they could recall about Kerchier's disappearance and the ensuing hunt for him and the money. It was a far fuller account than the one Chaloner had been given, and included the fact that Kerchier had often voiced an intention to 'rid the cathedral of the carbuncle that was St Gregory's'.

'You did not tell me this yesterday,' said Chaloner crossly, irked that something so important should have been kept from him. 'How did he plan to do it?'

'He never said,' replied Tillison serenely. 'And I did not mention it before, because I only remembered after you had gone. At my age, the brain needs a bit of time to get itself up and running at full speed.'

'Mine does, too,' put in Henchman. 'Even though it is thirty years younger than his.'

'Where is Canon Stone?' asked Thurloe, before Chaloner could say he did not believe their excuses. 'It is imperative that we speak to him as soon as possible.'

'I am afraid he left the city last night,' said Cartwright. 'I met him as he was clambering into a coach with his bags. He told me that he had been summoned by an ailing sister, but he promised to be back the day after tomorrow – Tuesday.'

'Where does this sister live?' demanded Chaloner.

'It is not for lowly vicars to interrogate senior canons about their personal lives,' replied Cartwright, looking anything but lowly. 'So I did not ask.'

Although the young vicar's tale roughly corresponded to what Paget had said, Chaloner had the distinct sense that he was lying. But why? Cartwright could not be involved in Kerchier's death, because he was not old enough. Or was the mystery bigger than ancient murder, and had stretched its tentacles to entwine others, too? In which case, perhaps it *was* significant that Upton had died on the day that Kerchier's bones had been discovered, that both men had been killed by blows to the head, and that Bing thought Upton might have been in possession of information about Kerchier's demise.

'I think Stone has a sister in Scotland,' said Henchman, scratching his pink and white head. 'But there may be another. Owen will know – he and Stone are particular friends.'

Thurloe moved to yet another matter. 'What can you tell us about Harbert, whose death resulted in the discovery of Kerchier's body? I understand he died while fighting the royal Keeper of Fish.'

'We did not see the fracas ourselves,' replied Henchman, then added gossipingly, 'although witnesses say it was over very quickly.'

'What witnesses?' asked Chaloner. 'Because Denton denies it happened.'

'Well, he would,' put in Cartwright slyly. 'Duelling is illegal.'

'Denton's friends were there, by all accounts,' said Henchman, ignoring him. 'Kirton, Gaundy and Wildbore. They will be at St Gregory's now, ringing the bells. You can catch them if you hurry.'

Leaving Thurloe to continue questioning the clerics alone, Chaloner aimed for the door. The ex-Spymaster caught his arm before he went.

'Tillison is no liar,' he whispered. 'Yet I have the sense that we are not being told the whole truth even so. There is dark business afoot here, Tom. I feel it with every fibre of my being.'

The ringers were not in St Gregory's, and enquiries revealed that the service had been postponed, as Masley needed to bury all those who had died the previous night first – some ten souls from his own parish, plus another two from St Faith's, the vicar of which had fled shortly after the first case of plague had been confirmed back in April.

Unwilling to witness a dreary mass committal, Chaloner went to the cathedral to wait, where it was cooler. He prowled aimlessly for a while, but as he passed the Lady

Chapel, he saw all three Hall brothers and the drink-sodden Owen, talking in suspiciously low voices. Unfortunately, eavesdropping quickly proved to be impossible, so he strode inside instead, and spoke deliberately loudly in an effort to disconcert them.

'Just the men I want to see,' he announced, noting the guilty starts and anxious looks as the four clerics tried to determine whether they could have been overheard.

'About Kerchier again?' Owen was clearly inebriated, with glazed eyes and unsteady hands. 'But we know nothing to help you.'

'*I* do,' countered John stiffly. 'Our poor friend was murdered because he wanted to drag the cathedral into the seventeenth century. His devotion to progress terrified the Maurice Men, and one of them killed him for it.'

'True,' nodded Francis. 'They were afraid of innovation twenty years ago, and they are afraid now. Nothing has changed.'

'His murder was a wicked crime,' put in William. 'Not only because it deprived us of a great visionary, but because the culprit stole all the money we had raised.'

'*He* is our treasurer now,' said Owen, jerking his thumb at William. 'But I hope he is more careful than Kerchier was, because I should hate to lose another hoard.'

'If Kerchier had lived,' said John, glancing around him, 'this crumbling ruin would be demolished by now, and an exciting new basilica would be standing in its place.'

'But *you* like this building,' surmised Francis, watching Chaloner wince at the notion. 'Why, when you can have something better? I mean, just look around you – cracks in the walls, a leaking roof, shoddy craftsmanship . . . If the south transept survives another winter, I shall dance naked in the chancel.'

187

'How about dancing in St Faith's instead?' asked Chaloner coolly, recalling where he had last seen Francis. 'Or the undercroft of St Gregory's?'

There was a short silence, then Francis gave a brittle laugh. 'It would certainly ensure that no one saw me – neither attracts many visitors. However, the point I was trying to make is that this old heap is not worth saving. We must knock it down and start afresh.'

'So what *were* you doing in St Gregory's crypt and St Faith's?' pressed Chaloner, aware that Francis had contrived to dodge the issue.

The Canon made a moue of irritation at Chaloner's persistence. 'I went to St Faith's for some solitary prayer, but I left when I saw it was in use. And I was never in St Gregory's – I do not like the place.'

Chaloner wanted to argue, but he was not completely sure that it *had* been Francis in St Gregory's, and it was clear that the canon would continue to deny it without evidence to the contrary. He moved to another question.

'Kerchier mentioned a plan to rid the cathedral of St Gregory's, and the last remark anyone heard him make was about its vergers doing it a serious disservice by digging a crypt, because it had rendered the church unstable. What did he intend to do to it, exactly?'

Francis met his gaze evenly. 'Nothing. It was just talk.'

'Actually, I think it was more than talk, Francis,' countered Owen tipsily. 'He never actually told me his plans, but I had the distinct impression that they were to involve gunpowder.' He shrugged at the exasperated expressions on his friends' faces. 'He never succeeded in blowing anything up, so what can it matter if we discuss it now?'

'General Monck told me that Kerchier tried to buy

188

powder from him,' said Chaloner. 'But the request was denied.'

'You see?' said Owen to the brothers. 'Kerchier might have *wanted* to blast St Gregory's to kingdom come, but he never did it, because he did not have the wherewithal.'

'Of course he did not have the wherewithal,' said Francis tightly. 'For a start, this was during the wars, when the military had a monopoly over the stuff. This line of enquiry is ludicrous, Chaloner, and you should abandon it before you waste any more of your time.'

'I need to speak to Stone,' said Chaloner, feeling that if the likes of Francis urged him to stop, then the matter was definitely worth pursuing. 'Where is he?'

'Gone to his sister,' replied Francis shortly. 'She has run out of money, so he had to take her some. But *he* will not be able to help you. He defected to the Maurice Men shortly after Kerchier disappeared, but Kerchier had already sensed the traitor in him, and had kept him out of all the important decisions.'

'Then he can tell me so himself,' said Chaloner, recalling that Cartwright had claimed that the sister was ill, so who was lying – Cartwright, Francis or Stone himself? 'Where does she live?'

'I have no idea. A village somewhere, I imagine.'

'Owen?' asked Chaloner. 'Surely you know? You are friends.'

'Not friends – colleagues,' corrected Owen. 'And he never talked to me about his family, so I cannot help you. However, I can say that he promised to be back on Tuesday.'

'Although do not expect to monopolise him immediately,' warned William. 'His cathedral duties must take precedence over an ancient crime.'

189

'Dean Sancroft would disagree,' retorted Chaloner.

'Speaking of the dean, have you discovered yet who wrote to him about the skeleton?' asked John. 'You promised to tell us when you found out.'

Chaloner had done no such thing.

'Harbert!' exclaimed Owen suddenly, and beamed. '*He* killed Kerchier! It is obvious now that I think about it. He must have learned that Kerchier planned to blow up St Gregory's, and brained him before he could light the fuses. Then he hid Kerchier in his own grave, knowing that the body would not be discovered until it was too late to matter to him.'

'That makes sense,' nodded Francis with an oily smile. 'Well done, Owen! You have saved the dean's envoy a lot of wasted effort.'

'I understand that you met Upton the stationer recently, Owen,' said Chaloner, ignoring their attempts to lead him astray. 'Why?'

'Cathedral business,' replied Owen, although Chaloner had rarely seen such furtive eyes. 'And thus confidential.'

'I carry your dean's authority,' Chaloner reminded him. 'So please answer the question. Or do you want me to tell Sancroft that you were obstructive?'

'No.' Owen swallowed hard. 'It was . . . Upton came to . . . we were not . . .'

William came to his rescue. 'He came to sell us paper. We use a lot of it, as I am sure you can imagine – there is a heavy administrative burden involved in running a diocese.'

'Not when most of the staff are away,' countered Chaloner, recalling what Tillison had said. 'Your supplies run down slowly.'

Something flashed in William's eyes, although it was

gone too quickly for Chaloner to tell if it was guilt or irritation. 'Quite right,' he said evenly. 'So Upton was thanked for his visit and sent on his way. Is that not right, Owen?'

The other canon nodded. 'He was disappointed, naturally, but I told him to come back when the plague is over and we are fully functional again.'

'So there you are,' said Francis with a smug smile. 'Now, is there anything else, or may we return to our religious duties?'

Chaloner looked at their clever, devious faces, and knew that pressing them further was futile. He gave a brief bow and took his leave.

He was about to return to St Gregory's to see if the ringers were there when he saw Thurloe. The ex-Spymaster shook his head when Chaloner raised questioning eyebrows: he had learned nothing new by lingering in the Deanery. Then a peculiar keening sound began to emanate from the south transept. It was Bing, squatting on his haunches with his hands over his head. He wore his clerical robes, but was barefoot and had reapplied the black paint around his eyes. He was singing to Dean Cary's tomb, while young Cartwright tried in vain to make him stop. Chaloner homed in on the violist.

'Tillison tells us that you saw Upton shortly before he died,' he began without preamble. 'Here in the cathedral, talking to Owen.'

'Upton, Upton, Upton,' chanted Bing, springing to his feet so fast that Cartwright stumbled backwards. 'The man who loved new things – new wives and new churches. It was all the same to him. He sold Owen paper. *Lots* of paper.'

191

'Are you sure?' asked Chaloner. 'Because Owen denies it, while Tillison says the cathedral does not need any – not when so many of its officers are away.'

A sly cant lit Bing's eye. 'There are many uses for paper. Oh, yes, there are.'

He gave one of his high-pitched giggles, and began to dance a reel that took him in ever increasing circles away from Chaloner and Thurloe.

'Blame the plague,' said Cartwright, watching Bing gyrate jerkily around a cracked pillar. 'It has sent him out of his wits.'

'Has he lost loved ones?' asked Thurloe sympathetically.

'Who has not?' shrugged Cartwright. 'But it is the thought of catching it himself that unnerves him. He does not have a blameless past, you see, and fears eternal damnation.'

'Does he indeed?' said Thurloe keenly. 'Would you care to elaborate?'

'I cannot – it is not my secret to share. You must speak to him about it.'

'How?' asked Chaloner, frustration making him testy. 'It may have escaped your notice, but he is mad – incapable of answering questions in a rational manner.'

'I doubt that will pose a problem for Dean Sancroft's envoy and a past Spymaster General,' said Cartwright, rather too acidly for Chaloner's liking. 'You both must be used to prising information from people who would rather not part with it.'

'You cannot help us at all?' asked Thurloe, speaking before Chaloner could offer to use the vicar himself to demonstrate how good he was at interviewing uncooperative subjects. 'Even though all we want is to bring a murderer to justice – one who killed a priest?'

Cartwright considered carefully for a moment. 'All right. Ask Bing about William Turner. I cannot say more without breaking a confidence, but it should take you in the right direction.'

'Who is William Turner?' asked Chaloner tersely, disliking the game the young man was playing with his devious half-revelations.

'I am afraid you must find that out for yourselves. Incidentally, it was not only St Gregory's ringers who witnessed the fight between Harbert and Denton. So did Bing – he told me so himself. Perhaps he will tell you what really happened there, given that you seem to have been regaled with conflicting tales.'

He smiled spitefully, giving the impression that, far from clarifying matters, he expected Bing to confuse them even more. Chaloner stared at him, wondering why he should want such a thing.

'Did *you* see Upton when he came to London recently?' asked Thurloe. He sounded as exasperated as Chaloner felt. 'Tillison answered that question in the Deanery, but you remained suspiciously silent.'

'Not suspiciously,' objected Cartwright. '*Respectfully*. My lower status prohibits me from thrusting myself into a discussion with my seniors.'

'Yes, yes,' said Chaloner impatiently, thinking that it had not stopped the young vicar from monopolising the conversation the first time they had met, and suspecting that Cartwright was 'respectful' only when it suited him. 'So did you see Upton or not?'

Cartwright nodded. 'But not here – in Kirton's book-shop. It was roughly three o'clock on the Sunday afternoon. I have no idea how long he stayed there, but just four hours later, I heard that he was dead of the sickness.'

'Were you not suspicious?' demanded Thurloe. 'The plague does not kill *that* fast.'

'Perhaps he was already ill when I saw him – I was too far away to tell. But Kirton will know, so question him about it. But now you must excuse me – duty calls.'

'He is ambitious,' said Thurloe, watching the young man stride away. 'And will do anything to further his career in the Church. He will not hesitate to mislead us, should it suit his purposes, so we should treat everything he tells us with caution.'

Chaloner agreed, then pushed the self-serving vicar from his mind, and turned to stare at Bing again. If the plague really had turned the violist's wits, then why had Tillison not sent him away? As a representative of the cathedral, he did it no favours, which was unfortunate at a time when people were looking to it for reassurance.

Chaloner and Thurloe approached Bing slowly, both aware that any sudden moves might cause him to bolt, and it was too hot to go haring after him.

'Cartwright says you witnessed the spat between Harbert and Denton,' Chaloner began quietly. 'Will you tell us what happened?'

'Weapons flashed and flew,' sang Bing, hopping from foot to foot. 'Duelling is evil. It happens when the devil roams unchecked.'

'What weapons? Swords?'

'Swords and sticks and Satan's pits,' chanted Bing. 'They skipped and leapt, but it was the dance of death. Harbert is in his grave now. Ask his corpse if you want to know more.'

'Do you know what they quarrelled about?' asked Chaloner, struggling for patience.

'The bells of St Gregory, which Harbert loathed and

Denton loves. The world is full of folk who adore what another hates, and who hate what another adores.'

'That is certainly true,' sighed Thurloe wryly, as Bing broke off to giggle.

The violist suddenly grew serious. 'You will never find the truth about Kerchier, Upton *or* Harbert. There are too many secrets and too many lies.'

'There are,' argued Chaloner. 'And you have one of your own – William Turner.'

Bing's jaw dropped in horror, and he began to back away, eyes wide with alarm. Then he turned and fled, robes flying behind him.

'Do you want me to catch him?' asked Chaloner without enthusiasm.

Thurloe shook his head. 'He may be more willing to talk once we know why this William Turner fills him with such horror. I have a few old spies who may be able to help, so I shall go home and send for them. Who knows? Perhaps one will know the whereabouts of Canon Stone as well. It is time we had some good luck.'

'Do you need any help?'

'No – you should talk to the ringers at St Gregory's.'

Chaloner winced as he walked across the churchyard, sure it was worse than the hottest day he had ever experienced in Spain, France or even Tangier. Then he saw a familiar face.

Fabian Stedman was a friend of sorts, in that he and Chaloner were both regulars at the Rainbow Coffee House in Fleet Street – or they had been before the plague. He was a printer who held Royalist convictions so rabid that Chaloner sometimes wondered if he was a government spy, employed to report on those who did not immediately agree that the King was a saint and all his courtiers angels.

'You are still alive then,' said Stedman with a smile as their paths converged. 'I have not seen you for so long that I assumed you were dead. I am glad you are not.'

'Likewise. Have you heard from the others – Farr, Speed, Thompson?'

'All well, although the Rainbow has been shut up three times now for serving men with fevers. Farr says none had the plague, but General Monck takes no chances and I do not blame him. The latest forty days will be up next week, thank God. How I miss its brews!'

Farr's coffee was bitter, powerful and very variable, although he had a band of loyal devotees who claimed they could not start their day without a dose of it inside them.

'Why have you stayed in the city?' asked Chaloner. 'Nowhere else to go?'

Stedman shot him a sour look. 'I had invitations galore from friends in the country, but there is work to be done here, and I am not a man to run away from danger.'

'Your printworks is still open?'

'No – the stationers are too craven to do business in London now, and refuse to send us any paper. We cannot work without it, so we have been closed since June. My duties now involve tolling the bells for the dead.'

'John Upton is a stationer,' remarked Chaloner. 'He was here last week, trying to sell supplies to favoured clients.'

Stedman blinked. 'I thought I saw him, but he was gone in a flash, so I assumed I was mistaken. What a pity! If he had come to us, we would have bought his entire stock.'

'Apparently, he visited the cathedral and Kirton, to name but two possible customers, although—'

'Kirton the bookseller?' Stedman's eyes narrowed. 'He never mentioned this to me.'

'You know him?'

Stedman nodded towards St Gregory's church. Absently, Chaloner noticed that the tower clock had stopped.

'We ring the bells together. It is where I am bound now.'

Chaloner fell into step beside him. 'You do this every Sunday?'

'We ring cross-changes every Sunday, but the rest of the time, we just toll for the dead. There are so few ringers left now that we are obliged to do it all day, every day. Look at my hands – full of blisters.'

Chaloner regarded him doubtfully. 'St Gregory's cannot have that many fatalities.'

'No, but we perform all over the city, as most of the churches have lost their own bands, and their vergers are too busy digging graves. And in the evenings, I work on a book entitled *Tintinnologia*. I shall expect you to buy a copy when it is published.'

'You do all this tolling with Wildbore and his cronies?'

Stedman grimaced. 'They say they help, but the reality is that they spend the time chatting to the mourners while I do all the work. I pity the folk they waylay, because Wildbore is very aptly named – he *is* a wild bore. He has no conversation, but worse yet' – he lowered his voice – 'he supported Parliament during the wars.'

'Gracious!' said Chaloner, not bothering to remind him that so had half the country.

'*And* he reeks of fish. I assumed it is because his trade

is selling the things, but it transpires that he wears a dried roach head around his neck to repel deadly miasmas. He should put his faith in good Virginia tobacco instead, as there is nothing quite like it for thwarting pestilential diseases.'

He pulled a pipe from his pocket, tamped it with a plug of brownish material, and produced enough smoke to fumigate the entire precinct. Some wafted over Chaloner, who jerked away, repelled.

'That is not "good Virginia tobacco"! Have you added something else to it?'

Stedman laughed. 'Sawdust, hemp and a drop of London Treacle for flavour. It has not been possible to buy real tobacco in the city for weeks now, so I have been experimenting.'

'I did not know that London Treacle could be smoked. I thought you had to drink it.'

'It dries into a sticky tar if you forget to put the lid back on, and it is too expensive to discard, so I devised another way of ingesting the stuff. You would think the cathedral would distribute it free of charge, as an act of Christian charity, but it costs twice as much now as it did in May. Still, all the canons take a daily dose, so it must be worth the expense.'

Chaloner knew they did not – Tillison prayed, while Henchman preferred Bayhurst's Lozenges.

'Of course, it is not just medicine that has doubled in price,' Stedman went on. 'So has food. Lawrence and Monck do their best, but there are simply too many felons at work. These profiteers are wicked, and when the King returns, he will hang the lot of them as unpatriotic villains.'

*

198

Access to St Gregory's ringing chamber was via a spiral staircase in the corner of the tower, and Chaloner followed Stedman up steps that were worn with age. Eventually, they emerged into a room with five ropes dangling through holes in the ceiling. Wildbore was there, holding forth about double-dodging and lead-ends to Kirton and Denton, who looked bored. All three brightened when Stedman walked in, expressions that turned wary when they saw that Chaloner was behind him.

'Where is Gaundy?' asked Stedman, glancing around. 'He is not usually late.'

'We can start without him if *he* steps in,' said Wildbore, pointing at Chaloner.

'I hope Gaundy does not have the plague,' said Kirton, white eyebrows drawing together worriedly. 'I always assume the worst when someone breaks an appointment these days.'

'Has John Upton broken one?' asked Chaloner casually. 'He went to your bookshop, but four hours later, he was dead. Did *he* promise to visit you a second time?'

'So the tale about his demise is true?' Kirton shook his head sadly. 'Poor man! He was newly wed and had great plans for his future. His wife was rich but old, so he hoped soon to inherit . . .' He trailed off uncomfortably. 'Lord! You do not know her, do you?'

'What were his "great plans" exactly?' asked Chaloner coolly.

'To amass a fortune and enjoy it. He did not explain how – it was just a passing remark, one he made as we concluded our business.'

'What business?'

Kirton shrugged. 'He sold me some paper.'

'And why did you not send him in my direction, pray?'

demanded Stedman archly. 'You know I would have bought some, too.'

Kirton made an apologetic gesture. 'He was so full of excited chatter about his wedding that I am afraid you slipped my mind. I am sorry, Fabian.'

'And four hours later, he was dead,' repeated Chaloner, watching the bookseller intently. 'However, he did not die of the plague – he was killed by a blow to the head.'

Kirton regarded him in horror. 'You mean he was murdered? How awful! You would think there was enough death in the city without felons adding to the toll with violence.'

Chaloner sensed instinctively that Kirton would be more talkative away from his cronies, so he decided to leave him until he could corner him alone. He turned to Denton instead, noting again the Keeper of Fish's resemblance to his piscine charges in St James's Park.

'Speaking of violence, I have witnesses who say that you *did* fight Harbert.' Chaloner included all the ringers in his stern glare. 'And that the rest of you watched.'

'Not me,' said Stedman at once. 'Although I wish I had. It would have been a delight to see that miserable old dog put in his place.'

'Your witnesses are mistaken, Chaloner,' blustered Denton, although his eyes were uneasy, and he swallowed hard. 'They probably swallowed too much *sal mirabilis*. I understand that some of it contains a lot of very strong wine.'

'Because powerful diseases must be fought with powerful ingredients,' gabbled Wildbore in a transparent attempt to swing the conversation away from Harbert. 'Or so the makers of these remedies claim. Personally, I find that hanging a dried roach head around my neck does the trick. Deadly miasmas are attracted to it, rather than me, thus keeping me safe.'

'And Gaundy advocates London Treacle,' put in Kirton. 'But I think—'

'Harbert,' interrupted Chaloner firmly, refusing to let them side-track him. 'I want to know what really happened the day he died.'

'It is all right,' said Stedman, when the others looked as though they would continue to prevaricate. 'Chaloner works for the Earl of Clarendon, and he is a good Royalist. You can tell him what you told me – the truth.'

Denton looked as though he might be sick. 'I did not . . . that is to say . . .'

Tutting impatiently, Stedman answered on their behalf. 'There *was* a fight, because Harbert stormed up to my friends here, and accused them of making an ungodly noise with the bells. He was rude and aggressive.'

'So you challenged him?' Chaloner kept his eyes fixed on Denton.

'Of course they did not,' declared Stedman impatiently. 'Harbert challenged *them* – he drew his sword and threatened to cut them to pieces. But he was a ridiculous fellow, and they knew they were in no danger. Tell him what you did, Denton.'

'I grabbed a stick and waved it back at him,' supplied Denton reluctantly. 'It was a joke – *Harbert* was a joke. Then I feinted, expecting him to jump away, but he just stood there and I inadvertently jabbed him in the side . . .'

'After which he sheathed his weapon and scuttled away, swearing,' finished Kirton.

'Then why did you not tell me this when I first asked?' demanded Chaloner crossly.

'Because I do not want to be hanged for assault,' explained Denton wretchedly. 'I know how these things work – the word of a Keeper of Fish against a wealthy baronet.'

Wildbore's porcine features creased into a scowl. 'I suspect Harbert went home to bed, and one of his servants dispatched him, safe in the knowledge that poor Denton would be accused instead. I know for a fact that they hated him.'

'So did his brother Matthew,' put in Kirton. 'They had not spoken in years.'

'And let us not forget the canons,' added Stedman. 'Harbert had a sharp tongue, and those haughty Hall brothers will not forget an insult. Nor will Stone and Owen.'

'Perhaps that is why Stone left London,' suggested Wildbore. '*He* murdered Harbert, and fled when Dean Sancroft's envoy arrived and began asking questions.'

'Apparently, Stone has gone to visit his sister,' said Chaloner. 'Who is either ill or needs some money, depending on who you believe.'

'It is more likely that he has gone to share her food,' averred Wildbore. 'There is virtually nothing to eat in the city, and he likes his victuals.'

'Especially fish,' sighed Stedman, 'which you cannot get for love nor money these days. And to think we had such plenty at the beginning of July.'

At that moment, Vicar Masley arrived, his arms full of paper. He faltered when he saw Chaloner, mismatched eyes blinking warily.

'You are brave,' he remarked, 'lingering for a mystery that will never be solved.' He turned to the others before Chaloner could respond. 'Why are you not ringing? The service will start soon. Where is Gaundy?'

202

'Late,' replied Wildbore, and pushed a rope towards Chaloner. 'But we have a replacement, so do not worry. Are you ready, boys?'

He called for Plain Bob, and Chaloner winced when, instead of evenly struck notes, there was a staccato jumble of clangs. Wildbore was the chief culprit, but the ringing master was too busy criticising everyone else to correct himself. Chaloner came in for more than his share of abuse, and by the time they had finished, tempers were running high.

'I did *not* miss my dodge, Wildbore,' snapped Stedman. '*You* did.'

'Because you were slow to lead,' Wildbore barked back. 'And you had better improve by next time, or I shall fine you. Now go and wind the clock. Gaundy must have forgotten to do it, because I noticed on my way here that it had stopped.'

Stedman stamped away with poor grace, while Wildbore and the others continued to blame each other for their poor performance. They were interrupted by a sudden yell, after which Stedman came hurtling down the steps.

'Gaundy!' he gasped. 'I have just found him. Dead!'

# Chapter 7

Gaundy was indeed dead. He lay behind the complex jumble of levers and cogs that formed the clock's innards, and had been discovered only because Stedman had glanced there to see if he could find out why the winding mechanism had jammed. There was a wound on the back of the verger's head and a white wave of froth on his lips. While his cronies clustered in a horrified semicircle by the door, Chaloner looked around the clock chamber.

A stool stood nearby, around which lay a number of empty flasks, while the whole place reeked of tobacco. It did not take a genius to guess that here was Gaundy's secret refuge, the place where he went for a quiet smoke and drink, safe in the knowledge that everyone would assume he was busy tending the clock.

On the floor next to the stool was a pot marked *sal mirabilis*. Chaloner picked it up and sniffed at it carefully. The foul stench made him recoil. He dribbled some on the floor, and watched as it hissed and released tiny tendrils of vapour. He donned gloves and prised open Gaundy's mouth to see it was full of bleeding lesions.

He sat back on his heels, recalling what Landlord Paget

had said when he had poured away the poisoned wine in the Mitre – that it had smoked. As there were unlikely to be two poisoners at large in and around St Paul's, it was not unreasonable to assume that whoever had tried to kill him had succeeded in dispatching Gaundy – which in turn meant that the verger was connected to the mystery surrounding Kerchier's bones. Had Gaundy found clues with the skeleton and guessed the killer's identity? Then why not tell the authorities? Because he had tried to blackmail the culprit, and had paid for it with his life?

Chaloner was angry with himself. He should have pressed Gaundy harder about finding the bones, as then not only might the poisoner now be safely locked away, but the hapless verger would still be alive.

So what had happened, exactly? There was no sign of a struggle, so the culprit had either crept up undetected or Gaundy had not considered himself to be in danger until it was too late. Chaloner examined the verger's head again. The wound did not look serious, and he was inclined to suspect that he had been hit first, and the poison poured into his mouth while he was momentarily stunned.

He slipped the pot into his pocket. Perhaps Prayse Russell or Rycroft would be able to identify the toxin, and if it was an unusual one, it could be used to trace the killer. Then he stood, and explained to Gaundy's friends what had happened. As all except Stedman were on his list of suspects – he already knew the printer had been a child in Herefordshire twenty years ago – he watched their reactions closely. Kirton was horrified, and kept casting agitated glances at the others; Wildbore was all blustering indignation; Denton was impassive.

'So the *sal mirabilis* killed him?' asked Denton doubtfully. 'Are you sure? I thought he was an advocate of London Treacle, like me. It is costly, but we toll too many bells for people who put their trust in other remedies, none of which do what they say on the pot.'

'True,' agreed Wildbore grimly. 'Which is why a roach head—'

'But his poor mouth,' interrupted Kirton unsteadily. 'How could he swallow something so caustic without the agony waking him up?'

'Chaloner explained that,' said Stedman. 'He was knocked silly first. And I wager anything you like that he had been at the wine, which would also have dulled his senses.'

'That is possible,' nodded Denton. 'Gaundy loved his claret, just like his father.'

'It is the Executioner's work,' whispered Kirton, his voice hoarse with fright.

'The Executioner is a tale for children,' scoffed Wildbore. 'He does not exist.'

'But *four* men lie dead of head wounds,' insisted Kirton fearfully. 'Kerchier, Upton, Harbert and now Gaundy. It cannot be coincidence.'

'Harbert?' interposed Chaloner sharply. 'He was struck on the head, too?'

'We would not know,' said Denton quickly, shooting the bookseller a warning glance. 'His death had nothing to do with us, as we have already told you. And Kerchier died twenty years ago, Kirton. There cannot possibly be a link between his demise and the other three. You are letting your imagination run riot.'

'No, I am not,' argued Kirton unsteadily. 'It is the Executioner. I *know* it.'

'I am unfamiliar with this story,' said Stedman, his eyes alight with interest. 'Who is the Executioner and what did he—'

'It is a yarn put about to titillate fools and children,' interrupted Wildbore shortly. 'There is no truth to it.'

'Tell me anyway,' begged Stedman.

Denton sighed testily. 'A public hangman is alleged to be buried in the cathedral, one who loved his work so much that he sometimes leaves his tomb to dispatch sinners. But it is an asinine story. For a start, only nobles, royalty and very rich merchants are interred in St Paul's. Hangmen go in their parish cemeteries.'

'There!' said Wildbore triumphantly. 'You see? Nonsense, just as I told you.'

'That is not the tale I heard,' countered Kirton. 'Which is that the Executioner—'

'Stop!' interrupted Denton, fishy eyes cold and hard. 'There is no Executioner. How many more times must we say it?'

Kirton threw up his hands in surrender, although it was clear that he remained sceptical. Chaloner determined to corner him alone as soon as he could, as it was patently obvious that the three older ringers harboured some sly secret – Kirton was the weak link, who would most easily be persuaded to share it with him. He gestured to Gaundy's body.

'Who else knew that he liked to come up here alone?'

'Just us and the cathedral— Hah!' Wildbore slammed one fist into the other. '*Pemper* did this. He is jealous of our better striking, so he decided to attack us by depriving us of our second-best ringer. The first-best being me, of course.'

'It was not Pemper,' said Kirton shakily. 'This goes

beyond petty rivalry. And there *are* connections between these four deaths, Denton. First, Gaundy found Kerchier's bones in the vault *he* built for Harbert – he was a mason before becoming a verger if you recall. And second, Gaundy met Upton last Sunday. I saw them together myself.'

'So?' shrugged Denton. 'Gaundy was probably buying stationery for his vicar. Do not make a mountain out of a molehill.'

Chaloner was listening with interest, but Kirton finally realised that bleating his fears in front of Sancroft's investigator was impolitic and fell silent. Stedman helped Chaloner to carry Gaundy down the stairs, and by the time they had laid the verger on a bier in the nave, the other three ringers had disappeared.

'They are silly men,' averred Stedman, mopping his brow. 'I would not pay any attention to what they say if I were you.'

Chaloner would make up his own mind about that, and immediately set off towards Kirton's bookshop.

To reach the shop, Chaloner was obliged to pass the plague pit in St Paul's Churchyard, where the stench of death was enough to make him gag. The only sounds were the hum of flies and the rasp of the gravediggers' spades. Bodies, some wrapped in blankets but most just wearing the clothes in which they had died, had been dumped in piles, waiting to be tossed on top of those who had gone before them.

It might have been a filthy, soulless operation, but one man was there to give it dignity. William Hall – clad in a protective cloak, although his face was uncovered – had taken charge. Under his stern eye, the burial detail was more respectful than they might otherwise have been, and all paused every so often, so he could recite the necessary prayers. Grateful mourners pressed coins into his hands, causing Chaloner to wonder if William was acting from compassion or a desire to augment the fund for his new cathedral.

Finding Kirton's shop was easy. Only two booksellers remained from the dozens that had operated in the area just a few months ago, and one was a cramped, mean place that sold nothing but radical religious tracts. Kirton's was larger, cleaner and newer, but was clearly suffering from a lack of trade: its paint was peeling, roof tiles were cracked and one chimney leaned at a worrisome angle.

A customer emerged as Chaloner reached the door. It was Samuel Pepys, the admiralty clerk, whose occupation prevented him from decanting to the safety of the countryside – Britain was currently at war with the Dutch, so Navy Office officials were obliged to remain in the city, overseeing the building and provisioning of ships.

'Have you see the latest Bill?' Pepys asked, as he and Chaloner passed each other. He kept a wary distance, and a herb-filled pomander was ready to be deployed at the first hint of a cough or a sneeze. 'The plague within the city walls is increased, and likely to continue so. My waterman fell sick as soon as he had landed me on Friday morning last, and both my servants have lost their fathers. All doth put me in great apprehensions of melancholy.'

'You are brave to have stayed,' remarked Chaloner.

Pepys smiled. 'My captains take their turn at the sword; I must not therefore grudge to take mine at the pestilence.'

He went on his way, taking a sudden and very wide detour when two men carrying a body on a stretcher stepped into his path.

Chaloner opened Kirton's door, glad to exchange the reek of death for the cleaner scent of ink and paper. The shop was dim after the brightness of the sun outside, and he blinked, waiting for his eyes to become accustomed to the gloom. When they did, the first thing he noticed was that most of the shelves within were singularly bereft of tomes.

Kirton was talking to two people. One was the crook-backed apprentice who had yelled radical opinions outside Lawrence's house a few days earlier; the other was the man Chaloner had seen in Masley's house, on both occasions mistaking him for the bookseller. All three turned when Chaloner entered, and Kirton's expression was one of open horror.

'Chaloner,' he blurted. 'What do you want now?'

'Stedman's book,' replied Chaloner pleasantly, opting for a gentle start to the interrogation in the hope that it would put the man at ease. '*Tintinnologia.*'

'It is not printed yet,' gulped Kirton. 'So if there is nothing else . . .'

'What did Pepys buy?' persisted Chaloner, acutely aware that a vendor so obviously in need of customers should not be trying to send one away without making a sale. 'He has good taste, so perhaps I should have what he bought.'

'*Institutes of the Lawes of England,*' replied Kirton, naming a dull treatise that Chaloner had studied at Cambridge. 'But he had the last copy.'

'Then I shall just browse,' said Chaloner, although that would not take long – Kirton's entire stock seemed to comprise two copies of Margaret Cavendish's *Poems and Fancies* and a stack of *The Plague's Approved Physitian*, which were unlikely to sell when Lawrence was giving them away for free. There were several piles of paper on the table, though, which he assumed were loose quires – books that had been printed but not yet bound. The paper was the cheapest available, and was a dirty grey-brown.

'You cannot browse, because we are closed,' said the man who looked like Kirton – so much so that Chaloner could only assume they were kin. 'Come back another time.'

'What is this book?' asked Chaloner, picking up one of the pages from the table.

'Nothing!' snapped the kinsman furiously, snatching it from him and slapping it back down, although not before Chaloner had seen that it was blank. 'It is not for sale.'

'Then do you have *The Compleat Surveyor* by William Leybourn?' pressed Chaloner. He owned several copies already – Leybourn was a friend and kept pressing them on him – but it was a volume that any reputable book-seller should have in stock.

Kirton regarded him suspiciously. 'Why do you want that? So you can conduct your own analysis of the cathedral?'

'Tillison has one,' said the kinsman before Chaloner could reply. 'Borrow his. Now please leave. Randall here feels unwell, and he might have the plague.'

The hunchback blinked his surprise at this claim.

Tiring of the game they were playing, Chaloner turned to Kirton. 'What is wrong?' he asked gently. 'I may be able to help.'

'No one can help,' blurted Kirton. 'We are all doomed to—'

'Shut up, Will!' snapped the kinsman angrily, and scowled at Chaloner. 'You do not know who I am, do you? You would not defy me if you did.'

'Is that so?' murmured Chaloner, eyeing him in distaste.

The man drew himself up to his full height. 'I am Joshua Kirton, Master of the Company of Stationers. Brother to Will here.'

Chaloner wondered if he had missed something, because he failed to understand why he should be in awe of a stationer, Master of the Company or no.

'Then you will know John Upton,' he said pleasantly. 'He was also a stationer. Kirton saw him talking to Gaundy on Sunday, and as both men are now dead, you will understand why I want a full account of what transpired between them.'

'But I cannot give you one,' bleated Kirton, licking dry lips and glancing nervously at his sibling. 'I was too far away to hear. However, Denton was probably right – Gaundy was buying supplies for his vicar, and I was wrong to think there was anything odd about the encounter. Now if you will excuse—'

'Upton visited *you* that day as well,' interrupted Chaloner. 'Was it before or after he met Gaundy?'

'Probably after,' replied Kirton. 'And now you really *must* leave. We are very busy.'

'With what?' Chaloner gestured around the empty shop. 'You have no customers and no books to sell. So what is happening that has put you in such a fright?'

'We are not in a fright,' averred Kirton, although his shifty eyes and unsteady hands belied the claim. 'We are just afraid of the plague, like all sane men.'

'I shall not tell you again,' snapped Joshua. 'I am a close friend of Dean Sancroft, so you would be wise not to vex me with your nosy questions.'

'It was Sancroft who sent me here.' Chaloner struggled to prevent the surly Joshua from getting under his skin.

'So unless you want me to tell him that you have been deliberately obstructive, you will cooperate. Why did Upton come to the city? And do not say it was to sell paper, because I know that would be a lie.'

'But it is true!' cried Kirton, agitated. 'What other business could a stationer have with me? He sold me the sheets you see on the table. It—'

'Your fiscal arrangements are none of his business, Will,' snarled Joshua. 'So say no more.' He glared at Chaloner. 'And if you persist in making a nuisance of yourself, it will be *you* who has the next encounter with the Executioner.'

'The Executioner?' pounced Chaloner, while Kirton shot his brother a stricken glance. 'I have been assured that he does not exist.'

At that moment, Randall began to cough. It was blatantly contrived, but Joshua seized the opportunity to bundle Chaloner out through the door anyway. Chaloner could have resisted, but he did not bother – Kirton would not answer questions as long as his obnoxious brother was there, so the only way forward was to corner him alone. He walked to Paul's Gate, found a shady alcove, and settled down to wait.

Not for the first time since starting work for the Earl of Clarendon, Chaloner wondered if he should have chosen another occupation. Despite the shade, his alcove was uncomfortably hot, and the stench from the plague pit was all but overwhelming. He wondered how William Hall, who was still officiating there, could bear it, and could only suppose that the canon was reluctant to leave when so many grateful mourners continued to press money on him.

213

Idly, he listened to scraps of conversation as people passed through the gate. There were many angry mutters about the paucity of food, and two butchers were in a loudly rebellious mood about the fate of one hapless family, who had been shut up inside their house but had waited in vain for provisions from the parish – the men charged with delivering them had stolen the lot.

'Bastards! They did not take it because they were hungry, but to curry favour by hawking it to the Mims. Well, I can tell you now – if I catch the plague, I will not lie down meekly and starve. I will go out and breathe on those Mims until they feed me.'

'I shall leave the city soon,' confided his friend. 'It is nothing but one big grave, and what use is a butcher with no meat to sell anyway?'

'You cannot leave. Monck's soldiers will stop you.'

'Not if I have a Certificate of Health.'

The first laughed harshly. 'And how will you get one of those? They cost a fortune.'

'I know where to buy one for a shilling. Or maybe I shall save my money and wait for Wednesday instead, when there is talk of an exodus. Monck's men will be so overwhelmed by the volume of folk wanting to leave, that they will have no choice but to let us all out.'

'And then what?' asked the first sneeringly. 'The villages do not want you – they shoot strangers on sight. There is nowhere for you to go.'

'I shall walk until I find a place that does welcome visitors,' said the second stoutly. 'Because anything is better than waiting here to die.'

They were not the only ones ready to defy the laws that had been devised to prevent the sickness from spreading across the whole country: four women debated how to smuggle out their ailing children, while a pair of clerks had been busily rinsing away the lime that Monck's soldiers had spread over their streets, on the grounds that it created a caustic dust. Meanwhile, two apprentices grumbled that the Mims had such a stranglehold on the black market that it was impossible for anyone else to get in on the act.

'I had a lovely racket going back in July,' growled one, a hefty lad with bad teeth. 'There were fish of all shapes and sizes, so I bought lots, and sold them for twice the price in the Fleet Rookery. But then the fishmonger's supply dried up, and could I find another? No, because the damned Mims were always there first.'

'I am leaving the city on Wednesday,' confided the other, a puny boy with spots. 'There is nothing for me here now. My family is dead and so is my master.'

'Do you have a certificate then?' asked the first curiously.

'I will not need one – not on Wednesday.'

'There is Monck,' hissed the first suddenly, and Chaloner followed his pointing finger to the pit, where the general's bulky figure was distinctive even in his protective cloak and scarf. 'Gloating over the bodies of them who would still be alive if he had not kept them penned up like animals. Him and Lawrence.'

'Lawrence is all right,' said Spots. 'He gives me free *sal mirabilis*, and his wife lets me have scraps from her kitchen.'

'Do not take *sal mirabilis*,' cried the first. 'It is poisonous. The only remedy that works is London Treacle. Of course, it costs ten times as much, so I doubt Lawrence will be giving you any of *that* for no charge.'

'Some of us will visit the cathedral before we leave on

Wednesday,' said Spots slyly. 'There is to be a special plague service, and while its priests are busy officiating, we shall help ourselves to their overpriced London Treacle.'

When they had gone, Chaloner watched Monck and Lawrence, who had come to assess the city's burial arrangements. William positively glowed under the praise they lavished on him for his compassion, and Chaloner found himself wondering if that was why he had volunteered for pit duty that day – he wanted important men to witness his courage, perhaps in the hope that they would reward him with a donation to the cause of his choice.

But Monck did not stay long, and was soon riding back to Westminster, although Lawrence went to murmur words of encouragement to the gravediggers, going so far as to clap them on the shoulders and shake their hands. Afterwards, they went about their grim task with more vigour and even a little pride.

'He loves us and he loves our city,' murmured a passing sweep, watching approvingly.

'Monck does not,' said a laundress. 'The other day, I heard Lawrence tell him that he would like us to have a nice new cathedral, but Monck said that we were already getting what we deserve – the plague. Someone should shoot that miserable old cur.'

'Just as long as they do not hit Lawrence by mistake,' said the sweep. 'You complain about the lack of food, but without him, we should have none at all.'

'He does his best,' acknowledged the laundress. 'But it is not nearly enough.'

Joshua left his brother's shop eventually, and to make sure he did not double back, Chaloner decided to follow him for a while. Joshua bought an apple – at an outrageous price – from a passing Mim, and ate it as he walked around the south side of the cathedral. He rapped on the Deanery door, which was answered by Bing. The violist tried to close it again when he saw who was there, but Joshua shoved past him and stalked inside. Bing performed an agitated jig before closing the door behind him.

Chaloner returned to the bookshop and entered without knocking. Kirton took two steps towards the back door before realising that running would be futile – Chaloner was younger, fitter and would almost certainly be faster. There was no sign of the apprentice.

'Just talk to me,' urged Chaloner. 'Then I will leave you in peace.'

'But I do not want to talk to you,' cried Kirton, his eyes huge in his pale face. 'Joshua would not like it.'

'Then do not tell him.'

'He will find out – he always does. You do not understand what is happening here, Chaloner.'

'Then enlighten me, because I am not going anywhere until you do.'

Trapped, Kirton began to speak in a faltering, unsteady voice. 'There is a plot afoot involving St Paul's and large amounts of money.'

'What sort of plot?'

Kirton shot Chaloner an agonised glance, but then relented. 'One to rebuild the place. Do you recall Rycroft telling you about the Agents of God – the hush-hush society founded to finance Inigo Jones's work? Well, it has been revived, to see Christopher Wren's proposals through.'

Chaloner was nonplussed. 'Then why the subterfuge? It is not illegal to raise money for worthy causes.'

'No, but the scheme is unpopular with Londoners, and the Agents . . . well, they will not walk away empty-handed. You know how it is with large sums of cash – some will be creamed off for expenses and bribes. Moreover, the *King* wants a new cathedral and will reward those who facilitate it – with knighthoods, honours and country estates.'

'So who are these Agents? You and your brother, I presume. And your fellow ringers?'

'My brother, yes. But not the rest of us – we are not rich enough.'

Chaloner did not believe him, given the lies and furtive behaviour, but he let it pass. 'Who, then?'

Kirton would not look him in the eye. 'The same folk who were in the original organisation, I suppose – Owen and the three Hall brothers, to name but four. Plus others who see the venture as an opportunity to curry royal favour.'

'So why could you not have told me all this when I first asked? It is not so terrible.'

Kirton cast an uneasy glance towards the door. 'Because of the Executioner. Denton is wrong – he *does* exist. And he terrifies me. *He* is your murderer, Chaloner, a man so determined to have a new cathedral that he will do anything to get one. Even kill.'

'I see. So who is he?'

'I do not know – if I did, he would not be so terrifying. However, it stands to reason that he will be a cathedral man. Of course, he may not even be in London at the moment – he could be managing his nefarious business from the safety of the country. Tunbridge Wells, for example.'

Chaloner blinked. 'You think he is Dean Sancroft?'

Kirton rubbed his eyes tiredly. 'Well, he does refuse to say whether he wants a new cathedral or is happy with the old one. It is suspicious.'

'Or it might just be that he has no strong feelings one way or the other.' Which is what Sancroft had claimed himself when he and Chaloner had discussed it together.

'Everyone has strong feelings,' argued Kirton, and became fearful again. 'I just *know* that those four men were killed by the same hand – all were hit over the head, and Kerchier, Upton *and* Gaundy wanted a new cathedral. It cannot be coincidence, no matter what my fellow ringers claim.'

'How do you know that Gaundy and Upton wanted a new cathedral?'

'Because they told me so. Gaundy longed to abandon vergering and put his masonry skills to use again, while Upton was always saying how he hated old things – which is why I was amazed when he told me that he had wed an elderly woman, even if she was extremely wealthy.'

'But Harbert did not want a new cathedral – he liked the current one.'

'True,' acknowledged Kirton unhappily. 'So I am not sure how he fits in.'

Chaloner was thoughtful. 'Tell me why you think that all four men were hit over the head.'

'You told me that Upton was; Gaundy told me that the skeleton was; and I saw Gaundy for myself.'

'And Harbert?'

Kirton looked away. 'Denton did not kill him, no matter what the gossips claim, and he was too careful to have caught the plague. It seems a logical assumption to make.'

Chaloner mulled over the information, but then shook

219

his head impatiently. 'Your tale makes no sense, Kirton. You say the Executioner is an Agent of God – a man determined to have a new cathedral – but if you are right, then why would he kill Kerchier, Gaundy and Upton? They were on his side.'

Kirton shrugged. 'Then perhaps I am wrong, and he is really a Maurice Man.'

Chaloner was not sure what to believe, other than that Kirton's conclusions were muddled, tenuous and illogical, and needed to be viewed with extreme caution. He turned to another matter.

'Now tell me what really happened when Harbert and Denton fought.'

'It was as they told you,' replied the bookseller miserably. 'With one slight difference – it was Denton who attacked first. He jabbed Harbert – rather hard, actually – with a stick, and only then did Harbert draw his sword.'

'Then what?'

'Nothing. Harbert waved his blade around for a bit, but was so unnerved by the prospect of having to use it that he backed away and fled. Denton was no danger to him, but Harbert was a rank coward.'

Not unlike you then, thought Chaloner sourly. He glanced out of the window, and saw that dusk had fallen. 'I will speak to Denton tomorrow. Where does he live?'

'Next to St James's Park. However, once all his fish had been boiled to death in the heat, he decided to take temporary lodgings in Outridge's Coffee House on Creed Lane instead. He can be found there whenever he is not tolling the bells for the dead.'

'Or when he is not chatting about cross-changes with you,' muttered Chaloner. He recalled what Stedman and Pemper had claimed, and what he had seen himself at

220

the church on Knightrider Street. 'Or gossiping with his friends while Stedman does all the work.'

Kirton gave a rueful smile. 'Stedman is younger than us. Why should we not make use of his greater vigour?'

Chaloner left the bookshop pondering what he had been told, and trying to sort fact from fiction. He believed that the Agents of God had been revived – there was certainly a fund for building a new cathedral, as it was common knowledge that William had control of it. But what about the Executioner? Had he killed Kerchier all those years ago, and then resumed his murderous activities when the Agents were re-founded? If so, did it mean he was a Maurice Man? Or just someone interested in stealing the Agents' hoard, perhaps for a second time?

Chaloner lengthened his stride, aware of the gathering gloom and the dangers it might hold. He reached the Mitre and went to the garden, where he fed his hens and shut them in their coop for the night. He was just securing the flap when he heard a sound behind him. He whipped around fast.

He was startled to see Kirton's crook-backed apprentice Randall trying to creep up on him. The little man carried a knife in one hand and a bucket in the other, and his eyes went wide with alarm when he found himself at the wrong end of a sword. Around his arm was a green ribbon, which had certainly not been there earlier.

'What are you doing?' demanded Chaloner, wishing the Mims would leave him alone. Had they not learned yet that sending amateurs against him was futile?

'The Mims promised to make me a full member when I bring them your head,' explained Randall, eyeing him up and down appraisingly, as if trying to decide where best to plant his blade. He indicated the pail. 'I brought something to put it in. These are my best clothes, and I do not want them spoiled.'

'Very practical,' said Chaloner, resisting the urge to laugh. He sheathed his sword – he was in no danger from Randall, no matter how deadly the man considered himself. 'Did they tell you why they want me dead?'

'Of course, or I would not have agreed to do it. I have standards, you know. They were hired by a generous customer to make you stop posing irritating questions.'

'Irritating questions about what?'

'Oh,' said Randall, crestfallen. 'I did not ask that.'

'Then who is the generous customer?'

A satisfied expression crossed the apprentice's face. 'Now that is something I *did* demand to know. Unfortunately, all they could tell me is that he is very rich, because I shall have half of what he paid them when I dispatch you. Three whole shillings!'

'My word,' said Chaloner, offended that he was not worth more. 'But unfortunately for you, I am not ready to die just yet.'

Randall persisted anyway. His arm went back, but it was the bucket, rather than the dagger that flew from his hand. Horrified by the mistake – and alarmed by the resulting clatter as the pail missed the startled Chaloner and hit the henhouse – he turned and hobbled through the garden gate. Chaloner started to follow, although he was sure that even Randall would not be stupid enough to dash straight to those who had set him the challenge.

He was wrong.

Randall left the Mitre and headed south, not once looking behind him to see if anyone was in pursuit. He was

222

absurdly easy to follow, partly because he was not very fast, but also because he had a curiously slapping gait that meant he could be heard even when he was out of sight.

He scuttled down Paul's Chain and turned left along Carter Lane, aiming for the alley that led to King's Head Court. Somewhere, a baby was crying, a persistent, angry wail that grated on the nerves. A bell tolled in the distance.

Randall trotted across the yard and entered the tavern. The building had a wealth of windows and doors, all of which provided excellent views of what was happening within. Clearly, the Mims had a lot to learn about evading the forces of law and order, and Chaloner saw that Paget was right about them having no real leader – a competent chief would have shunned the place as entirely inappropriate for criminal gatherings.

Inside, a parlour that had been handsome not long ago was now shabby and disreputable, rather like its current patrons, all of whom sported green ribbons. None were pleased by Randall's appearance.

'And you came straight here?' one was demanding angrily. It was Tommy Suger, the man who Chaloner had caught and questioned after the failed ambush outside the Mitre.

'I promise I was not followed, Mr Suger,' declared Randall confidently. 'He tried, of course, but I threw him off my scent with ease. I am not stupid, you know.'

Suger nodded at two of his cronies, who left to check the tavern's environs for themselves. Once outside, they embarked on a disorganised search that was simplicity itself to evade. Indeed, Chaloner was obliged to duck out of sight so briefly that he missed nothing of the conversation that continued within.

'So the rogue wins yet again,' spat Suger, disgusted.

'We shall have to give the money back at this rate. *Six* attempts, and still he struts around our city.'

There had only been four, if Randall's paltry effort could be included, so Chaloner assumed that either someone had claimed payment for assaults that had never taken place, or they had been so pitiful that they had gone unnoticed.

'He is too slippery for us,' said a Mim with a bandaged arm – Suger's partner outside the Mitre. 'And dangerous. We should be demanding *more* money, not offering to hand it back. Look at what happened to the Edwards lads when they tried to shoot him – poisoned horribly within hours.'

Chaloner saw he had been right to suspect that his first would-be assassins had not died of the plague. Had the killer of Kerchier and the others – the Executioner, for want of a better name – dispatched the two gunmen with the same toxin that had then been offered to Chaloner in a jug of wine? And if so, had *he* been the masked stranger or had he hired some Mim to do the honours? Somehow, Chaloner suspected the latter – the Executioner did not seem like someone to put himself at risk when he had minions ready to oblige.

'Poisoned by Chaloner?' Randall was asking in a hoarse whisper.

'Of course by Chaloner,' snapped Suger. 'Who else could it have been? But you promised us victory and you bring us defeat. And to add insult to injury, you wear our sigil before paying the admission fee – namely his head.'

'I wore it to unsettle him,' explained Randall earnestly. 'And it worked, because he was terrified when he saw me. It is a pity my blade missed him in the dark.'

'So when will you try again?' demanded Suger, reaching out to rip the offending ribbon from the apprentice's sleeve.

'Not for a day or two,' replied Randall, watching with obvious regret as the strip of material fluttered to the floor. 'He will be on his guard now, so I must wait until he lets it down again. However, I shall do something else for you in the interim – go to the person who hired us and demand more money.'

Suger gazed at him in wonderment. 'I might just let you do it – you are brash and stupid enough. Unfortunately, he contacts us, we do not chase after him. Now get out of my sight before I lose my temper.'

'But I *need* to be a Mim,' cried Randall, not moving. 'Kirton cannot pay me, because no one is buying books, and I never get enough to eat. I am tired of being hungry all the time. I want to be fat, like you.'

He was lucky to escape with no more than a clout, given Suger's offended indignation. He scurried away howling, colliding with the Mims who had just concluded their fruitless search and were coming back. During the ensuing commotion, Suger slipped into an adjoining chamber. Chaloner located its window, put his eye to a gap in the shutter, and saw that someone had been listening to the entire discussion from behind a door.

'You must send someone else to dispatch Chaloner,' Pamela was saying crossly. 'His death is worth a lot of money to me.'

'But no one dares go, miss,' bleated Suger. He was a large man with the kind of scars that suggested he liked to brawl, so the fact that he was intimidated by the tiny, bristling figure in front of him said a great deal about her personality. 'He is out of our league.'

'Do not make excuses to me, Tommy Suger. You promised to do what I wanted, so you will honour that vow or be sorry. Do you hear?'

'Yes, miss,' whispered Suger, hanging his head sheepishly. Then he gave a feeble grin. 'He plans to take a boat over the river in a couple of days, so we will capsize it and drown him. I know for a fact that he cannot swim.'

Chaloner could swim perfectly well, and had never expressed any intention to cross the Thames by boat. Suger was lying, to buy himself more time.

'I hope for your sake that it works,' said Pamela coldly. 'Because our benefactor will not be pleased if you let him down again. And nor will I.'

'Who is he, miss?' asked Suger unhappily. 'If I know his identity, I can make sure I stay out of his way.'

Anger suffused her small face. 'He wears a mask whenever we meet, almost as if he does not trust me – *me*, Pamela Ball! However, I shall have a name out of him soon, because I am no man's puppet.'

'This medicine you promised us,' said Suger with an obsequious smile. 'Do you have it here? Only it is getting late, and the lads are becoming fractious.'

'Have I ever let you down?' she demanded, hands on hips. 'When I give my word, it means something. Unlike you, it seems. Now, before I dispense your *sal mirabilis*, would your men prefer a hymn or a sermon first?'

'*Sal mirabilis*?' asked Suger, twisting his hat so agitatedly that it seemed he might tear it in two. 'I thought we had agreed on London Treacle instead this time. There are rumours that *sal mirabilis* is poisonous, see. It killed a verger in St Gregory's.'

Pamela regarded him thoughtfully. 'You are right. *Sal mirabilis* is dangerous, and I no longer take it myself for that reason. But London Treacle costs ten times as much . . .'

'Then maybe you can buy it with the money *he* paid you for getting rid of Sancroft's spy,' suggested Suger. 'You did keep most of it back for yourself, after all.'

'Yes, I kept it back,' flashed Pamela, angry again, 'but not for my own benefit. I aim to use it for spreading the word of God, as I have told you before.'

'Of course,' said Suger flatly. 'But we *need* London Treacle, and we dare not go to St Paul's to buy it ourselves, lest the canons are still irked with us over that poor box that went missing a few weeks ago . . .'

'Very well,' conceded Pamela. 'You may have a dose of London Treacle tonight – from my *personal* supplies. However, you will not get another until Chaloner is dead. Do you understand? Now, I ask you again: do you want a hymn or a sermon before I dole it out?'

Suger cleared his throat uncomfortably. 'This religious lark does not really suit us, miss. We would rather drink than pray, generally speaking. Besides, Quakers are unpopular in London, and we do not want to be part of—'

'You are Quakers now, and Quakers you will remain,' declared Pamela dangerously. 'Or I shall curse you, and you will go the same way as Jasper. You did hear that he died today? I had the sad duty of taking him to the plague pit myself.'

She did not sound sad, and Chaloner frowned. Was this her way of telling Suger that *she* had killed Jasper – perhaps by poison, given the froth on his lips? And as the Edwards boys' mouths had also been flecked with foam, was it she, not the mysterious benefactor, responsible for dispatching them? Regardless, Chaloner decided to arrest her as soon as she was no longer surrounded by Mims – even if she was not the Executioner, she was far too deadly to leave at liberty.

Like many religious fanatics, Pamela Ball did not know when to shut up, and her reluctant congregation grew increasingly restive as time ticked by and her homily showed no sign of ending. Obvious culprits were stilled with a sharp-eyed glare, although not even she could stem the rising tide of grumbles after an hour.

'Right,' she said at last. 'Now you may have your medicine. London Treacle – the best plague preventative money can buy, so you had better be grateful. One dose will keep you safe for the next three days, and Suger will let you know if you are entitled to more in due course. Let us hope for your sake that you are.'

The Mims surged forward en masse. Some tried to take more than their due, and spats broke out, which Suger was wholly incapable of quelling. Pamela was not, though, and Chaloner marvelled yet again that so diminutive a person should possess such a forceful personality. Once the medicine had been distributed and swallowed, most Mims settled down to drink, dice and plot their next crimes.

Chaloner waited with growing impatience for Pamela to leave the tavern, but instead she sat at a table on her own and began to write. Judging from the pile of papers in front of her, she intended to be busy for some time. Exasperated, he wondered if she was reluctant to return to the house where she had murdered her unloved husband, and so aimed to pass the night in the dubious but non-judgemental company of fellow criminals.

Midnight came and went, then one o'clock, but neither

Pamela nor her 'flock' showed any inclination to go home. The atmosphere grew raucous as more ale was consumed, although that did not seem to disturb Pamela, who continued to write steadily. At one point Suger asked what she was doing, and she informed him that she was composing a sermon for their delectation the following day. The Mim excused himself quickly, evidently afraid that he might be honoured with a preview.

Eventually, Chaloner was forced to concede that he had set himself a hopeless task. He considered various plans to coax her outside, but she was not stupid, and there was no point in alerting her to the fact that he had her in his sights. Reluctantly – resenting the time he had wasted by waiting – he decided to postpone tackling her until morning. And if she was still surrounded by rowdy felons, he would just have to beg help from Lawrence.

He had just reached Paul's Chain when he saw Cary with two guards, supervising the loading of one of the dead-carts. Cary abandoned his grim duties and came to talk. He regarded Chaloner wonderingly.

'You are bold – wandering about alone at this time of night when you know someone wants you dead.'

'It was Pamela Ball who hired the Mims to dispatch me,' reported Chaloner, 'although on the orders of a benefactor who only appears to her in disguise. I think they keep the Mims in thrall by supplying them with free plague remedies.'

Cary shook his head in weary disbelief. 'Every day, I am astounded anew by the depths to which some folk go to profit from this crisis. I assume you have her in custody?'

'Not yet – she is surrounded by felons. I was hoping

to take advantage of Lawrence's offer, and borrow some of your soldiers.'

Cary rolled his eyes. 'I suppose we can oblige. Do you want to do it now?'

'In the morning.' Chaloner was not in the mood for the pitched battle he was sure would follow if they tried to snatch her from the King's Head that night. 'And when she is safely under lock and key, we can question Pamela about the death of her husband as well. I am fairly certain that she killed him.'

Cary was plainly shocked. 'Jasper is dead? Then I am more sorry than I can say, because he was a decent man. And if your accusation is accurate, we should apprehend Pamela at once – we cannot have killers roaming free. What if she uses the delay to escape?'

'Unlikely – she has no idea that she is under suspicion. Besides, we will need our wits about us when we confront her, and I am too tired to do it tonight.'

Cary nodded acquiescence, although it was obvious that he thought Chaloner was making a mistake. 'My spies tell me that you have been asking after Canon Stone,' he said, changing the subject. 'Why? Is he no longer in the city?'

'He went to visit his sister. Tillison says it is because she is ill, the Hall brothers think she needs some money, while Wildbore is of the opinion that he has gone to eat her food.'

Cary raised his eyebrows. 'Did Stone provide these excuses or did the others invent them?'

'I am not sure. Why?'

'Because both Stone's sisters died years ago. So let us hope he is safely in hiding somewhere, and not dead in someone else's grave, like Kerchier.'

'I have been told that some of the murders might be connected to the revival of an organisation called the Agents of God. Have you heard of it?'

'I remember it from twenty years ago, when Kerchier was still alive. Its members were a nuisance – thought they were above the law because they were rich. And you say they are at it again?' Cary scowled angrily. 'Why did they have to resurrect it now? It is not as if we have nothing else to worry about. Very well. I will look into *that* tomorrow as well.'

He nodded a curt farewell and returned to his men, shoulders bowed under the weight of his ever-increasing responsibilities. Chaloner continued north, and saw Masley in his house, labouring away by lamplight, assisted by Joshua Kirton. He was tempted to knock on the door and ask why the Master of the Stationers' Company chose to play skivvy to a vicar, but decided there was no point in deliberately antagonising either man.

In the house opposite, Rycroft was also at work, windows thrown open in an attempt to dissipate the acidic yellow fug that hung within. He glanced up when Chaloner hailed him.

'Will this weather never break?' the alchemist asked wearily, wiping sweat from his brow with the back of his hand. 'It is like a foretaste of hell.'

'So is your laboratory,' said Chaloner, eyeing the swirling fumes.

Rycroft laughed, which made the years fall from his face, and for a moment, Chaloner saw the younger man he had fought at Newbury. 'The stench keeps the plague at bay, so I shall not complain. But I had better get back to it. Francis Hall says it will be my fault if the Mortality

Bills do not drop this week – for not supplying enough London Treacle.'

'Perhaps the fault is his – for not blessing it properly. I am sorry about Jasper, by the way. I only met him twice, but he seemed a pleasant man.'

'He is dead already?' asked Rycroft in dismay. 'I did not think it would be so soon. I promised to visit him tomorrow, and sit with him until . . . Are you sure?'

'I heard Pamela say that she had taken him to the plague pit herself.'

'The plague pit?' cried Rycroft, far too loudly for a time when his neighbours would be abed. 'But he wanted to go in a private grave at St Gregory's, and I swore that I would arrange it for him. Damn that accursed woman!'

'I will ask why she did it tomorrow. She has plenty of other questions to answer, so a few more will make no odds.'

'I shall tackle her now,' countered the alchemist furiously. 'After which she can come to the pit and help me get him back.'

He flung out of his house, all righteous outrage, but he used his back door, which meant Chaloner could not stop him. Chaloner ran to Carter Lane to head him off, sure the alchemist would put himself in danger if he stormed among the Mims in such a frenzy, but Rycroft never materialised. Supposing he had missed him, Chaloner hurried to King's Head Court.

Pamela was still writing at her table, surrounded by drunk and noisy felons, but there was no sign of Rycroft. Chaloner waited a little while longer, and when the alchemist still did not appear, he assumed the man had come to his senses. He abandoned his vigil and returned to Paul's Chain, but Rycroft's house was in darkness, and there was no reply to his knock. So where was he? Chaloner considered going back to King's Head Court, but then decided against it. Rycroft was a grown man, and should be able to look after himself. Tiredly, he turned and trudged across St Paul's Churchyard towards the Mitre.

As he passed the Deanery, an upstairs window was flung open and Owen leaned out, silhouetted against the lamplight. The canon pulled a flask from his coat and drained it, at which point someone appeared at his side.

'What are you doing?' hissed Francis irately, grabbing his colleague's arm and jerking him back inside. 'Do you want half the rogues in London to know what we have in here?'

'How? We are on the first floor – no one can see in,' retorted Owen waspishly. 'Besides, I need some air. We have all had a terrible shock, after all.'

'Yes, we have.' Francis's voice was softer. 'But come back and help us or we shall be here all night. I had no idea that William had been so assiduous.'

He closed the shutter, which was so well-fitting that it muted any sounds from within. Chaloner circled the building, aiming to break in and find out what was happening, but the front was unusually secure, while the other three sides were surrounded by a garden in which prowled two noisy dogs. He tried to slip past them, but was forced to concede defeat when they set up such a cacophony of barks and howls that the canons came to investigate. Unwilling to be caught spying, Chaloner slunk away.

He reached the Mitre, but his room was so hot and stuffy that he went to the garden and lay on a bench instead. He looked up at the stars, a brilliant dome of

233

twinkling lights, although some were rendered indistinct by a haziness in the air. Was it a deadly miasma stealing across the city, infecting yet more victims? Or just a sign that the weather was about to break?

# Chapter 8

Chaloner woke more refreshed than he would have expected after only three hours' sleep, all of them taken outside. Dawn was breaking, so he fed his hens and collected the eggs, which he and Paget ate with a stew that, as far as he could tell, had been made exclusively from veins and mint.

When they had finished, Chaloner planned his day. The first thing was to arrest Pamela, preferably with Lawrence's help lest her Mims were to hand. Once she was in Newgate, he would bring her to heel by charging her with the murders of Jasper and the Edwards boys, and then question her about her benefactor. She had told Suger that she did not know his name, but she might have been lying. And if not, she still might know something that would allow Chaloner to identify him. And identify him he must, because the more he thought about it, the more he became certain that the Executioner and her benefactor were one and the same.

Once Pamela was safely under lock and key, he would turn to other lines of enquiry. First, see if Thurloe had learned anything useful. Second, track down Denton and demand the truth about the spat with Harbert. Third, visit Harbert's house and talk to his servants. Fourth, question the Hall brothers and Owen about the Agents of God. And finally, find out where Stone had gone.

He left the Mitre and walked along Cheapside to Lawrence's mansion. Cary was there, already issuing the day's orders to an army of harried clerks. The secretary wound up his briefing when he saw Chaloner waiting, and called for six volunteers to accompany them to King's Head Court. The clerks continued to clamour questions at him while he and his guards readied themselves for the assault on Pamela.

'Use beetroot juice instead,' he snapped at the man who was complaining about a lack of red paint to make crosses on plague victims' doors. 'I imagine Rycroft will lend you some if you ask nicely.'

'You tell me to build bonfires for fumigating the air, but I have neither the wood nor the men to help me,' grumbled another. 'What do we—'

'Break up the abandoned stalls in St Paul's Churchyard,' interrupted Cary with asperity. 'God's blood man! Have you no initiative of your own? Chaloner – lend me a guinea.' He snatched the coin and thrust it at the clerk. 'There. That should buy you more than enough labour to see the scheme completed.'

'Can you borrow another off him?' asked one of the soldiers sullenly. 'Because me and my mates haven't been paid for three weeks now and—'

'I will raise the matter with Lawrence the moment I return from Newgate.' Cary's face was turning redder, and Chaloner suspected it would not be long before his temper broke. He only hoped he would not be there when it happened. 'You will get your money, never fear.'

'*If* you return from Newgate,' the man muttered darkly. 'There is plague in that prison.'

Cary set a cracking pace to King's Head Court, clearly aiming to be done with Pamela as soon as possible, so that he could return to more pressing duties. Chaloner opened the tavern door and stepped inside, only to find it empty – other than a lone Mim who was fast asleep on the floor. Chaloner prodded him awake with his toe.

'Mrs Ball is gone?' the felon asked groggily as he struggled to rally his wits. 'I suppose she went with the others then.'

'Went where?' demanded Chaloner.

Cary did not speak, but Chaloner was aware of the disgust coming off him in waves, and his face was puce with suppressed annoyance. And he had a right to be irked: Chaloner's disinclination to tackle Pamela the previous night had not only allowed her to escape, but had wasted valuable time that morning.

'I don't know,' shrugged the Mim. 'Out trying to persuade more folk to become Quakers, I suppose. That is how she usually spends her mornings.'

'Where is the landlord?' asked one of the soldiers, looking in distaste at the dirty floor and unwashed tankards. 'I cannot see him being impressed with this mess – he usually keeps a tidy house.'

The Mim sneered. 'At the first glimpse of a bubo, he bought himself a Certificate of Health and went to stay with his brother in Islington.'

'Which explains why his tavern has become the haunt of criminals,' said Cary to Chaloner. 'He would not have let them in before.'

Chaloner led the way to Pamela's house. No one answered his knock, so he picked the lock on the door

237

and opened it. A quick search revealed that no one was home, although crumbs on the table and a half-empty cup of ale suggested that Pamela had enjoyed a quick breakfast before heading out again.

'We should have arrested her last night,' exploded Cary accusingly, no longer able to contain himself. 'When we knew exactly where she was.'

'She was surrounded by Mims,' replied Chaloner defensively. 'There would have been a fight, and you do not have enough men to expose them to needless risks.'

'But now she might be anywhere,' snapped Cary, unappeased. 'Especially if she learned what we intended, and took the opportunity to escape. Did you tell anyone else?'

'Of course not. Other than you.'

But that was not strictly true: Chaloner had told Rycroft. Had the alchemist warned her? Or had someone else – a Mim, maybe – overheard one of the discussions?

'I will leave a couple of men here to wait for her,' said Cary, taking a deep breath and struggling to rein in his temper. 'But I hope she comes home soon, because I cannot afford to lose two pairs of hands for long. Not today of all days.'

'Why? What is happening today?' asked Chaloner.

'You will see,' said Cary grimly.

Chaloner did see, as he passed St Paul's a short while later – Thurloe had not been home, so he had gone to see if the ex-Spymaster was at his daily devotions in the cathedral. The men who usually worked at the plague pits had been pulled off their unenviable duties, and were assembling an enormous pile of rubbish and dismantled stalls. Even dead rats were being tossed on to it, along with miscellaneous items that had been blocking the drains for weeks. Presiding over the operation was Lawrence, his womenfolk at his side.

Abigail had chosen to wear orange that day, a colour that did not suit her colouring at all. The girls had known better than to follow her example this time, and had dressed in green instead, although the cut of their gowns did nothing to disguise the fact that they were all very plump lasses.

'What is going on?' asked Chaloner.

Lawrence dragged his eyes from the labouring men. 'Have you not heard? The government has ordered us to light massive bonfires in specific places to purify the air. We are to keep them burning for a week, after which the disease will be gone. God willing.'

Chaloner regarded him askance. 'You do not think they will make the atmosphere in the city even worse? It is airless enough already, but to add thick smoke . . .'

Lawrence grimaced, an expression that suggested he thought much the same, but knew better than to say so. 'The King has consulted the best medical men in the country. Who am I to question their learned opinions?'

'Men who skulk in Oxford,' muttered Chaloner in disgust. 'How can they know what will help when they are not here?'

Lawrence rubbed his temples with his forefingers, a gesture that revealed his utter exhaustion. Cary was not the only one who was wearing down as the crisis continued and there was no end in sight.

'To be frank, we are so desperate that we will try anything. The Mortality Bill will be higher than ever this week, and there are rumours of trouble planned for the day after tomorrow. We must be *seen* to be doing some-thing, whether futile or not, or we are lost.'

'Trouble timed to coincide with the special service in the cathedral,' put in Abigail indignantly. 'The one where we shall pray for an end to this dreadful visitation. How dare rioters use the petitions of the godly to further their own ends! Have they no shame?'

'Some folk will try to steal the cathedral's supplies of London Treacle then, too,' said Chaloner, recalling what his eavesdropping at Paul's Gate had told him.

'The villains!' cried Abigail furiously. 'A plague on them all for their wickedness!'

Lawrence was more sanguine. 'They are desperate and frightened, and who can blame them? The disease shows no sign of abating, food and medicine grow ever scarcer, and Monck claims that most Certificates of Health presented at the gates are forgeries, so he intends to reject them all from now on. I understand why folk are angry.'

'They should tighten their belts and put their trust in the Lord,' declared Abigail, who had probably never wanted for victuals in her life. 'If they spend their money on London Treacle, it will bring them safely through this calamity.'

'And there is another problem,' sighed Lawrence. 'Tales now abound that *sal mirabilis* is poisonous, so people are refusing to take it – which means that even more of them will fall ill. And most Londoners *cannot* buy London Treacle, dearest, because it costs too much. Or would you have me sell the last of your jewels to purchase it for them?'

'Certainly not,' said Abigail shortly. 'However, I have known for weeks that *sal mirabilis* is a waste of money. It is nothing more than a sop for paupers. And whores.'

She cast a challenging glance at her husband, reminding Chaloner that Lawrence had provided Mrs Driver with some.

'Is Pamela Ball in custody, Chaloner?' asked Lawrence, hastily changing the subject. 'One of my clerks told me that you and Cary set off to arrest her earlier.'

'She is a Quaker,' spat Abigail. 'You should have expelled the lot of them in April, as I told you. Then the plague would not now be raging in our poor city.'

'I think it would,' countered Lawrence tiredly. 'The Quakers are not—'

'Look!' cried one of the girls shrilly. 'Here comes the flame!'

They all turned to see a man with a torch. Gingerly, the fellow touched it to the teetering pile and jumped back as the tinder caught. Gradually, thick white smoke began to ooze out of it.

At that moment, St Gregory's bells began to toll, marking the first of the day's burials. Through the belfry window, Chaloner saw Stedman diligently hauling away, while Wildbore and Kirton gossiped with their friends in the porch below. Denton was nowhere to be seen, which was a pity, as it would have saved Chaloner a walk. Lawrence tugged on his sleeve.

'Have you seen Mrs Driver?' he whispered. 'I am in sore need of the comfort that only she can provide, but she is never at home.'

'I am afraid not,' replied Chaloner, although Abigail's sharp ears had picked up the question and spite gleamed in her eyes. Had she warned her rival to stay away? Or had Mrs Driver heard that *sal mirabilis* did not work, so had fled the city while she still could?

*

241

Lawrence's pyre was soon well and truly ablaze, producing a dense white smoke that swirled so thickly that Chaloner could barely see his hand in front of his face. Coughing, he beat a hasty retreat, but when he reached Paul's Chain he encountered another problem.

Using the excitement generated by the bonfire as a diversion, four men were preparing to mount a raid on Rycroft's shop. All wore green arm-ribbons. Unwilling to stand by and watch as unscrupulous thieves stole the medicine that might save lives, Chaloner stepped forward, pulling the pistol from his pocket as he did so – four Mims would be no match for him, given their dismal past performances. The thieves stopped their purposeful advance and eyed him malevolently.

'One bullet,' sneered the largest. 'One victim. How will you deal with the rest of us?'

Chaloner had hoped to thwart them without recourse to violence, but was about to draw his sword as well, when the spokesman's eyes flicked briefly to the left. He whipped around to see a fifth thief, who was holding a dag. There was a puff of smoke and a sharp report, and Chaloner had no idea how the fellow had managed to miss him.

While he was distracted, the others attacked en masse, and he realised he had made a tactical mistake in underestimating them – these four were a different kettle of fish to Suger and his inept cronies. The gun was knocked from his hand before he could use it, and hands clawed at him, preventing him from reaching his sword. Belatedly, he wished he had minded his own business.

He fought hard, injuring at least two with the dagger from his sleeve, and gradually felt them begin to lose ground to his onslaught. Then someone hurtled out of nowhere, fists flailing. It was the Greek. Rycroft was hot on his heels, waving an ancient musket in a way that was more likely to harm himself than the robbers. Seeing the odds stacking up against them, the Mims beat a prudent retreat.

Chaloner began to give chase, but one whipped around and hurled a stone, which caught him on the temple. His vision swam. He was aware of the Greek explaining to a gathering crowd that a robbery had just been thwarted, and thought he could make out Lawrence calling for soldiers to pursue the culprits. And then Rycroft guided him inside his house and he heard no more.

When Chaloner's senses finally cleared, he found himself sitting on a bench in Rycroft's laboratory. There was no sign of the Greek, but the alchemist was at the table, spooning medicine into bottles – dozens of them. All had labels glued to the sides, bearing a drawing of the cathedral, and the words 'London Treacle – a Most Excellent Pectorall against the Pestilence'. There was a blank spot for the price to be written by hand, and someone had costed the current batch at two shillings and sixpence a pot, indicating that making plague remedies was a very profitable business.

Chaloner took a deep breath, keeping his eyes fixed on the book that lay next to him when his vision began to blur again. It was *The Compleat Surveyor* by William Leybourn, although it had suffered from being in Rycroft's care, as it was heavily pockmarked and one burn went almost all the way through.

'Gunpowder,' explained the alchemist ruefully, seeing where he was looking. 'I like to include a pinch in my recipe, and accidents will happen.'

'The thieves,' said Chaloner, more to avoid remarking that explosives seemed an odd ingredient to add to any medicine than to solicit information. 'Will Lawrence catch them, do you think?'

Rycroft grimaced. 'Unlikely – they had too great a start. Thank you for trying to stop them, by the way. I imagine they aimed to steal the lot, which would have been a disaster, as the canons need every drop I can brew.'

'Did you confront Pamela last night?' Chaloner wished his wits were sharper, because he knew he should have them about him when he questioned Rycroft. 'Over Jasper?'

'I decided it would be a mistake to challenge her when I was blind with grief,' replied Rycroft smoothly. 'So I elected to leave it.'

'I tried to follow you. Where did you go?'

'Oh, here and there,' replied Rycroft evasively. 'But Lawrence told me that she will be arrested today, so I shall nab her in Newgate.'

'Maybe.' Chaloner tried to read the alchemist's face, but he was standing with the light behind him, making it impossible. 'She was not in the King's Head or her house when we went to lay hold of her this morning, and I cannot help but wonder if she knew we were coming and contrived to be out.'

'Well, she will not stay out for ever,' shrugged Rycroft, 'and Lawrence's men are lying in wait for her. It is only a matter of time before she is caught.'

'You saw Jasper when he was ill,' said Chaloner. '*Was* it plague or could he have died from some other cause? Poison, perhaps?'

'How strange you should ask,' said Rycroft, frowning.

'Because Jasper wondered the same thing. However, I saw nothing to suggest anything untoward. Poor Jasper! He was the best of men, and I shall miss him more than I can say. I wish I could have buried him in St Gregory's, as he wanted, but Cary would not let me hunt through the pit for his body.'

Thank God for that, thought Chaloner with a shudder at the notion, and tugged his thoughts back to the skirmish. 'That Greek. Where is he?'

'Do you mean me?'

Chaloner looked up to see someone standing at the door – the foreigner, but without his black hair. He blinked, sure his eyes were playing tricks. But no, he had seen aright: the 'Greek' was none other than Will Leybourn, surveyor, author, mathematician and friend.

'I am back,' declared Leybourn grandly, although Chaloner could see this for himself. 'I went to live in Uxbridge, if you recall, but I have decided to return to London.'

'I am glad to see you, Will,' said Chaloner warmly, and received an affectionate clap on the back in return. 'But why choose to do it while the plague rages?'

'For the best of reasons,' replied Leybourn happily. 'A woman.'

Leybourn's sole ambition in life was to find himself a wife, but he had an unfortunate tendency to choose entirely the wrong kind of woman. Chaloner was not very good at picking suitable partners himself, but he was an expert compared to the luckless surveyor.

'Then she must be quite a lady.'

Leybourn beamed. 'She is, and I am head over heels in love. She is a decent lass this time, not like the other one I planned to wed. What was her name?'

245

'Mary Cade,' replied Chaloner shortly. *He* was unlikely to forget such a person, and was astonished that Leybourn had, given the agonies he had suffered on her account.

'A heartless wench,' declared Leybourn, and then waved an airy hand. 'But this one is different – a widow named Mrs Nay.' He lowered his voice conspiratorially. 'Although she does not say "nay" to me, of course.'

'You are talking about my sister,' said Rycroft coldly. 'And you promised me faithfully that you would treat her with the utmost respect.'

While Leybourn made a stammering apology that only dug him a deeper pit, Chaloner studied his old friend. Leybourn had changed little in the time since they had last met, although his face was fuller, and his brown hair had started to thin at the temples. But his legs were still too long, and he had not lost his puppyish grin. As he spoke, he picked up a cloth and began to scrub at the dye that artificially darkened his skin.

'You will need more than a quick wipe with a rag to remove walnut juice,' remarked Rycroft, a little spitefully. 'It is permanent.'

Leybourn regarded him in alarm. 'But Ester does not like me looking this way! She wants me back to normal.'

'What a pity,' said Rycroft flatly. 'Because you will be swarthy for weeks.'

'Ester?' asked Chaloner warily. 'Not the Quaker who lives in King's Head Court?'

'You have met her?' cried Leybourn, and laughed joyfully. 'Is she not the most perfect creature you have ever seen?'

She was not far from it, and intelligent, too, which made Chaloner wonder why she had taken up with Leybourn. The surveyor had many virtues, but he would not be a good companion for a lively and clever lady like her. Yet again, Chaloner suspected that Leybourn had made a mistake – not for himself this time, but for Ester. And Chaloner was honest enough with himself to admit that he was rather dismayed by the news.

'You have been following me, Will,' he said, changing the subject abruptly, lest Leybourn could somehow read his guilty thoughts. 'Why?'

'In case you needed help. Thurloe told me that there have been attempts on your life.'

'Thurloe?' demanded Chaloner, irked. '*He* knows what you have been doing?'

'He knows I am in the city.' An anxious expression crossed the surveyor's face. 'You will not tell him about my disguise, will you? He forbade me to play the role of spy, but I could not resist it. I did it for your benefit anyway, to be on hand if you required assistance – which you did. You would be dead by now if I had not raced to the rescue.'

Chaloner sincerely doubted it – he had been winning the scuffle when Leybourn and Rycroft had intervened. Moreover, he was annoyed that the surveyor had not come to him openly, like any normal person would have done. He fought down his irritation, telling himself that Leybourn had acted out of friendship, not a desire to be a nuisance.

'Why stay in London?' he asked, struggling to regain his equanimity. 'Surely it would be better to take your Ester to Uxbridge, away from the plague?'

'Unfortunately, she refuses to leave him.' Leybourn nodded towards Rycroft. 'And *he* will not leave because he is needed to make London Treacle. Plus there is this dark business with the cathedral, of course.'

'Damn it, Will!' snapped Rycroft angrily. 'We told you that in confidence.'

'You can trust Tom,' said Leybourn comfortably. 'And Thurloe.'

'Cromwell's spymaster and a boy from the New Model Army?' Rycroft eyed Chaloner coolly. 'Oh, yes – I have not forgotten the Second Battle of Newbury. I recognised you instantly, although I think it took you longer to place me.'

'Do not say you met on the field!' exclaimed Leybourn, looking from one to the other. Then he shook his head. 'Those stupid wars! Will we never be free of them?'

'What dark business with the cathedral?' asked Chaloner, keen to change the subject. Rycroft had been fighting for the King, while Leybourn had always been a Royalist – Chaloner did not want either to dwell too long on the fact that he had been on the other side.

'We should tell him,' said Leybourn, and raised his hand for silence when the alchemist immediately began to object. 'We have been struggling with the matter for ages, Matt, yet we are no further forward. We need help if we are to do something about it.'

Rycroft did not tell his story willingly. He grabbed Leybourn's arm and hauled him to a corner, where the pair of them began to speak in furious whispers. Chaloner pretended to flick through *The Compleat Surveyor* while he waited for the spat to finish, although the truth was that he had unusually acute hearing, and had no trouble eavesdropping on the entire conversation. Rycroft began by informing Leybourn that it was not his own safety that concerned him, but Ester's. Apparently, she had been the first to notice something amiss.

'Then she is in danger for as long as we try to handle this alone,' argued Leybourn. 'Especially as we are having no luck. Besides, I suspect that Tom and Thurloe are looking into the matter anyway, so pooling our resources makes sense.'

'But *he* is employed by Dean Sancroft,' objected Rycroft, stabbing an angry finger in Chaloner's direction. 'And there are rumours that Sancroft is the Executioner.'

'How can he be?' asked Leybourn impatiently. 'He is in Tunbridge Wells, waiting for the plague to abate.'

'The culprit does not have to be here in person,' Rycroft flashed back. 'It is easy to hire helpmeets and monitor events from afar.'

'Then why did he recruit Tom to look into it?'

'To throw us off the scent, of course! Besides, why choose Chaloner? Why not use one of his own people? It is suspicious.'

Leybourn waved a dismissive hand. 'You have grown overly wary, Matt, and it is clouding your wits. The Executioner is here in London, busily dispatching anyone he sees as a threat, which is why we *must* talk to Tom. Or you, me and Ester might be the next victims. And if you do not care about me or yourself, then at least consider her safety.'

Rycroft was silent for a moment, then inclined his head, albeit reluctantly. 'Very well. But if anything happens to us, it will be *your* fault.'

He and Leybourn returned to Chaloner, one still scowling, the other all happy relief.

'Shall we start at the beginning?' asked Leybourn brightly, sitting on the bench. 'It is all about whether the cathedral should be repaired or rebuilt.'

Chaloner narrowed his eyes. 'What is?'

'The plot that Matt, Ester and I have been struggling to expose. But do not interrupt, or we shall be here all day. Now, the cathedral. To rebuild *or* repair it requires large amounts of money, as Canon Kerchier knew twenty years ago.'

'So he enlisted the help of rich and powerful men.' Rycroft spoke reluctantly. 'Men who would not only donate funds, but would use their influence to get things moving.'

'Yes – the Agents of God,' said Chaloner. 'A society that foundered after his death, but that has recently been resurrected. I plan to ask some of the canons about it today.'

'Oh,' said Leybourn, crestfallen. 'You already know. But were you aware that *other* rich and powerful men aim to stop them?'

Chaloner nodded. 'They call themselves the Maurice Men.' He watched Leybourn's face fall a second time.

'The point is that the Agents have raised a lot of cash for their new cathedral,' said Rycroft, 'and they are keen to knock the old one down so they can make a start.'

'And do you know why?' asked Leybourn, then answered before Chaloner could tell him that he did. 'Because they want to give lucrative contracts to their cronies, win the King's gratitude, and be rewarded with honours, titles and country manors. At the same time, a person known as the Executioner is running around, frightening the life out of people.'

'And killing them,' put in Rycroft pointedly. 'Do not forget that.'

Chaloner looked from one to the other. 'What does all this have to do with you?'

'This Executioner is a criminal,' said Rycroft shortly. 'And none of us are safe if that sort of fellow is allowed to roam free. Obviously, we feel morally obliged to stop him.'

'And we do not want the Agents to succeed,' added Leybourn. 'St Paul's has always been here, and it is not for them to pull it down.'

'However, we do not want their money to be misused by the Maurice Men either,' said Rycroft. 'It was raised to make the cathedral better, not to be squandered on useless repairs.'

'There will be a middle way,' elaborated Leybourn. 'One that will ensure our glorious cathedral will survive in a more sensible form for centuries to come.'

'So those are the objectives we have set ourselves,' finished Rycroft. 'To catch the Executioner, and then to thwart *all* the fanatics with radical opinions about the cathedral. For London's sake.'

Chaloner was silent. He was not sure what to make of Rycroft. Was he really motivated by a desire to combat killers and zealots, or did he have a different agenda altogether, using Leybourn as his unwitting helpmeet? The surveyor was gullible, and would certainly throw himself into a reckless scheme, believing it would win him the favour of his latest lady.

'But you can take over now, Tom,' Leybourn went on generously. 'Because Matt is too busy making London Treacle, Ester has her Quakering duties, and I must watch over Ester.'

'Very well,' agreed Chaloner, glad Leybourn was prepared to step back, although Rycroft did not look happy with the arrangements being made without his say-so. He addressed the alchemist. 'William Hall told me that you have a habit of disappearing on private business when you should be working. Is this what has been taking up your time?'

Rycroft nodded. 'And I suppose passing the matter to you will allow me to produce more much-needed medicine. So how will you solve the mystery that has defeated poor stupid Will and me?'

'I shall start by speaking to William Hall,' replied Chaloner, ignoring the sarcasm. 'He is self-appointed keeper of the Agents' money, so he can tell me who stands to benefit most if the scheme swings into action early.'

'William Hall is dead,' said Rycroft. His voice was neutral, but there was a flash of gratification in his eyes that Chaloner's enquiries would not be all plain sailing. 'He got the plague and died yesterday.'

Chaloner gaped at him, then recalled the brief conversation he had overheard at the Deanery the previous night. Owen had talked about 'a terrible shock' – William's unexpected demise – and Francis had then remarked that his brother had been 'assiduous in what he had gathered'. Evidently, the Agents had gone to assess the money that William had collected, and had been pleasantly surprised by what they had found – which explained why Francis had been afraid that 'half the rogues in London' would be interested in it.

'It is a pity,' sighed Leybourn, 'because I think he might have known the Executioner's identity. I half-heard a discussion between him and Gaundy, you see.'

'What discussion?' asked Chaloner, eyes narrowing.

'One that took place in the cathedral – Gaundy mentioned the Executioner and William seemed to know who he meant.' Leybourn glared at Rycroft. 'I wish you had not stopped me from interrogating them. If I had, we might have a solution by now.'

'We would not, because they would have refused to answer.' Rycroft shot Chaloner a look that was none too pleasant. 'Although I concede that Sancroft's man might have persuaded them to talk. I know all about the sly tactics of professional spies.'

'When did William die, exactly?' asked Chaloner, electing to overlook the jibe.

'His body was found at about nine o'clock,' replied Leybourn. 'His brothers refused to let him go in the common pit, so he will lie in St Gregory's crypt until a private burial can be arranged.'

'Why there?' asked Chaloner. 'Does the cathedral not have a vault of its own?'

'Not one that locks,' explained Leybourn. 'And no one wants plague victims lying around in insecure places. Masley refused to accept the body at first, but Francis offered him a donation "for the poor", so he changed his mind.'

'And are you *sure* William died of plague?' pressed Chaloner.

'Well, he officiated at the common pit yesterday,' replied Rycroft, 'so it is highly likely. We all know how fast the sickness can strike.'

Chaloner reflected on what he had seen: William wearing a cloak, but not a mask. Had that been a fatal mistake? Yet surely it was suspicious that a fifth man connected with the cathedral and its mysteries should die so soon after the fourth? He sighed. There was only one way to determine if William's death was suspicious: visit St Gregory's crypt and look at the body for himself. He decided to do it as soon as he had consulted with Thurloe.

*

Taking Leybourn with him, Chaloner set off for Carter Lane, leaving Rycroft to his alchemy. A bell tolled in the distance, and Chaloner supposed that Stedman was hard at work again.

'I know a lot of ringers,' said Leybourn conversationally as they went. 'I met three lively fellows – Joyce, Day and Roan – on my way from Uxbridge two weeks ago. All had decided to flee the city, on the grounds that chiming for funerals is far too deadly a business.'

He said no more because one of Lawrence's huge bonfires was at the west end of the cathedral, and a waft of wind enveloped them in choking fumes. Both began to cough, and were relieved when they reached Prayse's house, where the air was scented with herbs rather than the thick stench of incinerating rubbish.

'I told you to leave Tom alone,' said Thurloe crossly when he saw the pair of them together. 'He has a lot of work to do, and we cannot afford him to be distracted. I sense something very unpleasant in the offing, and we will not stop it by—'

'It was not my fault,' interrupted Leybourn defensively. 'We . . . ran into each other.'

'I told you not to wear that ridiculous disguise, too,' scolded Thurloe. 'Wigs and face-paints are supposed to make you invisible, not stand out like a sore thumb.'

Thus admonished, Leybourn fell silent, so Chaloner began to outline all he had learned since he and the ex-Spymaster had last met. When he had finished, Thurloe confessed that he had made no headway in the matter of Upton, despite begging reports from a wealth of former spies.

'Upton the stationer?' blurted Leybourn. '*He* is the kinsman you aim to prevent from harming your family's reputation?' He assumed a martyred expression. 'Then this is exactly why you *should* confide in me, because I have information about him – information that I could have shared days ago if you had—'

'What information?' interrupted Chaloner quickly, seeing Thurloe's blue eyes take on a distinctly dangerous glint.

'I heard him tell Denton, the King's Keeper of Fish, that he was in London to get rich, although he did not say how. He also brayed that he had recently married for money.'

An expression of disgust suffused Thurloe's face. 'The rogue was frank about his designs on Ursula's wealth?'

'He was to Denton,' said Leybourn. 'But now I understand why you have risked life and limb coming to the city. His antics might well damage your family – it could encourage other unscrupulous and greedy suitors to chance their hands with your womenfolk.'

'Thank you for pointing that out,' said Thurloe curtly, and turned to Chaloner. 'It is clear what we must do next: examine William's body and ascertain exactly how he died.'

'I will help,' said Leybourn keenly. 'I need to impress Ester with my courage and intelligence, you see, so that she—'

'No,' said Thurloe in the tone of voice that brooked no argument. 'Take her for a walk in St James's Park instead. There is nothing more pleasant than a stroll with one's lady.'

Leybourn opened his mouth to say that it was far too hot for romantic ambles, but closed it again when Thurloe fixed him with a steely glare. With wounded pride, he bowed and took his leave.

255

'I have a bad feeling about this cathedral affair, Tom,' Thurloe said, when the surveyor had gone. 'And I wish Will had stayed in Uxbridge. He is ill-equipped to meddle in such matters, and his presence is a worry we could do without.'

Chaloner agreed. 'Can you not devise a pretext to send him back?'

'He refuses to leave Ester, and she refuses to leave her brother. However, I have a few irons in the fire, which hopefully will see all three in safer pastures soon.'

Chaloner experienced a pang of regret that Ester might leave the city, but then reminded himself that she was his friend's beloved, and it was not for him to swoon over her. He changed the subject abruptly enough to make Thurloe regard him appraisingly.

'Have you discovered where Stone went?'

'Not yet, although he told several friends that he intended to return tomorrow. However, I suspect that is unlikely, and I am fairly sure he is dead.'

'Or he has gone into hiding in the hope of avoiding the same fate as Kerchier and the others,' suggested Chaloner, disinclined to be quite so pessimistic.

'Either way, we cannot expect help from him in thwarting the Executioner.'

'What about Bing's secret past? Have you found out what that entails? Or the identity of the mysterious William Turner?'

'No, but a contact in the cathedral choir told me that Bing once did something of which he is deeply ashamed. I shall continue to dig, although I have the sense that it will transpire to be irrelevant.'

'Cartwright seemed to think otherwise.'

Thurloe eyed him lugubriously. 'Cartwright has his

own agenda, which does not include helping us. But we cannot stand here gossiping like politicians. We must go to St Gregory's and look at William's corpse. I shall ask Prayse to come with us – he is far better qualified for that sort of thing than we are.'

'Would he inspect Harbert as well?'

Thurloe looked doubtful. 'Not if the body is sealed inside its vault.'

'Gaundy died before he got around to it, and I doubt Masley has bothered. We need to know if Harbert died as a result of fighting or from some other cause. Of course, these examinations are best done in secret, so we shall have to devise a way to empty the church.'

'Easy! I shall walk in and announce that I have a fever. The place will clear before you can snap your fingers.'

Prayse Russell was in his parlour, impeccably dressed, but in clothes that were so austere that he could be nothing but a religious fanatic. He was reading a tract of the kind that would probably appeal to Pamela, and Chaloner wondered if they knew each other.

'The Muggletonian?' asked Prayse. 'Or is she a Ranter now? She changes her allegiance so often that I cannot keep pace.'

'Quaker,' supplied Chaloner.

Prayse was aghast. 'Then you must convince her to join another denomination! We are respectable folk, and she will bring us into disrepute.'

Thurloe explained what he wanted the physician to do, finishing with, 'Tom will keep you safe while you work, but wear a less striking hat, if you please. Yours is the only one of its ilk that I have seen in London for a decade, and it makes you very conspicuous.'

'It is the only one I have,' said Prayse haughtily. 'I do not approve of this modern desire to own several – we all have only one head to put them on, after all.'

'Then borrow this,' suggested Chaloner, offering the old felt cap that he kept in his pocket for those occasions when he needed a disguise.

'I most certainly shall not,' declared Prayse, eyeing it in distaste. 'You aim to make me look like a courtier, but my principles will not allow it. You must take me as I am.'

'It is not—' began Chaloner, wondering which courtiers Prayse had met, as none of the ones he knew would deign to touch such a grubby item, let alone put it on their heads.

'Cavaliers are empty-headed fools,' Prayse ranted on, 'who hide their inadequacies behind frills and lace. And that includes the turncoat Monck, who does nothing to help Lawrence fight the plague. He might as well be on the moon.'

'I understand you examined Upton's body,' said Chaloner, aiming to stem the flow before they lost half the day to it.

'It was I who found out that he died from a blow to the head,' said Prayse, all smug confidence. 'And that was not all. I conducted certain experiments afterwards, which have told me much more about his demise.'

'Did you?' Thurloe sounded irked. 'You did not mention these to me.'

Prayse smiled, an alarming expression with too many teeth and no humour. 'Because I was not sure if they would bear fruit, and I did not want you disappointed if they did not – not with family honour at stake.'

'And?' asked Thurloe, clearly unappeased.

'And I learned that Upton swallowed a whole pot of *sal mirabilis* before he died – I found the empty container caught in his clothes.'

'*Sal mirabilis*,' mused Thurloe. 'There are rumours that is useless against the plague.'

'It is,' averred Prayse. 'Its manufacturers claim otherwise, but they are liars, who will be damned for all eternity. However, Upton's *sal mirabilis* was not medicine at all, despite what it said on the label.'

'What was it then?' asked Chaloner, when the physician paused for dramatic effect.

'A highly acidic poison,' replied Prayse importantly. 'I thought at the time that the wound on his head was not sufficient to kill him, and I was right. What happened was this: he was knocked silly, and once he lay unresisting, he was fed the toxin. Once it passed his lips, his fate was sealed, because it seared away his innards.'

Chaloner stared at him, then handed over the pot that he had taken from St Gregory's tower. 'Does this contain an acidic poison, too? There was froth around Gaundy's mouth and bleeding blisters inside it.'

'Then I imagine it does,' said Prayse, taking the bottle and setting it on the table. 'I shall analyse it properly the moment I return.'

St Gregory's was pretty in the morning light, with sunshine flooding in through its east window to dapple its creamy flagstones. Yet there were small signs that the church was without a verger – the floor needed sweeping, the flowers on the altar were dead, and prayer books were scattered untidily over the back pew. There were perhaps a dozen people there, all on their knees with their hands clasped in prayer. Prayse nodded approvingly.

Chaloner was about to suggest that he and Prayse stood near the crypt door, ready to slip through it as Thurloe staged his diversion, when Randall the hunchback sidled up to them. Anticipating another rash assault, Chaloner's hand dropped to the hilt of his sword, but Randall ignored him and addressed Prayse.

'I need you, Mr Physician, sir,' he whispered. 'I think I have a bubo coming.'

Prayse sighed irritably, a response that was unlikely to be of comfort to an ailing man, but allowed himself to be tugged away for a private consultation. Chaloner followed at a discreet distance, lest Randall tried anything rash, but all that happened was a brief exchange of words, after which the apprentice slouched out of the church.

'Idle beggar,' growled Prayse. 'I guessed his game the moment I set eyes on him, and I was right: he wanted me to diagnose him with the plague, so he could be locked up in a nice house for forty days, with free food from the parish. I sent him away with a flea in his ear.'

Then Thurloe arrived, clad in his plague gear. He staggered up the nave, gabbling about a burning pain in his armpit. There was a concerted dash for the door. Only one man remained, doggedly refusing to abandon his devotions, but even he did not linger when Thurloe started to remove his mask.

'Now hurry,' Thurloe urged Chaloner and Prayse. 'I shall stay by the door to repel visitors, but I cannot do it indefinitely without suspicions being raised, so please do not dawdle.'

Chaloner trotted towards the crypt. He picked the lock and descended the steps in the dark, recalling that there was a lamp on a shelf at the bottom. He lit it quickly, then held it up to illuminate the way for Prayse. The shadows it cast were long and eerie, and he hoped the physician would not take too long to do what was necessary.

'Jesus Christ!' Prayse swore, as he stumbled down the last stair, an unexpectedly blasphemous exclamation that made Chaloner regard him in surprise; Quakers never cursed. 'Could you not have told me that it was uneven? Now I have twisted my ankle.'

'I assumed you would be careful,' said Chaloner defensively, staggering as Prayse leaned on him and began to flex the afflicted joint. 'Most church stairs are old and worn.'

'*These* should not be,' snapped the physician. 'The undercroft was only dug twenty years ago – for spite, in the hope that it would destabilise the cathedral above.'

Chaloner was glad that William had not been carried too deep inside the crypt, given that Prayse grumbled about the pain in his foot at every step. The canon lay in a beautifully crafted casket next to the Countess of Devonshire's tomb. Another corpse was with him, although this was just covered by a blanket. Gingerly, Chaloner pulled it off, and was surprised to recognise Gaundy – he had assumed the verger would go in the cemetery.

'His father is down here,' explained Prayse. 'He doubtless made arrangements to be buried next to him, and as he did not have the plague, his wish was granted.' He sniggered unpleasantly. 'Perhaps he hopes that he and his sire will spend eternity drinking together – they were both dreadful sots. Do you want me to look at him, too?'

'I suppose you had better,' said Chaloner reluctantly. There was a powerful stench of urine in the crypt, and he longed to be out in the fresh air – or as fresh as air could be with fires belching smoke and plague victims' bodies piling up everywhere.

Prayse began with Gaundy, although Chaloner did not think his examination was as deft or as competent as Surgeon Wiseman's would have been, and he wished it was his friend who was there instead.

'This was in his pocket,' Prayse announced, brandishing a scrap of paper. Chaloner reached out to take it, but Prayse jerked it away and placed it in a pouch he had brought with him. 'You may examine it when we are home again, in a room with decent lighting. However, I am optimistically confident that it is what is known as *a clue*.'

Chaloner could have wrested it from him, but that would take time, and he wanted the whole grisly business over with as soon as possible. Prayse nodded to say that he had finished with Gaundy, and moved on to William, who was dressed in a white shroud, hands folded across his middle. Chaloner was glad when that examination proved to be brief – and without commentary – and led the way quickly to Harbert's vault.

Kerchier's bones lay where he had left them four days ago – he had half expected Masley to have disposed of them, just to be rid of the nuisance they posed. Prayse poked desultorily at them, while Chaloner removed the nails from Harbert's coffin.

Even though the crypt was cool, Harbert had been dead too long to be pleasant company, and Chaloner jerked back with his sleeve across his face when the lid finally came off. Harbert had been a tall man in his sixties, with thin lips, a narrow face and an unfashionable beard. He wore a rough old long-coat and nothing else.

Prayse unfastened it to reveal a bruise – the wound that Denton's stick had inflicted. It looked painful, and had obviously been delivered with considerable force, which meant that Denton had lied about the seriousness of the encounter. Chaloner determined to speak to him as soon as possible.

At that point, he heard faint voices coming from the church above – Thurloe was talking to Masley. He indicated that Prayse was to hurry.

'Yet another clue,' declared the physician proudly, holding up a second piece of paper. It was stained with whatever had leaked from the body, so Chaloner made no attempt to take this one from him. 'I shall clean it up at home, and see what it says. I have also taken Kerchier's cloak. I shall explain why later.'

Grateful that the ordeal was almost over, Chaloner put all to rights, and ushered the still-limping Prayse back up the stairs. In the church, Masley and a masked Thurloe were deep in conversation. The ex-Spymaster had placed himself so that he could see the crypt but Masley could not, and made a gesture with his hand, warning Chaloner and Prayse to stay back.

'I see lamps lit in your house until very late, vicar,' he was saying sympathetically. 'The loss of your clerk must be a dreadful trial.'

'It is,' agreed Masley with the air of the martyr. 'The bishop offered me another, but I declined. I know the work now, and there is no need to put a second life at risk.'

'You must have lost hundreds of parishioners,' said Thurloe, trying to lead Masley away, so that Chaloner and Prayse could escape. 'I have visited many churches, but none of their officials work such long hours.'

'I have taken it upon myself to prepare proper letters

for the victims' next-of-kin,' explained the vicar, declining to move, 'which will be distributed when the pestilence is over. How else will they know what became of their loved ones? It is an act of human kindness.'

'And will be rewarded in heaven, I am sure,' said Thurloe ingratiatingly. He indicated the door. 'Will you show me one?'

Masley stood firm. 'They will be viewed by the families of the dead and no one else,' he said sternly. 'Are you sure you are a physician? Your voice is unfamiliar.'

'I am from Hull,' lied Thurloe. 'General Monck hired me to make a professional survey of the city, but this is my first time in St Gregory's.'

'Then tell him to rethink his foolish decision to reject Certificates of Health. He fears forgeries, but most are genuine, and it is cruel to prevent healthy folk from leaving. They will rebel. Indeed, I have heard that many plan to go out on Wednesday, all at the same time.'

'I shall tell him,' promised Thurloe. 'Now let us go to your house, so I can write my official report. It will carry more weight if you countersign it.'

Chaloner heaved a sigh of relief when the vicar finally led the way outside.

It was some time before Thurloe returned to Carter Lane, but Prayse stubbornly refused to tell Chaloner what he had discovered in the interim, on the grounds that he was unwilling to say everything twice. Chaloner paced restlessly, fretting at the passing time, while Prayse went to his parlour, where he bandaged his ankle and set about conducting more experiments. Thurloe arrived eventually, and Chaloner went to help him peel off his costume.

'Masley is an odd fellow,' Thurloe remarked, unbuckling the mask. 'He is a saint for the task he has set himself, yet there is something awry in his manner. There could be no harm in letting me read one of his letters, but he doggedly refused to show me any.'

'Perhaps being awkward makes him feel important.'

'His office is stuffed with paper, pens and ink, so I asked for the name of his stationer. He mumbled something about a sponsor who supports his philanthropic labours.'

'A sponsor named John Upton?'

'He said not, but I had the sense that he was lying. Then he dashed off a letter with astonishing speed for me to deliver to Monck.'

He held out the missive, and Chaloner was surprised to see that it was beautifully crafted, with even letters in a perfectly straight line. He had expected it to be all but illegible, like his own writing when rushed.

'Then *that* is why he is producing so many reports,' he said wryly. 'He aims to show off his fine penmanship to all the victims' kin, in the hope of impressing someone wealthy. In other words, he wants to win himself an influential patron.'

'So Masley is yet someone else who is using the plague to further his own interests,' sighed Thurloe. 'He is no different from a host of others.'

'He was angry when he found out that Sancroft had sent me to investigate the bones,' recalled Chaloner. 'Probably lest a whiff of scandal in his church should adversely affect his efforts. He demanded to know who had contacted him about them.'

'I should like to know the answer to that, too,' mused Thurloe. 'Because it is clearly a person who is eager to see justice done, and we need all the help we can get.'

'We do,' agreed Chaloner, and nodded towards the

parlour, where Prayse was humming to himself as he hovered over his pots and potions. 'So let us hope he can provide us with some sensible answers.'

'I imagine he will. I appreciate that he is a little . . . extreme in his opinions, but I trust him implicitly. He served me well during the Commonwealth.'

'He was one of your spies?'

'He monitored certain Royalists for me, when he visited their homes in a professional capacity. So let us see what he can tell us about the bodies in the crypt.'


'I have discovered a great deal that will interest you,' Prayse began importantly. 'First, Upton, Gaundy, Harbert *and* William were struck over the head and then poisoned. The likelihood is that they are all victims of the same hand.'

'Poisoned with what?' asked Chaloner.

'A substance that includes a highly acidic element called *acer*, after the Latin for "sour". A simple test confirms it.' Prayse handed over a packet containing white crystals. 'Here is *nix album*, which always bubbles when *acer* is added. Take it – then you will not need to bother me again, should your culprit claim another victim.'

Chaloner put it in his pocket. 'So who sells *acer*? Then we can visit their shops, and ask who has bought some recently.'

Prayse spread his hands. 'Apothecaries, alchemists, *medici*, tanners, ironmongers, painters, braziers, glass-blowers, pewterers, dyers, housewives . . . the list is endless, as *acer* can be found in many common materials.'

'Damn!' muttered Chaloner, although he should have known that answers never came that easily. 'So there is nothing unusual about it?'

'Nothing – although I confess that it would never have

occurred to *me* to use it in such a fashion. Your killer is resourceful, imaginative and intelligent.'

'So Denton was telling the truth about not killing Harbert?' asked Thurloe. 'Or rather, that Harbert did not receive a fatal wound during their fight?'

'Not a fatal wound, but a very vicious one,' replied Prayse.

'Which means that Denton lied about the seriousness of the quarrel,' mused Chaloner, 'and so did his friends. I will threaten to charge him with Harbert's murder today, to see if fright will shake loose the truth.'

Thurloe nodded his approval. 'You must talk to William's brothers, too, and assess if they are aware that it was not the plague that killed him. The murderer chose his time well, striking after William had spent a day officiating at the pit.' He turned back to the physician. 'Thank you, Prayse. You are been most helpful.'

'I have not finished yet,' said the physician archly. 'Because I have ascertained that Kerchier had an encounter with *acer* as well – when I looked at his bones, I happened to notice that tiny holes had been burned in his cloak.' He indicated the garment that now lay on the table. 'Holes made by *acer*.'

Chaloner regarded them sceptically. 'Not by moths?'

'No,' replied Prayse shortly, disliking his professional opinion questioned. 'The damage caused by insects is of an entirely different appearance to that caused by caustic substances, as any man of science will tell you.'

'So all *five* were dispatched in an identical manner?' asked Thurloe keenly. 'Despite the twenty-year hiatus between the first case and the rest?'

Prayse nodded. 'The victims could never have swallowed *acer* if they were conscious – it is too corrosive, and the pain would have stopped them. Hence the blow to the head, which stunned them first.'

Thurloe shuddered. 'Does the killer consider himself merciful by rendering his prey unconscious before burning out their innards?'

'I do not believe so. Kerchier suffered several blows to the head, which would have been both messy and distressing. None were fatal, and I suspect the killer panicked – he resorted to *acer* in sheer desperation. Then, recalling how well it had worked on his first victim, he elected to use the same technique on his subsequent ones.'

'Or maybe he just did not want blood splattering over him,' countered Thurloe. 'Or he is a frail man, physically incapable of the power required to dispatch his prey cleanly.'

'Or a frail woman,' suggested Chaloner. 'Pamela's husband and the Edwards boys had froth on their lips that—'

'I still have not finished,' snapped Prayse irritably. 'Or have I been labouring away all this time for nothing?'

'My apologies,' said Thurloe, although Chaloner wished the physician would stop doling out his findings in dribs and drabs.

'I searched the victims' clothes and found two pieces of paper,' said the physician pompously. 'The one from Gaundy is in good condition, although worn, suggesting that it had been taken out and studied repeatedly. The one from Harbert's leaky corpse required special cleaning, but I have managed to render it legible.'

He laid both on the table. Gaundy's read *Mind the Executioner*, followed by a crude depiction of a gallows. The ink had run on Harbert's, but it was still possible to see that it had carried the same message and picture.

'There was nothing on William?' asked Thurloe.

'No, but he was wearing a shroud – those do not come with pockets.'

'"Mind the Executioner",' mused Thurloe. 'Does it mean mind as in "take heed of", or mind as in "beware"? In other words, did the Executioner send these himself, ordering his victims to follow his instructions? Or was it sent by a third party, warning them that the Executioner was at large?'

'Or sent by the Executioner *after* the recipients had failed to do something he wanted,' suggested Chaloner. 'So who is he? Kirton and Rycroft think it is Sancroft, although I do not see the dean creeping about with a cudgel and a pot of *acer*.'

'My money is on Pamela,' said Thurloe. 'The woman who hired Mims to kill you, and whom we suspect of poisoning Jasper and the Mims. I know she claims to receive orders from a benefactor, but she could be lying.'

'I disagree,' said Prayse. '*Acer* kills in minutes, but you told me that Jasper lingered for hours. If she did administer *acer* to him, it would have to have been in a seriously diluted form.'

'Go to King's Head Court and see if there has been word of her, Tom,' ordered Thurloe. 'And while you do, I shall send for a few of my more reliable contacts and set them to finding out if Upton received one of these warnings. Meet me here this evening.'

'Are you not forgetting something?' asked Prayse. He held out his hand and waggled his fingers. 'I did not agree to go through all this unpleasantness for nothing.'

'You will charge a friend for your help in catching a killer?' asked Chaloner in distaste, although Thurloe

269

promptly reached for his purse. 'I thought Quakers put scant value on worldly riches.'

'We do,' replied Prayse, accepting Thurloe's coins with a nod of thanks. 'But that does not mean we should ply our God-given skills for no reward.'

# Chapter 9

As Chaloner left Prayse's house, he saw Suger loitering at the entrance to an alley. They locked eyes before the felon turned and loped away, glancing tauntingly over his shoulder. He had a peculiarly lumbering gait that was a brazen invitation to give chase, but Chaloner resisted – it was the oldest trick in the book to lure a victim into an ambush, and he was not about to misjudge a dangerous situation a second time that day.

Grimly satisfied that Suger would be waiting in vain, Chaloner started to walk towards King's Head Court, a route that took him between two of Lawrence's great bonfires. Both released billowing clouds of smoke, and flames danced so high that he wondered if the intention was to 'purify' the city by burning it to the ground. Then he saw Cary, dashing from one inferno to the other with a team of harried workmen at his heels.

'No news of Mrs Ball yet,' the secretary wheezed. 'But I shall make a concerted effort to hunt her down the moment we have contained these damned blazes.'

Chaloner regarded him in alarm. 'You mean they are out of control? In the midst of all these wooden houses and thatched roofs – every one bone-dry from the summer heat?'

Cary scowled. 'It was not our idea to set the things – blame the King's "clever" advisors. But I cannot talk now, or we shall have a disaster on our hands.'

Chaloner went on his way, sweat trickling down his back and stinging his eyes. A stray dog – an unusual sight now that so many had been slaughtered – tried to squeeze itself into the shade afforded by a wilting tree, but it was the only living thing abroad. He glanced at the sky, which was yellow-brown with smoke and made him feel hotter than ever. A bell tolled in the distance, the pattern of chimes telling him that a woman in her thirties had died.

He had not gone far when he saw Kirton with Joshua, so changed course to intercept them. They were deep in conversation and did not see him until he spoke.

'You should keep your apprentice in check, Kirton,' he said shortly. 'I do not appreciate being attacked in the dark.'

'Randall does not work for me any more,' said Kirton defensively. 'I dismissed him.'

'Which you should have done months ago,' declared Joshua. 'All he ever did was moan – about his wages, the quality of his food, the work he had to do . . . He is an ingrate, and I am glad he is gone.'

'Once the plague came and book sales plummeted, I was unable to pay him,' Kirton told Chaloner. 'Although I did provide a bed and as much food as I could spare. But last night I learned that he has taken to consorting with felons . . .'

'Mims, no less,' elaborated Joshua indignantly. 'Randall stood outside and howled his outrage for an hour before he finally slunk away.'

272

'He has always been cognisant of his rights and privileges,' said Kirton unhappily. 'And I fear he will bring trouble to London before this crisis is over.'

Joshua coughed. 'Whose idea was it to light these wretched fires? Some fool in Oxford, no doubt, making asinine decisions while he lounges by the cool, clean waters of the Isis.'

'Come, brother,' said Kirton. 'This is no place to linger and business awaits.'

'What business?' Chaloner called after them. 'I thought you had no customers.'

'Dusting shelves,' replied Joshua over his shoulder, when Kirton opened his mouth to provide an excuse but then closed it again without giving one. 'So they will be clean when his patrons eventually return.'

Chaloner reached King's Head Court, and was alarmed to see no sign of the soldiers that Cary had posted, although it did not take him long to find out why. They had contrived to stand sentry inside the tavern, and as the place was empty, no one had stopped them from having an ale to slake their thirst. Unfortunately, they had then gone on to drain the whole keg, and were now deep in a drunken slumber. Disgusted, Chaloner grabbed one's shoulder and shook it until the fellow's eyes fluttered open.

'Ale!' the man slurred with an enormous grin of satisfaction. 'Cold, clean ale, just like there used to be before the plague. Try some. It's bloody delicious.'

'I would,' said Chaloner shortly, 'but you have finished it all. Worse yet, you have failed to keep a look out for Pamela Ball.'

But he was talking to himself, because the man was

asleep again, the happy smile still plastered on his face. Chaloner felt like kicking them both awake, irked that they should so brazenly flout their duties, although he was not entirely surprised. He had heard them grumbling about their late wages, and it was unreasonable to expect good service from men who were not treated well in return.

He went to Pamela's house, and was just raising his hand to the door when it was ripped open by the lady herself, a bristling, scowling package of mean-tempered aggression. Chaloner blinked his astonishment, having assumed that she was too clever to return home when she must know that she was in serious trouble.

'What?' she snarled.

Unwilling to question her on the doorstep, where her Mims might come to intervene, Chaloner pushed past her into the house and closed the door behind him. She screeched her outrage at the liberty, and pummelled him with her little fists, although he was moving too fast for her blows to have much impact.

'You have no right!' she raged, although she had the sense not to persist with her assault when they reached the parlour and he turned around to face her, hand on the hilt of his sword. 'This is *my* house, and I do not care what my snake of a husband wrote in his stupid will. The parish poor *cannot* have it as a plague hospital.'

Chaloner frowned his bemusement. 'Jasper has disinherited you?'

'I shall contest it in a court of law,' she snarled. 'And I *will* win. He will never get the better of me. Never! I should have guessed he would do something like this. Why did I not check his will before I—'

She stopped abruptly and glowered at Chaloner, as if

she thought it was his fault that she had almost blurted something that she should probably keep to herself.

'Before you what?' asked Chaloner coldly. 'Fed him poison?'

Her scowl deepened. 'He died of the plague, which is what happens when you visit the sick, brazenly disregarding the explicit orders of your wife.'

'It was his job to visit the sick,' Chaloner pointed out, declining to remind her that most Quakers considered it their moral duty as well, and that she had actively encouraged it in one of her homilies, as an act of defiance against the government. 'He delivered their medicine.'

'It was not his job to slip them alms into the bargain,' she countered hotly. 'Money I could have used for my own purposes. And now he aims to steal my home. Well, it will be over my dead body.'

That could probably be arranged, thought Chaloner in distaste. 'Why did you send your Mims to kill me?'

'You have already asked that question and I have already answered it,' she retorted shortly. 'Those assaults had nothing to do with me.'

'Do not lie – I overheard you discussing them with Suger.'

Her eyes were gimlet hard. 'Then shame on you for engaging in such low antics.'

He was amused by her indignation. 'Eavesdropping is worse than hiring assassins?'

'It is when *I* am the victim,' she flashed. 'But since you know the truth, let me say that I am *proud* of trying to rid the world of a man who does sly work for the Church – the authority that wants to suppress me and my co-religionists. I only wish Suger had succeeded the first time, because then I would not have had to keep paying out for further efforts.'

'Lord!' muttered Chaloner, wrong-footed by the abrupt capitulation. 'Do you—'

'But it was not my idea,' she interrupted. 'I was asked to do it by someone else. However, I do not know his name, and I cannot describe him because he keeps himself masked against the plague. So you may as well go away, as I can tell you nothing more.'

Chaloner stood firm when she tried to push him. 'You keep the Mims supplied with plague remedies. However, I doubt you buy them yourself.' Too many people had mentioned her penny-pinching for that not to be true. 'Which means that someone else provides them. Who? The same person who told you to kill me?'

'What if it was?' she hissed. 'Now get out. I am too busy to answer stupid questions.'

So, thought Chaloner, again resisting her efforts to shove him outside, the Executioner controlled the Mims by making them depend on the medicine he provided, thus placing a ready-made army at his disposal – although not a very efficient one, given their feeble attempts at assassination. But why? And how did he intend to use them? Was it something to do with the trouble that was brewing, with riots and unrest in the offing for later that week?

When she saw that she was not going to remove him by force, Pamela contrived to bring her temper under control, and attempted a smile. The result was not pretty.

'Look, I am sure we can reach an agreement,' she said obsequiously. 'I have a little money, although if you take any, you will be doing London a grave disservice, as I need every penny for my good works. However, under the circumstances . . .'

'I do not want your money.'

She brightened. 'Good! Then let us drink to seal our new alliance. I have a pot of *sal mirabilis* here somewhere, which is just as good as wine.'

And with that offer, a number of things suddenly became abundantly clear in Chaloner's mind. He stared at her for a moment, then turned and ran lightly up the stairs. Pamela followed, screeching fresh indignation. He reached Jasper's bedchamber, flung open the door, and looked around. The little pot of *sal mirabilis* still lay on its side on the floor. He picked it up gingerly.

'What are you doing?' demanded Pamela, although her eyes were uneasy. 'You dishonour the memory of my husband with this nasty invasion. Out, at once!'

'Jasper would never have taken this willingly,' said Chaloner, waving the bottle at her. 'Why would he, when he worked for the alchemist who makes London Treacle?'

Pamela started to deny it, but then faltered into resentful silence when he tapped a couple of Prayse's crystals into the dregs at the bottom of the pot. After a moment, tiny bubbles appeared – it had contained *acer*, although a far less potent dose than had been fed to the other victims, which explained why Jasper had taken so much longer to die.

'Poison,' said Chaloner harshly. 'As I suspected. You murdered him.'

'No, I did not,' she countered haughtily. 'Someone gave me that pot for myself. Is it my fault that Jasper drank what was not intended for him?'

'Who gave it to you? The man who told you to send your Mims after me?'

'Yes, I think so,' she conceded sullenly. 'But I am not—'

'He is known as the Executioner,' interrupted Chaloner

harshly. 'You have thrown in your lot with a very dangerous man.'

'The Executioner?' she blurted. She rummaged about her person, and produced not one but two messages, both identical to those sent to Gaundy and Harbert. 'You mean the rogue who insists on telling me to mind him?'

'Others have received this warning and they are dead. You are in . . .'

He trailed off as he recalled what Jasper had babbled as he lay dying: that 'he' had been, and that he had wanted Pamela, but she had cheated him. Then Jasper claimed to know nothing of his wife's business, but it had killed him anyway. Chaloner looked at the empty pot in his hand, and then at Pamela.

'You suspected something was wrong with this, so you fed it to Jasper, to see if you were right. My God! That was cold.'

'Not so,' she cried, although the truth was in her eyes. 'He said he felt unwell, so I gave him medicine to help him recover. And how did he repay me? By amending his will to deprive me of my house. *Me*, Pamela Ball! Disinherited!'

'He told me that he had swallowed a dragon, which would devour him from within – as an alchemist's assistant, he recognised the effects of poison. And once you saw what the stuff was doing to him, you beat a hasty retreat and left him to die alone.'

'Well, it does not matter now,' said Pamela shortly. 'He is at peace, God rest his soul. But we have more important matters to discuss – namely how to prevent a third attempt on my life. I cannot abstain from medicine for ever, not while the plague rages.'

'A *third* attempt?' pounced Chaloner. 'Does this mean

that you fed the Edwards boys something the Executioner sent you as well?'

'Do not mourn them too deeply,' she flashed. 'They tried to shoot you.'

'On your orders.' Chaloner glanced out of the window, and saw that a number of Mims had gathered in the yard below. Now what? He could not arrest Pamela and drag her through them. She would demand their help, and there were too many of them to fend off.

'On *his* orders,' she snapped. 'I just relayed them. I am not the villain here – *he* is.'

Chaloner treated her denials with the contempt they deserved by ignoring them. Then a plan began to form in his mind. He assessed the bedroom quickly. The windows were too narrow for her to squeeze through, and the door had a very good lock. Without another word, he turned, walked out and secured it behind him. There was a startled silence followed by the pounding of angry little fists.

'What are you doing? Let me out at once! I have prayer meetings to convene.' The voice turned wheedling. 'Please! Jasper died in here, and there is an atmosphere . . .'

'Superstition,' called Chaloner, pocketing the key and bracing the door with a bench for good measure. 'A Quaker should know better.'

'I plan to leave them soon – they are too pious for me. But let us be reasonable about this. How much do you want to forget all this nonsense? Five shillings? Six?'

Chaloner had been offered many bribes during his career as an intelligencer, but none so insultingly meagre. 'Put it towards hiring a good lawyer.'

'You plan to steal my money,' she cried accusingly.

'Well, you will never find it. Not ever! I am far too clever for you.'

'Cary will be here soon, to take you to Newgate,' said Chaloner as he left. 'But do not expect rescue in the interim. Not when you have the plague.'

'The plague?' came the astonished response. 'But I am healthy.'

'That is not what your Mims are about to be told.'

Downstairs, Chaloner found some paint and slapped a large red cross on Pamela's door, at the same time informing her dismayed felons that anyone attempting to enter the house would certainly die of the pestilence – not the common form of the disease, but the nastier, more painful one, with pus-filled buboes and gangrenous limbs. They exchanged horrified glances and beat a prudent retreat. Not one thought to ask why the news should be announced by the man they had been trying to kill for the past few days.

Once they had gone, he went back inside and scribbled a note to Cary, telling him that Pamela was ready for collection. He was just waving it in the air to dry the ink when Ester arrived, fresh from her romantic stroll in St James's Park with Leybourn. Her sweat-streaked face and dusty clothes suggested that it had been a less than enjoyable experience.

'Is it true?' she demanded. 'Pamela has the plague? Just like Jasper?'

'Not quite like Jasper,' said Chaloner, and gave a brief account of his confrontation with her fellow Quaker, and the conclusions he had been able to draw. He supposed he should have been more cautious, given that he barely knew Ester, but he felt she deserved some explanation as to why her neighbour would soon be in Newgate. Moreover, he wanted Ester to know the truth lest Pamela spun a web of lies that would result in her being let out.

'Jasper kept insisting that she was involved in something nasty,' whispered Ester, shocked. 'But I thought he was just inventing excuses to leave her.'

'He did not need to invent them – not to anyone who knows her.'

'I meant inventing them to convince himself – he was not a man to abandon his duties lightly. Poor Jasper! He did his best, but eventually she exhausted even his kindly patience.'

She had exhausted Chaloner's within a few minutes of meeting her, and he secretly thought Jasper a fool for putting up with her for so long.

'I am glad that you have agreed to sort out the cathedral, by the way,' said Ester when he made no reply. 'Will, Matt and I got nowhere with our excuse for an investigation, and I sense that something bad will happen there soon.'

'So do I, but Pamela will play no part in it. It is a pity she knows nothing to lead us to the Executioner, though. Let us hope our other witnesses can oblige – Denton, Harbert's family, the canons . . .'

Ester held out her hand for the letter and the key to Pamela's door. 'I will take those to Mr Cary while you make a start. Clearly, there is not a moment to lose.'

The day was passing fast, so Chaloner hurried to Denton's lodgings above Outridge's Coffee House, trying to ignore the smoke that seared the back of his throat and the sun that beat down on his head. As he went, he ran through all the questions he wanted to ask about the spat with Harbert, and the tale Denton had invented about a hangman buried in St Paul's, when, all along, the Executioner was alive and busily poisoning his enemies.

Outridge's stood at the junction of Creed and Carter lanes, an unfortunate location that day, as it was inconveniently close to one of the great bonfires. The only upside was that if the belching smoke really was an effective way to eradicate the disease, then few places would be more thoroughly cleansed.

Thomas Outridge was a large, bluff man in his sixties, but his 'what news?' was wary, and Chaloner sensed that strangers were not welcome there, especially ones who entered coughing. Chaloner walked to where Denton sat with a dish of cold coffee in front of him. The Keeper of Fish looked up miserably, but made no effort to escape.

'You lied to me,' said Chaloner coolly. 'I have just seen Harbert's body. You delivered a serious blow, not the gentle prod you claimed.'

He was startled and acutely uncomfortable when Denton promptly burst into tears. The other patrons stared at him, but not for long – there were so many tragedies in the suffering city that a weeping man aroused scant curiosity. Chaloner waited until the sobs had subsided, then asked Outridge to pour Denton a fresh brew.

'Drink,' he said firmly. 'And then tell me what really happened.'

He took a sip from his own dish, but it had a peculiar flavour – it seemed that Outridge had compensated for the current dearth of beans by using alternative ingredients. He set it down in distaste, although Denton gulped his down, and some colour returned to his face.

'The story I told was mostly true,' he said eventually. 'Harbert *did* storm up to us with complaints about the bells, and he *was* so impertinent that I lost my temper . . .'

'But it was you who made the first hostile move,' said Chaloner. 'Yes, I know.'

Denton winced. 'I grabbed a stick and ran at him. I expected him to jig away, but he just stood there, so I ended up poking him much harder than I intended. He drew his sword then, and threatened to run me through, but he hobbled away when I feinted at him again.'

'So you lied to avoid a charge of murder,' surmised Chaloner.

'Yes, but to protect St Gregory's, not myself,' averred Denton, and hastened to explain when Chaloner looked sceptical. 'If I am accused of unlawful killing, Pemper will use it to harm the whole parish. He is a vile old scoundrel, whose spite knows no bounds.'

Having met Pemper, Chaloner was inclined to agree. However, Denton's tale had a lot of holes – the Keeper of Fish was still not being completely honest with him.

'Harbert had been criticising your ringing for years,' he said, 'so you must have been used to his tirades. What did he *really* say that induced you to attack him?'

Denton sagged in defeat. 'Fish,' he said in a strangled whisper, glancing around to make sure no one could hear. 'He mentioned my fish.'

'The ones in St James's Park?' Chaloner was bemused.

'He said that I killed them on purpose, but I never did! It was the sun – the water is shallow and the poor beasts were boiled alive. He threatened to write to the King, telling him that I dispatched them deliberately.'

'I doubt His Majesty would have believed such a claim,' said Chaloner, thinking that even if he did, he was unlikely to do anything about it. That would require effort, and His Majesty was an indolent man.

Denton sniffed to indicate that he disagreed, and poked some spilled sugar into a pile with a finger that shook. However, Chaloner knew that the Keeper of Fish was *still* holding back. For a start, Harbert's accusation was ludicrous, and would never have ended in a physical set-to between two men who were not natural brawlers.

'You did not kill anyone,' he said, watching Denton intently for his reaction to this particular piece of news. 'Harbert was hit over the head and poisoned, just like Gaundy.'

The relief that started to flood across Denton's face at the first half of Chaloner's revelation changed to horror at the second.

'No!' he breathed. 'Are you sure?'

Chaloner nodded. 'So unless you want to follow them to the grave, you must tell me what is really going on. I may be able to help.'

There was a moment when he thought Denton would lie again, but the Keeper rubbed a shaking hand across his face and began to speak in a voice that was raw with fear.

'I was rich once: I bred carp that were the talk of the country. Then war broke out, and the Roundheads came along and ate them all – although I managed to slip a few rotten ones in the oven, which resulted in several key generals being unavailable for an important battle. At the Restoration, the King appointed me Keeper of Fish – to reward me for my bravery.'

'You must have been pleased,' said Chaloner, wondering where the tale was going.

'Not really – it pays a fraction of what I earned from

my beautiful carp. My friends were also wealthy. Wildbore was London's leading fishmonger, Kirton's bookshop was the most celebrated in the city, and Gaundy was a master mason. The wars beggared us all . . .'

Slowly, Chaloner began to understand. 'That was back when Kerchier was persuading affluent men to help him rebuild St Paul's. You were all Agents of God.'

Denton nodded miserably. 'Kirton tells me that the society has been revived, but we have not been invited to join. Not now we are poor. Well, other than Joshua, who fared better than the rest of us when the Royalists took power, and is now Master of the Company of Stationers.'

'So how does all this relate to the quarrel with Harbert?'

'It doesn't – our quarrel really was about the King's fish. However, Harbert had strong opinions about the cathedral, and so did Gaundy. Perhaps Kirton is right to fear that the Executioner is at work again. He killed Kerchier twenty years ago, and now he is back.'

'It does appear that Kerchier, Upton, Gaundy and William were killed by the same hand. But so was Harbert and he was not an Agent of God – he wanted to preserve the cathedral as it stands, not pull it down and start afresh.'

Denton raised his hands in a shrug. 'Yes, but the Executioner is a deranged killer. His mind does not work like yours and mine, so it is no good looking for logic in his actions.'

'When we last spoke, you claimed that the Executioner does not exist, even going so far as to invent a tale about a hangman's ghost.'

Denton sighed unhappily. 'I believed it myself at the

time, but I have since reconsidered, and I think Kirton is right. The Executioner *does* exist, and he has set his beady eyes on me and my friends.'

'So who is he? A Maurice Man or a new Agent of God?'

'Or someone who hates both groups, and just wants to get his hands on all the cathedral's money. If you know what is good for you, you will walk away and leave the whole matter alone. It is just too dangerous.'

'I am afraid Dean Sancroft would not approve of that.'

'No?' asked Denton softly. 'Are you sure?'

His mind teeming with questions, Chaloner walked the short distance to Harbert's mansion. It was already showing signs that its master was no longer in residence: the glass in several windows was broken, weeds sprouted between the paving stones in the front garden, and the contents of the decorative flowerpots on the steps had been allowed to wither.

When no one answered his knock on the front door, he went to the back one. The kitchen window was open, and he looked through it to see four servants at a table, enjoying dried fruit, smoked meat, cheese and wine. As most Londoners had not seen such fine fare in months, he could only assume that they had raided their late employer's larders. None of them stopped eating when Chaloner entered and asked who was in charge.

'I am,' said a heavy-set man with a fringe. 'Henry Izod – Sir Arnold's steward. Why?'

Izod had adapted what had once been a smart livery to suit his personal comfort, and his appearance was as slovenly as his manners. His companions comprised a cook-maid who was so drunk she could barely sit upright; a groom in suspiciously lavish clothes that were more Harbert's size than his own; and a scullion who wore a solid gold necklace around her neck and rings on her fingers.

'Who owns this house now that Harbert is dead?' asked Chaloner sharply.

'His will has not yet been proved,' replied Izod with a smirk. 'And nor will it be while the plague rages, so we are minding the place for his heirs.'

'Thieves,' slurred the cook-maid, blinking hard as she tried to focus on Chaloner. 'The city is full of them, all desperate to take what don't belong to them.'

Chaloner glanced into the hallway beyond the kitchen. Marks on the walls showed where paintings had recently hung, and gouges in the marble floor told of furniture being dragged along it. Thieves were in the house already.

'You should go now,' said Izod, seeing what Chaloner was thinking and coming threateningly to his feet. 'We don't talk to strangers – they might carry the plague.'

'You will talk to me,' said Chaloner coolly. 'Because if you refuse, I shall report you to General Monck, who takes a very dim view of looters.'

'We aren't looters,' objected the scullion indignantly. 'We live here.'

'He will come with the inventory from Harbert's will,' Chaloner went on, 'which will itemise everything that should be here, right down to the last spoon. If anything is missing, you will be arrested for theft. And plague rages in the gaols.'

All four blanched.

'But that would not be fair!' cried the groom. 'Sir Arnold was a terrible master. He never paid us what we are worth, and he was unreasonable in his demands—'

'Such as not allowing us to drink on duty,' put in the cook-maid.

'—so we are within our rights to take what we are owed,' the groom finished.

'He was always searching our rooms to see if we had pinched anything,' said the scullion, quickly putting her be-ringed fingers under the table, out of sight. 'And he never gave us enough to eat. We would have left him years ago, but he threatened to give us bad testimonials if we did. He treated us like scum.'

'Perhaps we can reach a mutually beneficial arrangement,' said Izod, more canny than his fellows. 'There are a few things left that will fetch a pretty price. You may have them if you agree to go away and not return until Wednesday night – the day after tomorrow.'

'Why then?' asked Chaloner, although he suspected he already knew the answer.

'Because that is when we plan to leave the city,' explained Izod. 'Lots of people will go at the same time, and there will be safety in numbers – we have all heard the tales about villagers shooting strangers, lest they carry the sickness.'

'Not that they have cause to worry about us,' said the cook-maid. 'We have Certificates of Health, which means we are disease-free. I have them in here.' She patted her pocket.

'I doubt Monck's men will accept ones bought so far in advance,' remarked Chaloner. 'They are only issued on the day of departure, for obvious reasons.'

'Yes, but we will write in Wednesday's date just before we go,' explained the cook-maid blithely. The others made frantic gestures, warning her to silence, but she was too drunk to notice. 'Then they will be *new* documents, not ones that we have had for a couple of weeks.'

'Show them to me,' ordered Chaloner.

She started to refuse, but thought better of it when

288

he dropped his hand to the hilt of his sword. Reluctantly, and now aware of her cronies' dismay, she produced four documents. At first glance, they looked official, but the paper was the cheapest available, and the signatures of the physician and cleric were all but illegible. The date of issue and the name of the bearers were blank, and Chaloner had recently seen another just like it – the one that Lawrence's daughter had taken from Mrs Driver.

'How much did they cost?' he asked.

'A shilling each,' replied Izod, then added quickly, 'although we will not leave the city if we show any signs of the pestilence, of course.'

Chaloner pocketed them, earning himself four scowls, although he suspected that Izod would just go out and buy them some more.

'How long have you worked for Harbert?' he asked.

'About thirty years,' replied Izod warily. 'Why?'

'Then you will remember Canon Kerchier.'

Izod nodded with sudden eagerness, obviously hoping that Chaloner might be persuaded to overlook his misdeeds if he was cooperative. 'Oh, yes, very well, because Kerchier's friends accused Sir Arnold of killing him. He never did, though – Sir Arnold was nasty and mean, but never violent. Indeed, the very thought of fighting horrified him.'

'Did he ever talk about Kerchier's disappearance?'

Izod frowned as he struggled to remember. 'I think he once remarked that the devil had taken him to hell. He hated him for wanting to pull down old St Paul's in order to raise a new one, you see. But it was a very long time ago, sir . . .'

The others murmured that it was, and the cook-maid had to be reminded of who Kerchier was, although her blank expression showed that she was none the wiser when they had finished their explanations. Sure they had nothing useful to tell him about the bones in the crypt, Chaloner turned to another matter.

'What happened the day your master died?'

The groom spoke in a gabble, also desperate to ingratiate himself. 'He went after St Gregory's ringers with his tongue wagging like a fishwife's. He did it a lot, but Mr Denton must finally have had enough, because he hit Sir Arnold with a stick. Afterwards, Sir Arnold ran away.'

'I was watching through the window,' put in the cook-maid gleefully. 'And I laughed fit to burst. He sulked in his parlour for the rest of the day, drinking hard. He swore revenge, but he was dead by the morning. Perhaps it was the shame of being a coward that carried him off.'

'Did he have any visitors during that time?'

'No,' replied Izod. 'But he would not have let them in anyway – he was too angry.'

Chaloner regarded them sceptically. 'Were you all home when this was going on? Or did some of you slip out once he was too deep in his cups to notice?'

Izod indicated the groom and the scullion. 'We three might have nipped away for an hour or two, but Sir Arnold was not left alone, because she was here.' He pointed to the cook-maid.

Chaloner stifled a sigh as he addressed her. 'And how much of his wine did *you* drink, comfortable in the knowledge that he would later assume that he had had it himself?'

She eyed him belligerently. 'A cup or two – no more than I was owed by right. If he had not been so niggardly with it, I would not have had to quaff it on the sly, would I?'

So the house had been empty, apart from a woman who had almost certainly been drunk, thought Chaloner. The killer had entered unopposed, hit Harbert over the head, and dribbled poison between his lips as he lay senseless. It could not have been easier.

'Show me the room where he died.' Chaloner raised his hand to still the immediate clamour of objections. 'Or would you rather I fetched General Monck?'

He soon saw why they were reluctant to let him in the main house. Nearly all Harbert's belongings were gone, other than two ugly paintings, an ancient bureau and some books. The bedchamber had been stripped of anything remotely portable, including the hinges from the doors, and all that remained was a broken wine jug and a discarded jar of *sal mirabilis*. Chaloner picked the pot up carefully, and two of Prayse's crystals told him it had contained *acer*. The servants had followed, so he told them how their master had died, watching their expressions go from sullen resentment to alarm, terrified that they would be blamed.

'So who wanted him dead?' he asked.

'Lots of people,' replied Izod hoarsely. 'He was always saying unpleasant things, and he upset any number of folk.'

'His brother hated him,' put in the cook-maid, and her voice turned bitter. 'They had not exchanged a civil word in years, yet Sir Arnold still left Mr Matthew everything he owned. Of course, Mr Matthew does not know it, given that the will has not been—'

'Hold your drunken tongue, woman!' snarled Izod furiously. 'Do you *want* Mr Matthew to come here and throw us out before we are ready?'

'Why were they estranged?' asked Chaloner, watching

291

the cook-maid turn pale as she realised that she had revealed something she should not have done.

'We will tell you their history,' said the groom slyly. 'But only if you agree to stay away from Mr Matthew until Wednesday night.'

When they would have sold the last of Harbert's possessions, thought Chaloner in distaste. Fortunately, Izod saw the wisdom of continuing cooperation.

'They were never close,' he said quickly, shooting the groom a sharp look to shut him up. 'But the real rot set in over the cathedral. Sir Arnold loved it, but Mr Matthew thought it was an eyesore. Eventually, he joined a society that aimed to pull it down.'

'Matthew was an Agent of God?' asked Chaloner keenly.

'Yes, that *was* what they called themselves, now that I think about it,' replied Izod. 'Mr Matthew has always been richer than Sir Arnold, even though he is younger, and the society only enrolled very wealthy men. Sir Arnold inherited his money, but Mr Matthew earned his himself, by being a canny businessman.'

'He means Mr Matthew is a schemer,' put in the cook-maid. 'Him and his slippery friend George Antrobus. If there was even the hint of a scam, them two were in it. They did not join that society for the good of London or the cathedral, but to benefit themselves.'

It was fitting, thought Chaloner as he crossed the arid and very smoky expanse of St Paul's Churchyard, that the warring Harbert brothers should have chosen to live diagonally opposite each other: Harbert's mansion was just to the south-west of the cathedral, while Matthew's was just to the north-east. Their homes were as different

292

as any two buildings could be – Harbert's was old, venerable, dark and solid, while Matthew's was modern, light and airy.

Even a brief glance was enough to tell Chaloner that Matthew was rich. Lemon trees – an expensive import from Spain – stood in pots up the steps that led to the front door, all the windows had curtains rather than the more traditional shutters, and there was a private carriage in the courtyard. Its coachman carried himself with a lofty hauteur, and wore a metal breastplate and a helmet as part of his livery, to protect him as he drove past those who would resent such a brazen display of affluence.

As it was clear that Matthew could easily afford to leave the stricken city, Chaloner supposed he must have very pressing reasons for staying.

He was about to knock on the door when it opened and two men stepped out. They were dressed in identical suits of pale green with contrasting yellow lace, and they carried handkerchiefs that they flapped affectedly. Chaloner knew one was Matthew, as he was a younger version of the corpse in St Gregory's crypt. He was not surprised that this peacock and the dour Harbert had failed to stay friends.

'Servants go to the *back* door,' Matthew said curtly, as Chaloner approached, eyeing in distaste the spy's sweat-stained shirt and dusty breeches.

'I am Dean Sancroft's envoy.' Chaloner did not care what Matthew thought of his less than sartorial attire, as long as he answered his questions. 'Will you speak to me here or inside, out of the sun?'

'Neither,' retorted Matthew indignantly. 'We are busy.'

Chaloner put out a hand to stop him from pushing past. 'It concerns your brother.'

'I have no brother,' declared Matthew. 'And if you mean Arnold, he has been dead to me for years. Is that not so, George?'

George Antrobus, older and fatter than his friend, nodded. 'The only words they exchanged in three decades were hostile ones. Arnold was a foolish man who opposed any hint of progress.'

'Whereas I just *adore* anything new,' said Matthew, and allowed himself a small, proud smile. 'Indeed, it was I who introduced hand-painted wallpaper to London.'

Chaloner recalled the disaster in the Deanery. 'Not the best idea for a damp country, I would have thought.'

'There have been complaints,' acknowledged Matthew. 'But those are no concern of mine, as I never look back once a sale has been made.'

'Will *you* be leaving the city on Wednesday?' asked Antrobus, changing the subject abruptly. 'I recommend you join the planned exodus, because the only thing that awaits those who remain is certain death. How are you fixed for a Certificate of Health? We can arrange for one to be issued in your name if you like. For a price, of course.'

'Your brother was murdered,' said Chaloner to Matthew, aiming to bring the discussion back on track. 'Struck on the head and fed a poison that seared his innards. It was a terrible way to die.'

Chaloner was interested to note that neither man seemed particularly surprised by the news. Was it because they had hated Harbert and did not care that someone had snuffed out his life prematurely? Or could their lack of emotion be because they already knew exactly what had happened to him?

'But probably better than the plague,' said Matthew eventually. 'Which can take days.'

'And now we have an urgent engagement,' said Antrobus briskly, 'so you must excuse us. Perhaps we can chat another time, Mr . . .'

'Chaloner.' He glanced at the carriage. 'That is a nice big coach, with plenty of room inside, so I shall accompany you to your appointment, and ask my questions as we go. Then we will all be happy.'

Before they could disagree, he trotted down the steps and gestured for the driver to open the door. The fellow was too startled to refuse, so Chaloner climbed in and waited. There was a moment when he thought Matthew and Antrobus might decide their business could wait, but after a brief exchange of glances, they followed him in. Antrobus slapped the door with the flat of his hand, and the vehicle moved off.

The carriage was one of the most luxurious Chaloner had ever seen – more plush even than the Earl's. Its seats were padded in red velvet, while the springs were of such high quality that they absorbed all but the most severe of jolts. Unfortunately, they also resulted in an unpleasant swaying motion, and he wished he had not chosen to sit backwards.

'I shall not be pressing charges against Denton for my brother's murder,' announced Matthew, as if he thought he might have a say in the matter. 'Arnold almost certainly goaded him – he hated bells, and often railed against them.'

Antrobus agreed. 'Denton must have followed him home after the spat, where he did what you said – knocked him over the head and fed him poison.'

'Or Arnold's servants did,' mused Matthew. 'He treated them abominably, and it was only ever a matter of time before they could stand it no longer.'

'The only thing he loved was St Paul's.' Antrobus

shuddered fastidiously. 'I cannot imagine why. I mean, just look at it – it is nothing but a teetering ruin.'

'Yes, but have you seen what Wren wants to replace it with?' asked Chaloner, unable to help himself.

'A beautiful basilica with a lot of pretty white marble,' declared Antrobus. 'It will be much nicer to look at, and not nearly so shamelessly *sacred*. I find it tiresome to be reminded of religion every time I look out of my bedroom window at it.'

Chaloner could see there was no point in arguing with such rigidly held opinions. 'I understand you are Agents of God – men who aim to ensure that this basilica is built at it.'

'We are,' acknowledged Matthew. 'But it is a *secret* society, so how did you know?'

'People talk,' shrugged Chaloner. 'So tell me, which of your fellow members did Harbert especially annoy?'

'All of them,' replied Matthew promptly. 'And lots of others besides.'

'Including Denton,' said Antrobus, and smirked. 'He was an Agent once, but he is not as rich as he was, so he was not invited to reapply when the society was resurrected.'

'Resurrected by whom?'

'I cannot recall now,' said Matthew. 'Can you, George?'

'No, but it was an excellent notion, and I was delighted. So were the Hall brothers and Canon Owen.'

'Who else?'

Matthew wagged an admonishing finger. 'You just intimated that you know the other Agents' names already, so do not try to trick us into breaking confidences.'

'Not that we could tell you anyway,' said Antrobus.

'We usually communicate by letter, and we never meet in person. However, I do know that our membership currently stands at thirty-two. Most have gone to the country, where they will stay until the disease has burned itself out. Few folk are as brave as we are.'

At that point, the coach reached Ludgate, one of several places where Monck's men aimed to limit movement around the city. Chaloner did not hear what the driver said to the guards, but moments later, the carriage was on the move again.

'We have the right . . . connections,' explained Antrobus, seeing Chaloner's surprise at the ease with which the vehicle had been allowed through.

'Meaning you bribe them?' asked Chaloner in disgust, thinking it was small wonder that the plague had spread to other parts of the country, when rich folk considered themselves above the measures implemented to contain it.

'Of course not! We just know how to open doors. And gates.'

'We act for the good of London and Londoners,' put in Matthew defensively. 'After all, if commerce dies, the city dies with it, and how will that help anyone?'

'Is that why you stay on when virtually everyone else has gone?'

'We stay because it is the right thing to do,' declared Matthew piously.

'Of course, we would not advise anyone else to do it,' said Antrobus. 'If we were not involved in such *important* affairs, we would depart in an instant. Indeed, we have been busily recommending flight to anyone who will listen – including you.'

*

The rest of the journey was too punctuated by interruptions for further conversation. These arose not only from checkpoints, all of which were negotiated like the first, but from folk who did not have the luxury of hopping in a carriage to travel where they pleased, and resented those who did. They howled torrents of abuse as the coach rattled past, and when that provoked no reaction, bombarded it with stones.

'Are you sure your appointment is worth this risk?' asked Chaloner, after one particularly vigorous barrage. 'If your driver loses his nerve and runs away, you will have no mercy from these mobs. Even if you escape a trouncing, you run the danger of infection.'

'He is far too well paid to abandon us,' replied Matthew with conviction, and smirked. 'Besides which, we are in the process of arranging a safe haven in the country for his family. He will not dare risk that with cowardly behaviour.'

'Where are we going?' asked Chaloner, hoping it was not too much further. He did not have time for a long ride, and the swaying motion was making him queasy.

'Westminster,' replied Antrobus importantly. 'To visit General Monck.'

At that point, the driver decided that the best way to avoid further attacks was to go full pelt, so all was rattling wheels and violent rocking until they arrived at the palace gate. It was like a fortress, with armed men on guard and barricades across the road. A cannon stood nearby, ready to be rolled out and aimed up King Street in the event of trouble. A lot of people milled around outside, all dressed for travel with their worldly goods in packs over their shoulders. None were being allowed through.

'Certificates of Health,' barked the officer on duty as the carriage rolled to a standstill.

'Do you have one, Chaloner?' asked Antrobus sweetly, producing two handsome documents on thick, expensive paper. 'If not, you will be arrested and charged with spreading the plague – and rightly so.'

Chaloner smiled superiorly, and handed over the letter of authority that Sancroft had given him in Tunbridge Wells, although it was now badly creased and sweat had made the ink run. It was, however, on paper that was just as costly as theirs, and had the added advantage of being adorned with a big and impressive seal.

'I cannot read it,' objected the officer worriedly. 'Or see the date.'

'Today's,' lied Chaloner. 'And the signatories are Canon Hall and Dr Prayse Russell.'

The officer handed it back with a nod of thanks. 'You cannot be too careful these days. Three people have presented me with forgeries in the last hour alone.'

He stepped back and waved the driver through, much to the dismay of those who had been queuing for hours. Chaloner stuck his head out of the window as they rattled forwards, and saw that several guards had muskets at the ready. He had no doubt that they would open fire if there was any attempt by the crowd to rush them.

There was a fountain in the middle of New Palace Yard, an ornate structure with integral stone benches and a slate roof to shield it from the elements. No water tinkled in it that day, though, and when the coach stopped next to it, there was only silence. General Monck was lounging in its shade, jaws working determinedly on a plug of tobacco.

'This is where we part company, Chaloner,' said Matthew. 'Out you get.'

'But one final word of advice before you go,' put in Antrobus. 'Leave London and do not stop until you are a hundred miles away. Only then will you be safe from the plague.'

Chaloner alighted and made a show of walking away, then used a row of abandoned stalls to double back without being seen. He reached the fountain just as Matthew and Antrobus were perching next to the vigorously chewing Monck.

'Well?' Monck demanded with his customary gruffness. 'How many?'

'Eighteen,' replied Matthew, and handed over a sheaf of papers.

'Eighteen?' cried Monck angrily. 'I expected more than that. Do you not understand that they represent the end of our country and all that we hold dear?'

'Oh, come, General,' chided Antrobus. 'You give the matter an importance it does not deserve. But we shall continue our hunt, never fear.'

'Good,' growled Monck sullenly. 'Because otherwise we are all doomed.'

And with that, he stamped away, stopping only to direct a stream of brown goo at a waddling pigeon, and then to bawl a reprimand at a soldier for having the temerity to sneeze.

'Well, I am glad we risked our lives for *that*,' muttered Antrobus, climbing back into the coach. 'He was so grateful, and such pleasant, gracious company.'

'Risked your lives for what?' asked Chaloner, opening the opposite door and taking the seat he had vacated not long before.

Both men scowled to see him back again.

'I sincerely hope you were not spying on us,' said

Matthew indignantly. 'But if you were, you had better pray that Monck did not see you. He would hang you from the nearest tree, and good riddance.'

'Risked your lives for what?' repeated Chaloner, more forcefully.

'Revolutionary broadsheets, if you must know,' replied Antrobus irritably. 'Monck is afraid that they will inflame a city already in crisis, so he aims to gather them all up and burn them before they do any harm.'

Chaloner regarded him thoughtfully, sure they were not cooperating with Monck out of patriotism, but because they had some scheme in the making. But what? And was it relevant to his enquiries, or had he just happened across two of the most unscrupulous and self-serving men he had ever had the misfortune to encounter?

'Now get out, please,' Matthew ordered. 'We have carried you quite far enough.'

'Are you returning to the city?' asked Chaloner, leaning back comfortably. 'If so, you can drop me at the cathedral.'

'No, we are not,' said Matthew curtly. 'Now leave, before we tell Monck's soldiers to drag you out. And do not think the sight of your weapons will deter them. They are warriors, and there are far more of them than you can fight alone.'

He had a point, so Chaloner bowed a farewell and stepped out, although only to walk to the back of the coach and hop on to the rear footplate. And then they were off, rattling through the Westminster Gate, where they were waved through without having to stop. There was a howl of alarm when the officer noticed Chaloner, but the wheels were making far too much noise for the driver to hear.

*

301

The coach did not go far when it left the palace – just to St James's Park, which lay a short distance to the west. It was owned by the King, and the general public was kept out by high walls and iron gates. The driver jumped down, took a key from his pocket, and unlocked the main entrance. Then he drove to the edge of the straight, narrow strip of water called the Canal, and brought the vehicle to a standstill under the shade of a tree.

Chaloner was dismayed to see the park in such a sorry state. The rich, green meadows were now expanses of dead grass, trees wilted, weeds took the place of exotic shrubs, and the water level in the artificial lakes was far lower than it should have been. When he had last visited, the Canal had been thick with waterfowl, but the only bird that day was a solitary duck, which flew off with an irritable whirr of wings when it saw it was about to have human company.

The driver took a blanket from the roof and began to lay out a picnic, while Antrobus and Matthew climbed out of the coach and removed their shoes. Then they trotted barefoot to the Canal where they proceeded to paddle in its shallows, squealing their pleasure. It looked so refreshing that Chaloner decided to join them. He laughed when he saw their outrage. The driver stepped forward purposefully with a blade in his hand, but when Chaloner drew his gun, the fellow suddenly discovered a wheel that needed his undivided attention.

'Why will you not leave us alone?' demanded Matthew crossly. 'We have told you: we know nothing about my brother's death. Our paths had not crossed in years, and all I can say is that he was an objectionable man, who made himself many enemies.'

Chaloner waded further out, where the water was

cooler. Denton was wrong about his fish, he thought, detecting a flash of movement by his legs – they had not all been boiled to death. There were no large ones, but the smaller individuals had thrived, despite the heat, and the Canal was full of them.

'Come, Matthew,' sniffed Antrobus, taking his friend's arm and beginning to waddle up the bank. 'Dinner in the park has lost its appeal, and I want to go home – preferably *without* our stowaway.'

Chaloner had no intention of walking such a distance in the heat, or of devising ways around the various checkpoints, should his battered warrant be rejected. Reluctantly, he left the water, and forced his wet feet into his boots, while the driver hastened to fold the blanket and gather up all the elegant treats he had set out for his effete masters.

'Harbert named you his sole heir,' he informed Matthew. 'He left you everything he owned – money, house and possessions.'

'Lies,' declared Matthew contemptuously. 'He always said he would rather throw it all in the Thames. You will have to invent a better tale than that if you want me to believe you.'

Chaloner shrugged. 'Ask his servants. They have read his will.'

The pair exchanged a bemused glance.

'He might, you know,' said Antrobus quietly. 'He will not have forgotten that you are also his father's son, and you do not need me to tell you how seriously he took tradition.'

'I am his *sole* heir?' Matthew asked of Chaloner, still wary. 'But what about his retainers? Are they not to be rewarded for their loyalty all those years?'

'Apparently not,' replied Chaloner. 'But they will not depart empty-handed. They have already sold most of his furniture and they are in the process of—'

Matthew raced towards the coach and flung himself in, bawling at the driver to return to the city with all possible speed. Chaloner reached it just before the portly Antrobus, and settled himself in the forward-facing seat – he was not about to endure another bout of travel sickness by hurtling along backwards.

'You cannot come with us,' snapped Antrobus, trying without success to shove him out. 'Now remove yourself before I—'

'Leave him!' screeched Matthew, pounding furiously on the carriage door. 'Go. *Go!*'

The driver took off at such a lick that Chaloner almost ended up with Antrobus in his lap. He had intended to resume his interrogation en route, but it was impossible. They raced along at a breakneck speed, the driver yelling that they were on urgent business for Monck when the officers at the checkpoints tried to stop them. The general's savage reputation was such that none dared question the claim.

When they reached Harbert's mansion, Matthew and Antrobus jumped down from the carriage and tore inside, at which point Chaloner saw four people slinking down a nearby alley, all with bulging packs over their shoulders. The cook-maid made an obscene gesture to her erstwhile home as she went.

It was almost dark by the time Chaloner returned to the Mitre, and he was hot, tired and sticky. Paget's children had done their duty to his hens, which were safely ensconced in their coop, so he washed in a bucket of tepid water, donned clean clothes and set off for Cornhill, to check with Lawrence that Pamela had been collected and delivered to Newgate Gaol.

'Of course she has,' declared Abigail haughtily, as it was she who answered the door. 'We run an efficient business here, and the King should thank God for it, because there are not many who could manage this crisis as well as we.'

'Are your husband or Cary here?' asked Chaloner, thinking to give them a report of his discoveries that day.

'They are far too busy to lounge about at home. They will be supervising the fires. Or trying to quell the rumours about Wednesday's trouble. Or overseeing the distribution of food to the poor. Or—'

'Thank you,' interrupted Chaloner hastily, seeing the list might continue for some time. He bowed politely and took his leave.

He walked slowly towards Newgate, enervated by the sultry evening heat, although his senses were on full alert for any hint of danger. He stopped at Prayse's house on the way, where Thurloe sat at a table piled high with the reports he had commissioned from his vast network of informants.

'Would you like me to help you sift through those?' Chaloner offered.

'I can manage, thank you.' Thurloe grimaced. 'Most of them will transpire to be irrelevant anyway. Where are you going?'

'To Newgate. Pamela Ball is incarcerated there, and I should question her again, to see if she can tell me any more about her benefactor – the Executioner.'

'Leave her until tomorrow, and have an early night instead,' advised Thurloe. 'We shall need all our strength for the coming days, and you look exhausted.'

'And you are not?'

Thurloe gave an uncharacteristic chuckle, and Chaloner was suddenly assailed by the realisation that he was enjoying the opportunity to play at being spymaster again – unlike Chaloner himself, who just wanted to go home to bed.

'Do not worry about me, Tom. I have never felt better. Goodnight.'

# *Chapter 10*

Despite his weariness, Chaloner slept badly in the stifling heat, and fell into a deep sleep just before dawn, which meant he rose later than he should have done. Paget's children had already seen to his hens, so he ate a hurried and peculiar breakfast – pickled herrings and marchpanes – before setting off for the Deanery. Smoke continued to billow from the bonfires, and the whole precinct was thick with fug.

It was only just nine o'clock, but the day was already scorching, and he was startled and distressed when a sparrow fell dead to the ground in front of him. He glanced up, and saw a line of panting birds on the window sill of the house he was passing.

He knocked at the Deanery door and was admitted by Bing, who wore nothing but a clerical hat and a pair of boots. Chaloner supposed it was one way to stay cool.

'Stone, Stone, Stone,' the violist chanted. 'Speak to him, if you dare. He will tell you all about his old friend Kerchier.'

'I would love to,' said Chaloner testily, 'but no one knows where he is.'

307

Or even if he is still alive, he thought, recalling what Thurloe believed about the missing canon.

'Sweet kisses and promises,' sang Bing. 'The one who drives will know. Stone will not return until he has drunk deeply of the medicine of life.'

Chaloner watched in bemusement as Bing released one of his high-pitched giggles and gyrated off down the corridor. Like a demented acrobat, he thought sourly, wondering how the man had the energy for such antics on so oppressive a morning.

Bing's agitated cackling had attracted attention, and Tillison came to see what was going on, accompanied by Henchman and Cartwright. Henchman had evidently been out in the sun, because the pink parts of his face were red, and the white parts pink. By contrast, Cartwright was cool, debonair and handsome, despite the heavy vestments he was wearing in readiness for his daily duties at the altar.

'Go and play an air, Bing,' suggested Tillison kindly. 'It will soothe us all.'

Chortling, Bing scampered away, and a few moments later came the strains of a melody by Ferrabosco. All else flew from Chaloner's mind. As he had noted the first time he had heard it, the viol was unusually fine, but in Bing's hands, it became extraordinary. Tillison was droning on about the unseasonable weather, but Chaloner had ears only for the music, and followed it to a small room near the kitchens.

Bing sat on a stool, his face serene as he bowed. Chaloner closed his eyes, and was immediately transported to a place of such unmitigated delight that it was a shock when the playing stopped and the exquisite sound was replaced by Henchman's plaintive whine.

'Bayhurst's Lozenges are getting very difficult to come by, and the shortage is pushing up the price. If it continues, I shall have to sell some books to raise the money.' There was a pause, and the voice turned accusatory. 'Under normal circumstances, I would borrow from the cathedral, but its coffers are empty, thanks to you.'

'We had no choice,' said Tillison, the asperity in his voice suggesting that this was not the first time the subject had been aired. 'Pemper's death was the last straw, and we had to do something immediately.'

'Pemper?' blurted Chaloner, music forgotten. 'The bell-ringer? He is dead?'

'Killed by falling masonry,' explained Cartwright. 'It was his own fault. We closed the south transept off after Flower was struck by a piece of ceiling, but Pemper elected to ignore our barriers and that was the end of him.'

'I witnessed the mishap with Flower,' said Chaloner, recalling the old man's yelp when the plummeting scrap had landed on his head. 'So did Pemper.'

'The suspicion is that he thought his rival ringers from St Gregory's were in there, so he went to drive them off,' Tillison went on. 'However, they were all in Outridge's Coffee House at the time, with a dozen witnesses to prove it.'

'How do you know that is what he thought?'

'Because of me,' explained Cartwright. 'I happened to be passing at the time. I heard a shout, which sounded like "Wildbore", followed by a nasty cracking sound. I found Pemper with his brains dashed out and the offending lump of stone next to him.'

'Was anyone else with him?'

'He was alone – the poor fellow's eyes must have deceived him. Fortunately he has no kin to sue us for damages, but someone else might, so we have invested in some proper barriers now.'

Henchman eyed Tillison coolly. 'Rigid and very expensive barriers.'

'Are you sure it was an accident?' asked Chaloner. 'Bearing in mind the number of murders recently, all of which have involved blows to the victims' heads?'

'Oh, yes,' replied Cartwright confidently. 'As I told you, the piece of ceiling was lying right next to him, covered in his blood.'

'But someone could have picked it up from the floor and hit him with it,' Chaloner pointed out. 'God knows, there are enough bits to choose from.'

'Someone could,' acknowledged the vicar. 'But no one did. I was on the scene very quickly, and I saw no crazed killer looming over his latest victim.'

Chaloner regarded him thoughtfully. Cartwright seemed oddly unmoved by the death of a man he must have known well, and his tone was almost mocking. Was he telling the truth, and Pemper really had been in the wrong place at the wrong time? Or had *he* dispatched the old ringer with a convenient scrap of masonry, confident in the knowledge that there were no witnesses to his crime?

'Perhaps we *should* let Wren rebuild,' said Tillison unhappily. 'I love the old place, as you know, but we cannot have it killing our people. And you are right, Henchman: it is proving costly – for our own purses, as well as its own.'

'No, no – I would rather die a pauper than let Wren have his way,' gulped Henchman hastily. 'So let us say no more about it.'

'I know how to raise some much-needed cash,' declared Cartwright. 'By appointing *me* to Kerchier's stall. If you do, I shall donate every penny of my stipend to the cause – after subtracting a few necessary personal expenses, of course.'

'Whereas John Hall will use the money to support Wren,' mused Henchman. 'And their faction already has a fortune at its disposal. You are right, Cartwright. We should get you in post as soon as possible. I shall write to Sancroft again today.'

'Their faction?' asked Chaloner innocently. 'Do you mean the Agents of God?'

Henchman scowled. 'I see you have heard of them. It was an exclusive society founded by Kerchier, but it disbanded in disgust when he and their rebuilding fund disappeared together. Unfortunately, some rogue recently suggested that they reform – probably because the money in their coffers is now near the level it was at when it was stolen.'

'I take it you disapprove?' fished Chaloner, noting that there was real strength in the treasurer's pink and white hands.

'Of course,' declared Henchman. 'Wealthy laymen like George Antrobus, Matthew Harbert and their ilk have no business meddling in cathedral affairs. The Hall brothers and Owen should not encourage them. It is very wrong.'

'And those who back the Maurice Men with donations?' asked Chaloner. 'Should they be told not to meddle in cathedral affairs, too?'

'That is different,' said Henchman stiffly. '*We* have its best interests at heart.'

'Tell me about the Executioner,' said Chaloner, aware

that Cartwright was listening to the interrogation with unabashed interest, while Tillison was growing visibly alarmed by Henchman's intemperate replies. Bing only chortled to himself, rocking back and forth over his viol. 'The man who has murdered several of those who professed a desire to see your beloved cathedral demolished – Kerchier, Upton and Gaundy, to name but three.'

'Do not call him that,' ordered Tillison sharply, and his faded blue eyes were suddenly cold and hard. 'It serves to aggrandise his crimes, whereas the truth is that he is just a common criminal.'

'I agree,' said Henchman, and could not resist adding, 'although it is hard to condemn him for targeting those who aim to destroy St Paul's.'

'He jests,' said Tillison quickly, shooting the treasurer a warning glance. 'But why did you come here today, Mr Chaloner? How may we help you?'

'By telling me where I might find Stone.'

'We *have* told you,' said Henchman irritably. 'He is with his sister.'

'I have it on good authority that both his sisters are dead.'

Tillison smiled serenely, a beneficent old man once more. 'I doubt Stone lied to me, Mr Chaloner, so your "good authority" must be mistaken. However, he is due home today, so any misunderstandings about his whereabouts can be corrected then.'

'Then I should like to speak to Francis and John Hall instead,' said Chaloner, supposing it was time to tell the two clerics how their brother had died – assuming that they did not already know, of course.

'They are in the library with Wren's model,' said Henchman. 'Come, I shall take you.'

At that moment, Bing started to play again, so Chaloner stepped towards him, wanting a closer look at the instrument, but Bing jumped to his feet and pushed it behind him, as if to pretend it was not there. Unwilling to make a scene, Chaloner backed away, supposing he would have to inspect it another time – and inspect it he would, because he now knew exactly what Bing's 'dark past' entailed, and the viol would provide the evidence to prove it.

Francis and John were standing over Wren's prototype cathedral, talking in low voices to Owen, although all three fell silent when Henchman ushered Chaloner towards them. The treasurer did not stay, but the hair on the back of Chaloner's neck rose, and he was sure that Henchman was eavesdropping from behind the nearest bookcase.

'I am ill,' John announced, although he did not look it – unlike Owen, who had unnaturally bright eyes and flushed cheeks. 'Sick from taking *sal mirabilis*.'

'Why would you do that?' asked Chaloner suspiciously. 'You are one of those who believes that London Treacle is the only reliable preventative for the plague.'

'Yes,' acknowledged John loftily. 'But I felt compelled to give my allowance to a desperate parishioner. I took *sal mirabilis* instead, but it made me sick all night.' He gestured to a row of pots that had been set on top of Wren's peculiarly truncated model nave. 'I confiscated these from the choir, lest it did the same to them, but there are plenty more out there, waiting to harm others.'

Chaloner picked one up and dropped some of Prayse's crystals into it, but nothing happened. It did not contain *acer*, not even in its diluted form.

'Everyone knows that *sal mirabilis* is dangerous, John,' said Francis, watching Chaloner in mystification, but too proud to ask what he was doing. 'You should not have touched it. We cannot afford to lose a hard-working vicar.'

'I shall not do it again,' vowed John. 'However, it has proved once more that the only real remedy for the plague is London Treacle.'

'Did William take London Treacle?' asked Chaloner innocently.

Francis exchanged a brief and uncomfortable glance with his brother. 'Yes, but he died because he stood at the pits all day, reciting prayers for the dead. He was a brave man, and will be sitting with God and His angels as we speak.'

'Not even London Treacle can repel the foul miasmas that seep from mass graves,' added John. 'William's courage cost him his life.'

'He did not die of the plague,' said Chaloner, speaking softly so that Henchman could not hear; he smiled inwardly when there was a low hiss of frustration. 'He was killed by a blow to the head and poison – just like Kerchier, Upton, Harbert and Gaundy.'

The three clerics stared at him. He stared back, but could read nothing in their faces other than shock. Owen was the first to find his voice.

'How do you know?' he asked in a strangled whisper.

'His body was examined by a physician,' replied Chaloner, 'and the evidence was unequivocal. Will you tell me what happened the night he died?'

'He came to see us when he had finished in the church-yard,' began Owen, gripping the edge of the table for support. 'He was happy, because so many folk had made

314

donations for our new cathedral. He went home to count them . . . it was the last time I saw him alive.'

'John and I found him dead three hours later,' said Francis, whose face was as white as snow. 'At first, I assumed he was asleep. We could scarce believe . . . He had been laughing a short time before, joyfully showing us all the coins he had been given.'

'Like you, he was an Agent of God,' said Chaloner, and raised a hand when all three started to deny it. 'I know the society exists, because I have spoken to other members.'

'Who?' demanded John angrily. 'They are supposed to keep it secret.'

'Talk to me,' urged Chaloner. 'Help me find William's killer – the Executioner, if you will – before he dispatches anyone else.'

'How can we?' asked John sullenly. 'We know nothing useful to tell you.'

'Then show me the place where William died.'

The three exchanged more glances, after which John indicated that Chaloner was to follow him. Chaloner did, calling a jaunty farewell to the bookshelf as he went, just to let Henchman know that his eavesdropping had not gone unnoticed.

William had lived – and died – in the area just north of the churchyard, in a pleasant lane named Canons' Alley. He had occupied a sturdy, stone-built house with narrow windows, and when John unlocked the iron-studded front door the process required three separate keys.

'As you can see,' the vicar said, 'it is both private and very well protected.'

'It is,' agreed Chaloner, noting that the door could be

315

secured from within by four bolts and a bar. There was no other entrance on the ground floor, and even he would have found burgling it a challenge. 'Did he install these measures because he was entrusted with the Agents' money?'

John nodded. 'We did not want a repeat of what happened to our last hoard.'

'Which disappeared with Kerchier,' put in Owen, lest Chaloner should have forgotten. 'But it would have to be a very resolute burglar to get in here. And even if he did manage to enter the house, he would still have to fight his way past the gate to the cellar, which, as you can see, is unusually thick.'

Chaloner bent to inspect it, and saw deep gouges in the wood, showing that a determined effort had been made to hack through it. 'Yet someone has tried.'

'Yes,' acknowledged Francis stiffly. 'But William never mentioned it, so we can only assume that it happened after he died. It is why we moved the chest to another safe location – lest the rogue came back to chance his hand again.'

'The Deanery,' surmised Chaloner, recalling the conversation he had overheard from outside it, including the astonishment of the others that William had managed to augment their fund so handsomely.

Francis's lips tightened. 'It will not stay there – not if all and sundry know about it.'

'It is in no danger from me,' Chaloner assured him fervently. He had encountered vast sums of money before, and knew that no good ever came of them.

Owen addressed the brothers thoughtfully. 'We assumed that William died of the plague, forgetting to secure the front door in his delirium, so that an opportunistic thief followed him in here. But we were wrong: the rogue *killed* him in order to get inside, and we were lucky the cellar door is strong, or our money would now be gone.'

'Then the culprit is a Maurice Man,' said John tightly. 'One of *them* killed my brother and tried to steal our money – to squander on shoring up that worthless old ruin.'

'So how did he get inside the house?' asked Chaloner. 'It would be next to impossible to enter uninvited.'

'By pretending to be a friend,' replied John promptly. 'He must have claimed that he wanted a chat or had news to impart, and William trustingly believed him. Then once the rogue was inside . . .'

The three clerics watched in silence as Chaloner explored every inch of William's home, taking his time and working with meticulous care. It was scrupulously clean and surprisingly modest for a man who had earned a handsome stipend. There was a shelf for books, but it was empty, and when he raised enquiring eyebrows, John explained that they had been sold.

'For the new cathedral. We cannot expect others to give generously when we live in luxury ourselves. We pass every available shilling to the cause.'

William had breathed his last in his bedchamber, a dark, cheerless space with bare walls and a stone floor. There was nothing to show that violent death had occurred there, except some tiny droplets of blood on the door, coughed up as the poison had gone to work.

Adjacent to the bedroom was an office with a table that was piled high with papers. Chaloner rifled through them. Most were covering letters for donations, some large enough to take his breath away, which made him realise for the first time the true extent of the funds involved.

And at the bottom of the heap was a piece of paper bearing the familiar picture and words: *Mind the Executioner*.

'When did this arrive?' he asked, showing it to Owen, John and Francis.

'Last week,' replied Francis. 'We all had them, although I threw mine away. It is a paltry attempt to intimidate by some idiot of a Maurice Man.'

But Owen was staring at Chaloner in horror. 'You think it is genuine – that it came from the real killer? My word! Should I hire a bodyguard? Leave the city?'

'You cannot go,' said Francis sharply. 'None of us can – it is what our enemies want. We will *not* let them win this war, Owen. We owe it to William to stand firm.'

Owen looked as though he could not have stood firm to save his life.

It was noon by the time that Chaloner bade farewell to the three clerics. He trailed them back to the Deanery, trying to eavesdrop on their conversation, although with no success, as they spoke in low, hissing voices. At one point John laughed, which seemed an odd reaction so soon after being shown how his brother had been murdered.

'I do not like them,' came a surly voice at his side. It was Cary, who had come from the nearest bonfire. Its flames were not as high as they had been the previous day, although it still belched smoke at an appalling rate. 'They are sinister.'

'William Hall is dead,' said Chaloner, noting the lines of exhaustion etched in the secretary's smut-smeared face. 'Did you hear?'

Cary nodded. 'Of the plague. I saw him presiding at the pit on Sunday, which is something he had never done before. Doubtless he heard that Lawrence and Monck planned an official inspection that day, and aimed to impress them with his diligence and compassion.'

'*Were* they impressed?'

The secretary curled his lip. 'They praised him prettily enough, but I doubt they saw his efforts as any more heroic than those of the brave souls who have been doing it since the sickness first arrived. The rector of Christ Church has conducted more than four hundred funerals, while the vicar of St Katherine Cree digs graves himself, to spare his vergers.'

Chaloner moved to another matter. 'Thank you for taking Pamela Ball to Newgate, by the way.'

Cary shot him an irritable glance. 'I am still waiting for the guards to send word that she is home. I suppose I should have checked on them, but these bonfires . . . well, they are under control now, but it was touch and go for a while. Besides, I cannot put Dean Sancroft's business first *every* time, and it is unfair of you to be facetious with me.'

Chaloner blinked. 'I was being sincere – Abigail told me that Pamela was arrested.'

'Did she?' Cary was equally taken aback. 'But how could *she* know what . . . It will not be *her* fault. You must have phrased the question poorly. Or mumbled.'

Chaloner knew he had not. So why had she lied? Because she was loath to admit that she had not known the answer, so had made an assumption based on the fact that her husband and Cary were usually very efficient? Or was there a more sinister reason?

'I will speak to her,' Cary went on, looking pleased by the prospect. 'I am sure she will explain how you came to misunderstand what she told you.'

'You should speak to your guards, too,' said Chaloner, torn between amusement at Cary's reckless devotion and annoyance that he had been misled. 'Because they had drunk themselves insensible when I went to King's Head Court yesterday. Pamela had arrived home unnoticed by them, and was in her house.'

'So *you* took her to Newgate?' asked Cary, confused.

'I questioned her, then locked her in one of her bedchambers, ready for you to collect.'

'Then I doubt she will be there now. Her Mims will have let her out.'

'They think she has the plague,' said Chaloner. 'Or they did – I did not anticipate that she would have an entire night to convince them otherwise. I sent Ester Nay to you with a message and the key to the door.'

'The alchemist's sister? I have not seen her. Of course, she would have been hard-pressed to find me yesterday, given that I was haring all over the city.' Cary grimaced his irritation. 'I suppose we will have to go to King's Head Court now, on the off-chance that Pamela is still there, although do not hold your breath.'

'I will not,' muttered Chaloner acidly, falling into step at his side and silently cursing Abigail's antics.

'And when we have finished, London must manage without me for an hour,' said Cary, making it clear that Sancroft's enquiry was both a nuisance and an imposition, 'because I am going home for a nap. I am so tired I can barely think. Lawrence is the same, but he says tonight's music at the Mitre will restore him better than sleep.'

'It will restore me, too,' averred Chaloner, brightening at the prospect.

'While you waste time warbling, I shall trawl the

taverns again. We *must* learn more about what is planned for tomorrow – a concerted assault on the gates by hundreds of people, yes, but I have the sense that something darker and even more unpleasant is brewing.'

'Such as what?'

'If I knew, I would not have to skulk in alehouses to find out, would I? Hah! Look who is coming towards us: Ester Nay herself.'

Chaloner's stomach gave a peculiar twist when Ester rested her hand on his arm by way of a greeting. It felt pleasantly warm through his sleeve. Then he reminded himself sternly that she was Leybourn's intended.

'Chaloner says you have a message for me,' said Cary pointedly. 'And a key.'

'I gave them to one of your men,' replied Ester. 'He would not let me near the bonfire where you were working because he said it was dangerous, but he promised to hand them to you at the earliest opportunity. Surely he did not forget?'

'You did not watch, to make sure he did it?' asked Chaloner, unimpressed.

Something unreadable flickered in Ester's eyes. 'I tried, but there was too much smoke. What a rogue! He had better hope I do not see him again – I shall give him such a scolding.' Then she smiled. 'I met Mr Thurloe a few minutes ago. He sent me to say that he wants to see you immediately. Go to him – I can accompany Mr Cary to King's Head Court.'

'That will not be necessary,' said Chaloner shortly. Then, loath for her to know how disgusted he was, added, 'There are questions that only Pamela can answer, so I need to speak to her again myself as soon as possible.'

'Do not waste time on a woman who has already told

321

you everything she knows,' said Ester dismissively. 'Concentrate on the mystery surrounding the cathedral instead – the one you promised to solve for Will and my brother.'

Chaloner was sure he had done no such thing. 'Not until Pamela is—'

'Mr Thurloe wants to see you *now*,' said Ester, and gave him a shove. 'Will you ignore the urgent summons of a friend? Go!'

Chaloner could have argued further, but Ester was right: overseeing Pamela's arrest was not as important as finding out what Thurloe wanted. He nodded a farewell, watched her and Cary hurry away together, then aimed for Carter Lane.

Prayse's house was stifling, because all the windows were closed in an effort to keep out the smoke. Thurloe was in the parlour, looking hot, cross and perplexed.

'I have just learned that Upton had a message from the Executioner,' he reported tersely. 'I managed to trace one of his friends, who was there when he opened it. The friend saw the words and the drawing – he described them to me minutely, so there can be no doubt.'

'I see. Is that why you sent Ester to fetch me?'

'No, I wanted you to come because Prayse has gone. He has taken all his most valuable possessions and his travelling cloak. I think he has left the city.'

'Who can blame him? I do not want to be here myself.'

'But I am his guest! Why did he leave no message explaining his intentions? Would *you* decant to another place if I was staying with you?'

'Well, no,' acknowledged Chaloner. 'But I would not charge you rent either.'

Thurloe grimaced. 'Prayse has always been . . . thrifty. But he is a Quaker, and they consider the plague to be a test of their faith, so he would never abandon London willingly. I have a bad feeling that our investigation may have put him in danger, and I am concerned for his safety.'

'Perhaps he did leave a message, but you have not found it. Let me look.'

While Chaloner hunted, he told Thurloe all that had happened since they had last met.

'Cary is recklessly enamoured of Abigail,' mused Thurloe when he had finished. 'He will take the blame for the misunderstanding over Pamela, rather than see Abigail embarrassed. And Abigail has always bragged that she knows all her husband's business, regardless of whether or not it is true.'

'Then let us hope her conceit has not cost us Pamela,' said Chaloner acidly. 'Because if Pamela has escaped because of her . . .'

He trailed off as he found something that had slipped behind the clock on the mantelpiece – a single piece of paper that had been closed with a blob of bright red sealing wax, now broken. He unfolded it to reveal the familiar diagram and accompanying words of warning.

'But I saw that delivered,' said Thurloe, clearly bemused. 'Prayse and I were sitting here, chatting about old times, when the maid brought it in. He broke the seal, read it, finished our discussion and excused himself. He gave no indication that it was anything to unsettle him.'

The maid was summoned, but the missive had been left on the doorstep, and she had not seen it arrive. She had taken it to her master, who had summoned her half an hour later, and ordered her to help him pack.

'Pack?' echoed Thurloe. 'So he *has* gone? Without saying a word to me?'

'He told me to mind the house until he returns,' she replied. 'And to make sure that you are comfortable. I am to clean your room and launder your clothes, but only cook if you give me the money for food and fuel.'

Chaloner turned away to hide his smile, amused by the physician's dogged parsimony.

'He said nothing about where he is going?' pressed Thurloe, less inclined to see the funny side of the situation.

The maid shook her head. 'Only that he might be gone for some time – perhaps until the plague is over.'

She could tell them no more, and Thurloe nodded to say that she was dismissed.

'I do not understand,' he said, for at least the third time. 'Why did he not tell me what he was doing? His behaviour makes no sense.'

'Perhaps he was afraid that you might urge him to stay and do his duty,' shrugged Chaloner. 'Or he was angry with you for putting him in the Executioner's sights. Of course, you and I have been sent no such messages, and we are the ones investigating the man . . .'

'But the Executioner *did* send them to you,' argued Thurloe, 'in the form of Pamela and her murderous Mims. Poor Prayse! I should have stayed at an inn, not foisted myself on him. But a friend's house seemed so much safer than a tavern . . .'

At that moment, the maid reappeared to conduct Leybourn and Ester in to see them. Leybourn was his usual ebullient self, delighted to have his latest lady-love on his arm, but Ester was obviously distressed.

'It is Pamela,' she blurted. 'She is dead.'

Chaloner regarded her guiltily. 'Not because she was locked up for hours in a hot house with nothing to drink?'

'Of course not! I sent victuals up to her in a basket before I went to find Mr Cary with your note and the key.'

'You saw to her comforts, even though she killed Jasper?' asked Chaloner sceptically. 'Your brother's much-loved assistant?'

Ester regarded him with such reproach that remorse speared through him. 'I am a Quaker, Thomas. We leave vengeance to the Lord.'

'So what happened to her?' asked Thurloe, more interested in facts than recriminations.

It was Leybourn who replied. 'I joined Ester and Cary when I learned where they were going. We all trooped up Pamela's stairs, but when we reached the bedroom, it was to find the door wide open and her dead on the floor.'

'Usually, I would have noticed anyone visiting her house,' said Ester unhappily, 'But Jasper's death has left my brother without an assistant, so I have been out delivering medicines to the sick for him.'

'There was froth on Pamela's lips,' Leybourn went on, 'and it appeared that she had been drinking from these.'

He handed Chaloner two pots, one labelled London Treacle and the other *sal mirabilis*. Chaloner tested them quickly, and discovered *acer* in the *sal mirabilis*, although the London Treacle was innocent. When he had finished, Ester picked up the bottle of London Treacle and studied the label in puzzlement. Then she sniffed the contents carefully.

'This is not London Treacle!' she exclaimed in sudden anger. 'Someone has put together a lot of rubbish and is passing it off as the real thing!'

'How can you tell?' asked Leybourn.

'I know my brother's goods. First, this label is an inferior imitation – the image of the cathedral is blurred and the ink has smudged on the lettering. And second, whatever is in the pot stinks of urine. Matt would never use urine in something that is meant to be swallowed.'

Leybourn shook his head in disgust. 'The depths to which some folk plummet! Making counterfeit medicines indeed!'

Chaloner was surprised it had not happened sooner, given that there was an enormous demand for the stuff and Rycroft was struggling to produce enough of it. He moved away from Ester, because he was growing rather too aware of the musky scent of her body.

'Well, it is irrelevant to Pamela's death,' he said briskly. 'The *acer* was in the *sal mirabilis*, not the London Treacle.'

'She would never have taken *sal mirabilis* willingly,' said Ester. 'She knew that London Treacle was better. Ergo, someone must have fed it to her by force.'

'Just like the other victims,' mused Thurloe, looking at Chaloner. 'The Executioner must have wearied of sending her poison that she kept feeding to other people, so he reverted to his tried and tested methods. I do not suppose you noticed her head, did you, Will?'

'I noticed that it was still attached,' replied Leybourn, not very helpfully.

But Ester was more concerned with the fake London Treacle. 'We must locate whoever made this rubbish and stop them. People will swallow it in the expectation that it will protect them, but it will not, and they will die.'

'Take it to your brother,' suggested Thurloe. 'Ask him to analyse its contents. Perhaps that will allow him to identify the source.'

'Let us hope so,' said Ester tightly. 'Of course, it will take up time that he does not have to spare . . .'

'I had better visit Pamela's house,' said Chaloner, 'to see if the Executioner left any clues as to his identity. He has been careful so far, but he will make a mistake eventually.'

'I will help,' offered Ester. 'As soon as I have taken this vile substance to Matt.'

Chaloner smiled his thanks.

'We shall all go,' determined Thurloe, so firmly that Chaloner had the uncomfortable sense that the ex-Spymaster knew of his growing attraction to Ester and disapproved of it.


Pamela had been found sprawled on the floor, but Ester and Leybourn had picked her up and laid her on the bed, to preserve her dignity. There was white foam on her lips, and a quick inspection revealed the trademark blow to the head. The brace Chaloner had put across the door had been removed, and the lock smashed. There was no sign of a struggle, and the room was almost exactly as it had been when he had last been there – the only differences being the body on the bed and a handgun that sat on the window sill. The dag was an elegant piece designed for a lady's smaller hand. It was loaded, and he wondered why Pamela had not used it when her killer had arrived.

'Perhaps she thought he was coming to rescue her,' suggested Leybourn. 'Meaning that she knew him, and trusted him not to harm her.'

'Not necessarily,' countered Ester. 'She was an arrogant woman with an inflated sense of her own worth. If a stranger came to open the door, she would merely have assumed that he was doing it because she was Pamela Ball. It might never have crossed her mind that she was in danger.'

'I think it would,' argued Chaloner. 'She had received two written warnings from the Executioner, and he had twice sent her poison. She most certainly *was* on her guard.'

'Which would have dropped the moment the killer made a flattering remark about her importance,' stated Ester. 'It would not have been difficult to convince her that he was an admirer. Believe me – her vanity knew no bounds.'

Chaloner was not sure what to think, but was disinclined to waste time debating the matter. He searched the rest of the house quickly, but discovered nothing useful. He was about to suggest that they leave when there was a sudden hubbub, and Mims began to pour through the front door.

'Have you found it?' demanded one. When Chaloner looked blank, the man added impatiently, 'Mrs Ball's hoard. Have you found it?'

'No,' replied Chaloner. 'But she died of the plague, so you should not be in here. You might catch it if you paw through her—'

'We won't, because she never had it,' interrupted the Mim, and jabbed a finger at Leybourn. '*He* told us she was murdered, so do not think to frighten us away with lies a second time. All you want is to find the cash and keep it for yourself.'

Before Chaloner could deny it, the man hurried away to open cupboards and haul out their contents. Crashes and thumps from the other rooms suggested the same was happening in them.

'I thought telling the truth might help us catch the killer,' explained Leybourn defensively, when Chaloner and Thurloe turned accusingly to him. 'And Ester said it was a good idea. Unfortunately, no one saw a thing.'

The Mims were not the only ones interested in locating Pamela's hoard, and within a very short space of time the house was packed with people from far and wide. When her fabled wealth failed to materialise instantly, some folk decided to avail themselves of her belongings instead, so there was soon a steady stream of items being toted through the door. Repelled by such brazen criminality, Thurloe drew breath to put an end to it.

'No, let them be,' said Ester, putting out a hand to stop him. 'Pamela and Jasper have no more need of it, and these folk have little to call their own. What harm can it do?'

'It can destroy evidence that might lead us to the Executioner,' said Thurloe tightly.

'There is nothing here – if there were, you would have found it,' countered Ester. 'And you should not waste time on futile undertakings when you have the cathedral business to sort out. Your energies should be focused on that now.'

'They are,' retorted Thurloe coolly. 'Because the best way to resolve that particular problem is to identify the Executioner. He lies at the heart of all this trouble.'

'Does he?' asked Ester archly. 'Or is he a clever hoax – something thrown into the mix to lead you astray – which is what my brother believes. And Matt is not usually wrong. *He* is a very clever man.'

'Ester and I will continue looking for clues here,' said Leybourn quickly, before Thurloe could take the last remark as an insult, 'while you and Tom go back to whatever you were doing before we came to tell you about Pamela.' He turned to Chaloner. 'Lend me your gun.'

'Not likely,' said Chaloner, disliking the notion of a firearm in the surveyor's clumsy paws. Leybourn was more likely to shoot himself than an opponent, and would almost certainly forget he had it in the blind terror of an attack.

'Come on,' said Leybourn impatiently. 'You do not need it, not when you carry a sword and God knows how many knives. Besides, you are always telling me that you do not trust dags. Give it to me – you will not miss it.'

'Yes – he should have some protection,' put in Ester. 'Or do you want him in danger?'

Chaloner was certainly loath for her to think he did. However, he was not about to hand over the powerful weapon that Cary had given him, so he lent Leybourn the smaller one from the window sill instead.

'It is loaded,' he warned, then leapt away in alarm when the surveyor grabbed it by the barrel. 'Christ! Are you sure you know how to use it?'

'Point and shoot,' replied Leybourn glibly, shoving it into his belt with such reckless insouciance that Chaloner was sure he would emasculate himself before the day was done.

'Where will you go now?' asked Thurloe, once they were away from the hectic stripping of Pamela's house. His plague mask hid his face, but there was no mistaking the anger in his voice – he was livid that Ester's intervention had prevented them from conducting a more thorough search, and nor had he appreciated her challenging his conclusions.

'The Deanery,' replied Chaloner. 'To confront Bing with the evidence of his "dark past" – which I shall threaten to make public unless he tells me what he knows about Stone, Upton and the rest of it.'

'Blackmail?' asked Thurloe in distaste.

'Bing has information that might lead us forward, and Ester is right about one thing – time *is* running out. We do not have time for games, so Bing will share what he knows, in a way I can understand, or he will suffer the consequences.'

'Then I shall come with you,' determined Thurloe. 'Neither of us fared very well with Bing singly, so let us see what we can achieve together.'

It was nearing six o'clock – Chaloner had spent much longer than he had intended at King's Head Court. The evening sun drenched the city in hot red rays, while the smoke seemed thicker than ever, and when he saw one old woman gasping for breath, he wondered if the fumes would kill more people than they saved.

Bing answered the Deanery door himself, although this time he wore shirt and breeches with his clerical hat, so Chaloner supposed that someone had remonstrated with him for performing his duties virtually naked. Sweat had made the ink run around his eyes, with the result that his cheeks were streaked with black rivulets.

'Stone, Stone, Stone,' he chanted, jigging up and down. 'He is the one.'

Chaloner pushed past him and aimed for the room where the musician had played not long before. The viol was leaning against a wall, and Bing released a wail of distress when Chaloner took it in his hands.

'No, no, no!' he howled. 'She is mine, mine. Not for the likes of you.'

'No,' agreed Chaloner, inspecting the instrument closely. 'She is far superior to anything I am ever likely to own. Cartwright said you had a secret that involved William Turner, and now I know what it is.'

'You do?' murmured Thurloe irritably. 'I wish you had mentioned it sooner, Thomas. I just paid half a dozen spies to work out the answer to that particular question.'

'William Turner is dead,' wailed Bing, panic writ clear in his face. 'There are no secrets in the grave. Oh, no, no, no!'

'He was a viol-maker,' Chaloner went on, ignoring them both. 'Among the best in the world, and this is one of his finest creations. I recognised it when I heard you play earlier.'

'Oh, no,' groaned Bing, squatting down on his haunches and covering his head with his hands. 'The devil is out, out, out.'

'She will have cost a fortune, but copyists earn a pittance, and you have no wealthy patron to help you. Which means that you raised the money yourself – by sly means.'

Bing stood to look levelly at him, and suddenly he seemed perfectly sane. 'Oliver Cromwell was going to buy her – a Puritan, who deplored joyful music. I could not allow her to fall into such hands. No, no, no! What if he had later decided that viols were an affront to God, and ordered her destroyed?'

'He would never have done that,' said Thurloe, very coldly. 'He had a deep appreciation for beautiful things, and we often had music in his court.'

'He did not have a *court* – he had a gaggle of fanatics,'

countered Bing. He took the viol from Chaloner and ran loving fingers over its silky wood. 'And besides, she was made for Ferrabosco and Lawes, not dull devotional dirges.'

'So how did you outwit Cromwell?' asked Chaloner, cutting across Thurloe's indignant denial. 'By offering the seller a higher price?'

Bing closed his eyes briefly. 'A colossal sum,' he whispered, 'which I borrowed.'

'Borrowed from the funds that Kerchier had amassed?'

The violist nodded. 'But he never knew, because I took it the night he vanished. I was going to confess to him the following morning – he would have understood. Oh, yes, he would. But he disappeared, and everyone assumed he was a thief, a thief, a thief.'

'Yet even a fabulous instrument like this does not cost as much as a cathedral,' mused Chaloner. 'You did not steal the entire hoard, did you?'

Bing's expression was haunted. 'I did not *steal* any of it – I was going to repay every penny. I took what I needed, and was just leaving his house when I heard a strange thump behind me. Terrified, I ran away, away, away. In my haste, I neglected to secure the door . . .'

'Allowing someone else to take advantage of what you left unprotected,' finished Thurloe harshly. 'Which means that the theft may be wholly unrelated to the killings, and we have been barking up the wrong tree for the past five days.'

'You have been trying to make amends ever since,' said Chaloner, watching Bing's face fill with guilt and shame. 'You never left the cathedral's employ, even though you could have earned a fortune at Court. You have done something else for it recently, too – Sancroft.'

333

'Sancroft?' queried Thurloe.

'It was Bing who wrote to him about the skeleton in St Gregory's,' explained Chaloner. 'He guessed at once that the bones were Kerchier's, and when we first met, he said, "I love truth, but no one can ever know it." It was his way of telling me that *he* was the anonymous informer.'

Bing grinned, and suddenly the wildness was back. Or was it? Chaloner was no longer sure what to make of the man. 'Poor mad Bing. Who will ever guess?'

'You have told us several times to speak to Stone. Tell us what you think he knows, and we will leave you in peace. No one will learn from us what you did to get your viol.'

Bing considered, assessing the offer for loopholes or traps. Eventually, he nodded. 'Very well. There is a secret that connects St Gregory's to the cathedral, and when you know what it is, all will become clear. Kerchier once confided it to Stone, but Stone changed teams after Kerchier disappeared – he went from Agent to Maurice Man.' He giggled shrilly.

'What secret?' asked Thurloe, irritated by the violist's annoying manner.

'Kerchier never told me. Nor did Stone, Stone, Stone. Although he will share it with you if you ask.' Bing's face turned hard again. 'Especially if you bludgeon him, as you have bludgeoned me.'

'You will know when I have bludgeoned you, believe me,' said Thurloe coolly. 'And we cannot interrogate Stone, because he is almost certainly dead. You will have to do better than that if you want us to keep your confidence.'

'Stone *will* tell you,' cried Bing, distressed. 'He is *not* dead. He has just gone to drink the medicine of life –

sweet kisses and promises. You know what sort of man he is.'

Chaloner struggled to decipher the garbled revelations. Stone had told his friends that he was going to visit a sister, but they were no longer alive, which meant he had lied to conceal what he was really doing – something that entailed 'sweet kisses and promises'. Chaloner shook his head in disbelief as realisation dawned.

'You think he has gone off with a woman?'

Bing gave another high-pitched cackle. 'The one who drives.'

It was a phrase he had used before, and Chaloner was about to recommend that he speak in plain English before tempers frayed, when understanding came.

'Mrs *Driver*? Stone is cavorting with her?' He turned to Thurloe before Bing could reply. 'It is possible – I did once see them sneaking off together for an assignation. She *did* give him "sweet kisses" and he "promised" her an emerald necklace. She is also missing. Or at least, she has been unavailable to Lawrence, who has been asking after her for days.'

'Stone took her away,' sniggered Bing. 'Lustful Stone. He never could resist a handsome lady. But he will be sated soon, because not even the one who drives can keep *him* entertained for long. Now do what you agreed and leave me be.'

He reached for the viol and began to play, a soulful air that accentuated the fine quality of the instrument for which he had sacrificed so much. The music told Chaloner what words never could – that the confession had done nothing to lighten Bing's burden of guilt and he remained a soul in torment.

\*

335

That evening, while Thurloe settled down to read more reports, Chaloner decided to take a leaf out of Lawrence and Cary's book by visiting coffee houses and taverns, to see if he could learn anything about the mischief that was planned for the following day. Unfortunately, most were very poorly attended, and their patrons were more interested in keeping their distance from each other than exchanging news and gossip.

He soon gave up, and returned to the Mitre, where the Musick Hall was beginning to fill with guests. He stood in the shadows and watched, surprised by how many of them he had met since his arrival in the city just five days before. Some were on his list of suspects, although that was rapidly growing shorter as the Executioner picked them off one by one. Chaloner concentrated on those who remained.

First, Owen, who had brought a cask of wine with him, and was busily serving it to the others. He downed a cup himself for every one he poured for someone else, leading Chaloner to wonder if he was just a hopeless drunk or if he hoped that the claret would grant him a respite from his worries – whatever they might be.

Vicar Masley – not on the list, as he had not been in London at the time of Kerchier's death – was chatting to Antrobus and Matthew, who were. The pair had donned matching puce suits for the occasion, and Chaloner could smell their flowery perfume from the door. Henchman was with the St Gregory bell-ringers, although conversation was evidently strained, as the canon's smile was fixed, while the others looked uncomfortable and clearly wished they were somewhere else.

But no one did or said anything to help Chaloner's

investigation so, bored, his attention drifted to the other guests instead.

Not far away, Lawrence kept glancing hopefully towards the door, although Abigail's satisfied smirk suggested that she knew her rival would not be coming through it. Chaloner wondered if she had done something to encourage Stone to whisk Mrs Driver away. He threaded his way through the throng and went to talk to her.

'You assured me that Pamela had been arrested and taken to Newgate,' he said, not bothering to keep the accusatory tone from his voice. 'But she was not and now she is dead.'

'Plague?' asked Abigail, carelessly and without a flicker of remorse. 'She should have taken her London Treacle.'

'She did not die of the plague – she was murdered. It is a pity you lied to me, because if you had told the truth, she might still be alive.'

'I did not lie,' objected Abigail indignantly. 'I probably just did not hear you properly. You have a tendency to mumble and I am a very busy woman.'

She flounced away before Chaloner could ask why her hearing or his diction should be influenced by how much she had to do. However, there was clearly no point in pressing her further, so he went back to watching the other guests again.

'Pace yourself, man,' Masley was advising Owen. 'The last time you drank too much, you sang some very lewd lyrics to "Beauty Sat Bathing", which embarrassed us all.'

'Oh, please do it again,' chortled Antrobus. 'I had not laughed so much in weeks.'

'It was the funniest—' began Matthew, but stopped

337

when he saw Chaloner listening. His expression grew guarded, and he looked the spy up and down in distaste. 'I had not taken you for a madrigal man. I would have thought tavern songs were more to your taste.'

Chaloner knew he cut a less than sartorial figure – his shirt was dappled with smuts from the bonfires, his boots were dusty, and he had ripped a hole in his breeches while searching Pamela's house. Nonetheless, he resented the slur on his musical integrity.

'How was your inheritance?' he shot back. 'Was anything left?'

Matthew declined to be baited. 'The house will fetch a pretty penny, but the rest was rubbish anyway. Arnold had shocking taste, and the servants deserve some reward for putting up with him all those years. Have you packed to leave yet? You should do it soon, because all hell will break loose tomorrow.'

'The bonfires are the last straw,' put in Antrobus. 'People have been deprived of food, wine and medicine, but now they have lost access to clean air as well. They will leave en masse, and there will be nothing the authorities can do to stop them.'

'We shall depart for greener pastures soon, too,' said Matthew. 'So this is the last time we shall speak. I cannot say that knowing you has been a pleasure.'

He minced away, Antrobus and Masley at his heels. Then Chaloner saw someone else he knew – Leybourn and Ester. He weaved through the gathering towards them.

'Did your extended search of Pamela's house yield anything new?' he asked.

'Yes,' replied Ester, pursing her lips angrily. 'A huge cache of "London Treacle", which she had hidden down her well. My brother will analyse it tonight, but I suspect none of it is the genuine article – she was selling counterfeit wares to innocent Londoners.'

'Of course, anyone looking at the labels should be able to tell,' added Leybourn. 'They are so cheaply printed that the ink has smudged on every one, so that *London Treacle* reads *London Treade*.'

'There was no sign of her money,' finished Ester. 'Although the Mims continue to hunt for it as we speak. Shall we sing now? Time is passing.'

Ester transpired to be a rich alto, and Chaloner was more than happy to join her in a duet. He enjoyed it so much that he suggested another, but then a messenger arrived from Rycroft. Jasper had not yet been replaced, and he needed his sister's help with his next batch of medicine.


'You and Widow Nay sang well together, Chaloner,' remarked Lawrence, a short time later. 'It is a sign that you would do other things well together, too. You are a widower, are you not? That is a sorry state for a man – he should have a woman. So woo her.'

Chaloner laughed. 'I think Will Leybourn might have something to say about that.'

'He is a good man,' acknowledged Lawrence. 'But he is not the one for her. He sings like an old saw for a start, despite his claims to the contrary. If you have any liking for her – or for him – you will prevent such a disastrous union.'

Chaloner was startled by the blunt advice. 'It is hardly my place—'

'Life is short,' interrupted Lawrence. 'And none of us should reject opportunities for happiness. Take her away from this place of death and suffering. Tonight, preferably, before tomorrow's mischief falls upon us.'

Chaloner regarded him askance, the pitfalls of such a scheme running through his mind, not least of which was that Ester would object to being spirited away by a man she barely knew. 'Will would never forgive me.'

'Perhaps not, but Widow Nay would come to appreciate the wisdom of your actions in time. Here – have a slice of this fine cheese. We all know that cheese makes a man amorous, and it might encourage you to follow my advice before it is too late.'

Chaloner was sure it would do no such thing, but he took a piece for the sake of civility. He did not eat it, though, as there was still singing to be done, and dairy produce was bad for the voice.

'I did not know that cheese was still available in the city,' he remarked.

'It was a gift from a well-wisher.' Lawrence looked at the lump that was halfway to his mouth, then put it back on the plate untasted. 'Although it is difficult to enjoy such things without feeling guilty. I had better wrap it up and give it to the poor tomorrow. Perhaps a show of kindness will induce them to refrain from storming the city gates in the evening.'

'I have a bad feeling that nothing will dissuade them from that.'

Lawrence winced. 'I fear you may be right. Ah, here is Val.' He lowered his voice. 'I know he has a surly temper, but his heart is solid gold. He is a marvel, and I do not know how I would manage without him.'

Chaloner suspected he might have to try soon, because Cary was grey-faced with fatigue and was clearly nearing the end of his endurance. The secretary rallied when his eye lit on Abigail, though. He patted his thin ginger hair into place and stood a little taller.

'Well?' Lawrence asked him. 'What happened?'

'The malcontents *were* wagging their tongues in the Turk's Head,' Cary reported. 'They wore masks to hide their faces, but I recognised the voices of three: George Antrobus, Joshua Kirton and that stupid apprentice with the hump . . . I forget his name.'

'Randall,' supplied Chaloner, looking around to see that Antrobus was no longer in the Musick Hall, and nor was Matthew. Then it occurred to him that he had not seen either since the singing had started. Had it been his questions and insinuations that had driven the pair out of the Mitre early to cause trouble elsewhere?

'What did they say?' Lawrence was demanding. 'Exactly?'

'That we have no right to keep folk in this "City of Death" and that everyone should leave tomorrow evening after the plague service, which is at eight o'clock.'

'Did they advocate doing it violently?' Worry was etched deep in Lawrence's face.

'Randall did, but the other two advised buying Certificates of Health instead, on the grounds that Monck's men will be forced to accept them if they are presented by the hundred. They are right – Monck cannot check every one properly, and many will be forged.'

'Lord!' muttered Lawrence. 'What wretched timing! Monck started to reject them all, but it caused such outrage that I convinced him to reconsider, and a public announcement to that effect was made not an hour ago. We cannot retract it now – there would be a riot for certain. Damn these bloody troublemakers!'

At that moment, Abigail bustled up.

'Come and sing "Tobacco is like Love", dear,' she ordered. 'You need to laugh, and so do the girls. There will be time enough for weeping tomorrow.'

She tugged him away, and Cary watched them go with glistening eyes, clearly wishing it was he who had been invited instead.

'You should rest,' said Chaloner, wondering if the secretary worked so hard to take his mind off his aching heart.

Cary scrubbed at his face. 'I am almost too tired for sleep. Perhaps you can recommend a good book that will help me nod off. One you read at Cambridge, perhaps.'

'I did not read any good books at Cambridge,' said Chaloner, surprised that Cary should think he might, especially as the secretary had been a student there himself. 'But try *Institutes of the Lawes of England*. That should have you dead to the world within a few minutes.'

Lawrence and Abigail began to sing at that point, so Chaloner went to listen. Then the cathedral men performed a round in five parts, after which Masley managed a reasonable rendering of two songs from *The Book of Ayres*. Eventually, the strains of the last piece died away, and Lawrence announced that it was time his daughters were in bed. They wailed their disappointment, and Chaloner felt like joining in.

When the Mitre had emptied, Chaloner wished he had a copy of *The Lawes of England* himself, because his mind was far too active for repose. Not only was it full of questions about his investigations, but he was confused by his feelings for Ester, and there was the alarming knowledge that the following day might see an uprising in which sick people would pour out of the city to infect the whole country.

His room was unbearably stuffy, so he rose and went to the window. Moonlight streamed in, bright enough for him to see that a jug of wine had been set on the table beneath it. He frowned. Paget had not provided such a service before.

He took one of Prayse's crystals and dropped it in the jug. It began to fizz.

# Chapter 11

The knowledge that someone was still determined to dispatch him, even though Pamela Ball was no longer in a position to provide Mims for the purpose, meant that Chaloner did not rest easily that night. He started awake at every creak and groan, and eventually gave up trying to sleep. He went to sit in the window instead.

It was still dark, but the moon and the great fires illuminated the lofty bulk of the cathedral. He gazed at its elegant spires and pinnacles, trying to understand why anyone would want to pull it down. Or was he being as foolishly inflexible as Harbert, who had let the issue drive a wedge between him and his only brother?

Thoughts of Harbert led Chaloner to consider the other deaths, too, beginning with Kerchier, then moving to Upton, Gaundy, William, the Edwards boys, Jasper, Pemper and finally Pamela. Ten deaths: two canons, a stationer, a verger, an alchemist's assistant, a bell-ringer, a Quaker, a knight and two Mims. Three of the murders could be laid at Pamela's door, but who had killed her? And was the Executioner someone who wanted a new cathedral or was it the Agents' money that had caught his eye?

Chaloner lay on the bed, closed his eyes and reviewed everything he had learned to date, not just relating to the cathedral, but the city as a whole. Painstakingly he discarded rumour and supposition, and kept only facts. When he had finished, he had no specific answers, but a much clearer picture of what was happening. It seemed to him that it all boiled down to two separate but inter-woven issues. First, whether the cathedral should be repaired or rebuilt, and second, the looming trouble that would peak after its special plague service, which was partly aggravated by the high cost of its London Treacle.

He rose and went to the kitchen for something to eat, but decided against it when he discovered several dead rats in the pantry. He started to back out, but then stopped and inspected the rodents more closely. Teeth-marks scarred a number of items, including the piece of cheese that he had accepted from Lawrence the previous night – he had left it in the pantry before retiring to bed, thinking that one of Paget's children might like it. Every one of the little corpses had froth in its mouth.

He fetched Prayse's crystals and it did not take him long to deduce that the cheese had been impregnated with *acer*. He stared at it uneasily. He would have eaten the stuff if he had not been cognisant of the fact that it might affect the quality of his singing. And Lawrence had only demurred after Chaloner had made a chance remark about the scarcity of such victuals, bringing on an attack of guilt. The mayor had then expressed an intention to take the rest of it home for the poor.

Sincerely hoping that Lawrence was not in the habit of distributing alms before dawn, Chaloner left the Mitre and pelted along Paternoster Row towards Cheapside. A massive bonfire was burning near St Mary le Bow, so huge that it would have been a serious impediment to traffic had there been any. Flames leapt high into the air, fed by masked men, all of whom were coughing furiously.

He reached Lawrence's mansion and pounded on the door. It felt like a very long time before it was answered by a sleepy maid. Without pausing to explain, he shoved his way past her, only to be met by Cary with a handgun.

'Oh, it is you,' said the secretary, shoving the weapon back in his belt. 'I thought it was a mob come to lynch us. Whatever is the matter?'

'What is going on?' came an anxious voice from behind them. Lawrence was on the stairs, bare-chested and holding a poker. 'Are we under attack?'

'Yes – from poison,' said Chaloner, and explained what had happened.

Lawrence was pale with horror. 'But my girls . . . Rachel loves cheese. She might have gone to the pantry during the night and . . . I offered some to you, Chaloner! Christ God!'

'The Executioner is ruthless,' said Chaloner, when they had taken out the offending plate, and more of Prayse's crystals demonstrated that anyone sampling the cheese would have suffered the same kind of lingering agonies that had killed Jasper. 'He does not care about incidental casualties.'

Lawrence grasped his shoulder gratefully. 'I shall never forget this, Chaloner. I am in your debt, and so are my daughters.'

'I am, too,' said Cary, when the mayor had gone. His face was unnaturally white. 'Abigail might have had a bite, and then where would we have been? The city needs her.'

'What are you doing up so early?' asked Chaloner, itching to say that it needed Lawrence more. He still had

346

not forgiven Abigail her lie about Pamela being in custody.

Cary scowled sourly. 'I could not find a copy of *The Lawes of England*, so sleep eluded me. I was working when you arrived, reading reports from our spies.'

'About the trouble that will erupt tonight?' asked Chaloner.

'There will be marches, attacks on warehouses, riots and looting. Oh, and a mass exodus – Londoners have been buying Certificates of Health by the hundred, and nearly all of them are forgeries.'

'They will be irrelevant if the gates are stormed – a mob will not stop to show the guards its papers.'

'If that happens, Monck will deploy his cannon,' retorted Cary. 'So let us hope everyone comes to their senses before there is a massacre.'

The first glimmers of dawn were showing in the eastern sky as Chaloner hurried back to the Mitre, and he was aware that the mood of the city was changing before his eyes. More people were out than he had seen since he had arrived the previous Thursday, and there was an air of sullen expectation. Folk gathered in clots, muttering in low voices. Most wore scarves over their faces as a defence against the plague and the smoke. Anonymity emboldened them.

He stopped to buy a sack of overpriced barley, a large lump of gristly meat, six onions and a carrot, after which he took all the old food from Paget's pantry and dumped it in the midden at the end of the lane. Then he let his hens out and watched them hunt for tasty titbits by the compost heap, knowing it would be his only moment of peace in a frantic day.

As they scratched, he heard the clink of metal. A

moment later, it happened again, and he saw that their busy claws had excavated a pewter sixpence. The coin dated from the Commonwealth, and bore an inexpertly stamped image of Cromwell. A minute later, the big brown bird made another discovery, this time of a penny from the same era.

Many people had buried money in their gardens during those turbulent times, and he supposed the coins were part of a hoard. He poked about with a stick, but the ground yielded no more hidden treasure. He studied the grubby items in his hand. No tradesman would accept them as legal tender now, but Thurloe might like them as a memento of headier times. He slipped them in his pocket.

'A parcel has arrived for you,' said Landlord Paget shortly afterwards, crouching by the fire to stir the stew made from the ingredients that Chaloner had provided. His family clustered around him, eyeing the pot with hungry eyes.

'Has it?' Chaloner was at the table, composing another progress report to Sancroft. As an addendum, he could not resist saying that he had identified Bing as the man who had initiated the investigation with his unsigned missive. He did not state directly that Sancroft's decision to withhold the information had wasted valuable time, but the dean would have to be very stupid not to understand the rebuke in the words.

'A book with a note from the dean,' explained Paget. 'Mad Bing brought them while you were out with your chickens.'

Chaloner took the proffered package. It had been sent 'care of' the cathedral, and the wrappings were suspiciously loose – Paget was not the only one who had taken the liberty of looking inside. He glanced at the Bishop-mark – the stamp in the corner that told him when the parcel had been received by the Post Office. It was dated several days earlier, and he wondered what had caused the delay. The reluctance of post-boys to bring mail to the capital? Or the time it had spent being investigated by inquisitive clerics?

Inside was a short note ordering him to peruse the book carefully, as it might mean the difference between life and death. The tome was *The Plague's Approved Physitian* – one of the inexpensive editions printed on cheap grey-brown paper, intended for those without much money to spare. It had been produced in Oxfordshire, where its author was not obliged to put his advice to the test personally.

'Sancroft need not have bothered,' sniffed Mrs Paget. 'Mayor Lawrence bought hundreds of those with his own money, and gives them to anyone who will take one home and follow its advice. I could have got you a copy for nothing.'

It fell open to the list of remedies that were considered worth the expense: Oil of the Heathen God, Doctor Trig's Great Cordial, Dragon Water, Red Snake Electuary . . .

'I still say London Treacle is the best,' remarked Paget, peering over Chaloner's shoulder to read it. He raised his hand when his wife started to argue. 'I know you prefer *sal mirabilis*, dearest, but that is now deemed poisonous. It has killed several people, including Verger Gaundy, Sir Arnold Harbert and that mouthy Quaker woman . . .'

'Pamela Ball?' asked his wife. 'Good! It is her fault that the plague is here – she and her fellows told God to send it, so they could prove their faith. I heard them say so myself.'

'Not quite,' countered Chaloner, although he should have known better than to challenge a bigot. 'What Quakers actually maintain is that facing the plague without flinching is a sign of their trust in God. They certainly did not ask for it to—'

'I know the truth,' interrupted Mrs Paget shortly. 'The Quakers *are* responsible for all this death and misery. But they will not get away with it, because revenge is in the offing.'

'What do you mean?' demanded Chaloner uneasily, thinking of Ester.

'You will see.' Mrs Paget folded her arms to indicate that the discussion was over.

'Of course, now that *sal mirabilis* is out of favour, everyone is clamouring for London Treacle,' sighed Paget. 'Which means that not only has it grown scarce, but it is twice as expensive as it was last week. Hah! The stew is ready.'

It was not ready at all, and comprised a lot of half-cooked meat and crunchy vegetables. Chaloner ate it only because he did not want to face the day on an empty stomach. The moment he had finished, he hurried to his room, closed the door and slit open the spine of *The Plague's Approved Physitian* with a knife – he had understood perfectly the hidden meaning in Sancroft's terse message.

Inside, tightly rolled, was another letter. Sancroft began by expressing his sadness that the skeleton should have been Kerchier's. He had not been in London when the canon had disappeared, but he knew the tale, and had immediately put two and two together. He had not confided his suspicions, he went on, because he was loath for Chaloner to begin an investigation with preconceptions that might later transpire to be wrong.

'If he does not trust me to make sensible judgements, he should not have appointed me as his envoy,' muttered Chaloner to himself, irked.

Next, Sancroft listed all the men he knew to be Agents of God, most of whom were with the Court at Oxford. None were a surprise – all were wealthy and eager to please the King, so helping to fund a new cathedral was exactly the kind of scheme that would appeal to them.

The missive concluded with something that Sancroft had learned from the Earl of Clarendon – that several Agents had received messages *urginge them most stronglye to give all the moneys they cann, so that the Almightye's Wille maye be done upon St Paule's Cathedral. The message was embossed with a Gibbett, and all were warned to Mynd the Executioner's words on Perill of Death.*

So, mused Chaloner, the killer *was* interested in the fate of the cathedral, and he wanted a new one. Absently, he wondered how many Agents would rethink their membership of the society when they learned that the threat of death was not an idle one, and that others who ignored the Executioner's orders were already in the graves.

He left the Mitre and hurried towards Prayse's house, aiming to show Sancroft's letter to Thurloe. That day, the bonfires had been loaded with debris scoured from the banks of the Fleet River, which transpired to be excellent at producing thick, reeking grey fumes, much to the satisfaction of the men in charge. The smoke was so dense that the far side of the churchyard was completely lost to sight.

St Gregory's tenor bell began to toll as Chaloner

passed. He glanced towards the church, and supposed that Stedman was ringing it, as Kirton, Denton and Wildbore were standing outside, chatting to mourners. They made themselves scarce when they saw him looking their way. Then he noticed Ester and Rycroft aiming for the cathedral's west door, so he altered course to intercept them. They were pulling a handcart, which was piled high with crates. Both were pale and had dark rings under their eyes.

'We worked all night,' explained Rycroft wearily, stopping to massage the small of his back. 'Now that folk think *sal mirabilis* is poisonous, there is a huge demand for my treacle, and the canons say we are duty-bound to meet it.'

'Which is not easy without Jasper,' sighed Ester. 'I do my best, but I am no substitute for a skilled assistant.'

'This is the next batch.' Rycroft nodded at the cart. 'Ready not a moment too soon, as Owen says that some of his newer customers are very aggressive in their demands for it.'

'Probably because they are Mims,' surmised Chaloner. 'I heard Suger say that they were reluctant to come here themselves, because of some incident with a poor box, but now that Pamela is dead, they will have no choice.'

'I wonder if they will pay for it with money from her cache,' mused Rycroft. 'They conducted such a thorough search of her domain yesterday that they are bound to have found it. Personally, I think the canons should refuse to sell them any medicine until they replace what they stole – if they do have the hoard, they can easily afford it.'

'They can,' agreed Easter. 'Because I saw it once, and it comprised a fortune – Pamela was a very wealthy lady. Jasper hated the way she kept it all for herself, which is why he gave his own wages to the poor. He never wanted to be a Quaker, but he was a better one than she could ever hope to be – ethical, kind and generous.'

'I tested all the potions from her house, by the way,' said Rycroft. 'Her *sal mirabilis* contained *acer*, as you know. But her London Treacle was nothing of the kind. It contained urine and other rubbish, with tobacco juice to give it the kind of bite that makes gullible customers think it must be doing them some good.'

'Is it harmful?' asked Chaloner uneasily.

'Well, I would not drink it myself – you should see what it does to lice – but it will not kill anyone, if that is what you mean.'

'But that is not the point,' interposed Ester, full of righteous indignation, 'which is that anyone taking it will not be protected against the plague. It is a terrible thing to have done – an outrage that beggars belief.'

'Pamela must have sensed that her crimes were close to being exposed,' Rycroft went on, 'because she had planned to leave today. Show him the document you and Leybourn found, Ester.'

'Oh, yes,' said Ester. 'We forgot to mention it last night.'

She rummaged in her sleeve and produced a Certificate of Health, made out to Pamela Ball, and printed on cheap, grey-brown paper. It bore that day's date, and carried the signatures of Prayse Russell and Canon Stone.

'A forgery,' declared Rycroft, although Chaloner did not need to be told.

The page was so thin that he could see something had been written on the back. He turned it over to reveal neat rows of numbers. He recognised them at once – they were cross-changes, like the ones that Gaundy,

Wildbore, Denton and Kirton had been studying when he had first met them. He rubbed his chin thoughtfully as answers piled into his mind. He nodded a farewell to Ester and Rycroft and continued towards Carter Lane, eager to discuss his tentative conclusions with Thurloe.

Chaloner arrived at Prayse's house just as Leybourn was leaving. The surveyor had Pamela's handgun in his belt, which he whipped out and brandished triumphantly, causing Chaloner to flinch away in alarm.

'This is coming in very useful,' he declared gleefully. 'I went to the Ball house this morning, to make sure that Ester and I had not missed anything yesterday, and I met a Mim there named Suger. The rogue had gone to hunt for money, so I pointed this dag at him and asked a few questions. He could not stop talking when he saw I meant business.'

Chaloner would have bleated all his secrets, too, if *he* had been confronted by a gun-toting Leybourn. The surveyor would not kill anyone deliberately, but an accident was another matter entirely.

'What did he tell you?' he asked, wishing he had been there himself.

'That he and his fellows were never really Quakers, and only attended Pamela's prayer meetings to get the medicine she provided – they could have bought their own, as they had money from their profiteering, but hers was free, and they came to rely on it. He also said that she often demanded favours in return.'

'What kind of favours?'

'Mostly starting rumours – such as the one that *sal mirabilis* is poisonous – although he has no idea why. He never dared ask. Of course, then it transpired that *sal mirabilis* really is toxic, so they asked her to give them London Treacle instead.'

Leybourn's report told Chaloner little he did not already know. 'You did well,' he lied. 'Now give me the gun.'

Leybourn jerked it away when Chaloner made a grab for it. 'Not yet. Thurloe has asked me to investigate a tale about explosives being smuggled into the city, and I might need to put it to someone else's head for answers.'

'Explosives?' asked Chaloner, alarmed.

'The story came from a fellow named Randall, who used to work for Kirton the bookseller. When he was dismissed, he turned to crime. I am to track him down and question him carefully.'

'You will not need a weapon for Randall – a good punch will suffice.'

'Oh,' said Leybourn, crestfallen. He shoved the weapon at Chaloner barrel first, his finger frighteningly close to the trigger. 'You made a good impression on Ester last night, by the way. She could not stop talking about you this morning. She said she had never met a man whose voice better complemented her own, and cannot wait to sing with you again.'

Chaloner experienced a complex gamut of emotions, chief of which were a warm sense of pleasure and a vicious stab of guilt.

'She likes you very much,' Leybourn went on with a blithe grin. 'So you will be a regular visitor to our house when we are wed. What fun we shall have!'

Chaloner watched him lope away, then vented his disquiet on Thurloe by demanding to know why the surveyor had been allotted such a dangerous assignment.

'It is not dangerous, Tom,' said Thurloe soothingly.

355

'There is no truth to Randall's claim, but Will believes that he has been asked to do something important. It will keep him out of harm's way while you and I work to avert this brewing crisis.'

'How do you know there is no truth to it?'

'Because I heard Randall bray the tale myself, in the Turk's Head Coffee House this morning. It was a lot of stupid nonsense.'

Chaloner remained unhappy. 'But Randall was ready to chop off my head a couple of days ago, to prove himself to the Mims. I am not sure Will is equal to—'

'Randall came nowhere close to harming you, and his claim to have brought gunpowder to London under cover of darkness is an outrageous fabrication. First, he could never have outwitted Monck's sentries, and second, who would trust a lad like him with such a delicate mission?'

'So Will is safe? You are sure?'

'He is safe from Randall, although whether he is safe wandering around with a loaded gun is another matter.'

Chaloner patted his pocket. 'He no longer has that.'

'Good. Now do you have something to tell me? If so, speak quickly. One of my contacts thought he saw Stone in Wapping last night. He is probably mistaken, but I must see about checking the claim anyway.'

'I think I know why Upton came to London. Look at these.'

He handed Thurloe the copy of *The Plague's Approved Physitian* that Sancroft had sent him, along with the false Certificates of Health bought by Pamela and Harbert's servants. Thurloe started to shake his head in incomprehension, then looked at them more closely.

'The paper is identical!'

Chaloner nodded. 'And the book was printed in

356

Oxfordshire, where Upton was recently married. The paper is his, and *that* is why he was summoned back to the city – to bring urgent supplies for the forgers.'

Thurloe frowned. 'These pages do not prove that he was involved in the business of hawking false certificates – only that his paper is being used to make them.'

'Bing knows the truth. He gabbled about paper at one point, saying that it has many uses, and that we should ask the devil about them. I wish I had listened to him more carefully. He is an observant man.'

'I hardly think *his* testimony—' began Thurloe, startled.

'There were several piles of this paper in Kirton's shop,' interrupted Chaloner, waving the documents at him. 'I picked a piece up, thinking it was an unbound book. Joshua snatched it back, but not before I had seen that it was blank. Now look on the back of Pamela's certificate. Those numbers are cross-changes – and Kirton is a cross-change ringer.'

Thurloe rubbed his chin. 'Monck, Lawrence *and* Cary have mentioned a sudden and alarming proliferation of these false certificates. They cost at least a shilling apiece, so if they are produced in any quantity, it will be a lucrative business.'

'But a despicable one, if they result in infected people being let out of the city. I think we had better visit Kirton. It is time he told us more about his relationship with the Executioner, including why he is so terrified of the man.'

'You have not asked him that already?'

'Yes, but I suspect he was economical with the truth, just like everyone else in this wretched enquiry.'

'You think he is producing these certificates on the Executioner's orders? He and his friends?'

'It is possible. However, it is equally possible that the

Executioner disapproves of such antics, and dispatched Gaundy for his involvement in it. Kirton will tell me which.'

'If you are right, then Kirton has not grown fat on the proceeds of his crimes. His shop is falling into disrepair, and he could not feed his apprentice.'

'But Joshua is wealthy,' countered Chaloner. 'An Agent of God, no less.'

Thurloe was thoughtful. 'Joshua – an arrogant and determined man. Perhaps we need look no further than him for our Executioner. But tackle Kirton first, Tom. He will tell you the truth if you bring the right pressure to bear, and will break more easily than his brother.'

'Then come with me. He may be more willing to talk if there are two of us.'

Thurloe hesitated, disliking the notion of venturing out into plague-infested London without good cause. 'I have the Wapping lead to pursue . . .'

'But you do not need to go there in person.' Chaloner raised his hands in a shrug. 'This involves Upton – your kinsman by marriage. You will want to hear first-hand what dark business may affect your family.'

It was enough to convince, so Thurloe dashed off a letter to a former spy, asking him to enquire about the missing canon in Wapping, and ordered the maid to deliver it at once. Then he began the complex process of donning his plague costume.

'Give me Pamela's gun,' he ordered when he was ready.

'Why? Do you plan to shoot Kirton?'

'I might, if he lies, but I was actually thinking about my personal safety. The city has a brittle, unsettled feel about it today, and neither of us should be unarmed.'

*

London was indeed brittle and unsettled. There had been a distribution of free bread, but there had not been enough to go around, so tempers were running high. The bonfires were also causing much disquiet – flying cinders had damaged several properties, and the belching fumes, combined with the relentless glare of the sun, made life all but intolerable.

Work at the pit had stopped, and the burial duty leaned on their spades, bristling defiance as they smoked their pipes and declared that they would only return to work if they were paid double. As few men were willing to undertake such a dangerous and filthy job, Chaloner imagined it would not be long before Lawrence was forced to capitulate.

Meanwhile, the dead-carts were still bringing their sorry cargoes for disposal, and the heap of bodies awaiting attention stretched almost as far as the cathedral library. The bereaved knew better than to go near them, but gathered in distraught knots by Paul's Gate. Randall was there, too, scuttling from group to group; whatever he whispered to them earned nods of bitter agreement. The apprentice had not fared well since leaving Kirton's employ – his clothes were stained, his hair matted, and he had a sunken, hungry look.

'Does Will know he is here?' asked Chaloner. 'And that he seems to have abandoned his aspirations to become a Mim, and is now bent on a career as a rabble-rouser instead?'

'I told Will to search St James's Park first,' replied Thurloe, voice muffled inside his mask. 'With luck, it will take him hours.' Then his eye lit on the mounting heap of corpses. 'God help us! I doubt even Cromwell could have coped with a disaster of this magnitude. Lawrence is a remarkable man.'

This was praise indeed, as Thurloe was of the firm opinion that the Lord Protector had done everything better than anyone else.

They arrived at the bookshop to find that Kirton already had visitors – Denton and Wildbore were there. He had taken his fellow ringers to the very back of his shop, where they talked in low voices. However, he had chosen a spot that was ridiculously easy to approach without being seen, so it was simplicity itself for Chaloner and Thurloe to eavesdrop.

'. . . will never work,' he was gulping in agitation. 'I want to stop.'

'We cannot stop,' snapped Denton. 'You know why.'

'We could leave,' suggested Wildbore, although with more hope than conviction. 'We have Certificates of Health, and Kirton is right: to stay is to die.'

'To *leave* is to die,' countered Denton. 'The Executioner will hunt us down, and we will suffer the same fate as Gaundy. We are trapped here.'

'I hate London now,' whispered Kirton miserably. 'I have no books to sell – and no customers to buy them if I had. Food is scarce and costly . . . I had nothing but umbles and dried cabbage last night, but even those cost me sixpence.'

'Nor do we have the comfort of decent coffee,' sighed Wildbore. 'Outridge is now making his brews from the grounds retrieved from his midden.'

No wonder it had tasted so nasty, thought Chaloner, glad he had only taken a sip.

'Rioters will storm the city gates tonight,' said Kirton, brightening suddenly. 'We could slip out in the ensuing chaos and go to Scotland. He will never find us there.'

'He will,' predicted Denton. 'He has spies everywhere.'

360

'This is all your brother's fault, Kirton,' said Wildbore accusingly. 'We should never have listened to him. Stedman does not know his good fortune – if his print-works had been functional, he would have been dragged into this filthy business, too.'

'He would have refused,' said Kirton softly. 'As we should have done. Then we would not be in this terrible position.'

At that moment, Wildbore happened to glance at where Thurloe's shadow was etched against the wall, a ghastly vision with its pointed face mask and brimmed hat. He released a shrill shriek that made his cronies wail their own terror. Irked that they had been seen when there was more that might have been learned, Chaloner stepped out of the shadows. So did Thurloe, unfastening his mask as he did so.

'It is time you told me the truth,' said Chaloner sternly. '*All* of it, not just the bits you think I should know.'

'We cannot!' wailed Kirton, horrified. 'The Executioner will kill us.'

'I will kill you if you don't,' threatened Chaloner.

'But you will do it quickly,' countered Wildbore, and eyed Chaloner's weapons. 'With a sharp sword or a gun. He will make us suffer for days. Weeks, even. Joshua told us so.'

'The truth,' said Thurloe harshly, fixing them with icy blue eyes. '*Now*, please.'

Although not a large man, Thurloe had considerable presence, and even the most dedicated of traitors to the Commonwealth had cracked under his steely gaze. Wildbore and Kirton were no match for him, and the last vestiges of their resistance crumbled, although Denton continued to bristle in impotent defiance.

'The Executioner *made* us do it,' whispered Wildbore miserably. 'We know a lot of people, you see – from the churches where we ring the bells.'

'Desperate people,' added Kirton, his cheeks burning with shame. 'People who will pay anything to escape from the city – which they cannot do without the right documentation. It is a lucrative business, although we see none of the profits, of course.'

'I understand now,' said Thurloe to Chaloner in distaste. 'They toll mourning bells as a pretext to visit different churches, where they hawk forged Certificates of Health. After all, where better to meet frightened folk than the places they go for frantic prayers and to bury their loved ones?'

'It explains why Stedman is obliged to do all the ringing,' put in Chaloner. 'These gallant fellows are too busy with their lives of crime.'

Kirton put his hands over his face, Wildbore looked away, but Denton was still not ready to concede defeat. 'You are guessing,' he declared. 'You cannot prove any of it.'

'Oh, yes, we can.' Chaloner showed them Pamela's certificate, then turned it over to reveal the cross-changes on the back. 'You were careless.'

'Pamela Ball,' groaned Wildbore, and glanced at his friends. 'She demanded a certificate from me, but I did not have one to give her, so she shoved me against a wall and went through my pockets. I had used the back of a spare one to draft out some cross-changes, so she took that instead.'

'Who is the Executioner?' Thurloe made no effort to disguise his contempt. 'Joshua?'

'No!' cried Kirton. 'He is as frightened as we are – another victim of circumstances.'

'You are not victims,' said Thurloe scornfully. 'You are greedy opportunists who take advantage of the anguish of others. And for what? A quick profit!'

'But we have *not* profited,' sobbed Kirton in distress. 'Why do you think I have no books to sell? Why was Gaundy just a lowly verger? And why are we obliged to eat umbles and drink second-hand coffee? If we had been paid, we would be rich.'

'So the Executioner *blackmailed* you into a life of crime,' surmised Thurloe, more disgusted than ever. 'What in God's name have you done to give him such power over you?'

There was silence, and just when Chaloner thought he might have to resort to more forceful means of extracting the information, Wildbore spoke in a strangled whisper.

'Something terrible, which will see us hanged if the truth is ever revealed.'

'Say no more,' snarled Denton furiously. 'They can prove nothing. And if you feel your nerve failing, then think of Gaundy, Roan, Joyce, Day and God knows how many others who tried to break out of this wretched business. All dead – horribly murdered.'

The last three names were familiar, and Chaloner struggled to recall where he had heard them before. Then it came to him: Leybourn had met them on the road from Uxbridge.

'Roan, Joyce and Day are not dead,' he said. 'They left the city to escape the plague. They were seen by a very reliable witness.'

The three exchanged bemused glances. 'But Joshua told us . . .' began Kirton.

He trailed off, and there was silence as they digested the information. Meanwhile, Chaloner racked his brain for a crime so heinous that discovery would mean the scaffold. It was unlikely to be anything related to their occupations: Kirton's shop was all but defunct, Wildbore had had no wares to sell in weeks, while Denton's fish were dead from the heat.

He frowned. But that was untrue, because there *were* fish in St James's Park – he had seen them himself when he had paddled in the Canal. There were no large ones, but the smaller individuals still thrived in the cooler waters in the middle. And with that, he understood exactly what the ringers had done – and why they were so terrified of being found out.

'Fish!' he exclaimed. 'When the food shortages first began to bite, you caught and sold the ones in the park. Several people mentioned a plethora of handsome and unusual specimens a few weeks ago, a supply that suddenly dried up. And who better to enact such a scheme but His Majesty's Keeper of Fish and his friend the fishmonger?'

Denton began a stammering denial, but Wildbore turned a nasty shade of grey and Kirton hung his head, which told Chaloner all he needed to know.

'You stole the King's fish?' Thurloe was disgusted anew. 'What were you thinking?'

'That we needed money to flee the city and save our lives,' replied Kirton wretchedly, and raised a weary hand when Denton tried to interrupt. 'I am tired of living in fear. I want an end to it – one way or another.'

'Then your brother will fall with us,' vowed Denton in a voice that shook. 'Because it was all *his* idea.'

'It was easy at first,' said Wildbore, siding with Kirton. 'While Kirton and the other ringers kept watch, Denton caught the fish, and I sold them in my shop. Unfortunately,

364

the Executioner found out, and threatened to tell the King unless we gave him *all* the money we had earned. But even that was not enough – he then forced us to work for him, selling his certificates.'

'We did not know it was the Executioner to start with,' whispered Kirton. 'He refuses to deal with us directly, and uses poor Joshua to deliver his nasty messages. We only guessed it was him when we saw the warning he sent to Gaundy. I told Joshua what we had reasoned, and he agrees that we are right.'

'I bet he does,' said Chaloner drily. 'Because it is a conclusion that suits him perfectly. It keeps you where he wants you to be: too frightened to break free of him.'

Wildbore and Denton exchanged glances that suggested this was a possibility they had already considered, but Kirton doggedly shook his head.

'Joshua is in this mire just as deeply as we are.'

'Is he?' asked Chaloner. 'Surely you must be suspicious of the fact that it was *his* idea to steal the fish, and it is *he* who delivers orders from the "Executioner"?'

'Because he does not want us to be in the path of such a ruthless and determined villain,' explained Kirton earnestly. 'He acts as a go-between to protect us.'

Thurloe released a snort of disbelief. 'He has played you all for fools, and I can scarcely credit such gullibility.'

'I think we had better have a word with Joshua,' said Chaloner. 'Where is he?'

'With Vicar Masley,' replied Denton, and scowled when Kirton gave a whimper of dismay. 'They *should* question him, Kirton. You know that Wildbore and I have never been entirely happy with his role in all this.'

'Go to the park,' Chaloner told him. 'The fish in the Canal are small, but if you nurture them, they will grow. Who knows? Perhaps they will have reached full size by the time the King next sees them.'

'But *I* will never forget or forgive what you have done,' said Thurloe, the contempt in his voice crushing the hope that flared briefly in their eyes. 'Your selfishness has helped to spread the plague.'

'Will you arrest us?' asked Kirton in a small voice.

Thurloe scowled. 'No, but only because we do not have time to waste on you. I hope for your sakes that our paths never cross again.'

'You see?' asked Chaloner, once he and Thurloe were outside. 'I said they would be more forthcoming if you were there. Now come with me to Masley's house, and see if you can do it again.'

Chaloner and Thurloe cut through the cathedral to reach Paul's Chain. On their way, they passed a frantic commotion in the north transept, where Francis, John and Owen were selling the latest batch of London Treacle. Chaloner wondered whether there would be a riot if their supplies ran out before everyone had been served. He turned his thoughts back to their enquiries, aware of answers coming thick and fast now that they finally had the whole truth about the ringers' antics.

'Masley is always writing,' he began, 'and the first time we met, he told me that he was too busy to bother with the bones in the crypt. Kirton inadvertently threw me off the scent by suggesting that he is preparing a book about his plague experiences, while Masley himself claimed he is composing letters for the bereaved.'

'Letters he refused to let me see,' said Thurloe reflectively, 'on the grounds of confidentiality. Yet surely that stricture should not apply to a government representative, which I was purporting to be at the time?'

'Quite. And you noted that he can write unusually fast and to an exceptionally high standard. It seems to me that he has been using this talent to forge Certificates of Health.'

'I believe you are right. And Joshua has been helping him – I have seen him in Masley's house several times, working. What a revolting business! So which of them is the Executioner? The ruthless Joshua, who has no compunction in deceiving a devoted but stupid sibling? Or Masley, a vicar who would rather line his pockets than tend his flock?'

'Not Masley – he was not in London twenty years ago, and we know that whoever killed Gaundy, William, Upton and Pamela also dispatched Kerchier, as it is too unusual a method of killing for there to be two perpetrators using it.'

'Joshua then,' determined Thurloe, 'although we should arrest them both, as Masley will answer all our questions once he learns that it is the only way to avoid the noose. But slow down, Tom. Joshua will not roll over as meekly as your ringers – he will fight, so we must recruit reinforcements before we apprehend him. It would be a pity if we bungled and he escapes.'

'We will not bungle, and if we stop to organise help, he might find out that he has been betrayed and slip the net – which would be unfortunate, as I suspect he and Masley aim to add to tonight's trouble . . .'

'By hawking more forgeries, thus bringing extra pressure to bear on the guards at the gates,' finished Thurloe.

367

'Which is even more reason why we must make sure that nothing goes wrong. We cannot attempt this alone. Too much is at stake.'

Chaloner felt Thurloe was being needlessly overcautious, and was beginning to wish he had left him behind. He understood why the ex-Spymaster was reluctant to plunge into what might result in a physical confrontation – Thurloe's strength lay in solving problems with his wits, not his fists. But sometimes combat was unavoidable, and Chaloner was confident enough in his own abilities to make up for any shortcomings in Thurloe's.

'But who will help us?' he asked with asperity. 'Unless you have a private train band that you can call up at a moment's notice?'

'No – we ask to borrow some of *his* men.'

Thurloe nodded to the Lady Chapel, where Lawrence knelt in private prayer. The moment the mayor stood, he was mobbed by people demanding to know what he planned to do about the fact that the canons had just decided to double the cost of London Treacle.

'Now we can no longer take *sal mirabilis*, it is the only real preventative on offer,' wailed a laundress, while Chaloner imagined that this was precisely what had prompted the clerics to bump up their prices.

'You *can* take *sal mirabilis*,' Lawrence assured her, although his voice was not as loud or as strong as it had been a few days earlier. There were only so many morale-boosting speeches a man could bellow without going hoarse. 'Look! I use it myself.'

He brandished a pot and then quaffed its contents. Alarmed, Chaloner, Thurloe and the watching crowd held their breath, waiting for him to keel over. Instead, he tipped the vessel upside down, to show it was empty.

'You see? It is quite safe. Now, a free bottle of it will be given to anyone who comes to my house this afternoon, along with a copy of *The Plague's Approved Physitian*.'

'That book is useless,' came a disdainful voice, which Chaloner thought might belong to Antrobus, although he could not be sure, as the speaker wore a mask and a long cloak that covered his clothes. 'All it does is advise the reader to pray.'

'And what is wrong with prayer?' asked Lawrence, raising his hands in a gesture of quiet reason. 'Is that not the reason why we all are in here?'

'*We* are in here for London Treacle,' countered the laundress. 'But these thieving priests are charging too much for it. *Please* tell them to lower their prices. It is not fair!'

Lawrence hesitated, and Chaloner could see his quandary. He could hardly admit that his authority did not extend to telling canons what to do inside their own cathedral, lest it weakened the populace's faith in him and the measures he was struggling to implement. Yet the situation was patently iniquitous, and it was obvious that something had to be done.

But it was not the first difficult situation the mayor had been forced to handle, and he rose to the challenge magnificently, demonstrating the mettle that had allowed him to steer the city through crisis after crisis over the last few months. His voice became strong and confident again, and he seemed to grow larger and more commanding before their eyes.

'I shall buy every drop of their next batch,' he announced, 'and it will be delivered, completely free of charge, to anyone who leaves his name with my clerks. Now please go home. You know it is forbidden to gather in such large numbers, and if you do not care for yourselves, then think of those you love.'

Appeased, at least temporarily, the crowd began to disperse. Cary immediately hurried to Owen, and began to negotiate a deal. The canon named a price, but hastily suggested a lower one when his first offer was met with an indignant glower.

'That was clever,' remarked Chaloner, impressed. 'And generous. There are not many officials who would be so open-handed with their own money.'

'It is not generosity – it is fear,' harrumphed Thurloe. 'He knows the mob will turn on him if he cannot meet their demands.'

Chaloner was sure he was wrong. Lawrence had been quietly providing alms and medicines to the needy for weeks, and Londoners loved him for it. Of course, men like Antrobus and Randall could always turn the tables with their dissenting tongues . . .

'Regardless, we cannot bother him with our problems now,' he said. 'He has enough of his own.'

Thurloe took Pamela's gun from his belt to ensure it was loaded. 'I suppose I shall not mind shooting Masley or Joshua if they refuse to surrender peacefully.' His voice turned harsher still. 'And if Upton were alive, I would shoot him, too. How dare he drag my family's good name into this filthy affair!'

They reached Paul's Chain, where a quick glance through Masley's window showed the vicar writing at his table, while Joshua hovered at his shoulder.

'The back door,' murmured Chaloner, when they found the front one locked. 'We shall slip in that way, and catch them in the act. Then they cannot deny their involvement.'

Unfortunately, the back door was secured with a bar, but an upstairs window was open. Thurloe indicated that Chaloner was to climb up to it, then come downstairs and let him in – he was not in the habit of making undignified entries himself.

Chaloner did as he was told, and had just reached the pantry when he heard a sound behind him. He whipped around in alarm and saw Joshua standing there with a pistol. He started to reach for his own weapon, but Joshua made a warning sound, and Chaloner knew the stationer would shoot him long before he could draw. He cursed his own ineptitude. How could he have allowed himself to be caught like some rank amateur?

# Chapter 12

Chaloner was still berating himself for his stupidity when Masley arrived. The vicar also held a gun, although his hand shook dangerously. However, while Masley might be appalled by the situation in which he found himself, there was a gleam of vengeful satisfaction in Joshua's eyes – the stationer was delighted by the opportunity to silence the man whose questions had threatened his plans, and Chaloner glimpsed the sly ruthlessness of the individual who had so callously abused the trust of a loyal brother.

With deft, confident movements, Joshua relieved Chaloner of his weapons, then pointed to a door that led to a cellar. Chaloner started to refuse, but Joshua raised the gun with the clear intention of using it there and then. Chaloner raised his hands quickly and did as he was told.

As he climbed slowly down the narrow, uneven steps, he wondered what Thurloe had managed to hear, although there was little the ex-Spymaster could do from the wrong side of a locked door. He cursed the reckless overconfidence that had led him to think he could tackle the forgers alone – Thurloe had been right to recommend securing help first. Still, one thing was for certain – Joshua would not be knocking *him* over the head and dripping poison in his mouth. The stationer would have to use his gun.

He reached the bottom of the stairs, and assessed his surroundings quickly. The cellar comprised a single room that smelled of coal, and was bare except for three large metal hooks that dangled from the ceiling on ropes, of the kind used for hanging smoked meats.

'I told you he would be trouble,' Masley was hissing accusingly to Joshua, 'but you said you could handle him. God only knows what he has told Dean Sancroft.'

'Well, Chaloner?' asked Joshua. The gun was unwavering, and he was evidently no stranger to armed confrontations, as he had chosen to stand in a place where it would be impossible for his prisoner to rush him. 'What does Sancroft know?'

'Everything,' lied Chaloner. 'How you forge Certificates of Health, and coerce Kirton and his friends into selling them. How it is *your* fault that the disease has spread to Salisbury, Colchester, Cambridge, Petersfield, Deal and dozens of places in between. How—'

'Lord!' blurted Masley, pulling at his collar in agitation. 'He must have had all this from Kirton. The treacherous bastard! We should never have involved him.'

'Not just Kirton,' said Chaloner, aiming to rattle him further. 'You did your share of stupid things as well. For example, on the day that Gaundy was killed, you appeared in the tower with a sheaf of documents. They were forged Certificates of Health, but you could not hand them to your ringers for selling, because I was there.'

It was a guess, but Masley's horrified expression told him it was an accurate one.

'But I kept them pressed to my chest – you cannot possibly have seen what was on them. And you have the wrong idea about us, anyway – we have *saved* lives. Our certificates allow healthy people to escape to the country, folk who cannot afford the extortionate prices charged for genuine ones.'

'Do not pretend to be motivated by compassion,' said Chaloner contemptuously. 'You have used the suffering of others to make money for yourselves.'

'You preach virtue to *us*, when you work for the Executioner?' demanded Joshua. 'Oh, yes, we know it is Sancroft – which is why he sent you here, of course. He wants a cut of our profits for himself.'

Chaloner's mind raced. He had already reasoned that Masley was not the Executioner, but now it seemed it was not Joshua either – not if he thought it was the dean.

He struggled to make sense of it all. Were the certificates irrelevant to the killer's machinations, and he and Thurloe had inadvertently stumbled across a scheme that was unrelated to the murders? But there *had* to be a connection – there were too many strands linking them together for there not to be. So *was* Sancroft the villain behind it all? Chaloner wanted to say no, but the truth was that he did not know the dean well enough to judge.

'You must really despise your brother,' he said to Joshua, aiming to keep them talking for as long as possible, suspecting he would not survive long once they stopped. 'Terrifying him with tales that the Executioner is—'

'I did what was necessary,' interrupted Joshua curtly. 'Besides, it was his own fault. He should not have taken up with weak and greedy fools like Denton, Gaundy and Wildbore.'

'They stole the King's fish and sold them for food,' put in Masley. 'His Majesty will be delighted when he learns that Joshua and I have made them pay for their crimes.'

'Start talking, Chaloner,' said Joshua quickly. 'What have you told Sancroft?'

The abrupt question suggested to Chaloner that Masley did not know that stealing the fish had been Joshua's idea – Kirton and his friends were not the only ones to be victims of the stationer's penchant for deceit.

'He knows all about you two,' blustered Chaloner. 'And he will not let my murder go unpunished, so put down your weapons and let us discuss options. It is—'

'He will slaughter us, just like he did the others,' whimpered Masley, rubbing a shaking hand over his face. 'He has eyes everywhere. *I* did not know that Gaundy liked to skive in my church tower, but *he* managed to find out. He is all-seeing, and will—'

'Calm yourself, Masley!' snapped Joshua. 'A few more hours and it will all be over. Now, here is what we are going to do. I will kill Chaloner, while you go back upstairs and continue working. My brother will sell the last certificates at tonight's service, and we shall leave this miserable city with a fortune. Sancroft will never find us.'

'Leave how?' bleated Masley. 'Monck will block the gates.'

'Not even Monck can stop thousands of angry Londoners, all waving the documents that give them the legal right to pass. Now, go.'

'Sancroft also knows that your certificates are penned on paper supplied by John Upton,' Chaloner went on.

'Cheap, nasty stuff, to maximise profits. When you ran low, you wrote to him in Oxfordshire, demanding more.'

'Upton was the only stationer willing to brave the city and bring us fresh supplies,' explained Masley wretchedly, making no move to do as Joshua ordered. 'We had no choice but to call him away from his new bride – we were down to our very last reams.'

'But Sancroft killed him before he could deliver most of what we had ordered,' said Joshua bitterly. 'We might have gone on for months if he had stayed his murderous hand.'

Anger suffused his face as he reflected on the fortune that Upton's death had cost him, and Chaloner knew it would not be long before he avenged his losses by dispatching Sancroft's envoy. He took a step towards the nearest hook, addressing Masley at the same time in the hope of gaining a few more seconds.

'You said St Gregory's is a plum appointment. Why abandon it now?'

'It *was* a plum appointment,' replied the vicar miserably. 'But the city is dying, and soon there will be nothing left but corpses. I doubt it will ever recover.'

At that point, Joshua raised the dag and took aim, so Chaloner lurched closer to the hook, trying to make it look as though he was attempting to cringe away.

'Wait!' he cried. 'Just one more question. Kirton saw Gaundy and Upton talking together not long before Upton died. Were they discussing the certificates?'

'I doubt it,' replied Joshua shortly. 'Neither knew the other was involved. Goodbye, Chaloner. I cannot say it has been a pleasure.'

As Joshua's finger tightened on the trigger, Chaloner dived for the hook, swinging it forward with all his might.

At the same time, there was a blur of movement, and something flew down the cellar steps. It was a coal scuttle, which hit Joshua squarely in the back. Unfortunately, it jolted him forward, so instead of the hook striking his body, as Chaloner had intended, it struck his head. There was a sickening crunch, and he dropped to the floor.

Masley gaped at his fallen crony, before turning to tear up the stairs, where he met Thurloe coming down. Terror made him strong. He grabbed Thurloe and hurled him backwards, so that the ex-Spymaster went crashing down the steps. Afraid Thurloe might be hurt, Chaloner rushed to his aid, and by the time he had assured himself that his friend was unharmed, Masley had gone.

'Damn,' muttered Thurloe. 'You killed Joshua, too.'

'Not on purpose,' said Chaloner defensively. 'Although he *was* about to shoot me . . .'

'He would not have succeeded.' Thurloe showed him the gun he held. 'And I wanted him alive. There is a lot more he could have told us – such as why he thought Sancroft is the Executioner.'

'Then Masley can tell us instead.'

Chaloner ran up the stairs, retrieved the weapons that Joshua had taken from him, and dashed into the street. There was no sign of the vicar, but a woman was picking herself up from the ground to his left – someone in a hurry had bowled her over. It told him that Masley had headed towards the cathedral. He set off after him, aware of Thurloe panting at his side.

'Or better yet,' the ex-Spymaster gasped, 'we can ask Masley's master that question.'

Chaloner flashed him a bemused glance. 'What are you talking about? What master?'

'Masley does not have the courage to have organised

all this himself, while not even Joshua would exploit his brother without someone else whispering encouragement. Despite Joshua's hubris, he and Masley are mere cogs in a wheel, and a third party is directing their hand – a person to whom Masley is running as we speak.'

'The Executioner?' Chaloner glanced at him again. 'Not Sancroft?'

'We will find out soon enough.'

'How much of that discussion did you hear?'

'All of it.' Thurloe's words came in staccato bursts as he ran. 'I climbed through the front window the moment I heard you were caught. You are losing your touch, Thomas. I expected you to prise far more from them than you did.'

As they sprinted towards St Paul's, Chaloner noticed that several things had changed since he had been in Masley's house. First, clouds had rolled in for the first time in weeks, although they did nothing to lessen the heat. Second, no bells could be heard anywhere in the city, which was more disconcerting than their constant tolling. And third, there were considerably more people abroad than there had been earlier.

'There!' gasped Thurloe, pointing to the cathedral's south door, where Masley could just be seen disappearing inside.

'Where better for Sancroft to hide?' muttered Chaloner, beginning to run towards it. 'And no one will recognise him if he wears a plague mask.'

Thurloe grabbed Chaloner's arm. 'Slow down, Tom. Let us not make the same mistake twice. Follow Masley, but do not confront him. Wait until I arrive with help.'

He was looking back towards Rycroft's house. Chaloner

knew Ester was in there, because he had heard her singing as he had passed. His stomach lurched. She would insist on accompanying her brother when Thurloe demanded assistance, and he did not want her in danger.

'No!' he snapped. Thurloe's eyebrows shot up in astonishment at his vehemence, so he struggled to moderate his tone. 'Think of Will – he will disapprove if you put Ester at risk.'

'So will you, apparently,' retorted Thurloe. 'Now go, before you lose Masley. I will be but moments behind.'

Yet Chaloner still hesitated, caught by emotions he could not begin to understand. 'How will you know where to find me?'

'Oh, I shall know,' said Thurloe enigmatically, and trotted away without another word.

The nave was empty when Chaloner reached it, although the north transept was still full of people wanting to buy London Treacle. He was surprised the canons still had some left to sell, sure it should have run out by now. Then he saw Masley, robes flying as he pelted towards the chancel. Cartwright tried to waylay him with a question, but Masley shoved him away so hard that the young priest stumbled backwards into a pillar.

Masley ripped open the door that led to the northeastern corner of the churchyard, and shot through it. By the time Chaloner did the same, the vicar was haring past the plague pit. The gravediggers were back at work, but too languidly to make much impact on the mounting pile of corpses. Chaloner wondered if Randall was responsible for their sudden fit of indolence.

Masley had gained Paul's Gate before it occurred to him that he might have been followed. He stopped to look, so Chaloner was forced to duck behind a group of potters, who were grumbling furiously about the outrageous cost of London Treacle. Then Masley aimed for the smart new house on the corner – the one where Antrobus and Matthew lived.

Chaloner was disgusted that he had not guessed the pair's involvement sooner. After all, who had been spreading rumours about the looming crisis in coffee houses, and then urging all and sundry to buy Certificates of Health and leave? They were audacious, he thought, recalling how they had encouraged him – Sancroft's envoy – to get one; they had even offered to arrange it for him. Harbert's servants had called them canny and slippery, with a nose for scams, and they were right.

So was one – or both – of them the Executioner? Or were they just more cogs in the wheel, and the real culprit was laughing at Chaloner's efforts to catch him? All he could hope was that Matthew and Antrobus would provide answers, because he disliked the sense that time was ticking away while he rushed around in confused circles.

Masley was hammering frantically on their door, so Chaloner eased through the potted lemon trees, aiming to hear what was said when the urgent knocking was answered. He had just reached a good vantage point when the door was opened.

'What are you doing here?' hissed Antrobus, peering around in alarm. 'It is broad daylight, man! Go away!'

'Trouble,' gulped Masley, trying to force his way inside. 'Sancroft knows about us. His envoy admitted it, right before he killed Joshua. We must gather our spoils and leave at once. It is too dangerous to dally.'

'No,' said Antrobus fiercely. 'Tonight will see our best

sales yet, and we cannot abandon such an easy fortune. Now go and prepare the certificates you promised.'

'Sancroft *knows*,' snarled Masley furiously. 'Are you not listening to me? The Executioner knows! He will kill us, just as he killed Gaundy and Upton.'

Antrobus blanched. 'But he cannot know. We have been supremely careful.'

Chaloner closed his eyes in despair. Antrobus's alarm looked genuine to him, which meant *he* was not the Executioner either. Now what?

'It is Kirton's fault – he told the envoy everything,' rasped Masley, almost beside himself with agitation. 'And he will bleat even louder when he learns that his brother is dead. I said it was a mistake to use him – we should have hired Mims instead.'

'Respectable folk would not have bought certificates from Mims. Now stop blathering and let me think.' Antrobus took a deep breath to calm himself. 'If Kirton did break, then he did it today – it cannot have been before, because Joshua would have done something about it.'

'So?' demanded Masley shrilly. 'I do not see—'

'It means that Sancroft is still in ignorance – it takes time for letters to reach Tunbridge Wells. Ergo, he cannot possibly know about our activities yet, so we are safe. Now go home before you ruin everything.'

But Masley put his head down and barrelled past him into the house. 'No! I am finished with you. I want my money and then I am leaving.'

Antrobus scurried after him, shouting for him to stop. Chaloner hesitated. Should he follow them or go to tell Thurloe that the identity of the Executioner was still unknown? He decided to follow, unwilling to risk Masley or Antrobus escaping justice for what they had done. He trailed them along a corridor and out into the garden at the back, where Masley had grabbed a spade and was beginning to dig, while Antrobus struggled to stop him.

'Get away,' snarled the vicar, lashing out with the spade and catching Antrobus across the shoulders, leaving a shovel-shaped smear of dirt on the beautiful silk coat. 'I want my share, and I want it now.'

'Are you mad?' cried Antrobus angrily. 'You cannot walk through London with a box of coins. You will be mobbed before you take ten paces.'

'Let anyone try! Now get away from me.'

Although Thurloe had instructed him to wait, Chaloner felt he needed to take Masley and Antrobus into custody before any more precious time was lost on them. He stepped forward with his sword in one hand and Cary's gun in the other.

When he saw the spy, Masley fell to his knees with an anguished wail. Antrobus gaped his disbelief, then launched an assault that Chaloner might have found amusing if he had not been so fraught with tension. Seemingly oblivious to the fact that the spy was armed, Antrobus flailed and slapped with his hands in a manner more akin to one of Lawrence's little daughters than a grown man.

Then Matthew shot out of the house with a rapier. Chaloner swore under his breath. What was wrong with them? Could they not see the gun? He was tempted to shoot one of them, feeling it was no less than they deserved, but he manfully resisted the urge, and it was not many moments before he succeeded in flicking the sword from Matthew's grasp. The fight promptly went out of Antrobus, too, but Chaloner now had a problem: he could have marched two prisoners to Newgate on his own, but three was asking for trouble. He needed another pair of hands, so where was Thurloe?

'What do you want from us?' demanded Antrobus, while Matthew massaged his stinging hand and looked more irritated than alarmed. 'Money? Very well then. How much?'

'Your game is over,' said Chaloner coldly. 'We know all about the certificates that Masley has been forging for you. You have been impressively sly: you presented Monck with eighteen of them—'

'Those were revolutionary broadsheets,' interrupted Matthew. 'As we told you.'

'—which you claimed to have gathered as part of the effort to stamp out the trade,' Chaloner went on, ignoring the lie. 'You threw him off your scent by pretending to help.'

'It worked,' muttered Antrobus, eyeing him with dislike. 'And if you accuse us of anything, he will never believe you. He thinks we are on his side.'

'You have sold thousands,' Chaloner went on. 'So eighteen is a mere drop in the ocean. Even so, I imagine you hated parting with them.'

He wished Thurloe would hurry up. Or were he and Rycroft already there, listening? He made a sharp gesture with his gun to urge them forward. It was no time for another lengthy interrogation, especially as details about the crime could be demanded later, when the offenders were in gaol and the city was not on the verge of a crisis.

'We have no idea what you are talking about,' stated Matthew. 'Now go away.'

'You have been fomenting unease in coffee houses and

383

taverns,' Chaloner continued, when help failed to materialise. 'Encouraging folk to buy bogus documents and leave.'

'Prove it,' challenged Matthew.

Chaloner smiled with a calm he did not feel. 'Joshua Kirton is making a full confession as we speak. His testimony is all we need to convict you.'

Antrobus turned accusingly to Masley. 'You told me that Joshua was dead.'

'I thought . . .' gulped the vicar. 'I . . . I was *sure* I heard his skull smash!'

'Joshua,' sneered Matthew. 'He will regale you with all manner of falsehoods in an effort to save himself. But he is a liar, and no court of law will believe him.'

'That is right,' agreed Antrobus shakily. 'He will blame us, but the scheme was *his* idea. We had nothing to do with it. We are respectable men – Agents of God, no less. Do you really think we would stoop to such low activities?'

'I cannot imagine why you joined such a society,' said Chaloner in distaste, gesturing more urgently at the house's back door – the place where he thought Thurloe might be hiding. 'Not for altruistic reasons, certainly.'

'Because they aim to curry the King's favour,' supplied Masley quickly. 'Ask *me* your questions, Chaloner. I will tell you anything you want to know – in exchange for clemency.'

'Masley is a liar, too,' said Matthew sharply. 'And we *did* enrol in the Agents of God to benefit the city. Ask Canon Stone – he will tell you. He has known us for years.'

'He went to visit his sister, but he is back now,' put in Antrobus. 'I saw him in the cathedral not an hour ago.'

'*Please* let me go, Chaloner,' begged Masley tearfully. 'I will slip away quietly and you will never see me again. There is no need to tell Sancroft about me.'

'Or us,' put in Antrobus. 'Come on, man, be reasonable. We will give you more money than Sancroft will pay you in a lifetime. We have a fortune buried here in the garden – we have been hiding it away here for weeks.'

'Just take a spade and dig,' coaxed Masley, although Matthew looked less than pleased by his cronies' generosity. 'You should not work for a killer anyway, as it is only a matter of time before he decides that you are expendable, too.'

'Perhaps he already has,' interposed Matthew slyly. 'I understand that you have been attacked several times in the last few days.'

Chaloner struggled to mask his rising agitation. Where *was* Thurloe? 'How do you know the Executioner is Sancroft?' he demanded.

'Because Joshua told us so,' replied Masley, eager to cooperate. 'But he is right. Who else can it be, other than a high-ranking cathedral official? I have never liked Sancroft – too sanctimonious by half.'

'Was selling the certificates Joshua's idea?' asked Chaloner.

'Yes,' replied Antrobus quickly.

'No,' said Masley at the same time. He nodded at his cronies. 'It was theirs. They have been cheats and swindlers for years, and their claim to respectability is a sham. Why do you think Sir Arnold denounced them? It was not just a difference of opinion about the cathedral. Let me go, and I will give you a list of all the people they have defrauded.'

'Then you will swing with us,' flashed Antrobus. 'You

are a hypocrite! A vicar who does nothing but devise ways to deprive his parishioners of their money.'

They were still arguing when Thurloe appeared at last, along with Cary and four guards. Sweat beaded Cary's face, and Chaloner eyed him in concern. Did the secretary have a deadly fever, or was he just hot from racing around sweltering, smoke-filled streets?

Matthew took to his heels when he saw them. Panicked by his flight, Antrobus and Masley did likewise, and there followed an undignified and rather ridiculous chase around the garden. Chaloner did not join in, and nor did Thurloe.

'Rycroft had other urgent business to attend,' explained Thurloe, watching the spectacle in distaste. 'But I met Cary on my way here, and he agreed to help us instead.'

Chaloner was uneasy that the alchemist should have refused Thurloe, and was about to say so when Cary bellowed for his help. He went to oblige, covering the captives with his sword to keep them subdued while they were bound. All the while, Masley bleated his innocence, Antrobus spat fury, while Matthew maintained a cold and sullen silence.

When it was done, Cary nodded to his men. 'Good. Now take them to Newgate.'

'Newgate?' cried Masley. 'But the gaols are full of plague. We will die!'

'Just like the country folk, then, who have perished because *your* certificates allowed the disease to spread outside London,' said Thurloe coldly. 'It might be called divine justice.'

When the prisoners had been escorted away, Thurloe told Cary about their latest discoveries, while Chaloner pondered the claim that Sancroft was the Executioner. Could it be true after all? He rubbed his chin, not sure what to think.

'Scum!' spat Cary, when Thurloe had finished. 'The damage they have done with their greed . . . I hope they *do* catch the plague in prison. It would serve them right.'

'They must have sold hundreds of certificates to people who aim to use them tonight,' said Thurloe worriedly. 'How will you tell so many folk that they have wasted their money? You will have a riot, and indignant mobs will storm the gates anyway.'

Chaloner glanced up at the sky. It was already afternoon, and everything was predicted to come to a head after the service that evening – in just six or seven hours' time. Could they stop it? But how, when it involved so many people? They would be overwhelmed by sheer force of numbers.

'The cathedral and St Gregory's,' he murmured, his mind working frantically as he tried to sort through the mass of clues they had accumulated. 'Bing said there is a secret that connects them, and I think he is right.'

'What do you mean?' demanded Cary.

'Almost everything that has happened involves one or the other.' Chaloner spoke slowly, because he was still working out the details. 'The false certificates were produced by St Gregory's vicar and sold by his bell-ringers; the scheme was backed by two Agents of God; Pamela was attempting to cheat the cathedral with her fake London Treacle . . .'

Cary cocked his head as a wave of angry shouts came from the direction of the plague pit. 'I should go. And if you see Randall, either knock him senseless or lock the bastard up. He has been telling folk that the plague is the Quakers' fault, and we shall have a massacre on our hands unless he is silenced.'

Chaloner and Thurloe watched him go, exhaustion apparent in his every step.

'I hope *he* does not have the plague,' said Thurloe worriedly. 'Lawrence tells me that he cannot manage without him. Of course, it might not matter in a few hours. The city seethes with anger and resentment, and I have a very bad feeling about tonight.'

So did Chaloner. 'We *must* do something to calm the situation, because Monck's way of dealing with it will be to deploy his cannon. Using artillery on unarmed civilians will not only kill innocents, but it might ignite a violent backlash against the government.'

Thurloe was thoughtful. 'Then we must find Stone. I heard Antrobus say that he is in the cathedral, so let us go there now. Perhaps he can provide us with the answers we need to thwart the Executioner's nasty schemes.'

For the first time in weeks, it seemed the city might be in for a downpour. Clouds massed overhead, dark and heavy. The sun caught the undersides of some, turning them a sullen yellow-grey.

'Perhaps it will end this terrible heat,' panted Thurloe, who must have been roasting under his mask and cloak. 'The answer to our prayers at last.'

'We need gentle rain, not a deluge. If it falls too fast on dry ground, there will be floods – which is something we definitely do not need tonight.'

The cathedral was busy. Officials had arrived to prepare it for the ceremony, and more people than Chaloner could count were at their prayers, kneeling anywhere there was an empty spot. The Hall brothers were still selling London Treacle at a vigorous rate, while Owen counted their takings. Lawrence's men were toting two crates of it away, ready to be distributed to those who had left their names with his clerks.

'The canons must have stockpiled it,' said Thurloe, watching disapprovingly, 'to bring out when the price is higher. How else could they still have some left to hawk?'

Rycroft was there as well, feeding powder into huge plague-repelling braziers. They produced almost as much stinking smoke as Lawrence's bonfires, and made anyone near them retch. Chaloner supposed this was the 'urgent business' that had led him to refuse Thurloe's request for help.

'*Six* shillings a pot!' cried a potter to no one in particular, emerging in empty-handed dismay from the north transept. 'It was three shillings earlier. I cannot afford six!'

'The canons are no different from Joshua and his fellows,' muttered Thurloe. 'Profiting from the misery and despair of others. Shame on them!'

'Shame indeed,' agreed a voice from behind them, and they turned to see Lawrence. The mayor wore his usual burgundy suit, but it was stained with soot, and holes had been burned in several places from flying cinders. His hair was wild and his face dirty, but he was still a figure who commanded respect. 'They refused me a discount for the needy.'

'I thought Cary had already negotiated a reasonable price,' said Chaloner.

'So did I, but he dealt with Owen, who does not have the authority to make such arrangements, apparently. Only Francis does, but he declined to "cheat the cathedral of its revenues", so I had to pay the full amount.

I had no choice – I made a promise, and I cannot afford to break it. Not today of all days.'

Chaloner and Thurloe immediately reached for their purses, but Lawrence stopped them with a weary wave of his hand.

'Give it to the poor tonight, when we shall need every ounce of goodwill we can muster. People are beginning to turn against us, despite all we are trying to do for them.'

'The city has a dangerous feel,' agreed Thurloe. 'Perhaps you should cancel tonight's service. Then folk would not congregate in large and potentially uncontrollable groups.'

'If only I could! Unfortunately, the order to hold it comes from the King himself, and Monck refuses to countermand it. He says there will be no mass exodus, because he will prevent it.'

'Yes – with cannon,' muttered Chaloner.

'You should not be here, Lawrence,' said Thurloe. 'Some of the congregation might have the plague, and if you catch it, London really will be doomed.'

'I cannot lurk inside today. I must be seen, to convince folk that I am looking after their interests. I can lie around in bed tomorrow.' Lawrence smiled suddenly, and the strain ebbed from his face. 'Or perhaps I shall lie with Mrs Driver instead – I am told she is home again.'

'So is Stone.' Chaloner glanced around to see if he could spot the portly canon, but it was difficult to do when the cathedral held so many other people.

Lawrence's happy grin faded as Cary dashed up, breathing hard. 'You really should stop tearing around, Val. It is too hot.'

'Randall's vicious tongue has done its work at last,'

Cary gasped urgently. 'The Quakers in King's Head Court . . . They have taken refuge in Pamela Ball's house, but a mob aims to burn it down . . . with women and children inside.'

Chaloner knew his first duty was to find Stone, but how could he leave Ester to be incinerated? He took a step towards the door. Thurloe stopped him.

'There is nothing you can do against a horde intent on violence, Tom,' he said firmly. 'Let Lawrence deal with it.'

'I shall find a dozen good men, and lead them to King's Head Court myself,' declared Lawrence. 'Val – stay here, and monitor what is happening while I am gone.'

But gathering a troop of soldiers would take time, thought Chaloner in despair. The house might be ablaze by then, and those within would suffer a terrible death.

'Will you look for Stone?' he asked Thurloe. 'Try the Deanery first, and then the library. I will be back before you know it. I have a plan.'

He turned and tore towards the door before Thurloe could read the lie in his eyes.

Chaloner raced to King's Head Court, hoping that an idea to save the Quakers would occur to him en route. None did – at least, none that was sensible. His head throbbed from fear and tension, his shirt stuck to his back, and sweat stung his eyes. Worse, the air was so thick with smoke and dust that he could barely breathe.

When he arrived, he stared in horror. Heaps of wood had been stacked around Pamela's house, piled there by the rioters who were howling abuse at the frightened faces in the upper windows. One of the trapped Quakers began to sing a hymn for courage, but this only served to antagonise the mob even more. Many of the besiegers were Mims, and Chaloner wondered how much of their rage was really directed against Pamela, for forcing the cult on them against their will.

The crook-backed Randall was in the thick of the trouble, bawling encouragement to the rabble at the top of his voice. Leybourn was nowhere to be seen, for which Chaloner was grateful – he would not have wanted his friend caught up in such a mêlée.

Then he saw Ester, and breathed a heartfelt sigh of relief. She was not inside the house, but standing in the shadows of a nearby doorway, watching the scene unfold with stunned immobility. Moments later, Rycroft joined her there, gasping for breath. Chaloner supposed the alchemist had abandoned his smelly braziers when he had heard Lawrence calling for soldiers to accompany him to King's Head Court.

Frantically, Chaloner struggled to think of something – anything – that would prevent a flame from touching the wood, knowing that once it did, there would be no putting it out, as both fuel and house were tinder-dry. Then Randall appeared with a torch, and began to thrust his way forward. When he was stopped by the sheer press of numbers, Suger bulled towards him and lifted the little man on to his shoulders.

Chaloner fumbled in his pocket for the dag. He would discharge it in the air, and the report would cause the horde to scatter in alarm. Or would the sound of gunfire merely serve to inflame the situation even further? Then his groping fingers encountered something else: the two old coins that his hens had scratched up that morning. And *then* he knew what he had to do. He poured all the money he had with him into his hand, and plunged among the crowd, brandishing it aloft.

'Buried treasure!' he yelled, so loudly that his voice cracked. 'In Matthew Harbert's garden, by Paul's Gate. Huge chests of it, all for the taking.'

Nothing happened at first, but gradually the besiegers tore their attention away from Randall's bobbing torch to stare at him. He yelled his message again, and the Quakers' singing faltered into silence. All eyes were on Chaloner.

'He lies!' screeched Randall, incensed that his moment of glory should be interrupted. 'He is a Quaker, aiming to help his cronies escape. Ignore him and let us send these plague-toting villains to hell.'

'I speak the truth,' bawled Chaloner, waving the coins again and realising with a sick sensation that he would be torn limb from limb if his ploy failed, because there were far too many people to fight off. 'But hurry, or you will be too late.'

'Do not believe him,' shrieked Randall. 'He is a—'

'Gold!' boomed another voice, and Rycroft strode forward waving a newly minted guinea, which was a good deal more convincing than Chaloner's loose change. 'Look! And there are dozens more where this came from.'

'Of course there are,' sneered Suger. 'Just like there was a hoard in Pamela's house. Except there was not – we ripped the place apart, but never found a thing.'

Rycroft tossed him the guinea. Suger lunged to catch it, a move that dislodged Randall from his shoulders and sent him tumbling to the ground.

'Tell me *that* is not real,' challenged the alchemist. 'But I am not standing here to lose out while others get rich. Anyone who wants an easy fortune – come with me.'

393

He turned and raced away. There was a moment when Chaloner thought no one would follow, but then Suger hared after him, faster than Chaloner would have believed possible for so bulky a man. The other Mims were hot on his heels.

'No!' screamed Randall, scrambling to his feet. 'Stay here and roast Quakers. What is treasure when compared to ridding London of them who gave us the plague?'

But he was preaching to himself, because the remaining onlookers were streaming away as fast as their legs would carry them. In a furious gesture of defiance, Randall hobbled forward to light his pyre anyway, but Ester raced out from her hiding place and dealt him a clout around the ear that sent him flying. Chaloner battled through the stampeding horde towards them, but by the time he arrived, the apprentice had prudently made himself scarce.

'Thank you, Tom,' said Ester shakily. 'Now I must get my friends to safety before everyone realises that you have deceived them.'

'Hide them in Sir Arnold Harbert's house,' suggested Chaloner. 'That is empty, and his heir will not be needing it any time soon.'

He hurried back to St Paul's, passing Lawrence and his soldiers on the way, although he did not stop to tell them what had happened. They would find no angry mob to disperse, but they could still help Ester to secrete the Quakers in Harbert's mansion.

He glanced up at the sky as he ran. The clouds had brought an unpleasant humidity, which made the afternoon seem hotter than ever, and the air was so thick with smoke and dampness that it was difficult to breathe.

When he arrived back at St Paul's Churchyard, he saw that Suger and his cronies had reached Matthew's house, and were engaged in some serious plundering. Not everyone believed the tale of buried treasure, but a well-furnished mansion with an open door was reward enough. Chaloner could not see the garden, but he did hear the sounds of a frantic skirmish – something had been unearthed there, and the looters were fighting over the spoils.

He soon found Thurloe. Stone had not been in the Deanery or the library, so the ex-Spymaster was questioning lay officials about him. None were willing to stop for long, though, as they were frantically working to prepare for what was predicted to be the biggest ceremony they had hosted since the plague had broken out.

'There you are.' Thurloe's cool tone told Chaloner that he was in disgrace for haring off so precipitously. 'Stone was here two hours ago, but I cannot find anyone who has seen him since.'

'Then we shall ask them,' said Chaloner, nodding to where the purveyors of London Treacle had finally exhausted their supplies and were shutting up shop. Francis was guarding a very heavy money bag, John stacked empty crates and Owen swept the floor.

'We cannot sell you a bottle now,' said Francis briskly, as Chaloner and Thurloe approached. 'But come back after the service. It costs seven shillings a pint.'

'*Seven?*' exploded Thurloe. 'It was six a few minutes ago – and that was too high.'

John shrugged carelessly. 'Blame market forces – supply and demand. Besides, all the profits are for the cathedral, so where lies the problem?'

'You seem better,' remarked Chaloner, recalling that

John had claimed to be unwell the last time they had spoken.

The vicar smiled smugly. 'I would like to say it was a miracle, but the truth is that I just stopped taking *sal mirabilis*. My recovery was immediate.'

'More proof that London Treacle is the superior product,' put in Francis, and laid a satisfied hand on the money bag. 'And it grows more popular by the day. After all, what other medicine is blessed by high-ranking churchmen?'

'Stone,' said Thurloe curtly. 'We need to speak to him. Where is he?'

'We do not know,' replied Francis smoothly, although Owen's eyes were suddenly uneasy and John's face went suspiciously blank. 'We have not seen him since he went to visit his sister. But now you must excuse us. We are busy men with much to do.'

They bustled away. Chaloner started after them, aiming to put his questions more forcefully, but Thurloe grabbed his arm. Chaloner shook him off impatiently.

'They were lying. They *do* know where Stone is.'

'I suspect they know a lot more than that,' said Thurloe soberly. 'But leave them for now. Our priority is finding the Executioner.'

'Yes – which we might be able to do by interrogating Stone,' snapped Chaloner. 'But we cannot, because they refuse to cooperate. And you want to let them go?'

'London Treacle and *sal mirabilis* are by far the two most popular plague remedies,' said Thurloe with irritating calm, 'both generating huge sums of money. *Sal mirabilis* had the edge until recently, because it was cheaper, but now it has been implicated in several deaths, and folk are afraid to take it . . .'

Chaloner regarded him in disbelief. 'Do you really want to discuss this now?'

'*Think*, Tom! John was obviously lying when he said he took *sal mirabilis* because he had given his London Treacle away. First, he is not a man to make that sort of sacrifice; and second, the cathedral has masses of the stuff – he could just have collected another pot. It was pure invention, designed to damage the reputation of *sal mirabilis*.'

Chaloner shrugged impatiently. 'So he denigrated other medicines to stress the virtues of his own. What of it?'

'*Sal mirabilis* has suffered more than denigration – the Executioner has laced it with *acer*, and it has killed people.'

Chaloner gazed after the departing clerics. 'You mean that one of them is the culprit? They are, after all, the ones who will benefit from the rise of their medicine at the expense of the rest.'

Thurloe smiled grimly. 'Precisely! So let us follow them – discreetly – and see what we can find out. But no racing to confront them, if you please. This is a problem that can be resolved without recourse to violence.'

Chaloner nodded assent, but did not believe it for an instant.

It did not take them long to see where John, Francis and Owen were going: to St Gregory's, which was considerably quieter than the cathedral. The only people in the little church were two elderly women, who were gossiping gleefully about Masley's arrest. The vicar had been unpopular, and the hope was that a nicer one would now be appointed.

The three clerics aimed for the crypt, and when the

crones indignantly demanded to know what they thought they were doing, Francis whipped around and scowled at them.

'Have you not heard? Sir Arnold Harbert died of the plague, but his body still lies outside its vault. We are going to pray that none of you have inhaled the deadly miasma that has leaked from his rotting corpse.'

He did not need to add more, because the women were already hobbling out. Smirking his satisfaction, Francis unlocked the door at the top of the steps with a key he carried on a string around his neck.

'That means he is a regular visitor to the place,' murmured Chaloner. 'Why else would he keep it so conveniently on his person?'

'Quite,' Thurloe whispered back. 'And I suspect we are about to discover that Bing was right – there *is* a secret that links this church to the cathedral. Perhaps learning it will help us to thwart the Executioner's vile plans.'

The door had been relocked by the time they reached it, but Chaloner had it open in a trice, after which he and Thurloe crept down the steps to see the three clerics standing by the Countess of Devonshire's monument. There was no sign of William and Gaundy, suggesting that someone had arranged for them to be decently buried, while Kerchier and Harbert were at the far end of the crypt, well out of sight and smell.

Using the tomb as a workbench, John began to set out dozens of little bottles. Then Francis filled them with liquid from a nearby barrel and Owen stoppered them. They worked so efficiently that it was clear they had done it many times before. An unpleasant stench pervaded the air, one that Chaloner had encountered before. He felt like slapping his forehead in understanding. Urine! He had smelled it twice in the crypt already – once when he had been following Francis and once when he had been with Prayse. It had also been in the bottles of false London Treacle at Pamela's house. He turned to explain to Thurloe, but the ex-Spymaster was already nodding – he had made the connections for himself.

'Shall we see what they have to say for themselves?' Thurloe asked softly.

'I will,' said Chaloner. 'You stay back – a hidden weapon, if you will.'

He was glad when Thurloe agreed, as he was far from certain that the ex-Spymaster was right to think the situation would be resolved peacefully, and he sensed that his friend had had enough physical encounters for one day. He waited until Thurloe was safely concealed in the shadows, then stepped forward.

'You are cheating your customers if you claim that as London Treacle,' he said softly, watching the trio jump in alarm. Some of the liquid spilled from the jug. It was yellow-brown and sticky.

'How did you get in?' demanded Francis angrily. 'I locked the door.'

'Of course you did,' said Chaloner. 'You will not want anyone to see what you are doing down here – filling bottles with rubbish and passing it off as medicine. No wonder you had so much of it to sell today.'

'It is not the recipe that is important,' snapped Francis, irate but quick to regain his composure. 'It is the prayers we recite. *That* is what makes London Treacle efficacious. Besides, urine has many curative properties, and our potion also contains tobacco juice – another reliable confounder of the pestilence.'

'It is just as good as Rycroft's concoction,' stated Owen, although he did not look overwhelmingly convinced by his own claim.

Chaloner picked up a bottle, noting that the ink had smudged during the printing process, so its contents were branded *London Treade*, just like the ones that Pamela had stockpiled in her house. In the blank space left for the price, someone had handwritten *8s* – the canons were nothing if not diligent.

'Well, well,' he said. 'Labels printed on Upton's cheap paper. He *was* a busy man. No wonder you denied dealing with him – you did not want to explain what you did with the reams he sold you.'

John's expression hardened. 'You cannot tell anyone about this. If you do, folk will refuse to buy the potions that carry God's protection, and they will sicken and die.'

Chaloner shook his head in disgust. 'If you really believe that, you would have blessed *all* the available remedies, and the disease would never have taken hold in the first place. Instead, you slyly disparage your rivals, not to mention adding poison to them – poison that killed Upton, Harbert, Gaundy, Jasper—'

'Are you sure you do not have plague yourself?' interrupted John archly. 'Because you are raving mad to make such allegations.'

'All we have done is sell medicine.' Owen looked as though he might be sick, unlike the Halls, who were full of arrogant disdain. 'And for the best of causes: the cathedral.'

'Which you want demolished, so that another can be built in its place,' said Chaloner, not concealing his contempt. 'One that will be forever associated with *your* names.'

'Yes, because London deserves the best,' argued Francis passionately. 'The current one is falling to pieces, and we risk death every time we step through its portals.'

'And if you disagree, look at what happened to poor Pemper,' put in John.

'St Paul's cannot be saved,' Francis went on. 'It has been allowed to rot for too long. And do not accuse us of bringing that to pass – it has been centuries in the making.'

Chaloner gestured around him. 'But why hide your cache down here? Why not in William's fortress-like home? Or somewhere in the cathedral?'

'The stench,' explained Owen, although Francis glared at him. 'Our potion is necessarily pungent, as no one trusts anything that is bland. Rycroft's reeks, so ours also has to make its consumers' eyes water – to convince them that it is efficacious.'

'Which it is,' put in John quickly. 'Because of our prayers.'

Chaloner was about to bring an end to the debate by calling for Thurloe when he heard a yelp. He whipped around to see that someone else had been listening as well – someone who had then stumbled down the uneven bottom step.

'Christ God!' swore Prayse, bending down to rub the ankle he had twisted. 'Has no one seen to this damned stair yet? That is the second time I have nearly broken my neck on it.'

'Prayse!' cried Thurloe, emerging from his hiding place, much to the consternation of the three clerics. 'I *knew* you would never abandon the city you love. Quick – help us. These villains have just confessed to passing urine off as plague medicine and—'

'Shut up!' snarled Prayse. He hauled a gun from his belt and levelled it at the startled ex-Spymaster before addressing the clerics. 'Are you ready?'

Chaloner started to reach for his own gun, but raised his hands hurriedly when the physician saw what he was doing and made it clear that he would shoot Thurloe if he persisted.

'Ready for what?' he asked.

'For the final phase of our plan,' replied Prayse shortly. 'But you will not see it, because you will be down here. And unlike Kerchier, no one will find your bones.'

'*You* are the Executioner?' gasped Thurloe. 'No!'

# Chapter 13

The crypt suddenly seemed much colder and darker to Chaloner, and he was aware of the mounting sense that he and Thurloe would be powerless to prevent the plot that was brewing after all. And while the ex-Spymaster might be shocked by the revelation that his friend was part of the scheme, Chaloner knew they should have guessed sooner. After all, who better than a physician to dispatch his victims with a little-known toxin called *acer*?

He tensed, ready to whip out his gun the moment Prayse's attention wavered, but the physician was no fool and guessed his intentions at once.

'Throw down your weapons and step back against the wall,' he ordered. 'Now – or Thurloe dies.'

'Prayse, please,' said Thurloe softly, as Chaloner reluctantly began to disarm. 'Your city is in trouble. Let us work together to prevent—'

'You, too,' snapped Prayse. 'Or I shall kill you where you stand.'

Thurloe shook his head in disbelief as he tossed down his gun and went to stand next to Chaloner. Then John hurried forward and searched them both. He found no

403

more weapons on the ex-Spymaster, but Chaloner was relieved of his last two daggers.

'So you *are* the Executioner,' said Thurloe heavily to Prayse.

'I am not,' replied the physician curtly. 'And if you have not guessed his identity by now, you never will. However, he is someone I am happy to obey.'

'*What?*' blurted Francis, exchanging an uneasy glance with Owen and John. 'But you told us that you knew nothing about the Executioner.'

'I will explain later,' said Prayse tersely.

'No – explain now,' ordered Francis. 'And what have you done with Stone? You promised no harm would come to him if we brought him down here and—'

'And nor will it,' snapped Prayse impatiently. 'All will become clear soon – you just have to trust me. Now pack up those medicines and take them to the cathedral. Hurry! We do not have much time.'

'But you were sent one of those warnings, Prayse,' said Thurloe in bewilderment, as the clerics hastened to do as they were told, although all three were clearly unsettled by their accomplice's revelations. 'How can you follow such a man?'

The physician sneered. 'It was a ruse to lead you astray – you are too observant for your own good. Yet I wish you had lodged elsewhere, because I am sorry our association must end this way.'

While he spoke, Chaloner inched towards the gun that Thurloe had been forced to drop. One more step would put him within reach of it, at which point, he would shoot Prayse and subdue the clerics with his fists. But Prayse saw what he was doing and snarled an order at John. The vicar scurried over and kicked the weapon away. It skittered across the floor and disappeared under the Countess's tomb.

'What are you going to do, Prayse?' asked Thurloe. His face was pale: the betrayal was a serious blow to a man who prided himself as a good judge of character.

'Something that should have been done years ago,' came the brusque reply. 'Something that will hurt London in the short term, but that future generations will consider a blessing. The Executioner knows what he is doing.'

By this time, Owen, Francis and John were lugging their load of 'London Treacle' up the stairs. Prayse followed, his gun trained on Chaloner and Thurloe to prevent last-minute rushes; the lamp was in his other hand.

'At least leave us some light, Prayse,' said Thurloe reproachfully.

'Why?' shrugged Prayse. 'You will not need it, not if your eyes are closed in prayer.'

'And what should we pray for?' asked Thurloe. 'Our beloved city, which is about to suffer some dreadful outrage at your hands? Or for you, a man whose soul will be bound for hell unless he stops to consider his actions?'

'For yourselves,' replied Prayse shortly. 'You will be in Paradise soon, and you do not want to arrive burdened down by unconfessed sins.'

He reached the top of the stairs and slammed the door, leaving Thurloe and Chaloner in total blackness. There was a click as the key turned in the lock. Blindly, Chaloner stumbled up the steps towards it, Thurloe at his heels. However, he had only just located the door with questing fingers when there was a thump, and the wood trembled under his hand.

405

'A bench,' came Prayse's muffled explanation. There was a distinct gloat in his voice: he had known his prisoners would have reached it and would be listening on the other side. 'Jammed tightly between the door and the wall. You will not be able to move it, so do not waste your time trying.'

'Prayse!' cried Thurloe in despair. 'What are you—'

'You will find out soon enough.'

When the physician and clerics had gone, the silence in the undercroft was absolute. So was the darkness. Then there was a soft scrape and light flared: Thurloe had noticed where a spare lamp and kindling were kept. Unfortunately, there was very little fuel left.

'It will not last long, Tom,' he warned. 'So we need to escape fast – not just because it will be far more difficult to do so once the oil runs out, but because I am not sitting down here while the Executioner does London some irreparable harm.'

Chaloner began a furious assault on the door that involved kicks, shoulder-charges and levers, but Prayse had been telling the truth: it could not be opened from the inside. Meanwhile, Thurloe took the lantern and conducted an urgent but systematic search of the rest of the crypt, although he discovered nothing of use – the door was the only way in or out.

'I do not like the look of those cracks,' he remarked, glancing up to where the ceiling was a mosaic of fissures. 'Are you sure it is safe down here?'

An unsettling image of a younger Gaundy sprang into Chaloner's mind, feverishly excavating in an attempt to destabilise the cathedral's foundations above.

'It has lasted twenty years,' he mumbled, deciding to

keep his concerns to himself. 'There is no reason why it should crumble now.'

'Prayse,' said Thurloe, unable to push his erstwhile friend from his mind. 'His involvement makes no sense. He is a Quaker – they have no truck with cathedrals. What does he care if St Paul's is new or old?'

'He is not as devout as you think. He cursed – twice – when he tripped over that step, and truly religious men do not blaspheme. Nor do they charge their friends rent.'

'But Cromwell loved him like a brother! We cannot both have been wrong.'

The remark explained a good deal as far as Chaloner was concerned. Thurloe had worshipped Cromwell, and had trusted his judgement implicitly. Anyone who won the Lord Protector's approbation could automatically expect his Spymaster's as well.

'What did he mean when he said we would soon see Paradise?' Thurloe asked when there was no reply. 'Will he come to kill us later, with blows on the head and *acer*?'

'No – he said he was not the Executioner, and I believe him.'

'Why, when he has delighted in deceiving us at every turn?' asked Thurloe bitterly. 'He even examined the victims' bodies – *his* victims' bodies – and "found" clues to help us. And he identified the poison as *acer*. Every word of his so-called expert testimony was a lie.'

'No, it was the truth – Rycroft and our own observations confirmed most of it.'

Thurloe frowned. 'So why did he—'

'As Prayse did his "master" no favours by examining those corpses, it makes me wonder how long he has been aware that the man he has chosen to follow is a killer.

You saw a message delivered to him yesterday – one with a red seal – after which he packed up and appeared to flee . . .'

'And?' demanded Thurloe, when Chaloner trailed off.

'And I suspect it contained instructions, which he obediently carried out – including leaving a "Mind the Executioner" note, complete with a red seal, for you to find. Then, when he was somewhere private, he was told the truth.'

'Where he elected to continue following the rogue anyway, instead of turning to me.'

'Doubtless he is well paid, and he does like money.'

'So who is the Executioner?' asked Thurloe in despair. 'Are we back to Sancroft again? Or one of his clerics?'

'Not Francis, John or Owen – they were shocked by the revelation that Prayse is in cahoots with him. Prayse said it was someone he is happy to obey, so perhaps it is Tillison or Henchman. Or yes, it could still be Sancroft.'

Thurloe turned the lamp as low as possible. 'I have no idea of the time, but it will not be long before this crisis reaches its climax.'

'And then we will die,' predicted Chaloner. He had a deep-rooted horror of dungeon-like places, so he was unable to prevent the tremor in his voice. 'In the dark, because our fuel is almost exhausted already.'

'No,' countered Thurloe determinedly. 'We shall devise a plan to outwit our assassins when they come. Besides, St Gregory's will not remain empty indefinitely – someone will come in to pray. When they do, we shall holler to be let out.'

Chaloner began to experience a weary sense of defeat as more of the puzzle fell into place. 'You dismissed

408

Randall's claim about smuggling gunpowder into the city, but I have a bad feeling that it might be true.'

'The Executioner plans to blow something up?' Thurloe gaped in horror as realisation dawned. 'Not the cathedral?'

'I believe so. And most of this crypt lies directly beneath it.'

Thurloe continued to stare. 'But why would he do such a terrible thing?'

'Because if it "falls down", there will be no option but to build a new one.'

'But he cannot! People pray in it at all hours of the day and night. He will never find a time when it is empty.'

'He does not want it empty – he wants there to be casualties. And it will happen during tonight's service, when it will be full to bursting. Afterwards, the whole country will be so appalled by the scale of the "accident" that any parts left standing will be razed to the ground, leaving the land vacant for its replacement.'

'It will *never* be deemed an accident! An explosion large enough to demolish St Paul's will be heard from miles away. Everyone will know it was sabotage.'

'Any booms will be dismissed as the sound of the building tumbling down. Foul play will never be suspected, and the disaster will be passed off as an Act of God.'

'But this makes no sense, Tom. The Executioner has been killing Agents – folk who have been amassing money to rebuild. They were on his side.'

'Yes,' acknowledged Chaloner. 'And I cannot tell you why he turned against them, but I am sure I am right. I suppose we shall die in ignorance.'

'No,' said Thurloe with quiet determination. 'We cannot allow this to happen. Is there any false London

409

Treacle left? Perhaps we can use it to create an explosion of our own – one that will blow open the door. It does, after all, contain some very nasty ingredients.'

They returned to the Countess of Devonshire's monument, but although a powerful reek still hung around it, the clerics had used every last drop of the liquid in the barrel.

'The cask is empty, so why does this place still stink so?' asked Thurloe, then answered the question himself. 'Because they have another cache hidden away, of course! They will not want to run out now that they can charge top rates for it.'

'Francis!' blurted Chaloner suddenly. 'I saw him come down here a few days ago, but when I tried to find him, he had disappeared. It is possible that he hid and doubled back . . .'

'But you rather think he used an alternative exit?'

Chaloner nodded quickly. 'And remember why this undercroft was dug – in the spiteful hope that it would undermine the cathedral. Master Mason Gaundy might well have installed some sly device in the expectation that it would come in useful in the future.'

Thurloe patted the Countess's tomb. 'I never was convinced that she was banished from the chancel upstairs because of her colourful morals – she was moved for some other reason, so let us begin with her. It will be much safer than trying to ignite London Treacle.'

Heartened, Chaloner started to push and poke at the monument, hunting for evidence of a secret opening, while Thurloe explored the cracks with a dagger. His jabs grew increasingly frenzied as the minutes ticked by with no result.

'Is someone there?' came a very faint voice. 'Help me!'

'That came from inside,' gulped Thurloe. 'Pray God it was not the Countess.'

'Not unless she was a man,' said Chaloner, then yelled at the top of his lungs, 'Tell us how to open it.'

'Twist her nose,' came the muffled reply. 'Hurry! They have tied me up down here. It is pitch dark and I can barely breathe.'

Chaloner did as he was told, but the nose came off in his hand – the mechanism had been deliberately smashed.

'Who are you?' shouted Thurloe, indicating with an urgent flap of his hand that Chaloner should mend it.

'Ben Stone. Canon Ben Stone.'

Chaloner had no idea how long he sat astride the Countess of Devonshire, frantically struggling to loop two pieces of thin wire together through the tiniest of holes. Every time he thought he had succeeded, one would spring loose. Aware of Stone's rising panic at the delay, Thurloe asked questions in an effort to calm him.

'Who put you down here?' he called. 'Your fellow clerics?'

'I think so. At least, I was talking to Owen when someone crept up behind me and put a sack over my head. Then I was bundled down here and tied up.'

'Where have you been these last few days?'

'With my sister in Wapping. But why would Owen—'

'Your sisters are dead,' interrupted Thurloe. 'Do not lie. You were with Mrs Driver.'

'Oh,' came the sheepish response. 'You know. Well, a man must take what relief he can in these uncertain times. Surely you understand that?'

'Certificates of Health.' Thurloe moved to another matter. 'We have been told to question you about the

411

forgeries that Masley has been producing by the box-load.'

'*Masley* is the culprit? Well, damn me! I had no idea.' There was a short silence, then, 'Tillison asked me to be the cathedral's official investigator, and the profusion of false certificates was one of the matters he told me to explore. But Masley? Well!'

'Why did Tillison choose you?' Thurloe sounded sceptical.

'Because he said that someone had to find out what was going on, and I am the only one he trusts. He fears the others may be involved, you see, but he knows I am not, as I am always too busy visiting ladies.'

'What other matters did he charge you to look into?'

'Why Upton died so soon after arriving here, how William managed to amass so much money, and then – after the skeleton was found – the matter of Kerchier and his lost hoard. Unfortunately, I quickly learned that solving mysteries is not my forte.'

'You learned nothing about them at all?'

'Not really.' Stone's voice turned defensive. 'But then those arrogant Hall brothers mocked me, and called me a useless lecher. To save face, I *might* have exaggerated my progress a bit more than was strictly honest . . .'

Chaloner cursed under his breath as the wires flipped apart just when he thought he finally had them connected.

'To Bing?' asked Thurloe. 'And Antrobus?'

'Among others. But when Tillison requested an official report, I decided to slip away for a while, in the hope that he would have forgotten about it by the time I got back. It is one thing to *hint* that I had answers, but another altogether to put it in writing.'

'Did you know that the Halls and Owen have been

mixing urine and tobacco juice, and passing it off as medicine?'

'They have been doing *what*?' came the incredulous response. 'No!'

Thurloe turned to Chaloner in disgust. 'The Halls were right to sneer at his abilities as an investigator. Hunting for him was a total waste of our time.'

The two bits of wire slipped out of Chaloner's grasp yet again, and he released a series of pithy oaths. His back and shoulders ached from the cramped position he was obliged to hold, and his hands were slippery with sweat. He sat back for a moment and forced himself to relax.

'Tom!' snapped Thurloe. 'This is no time for sitting around with your eyes closed. If you do not hurry, we are going to be buried under thousands of tons of rubble.'

It was not a remark that helped.

'Gather up our weapons,' ordered Chaloner, thinking his task might be easier if Thurloe was not looming over him. 'We may need them.'

Thurloe obliged, while Chaloner took a deep breath and reached for the wires again. He moved them with infinite care, and there was a soft click as they reattached. He jumped off the tomb, grabbed the Countess's nose and watched in relief as the lid slid to one side. A powerful reek of urine wafted out.

'Thank God!' cried Thurloe, arriving with the weapons, and shoving several randomly at Chaloner. 'Now let us get away from this terrible place before we are crushed like snails.'

The inside of the Countess's tomb comprised a deep, stone-lined pit. It was similar to the one that was to have housed Sir Arnold Harbert, but with three significant differences. First, there was a barrel of stinking liquid in it – an enormous one, which explained why the cathedral always had so much 'London Treacle' to sell. Second, it had been furnished with steps that led to a small door. And third, there was no body in it – the Countess had been ousted.

Chaloner took the fading lamp and descended. The door led to a narrow tunnel, and Stone lay trussed up in its entrance. The canon wept with relief as Chaloner cut him free. The moment the last rope was severed, Stone staggered towards the stairs.

'We must use the tunnel to escape,' said Thurloe, putting out a hand to stop him. 'The door to the crypt is jammed shut.'

'No!' screamed Stone, so loudly and despairingly that Chaloner and Thurloe recoiled in shock. 'Then we are all dead! Why did you fill me with false hope?'

'False hope?' echoed Thurloe uneasily.

'The tunnel is packed with gunpowder,' wailed Stone. 'Can you not smell it?'

Chaloner supposed he could detect a faint whiff of saltpetre and brimstone over the rank contents of the barrel. 'You did not think to mention this sooner?'

'Of course not! You would have fled, leaving me to be blown to pieces alone.'

Weeping, Stone grabbed the lamp, thrust them aside and waddled away. Moments later, Chaloner and Thurloe heard hollow booms as he attempted to batter down the door, followed by frantic screams for help. But it was not long before he was back again.

'It was pride that brought me to this pass,' he sobbed, setting the lamp on the tomb and slumping down in defeat. 'I should have acknowledged my failure as a solver of mysteries, instead of bragging about discoveries I never made.'

'Pull yourself together,' ordered Thurloe sternly. 'Now, this tunnel goes east. Where is its other end? The Chapter House? The south transept?'

Stone was crying too hard to reply, but Chaloner knew the answer.

'St Faith's – probably the tomb of Rector Brown. You and I both saw Francis near it when we went down there to talk once. It was an odd place for him to loiter, and we should have been suspicious of it at the time.'

'We should,' agreed Thurloe. 'And I am sure you are right: the men who dug this corridor would not have put the other end in the cathedral, where it might have been discovered by their enemies. The parishioners of St Faith's, however, would have sided with St Gregory's . . .'

'Yes, it leads to St Faith's,' wept Stone. 'But we will never get there – not with thirty barrels of gunpowder barring our way.'

'Then stay here and take your chances,' said Chaloner harshly.

The tunnel was a terrible place. It was only chest height, which meant crouching awkwardly, and very narrow. This was a serious problem for Stone, who was portly and not very agile, and Chaloner had to stop several times to pull him on. Worse, it had collapsed in places, forcing them to crawl over piles of debris. Its air was hot, dusty and difficult to breathe, while the lamp grew dimmer with every step they took.

'Bing was right about one thing at least,' muttered Chaloner, to take his mind off the unpleasant prospect of scrambling along in the dark. 'He told us that Stone knows a secret that connects St Gregory's to the cathedral. He does – it is this passageway.'

'Gaundy built it,' panted Stone. 'When his crypt failed to bring down Inigo Jones's portico, he decided to target the south transept instead. But then the cathedral appeased St Gregory's by donating a piece of ground to use as a cemetery, so he abandoned his plans of revenge.'

'Is that why the south transept is on the verge of collapse?' asked Chaloner, glancing upwards uneasily. 'Over the years, this burrow has caused its foundations to slip?'

'Perhaps. It would explain all the roof-falls.'

Chaloner thought about the thousands of tons of cathedral above his head, all waiting to plummet. He took a deep breath to steady his nerves, but dust made him cough, and it was difficult to stop once he had started.

'Where is the gunpowder?' he managed to gasp.

'Not far now. Can you not smell it? It reeks of hell.'

Chaloner glanced at the fading lantern. What if it died before they could assess what they were dealing with? He stumbled on, trying to move more quickly.

'Who else knows about this place?' Thurloe was asking Stone.

'Originally, just a handful of men from St Gregory's and St Faith's, although they are all dead now. Gaundy was the last.'

'And various cathedral officials, obviously.'

'Yes, although none of us have been aware of it for long. And we would have remained in ignorance for ever, if it had not been for Pemper.'

'Pemper?'

416

'Gaundy used to come down here for a quiet drink, but one day he was careless – he let the nosy Pemper see him climbing down into the Countess's grave. Pemper ran straight to the Chapter House and told us about it.'

Chaloner was not surprised to learn that the spiteful cathedral ringer had stooped to spying on his rivals. Of course, he was dead now as well, ostensibly brained by a lump of ceiling in the south transept. Yet surely it was an odd coincidence that both Pemper and Gaundy should die just as the tunnel was about to play a major role in the cathedral's destruction?

'Who was in the Chapter House when Pemper made his announcement?' he asked.

'Tillison, the Halls, Owen and me,' replied Stone. 'But Tillison swore us to secrecy, because he thought it was not something that anyone else needed to know.'

Chaloner turned to peer at him. '*Tillison* wanted it kept quiet?'

'He was most insistent. Why?'

Chaloner glanced back at Thurloe. 'I think Gaundy's murder had nothing to do with the false certificates. I suspect it was to prevent him from talking about this place.'

'He kept it quiet for twenty years, Tom,' said Thurloe doubtfully. 'Why would anyone worry about him revealing it now?'

'Because Pemper's spying meant that Gaundy could no longer use it as a place to dodge work – he was forced to find an alternative refuge in the tower. It no longer mattered to him who knew about it, so the Executioner killed him, lest he was tempted to gossip.'

Thurloe nodded acceptance of the point as he gave Stone a prod, to get him moving again. 'And no one trusts a sneak, so Pemper's days were numbered, too. It is easy to make a deliberate blow to the head look like an accident in an unstable building.'

'I think Gaundy might have mentioned the tunnel to Upton, though,' said Chaloner. 'Kirton saw them talking together shortly before Upton died, and Joshua told me that it could not have been about the false certificates, because neither knew that the other was involved.'

'Upton *did* know about it,' said Stone suddenly. 'I forgot – I heard him bring it up to Tillison, when he came to sell Owen some paper. I am not sure why Owen wanted paper, as there should have been plenty in our store-room . . .'

'So there is our Executioner,' said Thurloe softly. 'Not Sancroft, but his deputy.'

'Is Tillison not too old to hit people over the head and force poison down their throats?' asked Chaloner, far from certain that their reasoning was correct.

'We shall have to find out. If we ever escape this tunnel, of course.'

They struggled on for what felt like an age, then Chaloner stopped. They had reached the first of the kegs of gunpowder. He yanked out the fuse that trailed from it, and pressed on, uncomfortably aware that the lamp was now so low that he could barely see the floor. Moments later, he came across a second barrel and a third, both connected by fuses. He pulled those out as well, and moved to a fourth . . . a fifth . . . a seventh . . .

Thurloe was a silent, stoical presence behind him, but Stone whimpered in terror as he tried to ease his bulk past the barrels without touching them. A tenth . . . a twelfth . . .

'So Randall did smuggle explosives into the city,'

murmured Chaloner. 'He was telling the truth for once.'

'He is incapable of such a feat,' argued Thurloe. 'He probably overheard the real culprit talking about it, and decided to claim the credit.'

'Or he helped the real culprit. He is desperate for money, and will turn his hand to anything to get some, even murder.'

Thurloe remained dubious. 'How could he – or anyone, for that matter – get hold of gunpowder? It is not something one buys at the market.'

'Monck will have some for his artillery,' shrugged Chaloner. 'And it is not difficult to corrupt badly paid guards.'

'Does that mean Monck will not be able to deploy his guns tonight? Thank God!'

'It will not matter,' said Chaloner, squeezing past the fifteenth keg. 'Because no one will storm the city gates. The rumour about a mass exodus is a lie – one intended to attract people to St Paul's, where they will either be blown up or left staring at ruins.'

At that moment, the lamp went out. Chaloner started to curse, but then realised that he could still see – there was a light ahead. He made an urgent sound at the back of his throat, warning Thurloe and Stone to keep quiet, and desperately hoped that they would not be forced to run back the way they had come. He heard voices, hurrying footsteps and a sharp bang. Then there was only darkness and silence. Other than a hiss.

'What is that?' whispered Stone in alarm.

'A fuse,' replied Thurloe tersely, but Chaloner did not hear Stone's response, because he was lurching forward, grazing head, elbows, shoulders and knees in his frantic haste to locate the source of the noise.

He soon found it. The fuse was a long one – the Executioner evidently did not want the cathedral to tumble about his ears just yet. Chaloner stamped it out and sagged against the wall in relief. But the hissing continued – there was another!

The next few moments were a wild panic, as he groped around in total blackness, using only his ears to guide him. He finally tracked the sound to an alcove at one side, where two more barrels of powder sat. He smothered the fuse with his hands and listened intently for more, but the silence was now absolute. Shaking with tension, he crawled back to Thurloe, then began to feel his way along the main tunnel again, hoping it would not be too far to St Faith's.

'And let us pray that they have not blocked that off, like they did in St Gregory's,' muttered Thurloe. 'I dislike the notion of hundreds of people assembled directly above so much powder. It is unpredictable and I want the place evacuated.'

'Twenty barrels,' came Stone's frightened voice. 'I counted twenty barrels down here, but my captors mentioned *thirty*. Ten are somewhere else. We may die yet!'

Fortunately, the rest of the journey was easier, despite the lack of light. There were fewer roof-falls to negotiate, and it was not long before Chaloner came smack up against a wall. His questing fingers located a handle, and when he tugged it, a wooden panel swung open. It transpired to be part of Rector Brown's tomb – they were right to surmise that Francis had been about to use it when he had been in St Faith's the previous Sunday.

Chaloner climbed through the opening, and was about to reconnoitre when Stone barrelled past him, shoving

420

him so hard that he was sent flying head over heels. The portly canon raced for the stairs, desperate to be away from the danger. Thurloe was hot on his heels, aiming to clear the cathedral before there was a bloodbath, but their way was barred by someone coming down the chapel steps.

'Cary!' shouted Thurloe in relief. 'Thank God! There is a plot afoot to blow up St Paul's. We must get everyone out.'

'Must we?' asked Cary shortly. 'Why?'

Chaloner had picked himself up and was about to follow Thurloe, but the secretary's words stopped him dead in his tracks. He ducked behind Rector Brown's grave to listen, heart hammering painfully. Now what?

'You should not have meddled,' said Cary sharply. 'I am afraid it will cost you dear.'

There was a groan of despair from Stone, although Thurloe was silent. Chaloner eased forward to see what was happening. The secretary held a gun, and four green-ribboned Mims were behind him. One was Suger, who toted a musket, while his cronies had cudgels.

Chaloner closed his eyes in despair. He and Thurloe had seen Francis in St Faith's, but Cary had been there, too – he had been on his knees and Thurloe had politely apologised for disturbing his prayers. How could they have forgotten?

'*You* are part of this monstrous plan?' Thurloe's voice was unsteady with shock, although his hand hovered over the dag in his belt, ready to draw it the moment Cary's attention wavered. 'I thought you loved London.'

'I do,' replied Cary. 'Which is why this must happen.'

While Suger covered Thurloe with the musket, Cary

stepped forward and relieved the ex-Spymaster of his gun. A distant part of Chaloner's mind noted that it was the one that Cary had lent him the previous week, although the secretary did not appear to recognise it. Chaloner himself had Pamela's. He pulled it from his pocket. It was smaller and much less powerful, but that did not matter – it would still drop Cary.

'Oh, God!' cried Stone, his horrified shriek cutting into Chaloner's thoughts. He was gazing behind a pillar. 'Owen!'

Two figures were sprawled there, both bleeding from wounds to the backs of their heads. Owen's eyes were already glazed in death.

'And Prayse!' breathed Thurloe in confusion. 'But why . . . he was on your side!'

'And he was well paid for it,' replied Cary calmly. 'He monitored you, he set the fuses in the tunnel, and he acquired the gunpowder on my behalf.'

Using Randall, thought Chaloner, recalling how the apprentice had approached Prayse in St Gregory's under the pretext of having a bubo. But Prayse did not tend plague victims, and would have refused such a consultation, especially with a man who clearly could not pay. The truth was that they had discussed the explosives – right under his and Thurloe's noses! And while Randall was incapable of carrying out such an audacious feat on his own, it would have posed no great challenge for the wily physician.

'Then why did you kill him?' asked Thurloe. He sounded exhausted, but Chaloner knew why he continued to bombard Cary with questions – he was playing for time, aiming to give Chaloner a chance to devise a plan to salvage the situation. Except that Chaloner's mind was alarmingly blank.

'Because he dabbled in other business as well,' replied Cary with a grimace. 'Namely the despicable sale of false London Treacle.'

The Mims had retreated to the steps, where Suger began to relate some tale that had the others sniggering their amusement. Chaloner assessed his options. Could he shoot Cary, then dart forward and disarm Suger before he could deploy his musket? Unfortunately, Suger was too far away, so that would not work. Should he shoot Suger first then? But Cary had two guns, and would simply kill him and Thurloe, after which there would be no one left to prevent the plan from succeeding – Chaloner knew he could not rely on Stone to help.

'The false medicine was not your idea?' asked Thurloe went on. 'To raise money for your new cathedral?'

'Of course not.' Cary sounded genuinely offended. 'I was appalled when Prayse told me about the scheme – braggingly, as if I should be impressed. I brained him and Owen on the spot. How dare they cheat my fellow citizens! *And* Lawrence, who was charged full price for the stuff, even though he was buying it for the poor.'

Thurloe blinked his bemusement. 'You object to Londoners being deceived, yet you aim to blow hundreds of them up? I think there is something awry with your reasoning!'

Cary did not answer. 'Where is Chaloner?'

'Killed by Prayse,' lied Thurloe. 'But why do you linger here, when ten barrels of powder are rigged to explode at any moment?'

He spoke loudly for the Mims' benefit, but they were cackling at some joke of Suger's and did not hear. Cary coughed, and when he raised one hand to wipe his mouth,

Chaloner saw that there was something wrong with it – the skin was raw.

'I am honoured to give my life for London,' the secretary replied calmly. 'You will also die, along with Francis and John, although they are blissfully unaware of it.'

'Unfortunately for you, we stamped out the fuses in the tunnel,' said Stone shakily but defiantly. 'Your blast will not be as massive as you hope.'

Cary regarded him disdainfully. 'Of course it will! When the other kegs ignite, they will set off the ones in the passage as well. It is how these things work.'

'Sacrifice yourself, by all means,' said Thurloe in distaste. 'But you have no right to demand the same of folk who come to pray. And while I know that Lawrence would like a new cathedral, I cannot see him approving of your way of getting one.'

Cary sneered at him. 'And who do you think will discuss it with him? You?'

'Abigail!' blurted Thurloe desperately. 'She will attend this service with her daughters. You cannot put them in danger – you love her.'

Cary smiled faintly. 'More than life itself. However, she thinks her mother is dying, and is riding to her bedside in Kent as we speak. She is safely out of harm's way.'

'Why are you doing this?' asked Stone tearfully. 'What harm have we ever done you?'

'Oh, plenty,' said Cary acidly. 'But that is in the past, and we should look to the future. To Christopher Wren.'

'The architect?' queried Stone stupidly.

'He has great plans, not just for St Paul's, but for the whole city. And when better to sweep away all that is ancient and rotten than when so many of its important residents are absent? What will happen shortly will be seen as a major turning point in our city's history.'

'Yes – one that deprives it of half its population,' said Thurloe caustically.

'Paupers,' shrugged Cary, 'who do nothing but complain about the free food and medicine we give them out of the goodness of our hearts. No one will mourn them.'

'But it is not the discontented who will gather here to pray,' objected Thurloe, as the first strains of organ music began to drift down into the undercroft; the service would start soon. 'It is the devout. If you must destroy the cathedral, at least let them out first.'

'I am afraid their blood is necessary – as is yours and mine. You see, parts of the building may survive the blast, but no one will want to restore them if they are associated with a thousand deaths. Kerchier had the right idea, but at the wrong time.'

Chaloner's mind raced. Kerchier had lost two fingers, perhaps from an encounter with explosives, although he had steadfastly denied it. *Had* the old canon found another source of gunpowder when Monck refused to provide him with a keg – a supply that had been dangerously unstable, and had resulted in a mishap as he had experimented?

'The last words anyone heard him say,' Thurloe was breathing in understanding. 'That St Gregory's might fall down of its own accord. Meaning that he had devised a way to destroy it and make it look like an accident . . .'

'He planned to rid himself of St Gregory's first, then turn his attention to the cathedral,' nodded Cary.

'So you killed him,' stated Thurloe flatly. 'Which means that *you* are the Executioner.'

# Chapter 14

There was silence in the crypt. Cary had shoved his own gun in his belt, and was covering them with the one he had taken from Thurloe, which was newer and more powerful. The ex-Spymaster stood proud and erect, unwilling to let Cary see his rising distress, while Stone cowered behind him. Suger and his cronies were in a cluster on the steps, whispering and blissfully unaware that they were about to be blown to kingdom come.

'I *had* to stop Kerchier,' explained Cary quietly. 'Inigo Jones had alienated people by ripping down St Gregory's, and Londoners would have hated any new cathedral designed by him on principle. Kerchier was about to light his fuses when I happened across him.'

'So you hit him on the head and dripped *acer* in his mouth,' surmised Thurloe.

Cary winced at the memory. 'I hit him several times, but he refused to die. It was awful. But I had a pot of *acer* with me – I was apprenticed to a tanner at the time, and always had some with me – so I sat on top of him and managed to drip some into his mouth. He struggled violently, and some spilled on his clothes. I have got better at it since then.'

426

'And then you hid his body in Harbert's vault.'

'It was meant to be temporary, but Gaundy's drunken father came along and sealed it up. He saved me a lot of bother.'

'How many lives have you claimed?' asked Thurloe, desperately encouraging the secretary to talk, while shooting an anguished glance at the shadows where Chaloner still hid. 'Gaundy, Pemper and Upton, because they knew about the tunnel . . .'

'It was vital to my plans – I could not have them braying its existence to all and sundry. Gaundy promised discretion, but then I overheard him blurt the secret to Upton in his cups. I cornered him in the tower, where he promptly confessed his role in hawking counterfeit Certificates of Health – which was yet *another* sly scheme designed to harm London.'

'And Pemper?'

'He certainly could not be trusted to keep his mouth shut. I took the precaution of yelling the name of one of his rival ringers before I struck the fatal blow. His skull must have been thinner than the others', because he died without needing the *acer*. Everyone assumed his death was an unfortunate accident.'

'The Hall brothers, Owen, Stone and Tillison also knew the secret, but you did not kill them.' Thurloe's voice shook with tension, and he glanced yet again in Chaloner's direction, urging him to do something fast.

'I reasoned that clerics were less likely to gossip than drunks, spies and dishonest stationers.' Cary shook his head slowly. 'I also assumed they were ethical men, although their disgraceful antics with the medicine have proved me wrong on that point.'

Thurloe returned to Upton. 'I assume it was you who

427

tried to have my kinsman buried with no questions asked?'

Cary's expression turned sour. 'I should have put him in the plague pit, but I thought a private grave might comfort his new bride. I should not have allowed compassion to cloud my judgement. It was a reckless mistake.'

Chaloner could tell that Thurloe was beginning to despair of rescue, but what could he do? One gun and one knife were no match for the arsenal that Cary and the Mims carried, and his suicide would help no one. Meanwhile, the organist was playing a thundering piece by Buxtehude, which suggested that there were enough people in the cathedral to warrant the trouble – people who would die when the powder ignited and the cathedral toppled. Chaloner gritted his teeth in an agony of desperation. He *had* to think of a way to stop it!

'But why kill William?' asked Stone tearfully. 'It was not because of the false London Treacle – you admitted that you have only just learned about that. And everything he earned went towards the rebuilding fund. He would have been an asset to you.'

Cary did not bother to reply, so Thurloe did. 'Because Cary aimed to steal that money for himself. And it is not the first time, is it, Cary?'

Although he knew he should be devising a plan to escape, Chaloner found himself reviewing what the secretary had confided about his past – the studies funded at Cambridge by his uncle the dean. But Cary's knowledge of the university was dubious, leaving Chaloner to wonder if he had ever been there, while all Dean Cary's fortune had been spent on his own tomb.

So *there* was the answer – Cary had used what he had stolen from Kerchier to buy himself an education, although not the respectable one he had claimed. More proof was in the slip Cary had just made himself – the confession that he was apprenticed to a tanner when he had claimed his first victim. Tanners did not usually rise to become personal secretaries to powerful merchants.

Cary glowered. 'William's thieving brothers kept awarding themselves illicit "commissions", so yes, I tried to remove it from their unscrupulous hands. However, it would not have been theft – every penny would have gone where it belonged.'

'This time,' said Thurloe acidly, telling Chaloner that the ex-Spymaster had also worked out what had happened to the first lot – or what had been left of it, after Bing had filched what he had needed for his viol.

'I did not *steal* Kerchier's fund either,' declared Cary crossly. 'I used a little to . . . to put myself in a position where I could dedicate myself to serving the city.'

'And the rest?'

Cary shrugged. 'My plan has been a long time in the making, and there have been expenses along the way – including helping Abigail and Lawrence to fight the plague. That has been very costly. And there is my uncle's tomb, of course. It will not be cheap to rebuild an exact replica in Wren's new chancel.'

'And how will you ensure that happens?' asked Thurloe. 'You will be blown to pieces along with the rest of us when your barrels ignite. Your uncle will be forgotten.'

'I have paid handsomely to see that he is not. He was a great man, and it is only right that some of Kerchier's hoard goes towards honouring his memory.'

'Harbert,' said Thurloe, his disdainful glance indicating exactly what he thought about the secretary's attempts to justify his actions. 'His murder was a mistake—'

'I received incomplete information,' interrupted Cary tersely. 'I thought *he* was the one selling false Certificates of Health, but it was his brother Matthew.'

He coughed again, raising his free hand to cover his mouth. He winced – even the light brush of lips on the inflamed skin caused him pain.

'You made mistakes with Pamela, too,' said Thurloe, and this time, the look he flashed at the shadows around Chaloner verged on the frantic. His fists were curled tightly at his sides, the knuckles white. 'Although she never knew your identity, given that you always approached her in plague costume.'

'The mistake was using her in the first place,' said Cary bitterly. 'I provided her with *sal mirabilis* to keep the Mims under control, but she sold it, kept the money for herself, and gave them coloured water. I sent her two warnings, which she ignored. I was sorry she fed my poison to Jasper, though. He was a good man, and deserved better.'

'Rycroft tried to retrieve the body from the plague pit, but you refused – not for reasons of public health, but because an alchemist would know the difference between plague and poison. The Edwards boys died the same way.' Thurloe raised his voice again, hoping Sugar would hear. 'You care nothing for the Mims. You let her dispatch them like rubbish.'

Cary smirked when Thurloe's ploy failed a second time. 'They *are* rubbish – incapable of completing even the most basic assignments. London will be better off without them.'

'But you managed to eliminate Pamela in the end.'

'Chaloner kindly locked her up and sent me the key. I was able to kill her like the others – a blow to the head and a drop of *acer* while she was not in a position to object. It was safer than sending her more of the diluted form. She died at once – unlike Jasper.'

'Leaving the pot of *sal mirabilis* behind,' finished Thurloe in a voice that shook with suppressed tension, 'which made folk think the stuff is poisonous. The canons' sales have gone through the roof, thanks to you.'

'That was a miscalculation on my part, but it will be rectified soon. Owen is dead, and his helpmeets in that disgusting scheme will follow him to the grave shortly.'

Like Thurloe, Chaloner was almost at his wits' end, but then his eye lit on the bodies. Owen was clearly dead, but Prayse's eyes were open – and they were full of rage. Chaloner felt the stirrings of hope. The treacherous physician would not be his first choice of allies, but he was hardly in a position to be picky. He edged to one side so that Prayse could see him, and made a series of gestures. Fortunately, the physician grasped at once what Chaloner wanted him to do. He nodded very slightly to indicate that he understood.

'Say your prayers, Suger!' yelled Thurloe suddenly, finally despairing of any invention from Chaloner, and so taking matters into his own hands. 'There will be an explosion any minute now, and you will die.'

'Shut up!' snarled Cary. He turned to the startled Mims. 'Ignore him.'

'Go to the door,' shouted Thurloe. 'You will find it locked. Cary is tying up loose ends, and no one who helped him will be left alive. Just *think* about it – why else would he murder Prayse Russell, a man who admired and respected him?'

When Cary turned to assure the felons that Thurloe was lying, Chaloner and Prayse made their move. Chaloner

431

pointed his gun at Cary and pulled the trigger. But Pamela's gun pulled savagely to the left, missing its target, so Chaloner lobbed the knife as well. At the same time, Prayse sat up and hurled two blades in quick succession, while Sugar discharged his musket and Cary fired his pistol.

Prayse's flying knives killed one of the Mims instantly and injured one more, while Chaloner's blade whipped past Cary and embedded itself in Suger's arm. Suger's musket ball took Prayse in the stomach. Cary's bullet went nowhere, but he fell to his knees, clutching the bloody remains of his hand.

There was a second of silence, followed by a cacophony of screams. Suger's were loudest, although his injury was by far the least serious. Cary released a keening wail of agony, while Stone shrieked from pure terror. The other two Mims howled their panic, too, and dashed up the steps to batter at the door, Suger staggering at their heels. Above their heads, the organ was blasting out a patriotic piece intended to inspire the faithful, which meant that neither gunfire nor cries were heard.

'You should have taken me into your confidence, Cary,' said Prayse in a low, rasping voice. He lay amid a spreading stain of red, and Chaloner knew the wound was mortal. 'Then I would not have examined your victims, and revealed things that led to you.'

'Confide in you?' sneered Cary, white-faced with pain. 'A corrupt and greedy physician who cares only for himself? I would sooner die!'

Thurloe knelt next to his erstwhile friend and murmured words of comfort, although he expected no deathbed apologies, and did not get them. Chaloner went to Cary, and began to search him for the key to the door.

432

'I do not have it.' Cary coughed again, and malice glowed in his eyes. 'You are too late anyway. Any moment now . . .'

'Fuses are unreliable,' said Chaloner with more confidence than he felt. 'They fizzle out for no reason.'

'Not these fuses – Prayse is nothing if not efficient. And even if by some miracle you do stop what I have set in motion, *you* will not survive. Not now.'

'You think you have the plague,' surmised Chaloner, 'which is why you chose to stay down here when any normal criminal would have run for cover.'

'Yes, and you have breathed my breath,' gloated Cary. 'You are doomed.'

'It is not the plague.' Chaloner pointed to the red-raw fingers on Cary's remaining hand. 'That is caused by *acer*. You must have spilled some on yourself when you dripped it into your victims' mouths, and your cough is from inhaling the fumes. You have managed to kill yourself! You should have paid more attention to your lessons as a tanner's boy.'

Cary stared at him in shock, but then shrugged. 'Well, it does not matter now, because none of us will escape – the door is barred from the outside.' He sneered. 'You think you are so clever, giving me the gun I lent you, so it is I who suffer. But you still cannot win.'

Chaloner gaped at him. 'You rigged it to misfire deliberately?'

'I expected you to use it days ago.'

Chaloner regarded him in disgust. 'All your other plans to kill me ended in disaster, too – Suger ambushed Lawrence instead of me at the Mitre; the *acer*-laced cheese at the Musick Hall ended up in *his* pantry; and as for Pamela's feeble efforts . . .'

433

A haunted look flashed across Cary's face. 'That cheese . . . Abigail might have . . . It does not bear thinking about.'

Chaloner began to clutch at straws in his desperation. 'She will not approve of what you aim to do tonight. She will be sickened by it, so tell me where the other kegs are hidden and we can——'

'They are somewhere you will never think to look,' jeered Cary. 'But Abigail will not think ill of me. She will believe that I died trying to save the cathedral. I shall forever be a hero in her eyes.'

Chaloner regarded him in incomprehension, struggling to equate the man who had worked so tirelessly for his city with the killer who aimed to blow up its most iconic building.

'But you helped me to eliminate all those names from Owen's list . . .'

'On Lawrence's orders – I did not volunteer. And I left you enough suspects to keep you busy.'

Knowing there was no point in trying to reason with Cary further, Chaloner ran up the stairs, elbowing the Mims out of the way. It took but a moment to see that Cary had been telling the truth: the door was barred from the outside, which meant the secretary had at least one more helpmeet, as he could not have done it himself.

Chaloner looked around wildly. A ladder lay nearby, used for cleaning the windows. He grabbed it and dragged it towards the door.

'A battering ram,' said Thurloe in understanding. 'Will it be strong enough?'

'Let us hope so – it is all we have.'

Without being told, Suger – now oblivious to his wound – grabbed one end, and snarled at his cronies to take the other, leaving the middle for Stone, Thurloe and Chaloner. The first blow did nothing except send a hollow boom echoing through the chapel. Cary staggered to his feet, and came to see what they were doing.

'It will not work,' he called mockingly, clutching a pillar for support. 'And do not think those thuds will be heard – I told Bing to play as loudly as he could. I thought of everything.'

'You told all our friends to come to the cathedral tonight,' said Suger, shaking with anger and fear. 'You promised us all free London Treacle after the service . . .'

'To ensure you all died,' said Thurloe bluntly. 'He did not want you as his private army, as we assumed, but so he could rid his city of thieves, profiteers and criminals.'

'London will be cleansed,' declared Cary with a fierce grin of triumph. 'They are scum, and will not be missed.'

His words did more than anything Chaloner could have said to encourage the Mims to greater efforts, and the next thump was delivered with such force that the hinges on the door squealed in protest. The third blow punched a hole through the centre of the wood.

Cary fell silent as Suger shoved his good arm through it and began to manoeuvre the restraining bar away. When the door swung open, Suger was almost knocked off his feet as his friends and Stone streamed past him.

'Clear the building,' shouted Chaloner to Thurloe, struggling to make himself heard over the resounding organ. 'I will look for the powder.'

They raced into the cathedral. It was eerily dark – night had fallen since they had been underground, but candles were in short supply and expensive, so very few had been lit. Then there was a brilliant flash and an ear-splitting roar, audible even over the organ. Chaloner glanced up in alarm, expecting to see the roof plummeting towards him. Then he recalled the storm that had been brewing.

'Just thunder and lightning,' he breathed in relief.

Thurloe headed for the organ loft. 'I will tell Bing to stop this infernal racket. Then we can make ourselves heard.'

Chaloner ran towards the nave, aware of a sharp, metallic odour in the air and the distinct sense that Nature was about to strike with a vengeance. He reached the crossing, and stopped in horror at the sight that greeted him.

There was a vast sea of heads – the service was far better attended than anyone could have imagined. People were packed together like fish in a barrel, most wearing scarves or masks to protect them against infection. The majority were poor, and at least half carried packs, suggesting that they planned to leave the city when the ceremony was over. How many had the plague? The child whose head lolled against his father's shoulder? The old woman who leaned so heavily on her son, her face fever-bright? Or the shivering Mim who stood surrounded by a gaggle of green-ribboned cronies?

'Have you seen any of our colleagues?' came a voice from behind him. It was Henchman, his pink face flushed with agitation; Cartwright was at his side. 'They have all disappeared, leaving us two to manage alone.'

The cathedral had evidently intended to put on a reassuring spectacle for London's beleaguered populace, as both clerics wore sumptuous ecclesiastical regalia. The reek of moth-repelling herbs suggested that the vestments had been hauled out of storage for the occasion.

'There will be an explosion at any moment,' Chaloner shouted at them. 'Get these people out. *Now!*'

Henchman opened his mouth to demand an explanation, but Cartwright heard the urgency in Chaloner's voice, and raced to obey at once, pulling the slower-witted canon with him. Moments later, the music stopped mid-fanfare, and Chaloner saw Bing and Thurloe clambering down from the organ loft. The low murmur of surprise from the congregation was drowned out by the next roll of thunder.

Chaloner began to search for the gunpowder, heart hammering so hard that he could barely hear what Cartwright and Henchman were yelling from the pulpit. He looked around in despair. The cathedral was enormous. How was he to find explosives that had – by Cary's own gloating admission – been very well hidden? He turned quickly when someone tapped his shoulder. It was Stedman.

'Where have you been these last few days?' the printer asked genially. 'I had hoped for some decent cross-change ringing while—'

'Get out!' Chaloner shouted, voice cracking with strain. 'The cathedral is about to collapse. Hurry, before it is too late! And take as many people with you as you can.'

Cartwright and Henchman were doing their best, but their warnings were mostly inaudible – a combination of the thunder and the irritable grumbles from the assembled masses when they failed to hear what was being yelled. Stedman grasped the situation at once, and his eyes took on a manic gleam.

'Tocsin bells! The congregation will certainly hear those. Wildbore! Kirton! Denton! Come with me. Your city needs you.'

His fellow ringers – masked against recognition – had been backing away, clearly afraid of what another encounter with Sancroft's envoy might entail, but Stedman was having none of it. He rounded them up briskly, and herded them towards the tower. Moments later, the thunder was joined by the urgent clang of alarm bells.

Fear rippled along the nave, and several people dived for the nearest exit. Their panic caused others to follow, and the doors were soon choked with folk trying to escape. Henchman, Bing and Cartwright scurried behind them like sheepdogs, rounding up the stragglers.

Desperately, Chaloner racked his brains, trying to think where the barrels might be hidden. Then Thurloe appeared, panting and wild-eyed.

'Cary tried to leave St Faith's, but Rycroft managed to stop him,' he gasped. 'He is no longer a problem. Have you searched the crossing yet? It is the heart of the cathedral, with an unstable tower above it. It is certainly the place that I would choose for a blast.'

Chaloner hurried there, dodging through the stampeding hordes. Then he heard someone calling his name. It was Leybourn, grinning his delight as he held a struggling Randall by the scruff of the neck.

'I have him at last,' he declared with savage glee. 'And he has a story to tell.'

'There are thirty kegs of gunpowder in here,' wailed Randall. 'Please! It is murder to keep me inside when the place is rigged to explode.'

'Tell them about the tomb,' ordered Leybourn, giving his prisoner a shake.

'Some of the barrels are in one,' cried Randall, growing more frantic by the moment. 'I heard Prayse Russell and

Val Cary talking about it. Now let me go. I do not want to die!'

'Which tomb?' demanded Thurloe urgently. 'There are hundreds of them in here.'

'I do not know,' wept Randall. 'They did not say. Mr Cary—'

'Cary!' exclaimed Chaloner. 'Of course! The nephew of Dean Valentine Cary – whose monument is in the south transept.'

Leaving Leybourn to escort Randall outside, Chaloner sprinted to the south transept, Thurloe at his heels. Together, they climbed over the barriers erected to keep people out. The floor showed signs of a fresh collapse, and when thunder boomed overhead, a shower of dust pattered down, shaken loose by the vibrations.

Chaloner inspected the tomb quickly. 'The mortar has been scraped away. It has been opened recently.'

He jammed his sword into the crack between lid and chest, and heaved with all his might. Nothing moved. Then Thurloe added his weight to the task, but the pressure was too great and the blade snapped. Thunder drowned out the ex-Spymaster's oath as he stumbled forward. Chaloner shoved the broken end of the weapon into the gap, and levered again, feeling the blood pound in his head with the effort.

The lid slipped an inch, just as another thunderclap reverberated through the building. There was a sharp snap and a puff of dust from behind them – more of the ceiling had fallen.

'Cary did not need explosives,' gasped Thurloe. 'The storm will bring the old place down without them. Listen to the rain!'

A deeper roar had joined the shriller crash of thunder, one that grew louder and louder until Chaloner could no longer hear the terrified wails of people trying to squeeze through the clogged doors, the furious jangle of the tocsin bells, or the frantic pleas of Henchman, Bing and Cartwright as they begged their flock to hurry. The lid shifted again. Heartened, he pushed harder, and eventually managed to shove the great slab back against the wall.

Dean Cary's final resting place comprised another stone-lined pit, and in it were the kegs, all lined up on top of a massive lead coffin. A fuse sizzled an inch from the nearest barrel. Chaloner leaned in and pinched it out just before it touched the wood. He staggered in relief, and gave Thurloe a weak grin. But Thurloe was still gazing into the vault.

'Nine,' he gulped. 'There are only *nine*! Where is the tenth?'

With horror, Chaloner saw he was right. He gaped at them in appalled disbelief, but at that moment, there was a sinister sound from above, even louder than the drumming downpour. He glanced up, and saw that an enormous crack had appeared in the ceiling.

'The rain!' he cried. 'It is adding too much weight to the roof.'

He grabbed Thurloe's arm and hauled him towards the barriers. The ex-Spymaster stumbled when a fragment of masonry caught him on the shoulder, but Chaloner dragged him on, and they reached safety just as a great lump of ceiling crashed to the floor. It was accompanied by an avalanche of water, some of which cascaded into Dean Cary's open tomb.

'Will that be enough to douse any—' began Thurloe.

He did not finish, because the floor of the south transept bubbled upwards, after which flames shot into the air, and there was a hot blast that blew them both from their feet. Smoke billowed, and burning debris began to patter down all around them. They lay with their hands over their heads until it subsided, then sat up carefully.

'They must have buried the last barrel under some of the rubble,' said Thurloe, yelling because the rain was pounding down even harder. Water splattered on the floor in a dozen places.

'The east wall,' cried Chaloner in alarm. 'It is coming down!'

They scrambled to their feet and ran, aware of a great crash behind them. They did not look back this time, but rushed over the crossing, into the north transept and out of the door on the other side.

They emerged into a scene of chaos. The rain teemed down with such force that people shrieked their terror. It bounced off the baked ground of the churchyard, and rushed in torrents towards the drains. And all the while, lightning flickered every few moments, and thunder crashed so loudly that many folk covered their ears with their hands.

Mayor Lawrence staggered towards them, hair plastered to his head and his fine burgundy suit sodden and stained.

'We are not ready,' he cried, pale with horror. 'If they rush the gates now . . . I thought we would have more time to prepare.'

'There will be no rushing,' shouted Thurloe, and nodded towards the library.

Cartwright and Henchman leaned out of its upper

windows, using them like pulpits, and whenever there was a respite from the din of thunder, they informed the cowering masses that the storm was God's judgement on those who aimed to flee the city. Without Antrobus, Matthew and Randall to bray otherwise, most folk believed them, and many began to hurry home, eager to be indoors, away from the elements.

'Is Monck standing by with his cannon?' asked Thurloe urgently.

'No, because I told him they would not be needed until after the service,' replied Lawrence unsteadily, 'which I thought was true. But folk started racing out of the cathedral before it had even begun . . .'

'You can blame your secretary for that,' said Thurloe, and gave a brief account of what had happened. Not surprisingly, the mayor did not believe him, so Thurloe invited him to St Faith's to see the culprit's body and the barrels in the tunnel.

Chaloner left them to it, and crept back to inspect the south transept. He was astonished to see that it still stood – it was only the ancient plaster that had fallen from the wall, and underneath were stones that gleamed clean and white. The roof was mostly intact, too, although it would require some serious restoration to make it waterproof again, while the floor was marred by a much smaller crater than he had expected.

'It will take more than one keg of powder to bring down this doughty old lady,' came a soft voice at his side. It was Bing. Rain had washed the black dye from his eyes, so he appeared almost normal. He rested one hand on a pillar. 'She will stand for a few more years yet. Oh, yes, she will.'

'You do not think the blast destabilised it?'

'The damage is superficial, and the Agents of God will not claim otherwise, because the loss of their leaders will leave them in disarray. She is safe at last.'

'How do you know some fanatic will not try again?'

Bing grinned, and the wildness returned to his eyes. 'One will, I am sure, because London is a city that breeds them. But not yet, not yet. You can sleep easy tonight.'

# Epilogue

The most violent storm that London had ever seen heralded a change in the weather, and it quickly became apparent that summer was over. Hints of gold and brown began to appear on the trees, and the evenings grew chilly. Having complained so bitterly about the heat, people now complained about the cold. Chaloner smiled at the banal predictability of it all.

He left the Mitre, much to Paget's dismay, and took up residence in Clarendon House while he waited for Sancroft to respond to his report. He took his hens with him, and installed them in the Earl's vegetable garden, where they began the process of denuding it of snails, worms, spiders and anything else that wriggled or crawled. He spent a lot of time there, taking quiet pleasure from their contentment.

Thurloe prepared to return to his family in Oxfordshire, but visited Clarendon House before he left, where he found Chaloner sitting on a bench near the potting shed, legs stretched comfortably in front of him. One chicken

445

preened on his knee, while the others scratched around his feet.

'You have found your true vocation, I see,' said Thurloe. 'Life as a poultryman suits you. I have never seen you so relaxed.'

'Probably because none of my birds are lunatics who want to blow things up,' replied Chaloner. 'Have you had any news from the cathedral? I have not been back there since . . .'

'Christopher Wren was summoned for an urgent consultation. Naturally, he was not told the truth, and all tales of explosions and gunpowder have been suppressed. Londoners think the storm did the damage.'

'Wren will be able to tell the difference. He is not a fool.'

'Well, if he did, he was too wise to say anything. In his opinion, the building is safe to use for now, although the south transept must be sealed off in the interests of public safety. However, he does not believe it will remain safe for long, and recommends that the Dean and Chapter demolish the whole thing and put his basilica in its place.'

'I bet he does,' muttered Chaloner. 'So Bing was right? The damage is superficial?'

'Yes, because most of the blast went upwards, towards a ceiling that is very high. It would have been different if all thirty barrels had ignited, of course. Then we *would* have been looking at rubble, because Gaundy's tunnel went perilously close to the crossing, and the whole central tower would have come down.'

Chaloner was silent for a while. 'Sancroft sent me to investigate a skeleton,' he said eventually, 'but we unearthed a plot to destroy his cathedral.'

'A plot that began with Kerchier,' said Thurloe, 'whom Cary killed because he felt it was the wrong time for a new St Paul's. He decided that five years after the Restoration *was* the right time, so he began to implement his first victim's scheme himself.'

Chaloner took up the tale. 'He poisoned Harbert by mistake, thinking he was involved in selling forged certificates; he killed William in order to remove the Agents' new hoard from men he felt were untrustworthy; he dispatched Prayse and Owen for their antics with false London Treacle; he planned to ensure that John and Francis were in the collapsing cathedral for the same reason; he got rid of Pamela for passing off coloured water as medicine—'

'And Upton, Pemper and Gaundy died to ensure that they never told anyone about the existence of the tunnel,' finished Thurloe.

'Speaking of Upton,' said Chaloner, 'what about the harm that his criminal antics did to your family? Protecting them is why you came to this plague-ravaged city, after all.'

Thurloe waved a dismissive hand. 'Oh, I had his union with Ursula declared null and void on a legal technicality five days ago. Now we can declare with complete truth that he was never one of us, and his penchant for easy money cannot sully our name.'

Chaloner turned his thoughts back to the Executioner. 'So where were Francis and John when they were supposed to be crushed with half of London? Have you seen them?'

Thurloe nodded. 'They suspected something was amiss when Owen failed to arrive for the service, and spent the crisis cowering at home. Sancroft offered them a choice: prison or exile. They chose the latter. He ordered them to give the Agents' hoard to Henchman, and it will be used to fund urgent repairs.'

'They handed it over willingly?'

'Oh, yes – they knew Sancroft would order their arrest if they refused. Meanwhile, Cartwright has been awarded Kerchier's canonical stall. He is young and energetic, and will do his best for St Paul's. Incidentally, I made some enquiries about Dean Cary. He had three legitimate sons, all of whom studied in Cambridge.'

'And how many bastards? Or should we call them "nephews"?'

'One – a boy who was apprenticed to a tanner, and so never enjoyed the privileged education afforded his half-brothers. It was a pity by all accounts, as he was by far the most talented. Dean Cary died forty years ago, ample time for our Cary to twist the truth about his heritage and forge himself a different career.'

'What was his real name? It was not Val Cary, or Owen would have included it on his list. I do not suppose it was Marmaduke Almond, was it?'

Thurloe blinked. 'How did you guess?'

Chaloner smiled. 'He made a remark about it being a ridiculous name when we spent the day working together, then told me that particular man – a tanner – had been dead for years. It was true, in a way. He must have changed his appearance dramatically, though, or people would have recognised him.'

'Henchman tells me that he did just that – it took him ten minutes of intense gazing before he was able to see the young tanner in the mature secretary's face. I have also learned that Cary changed his name when he entered Lawrence's employ – which he did by writing himself some glowing testimonials. But regardless of his deceit, Lawrence wants to bury him with his father in the south transept.'

'Why not? It will save space in some overcrowded cemetery.'

'Speaking of cemeteries, Matthew, Antrobus and Masley are in Newgate's – they died of the plague. It is difficult to mourn them when their selfishness may have killed thousands. There are new rules about Certificates of Health now – they will not be quite so easy to duplicate in future.'

'Have you heard from Will? Is he still in the city?'

'Gone back to Uxbridge, thank the good Lord. He will be safe there.'

'With Ester?' asked Chaloner, feigning a sudden and intense interest in his preening hen so he would not have to look Thurloe in the eye.

'Alone. Their betrothal is broken.'

Chaloner looked up in surprise. 'Really? Why?'

'Because they are ill-suited, and she is wise enough to know it. He is devastated of course, but he will recover. He always does. I rather think, though, that she met someone she decided she would rather have.'

'Did she?' asked Chaloner hopefully.

'But she realises that a union with him would be just as disastrous as one with Will, so she has elected to dispense with romance, and has hired a ship to ferry her and her fellow Quakers to Rhode Island instead. They will establish a community there, with its own church, market and farms. Rycroft will go with her.'

Chaloner experienced a sharp pang of loss. 'How will she fund such a costly venture?'

'She has received a windfall – a large legacy from an

elderly aunt. The old lady's death was most fortuitous, as the money appeared just when it was most needed.'

'Pamela's hoard!' Chaloner did not know whether to laugh or be angry. 'Ester must have known where it was all along. Down the well, probably, along with the fake London Treacle.'

'Yes, it was. But giving Quakers a chance to make new lives for themselves is a fitting use of it, and it is rather satisfying to know that Pamela would have been livid.'

'It is,' agreed Chaloner, and sighed. 'Perhaps I will sail to Rhode Island with them. I am tired of London and its intrigues.'

Thurloe held out a letter. 'I am afraid you cannot. The Earl wants you to join him in Oxford without delay, because there has been a murder in one of the Colleges. He says you are the only one who can catch the culprit and restore calm.'

'What about my hens?'

'You had better buy some cages. Perhaps we can all travel west together, and I shall host them in my garden until you are free to reclaim them.'

'We never did find the person who barred the door of St Faith's from the outside,' said Chaloner, reluctant to leave his haven of peace for the deadly undercurrents of Court. 'Perhaps I should stay here and look—'

'It was Tillison,' interrupted Thurloe. 'There must be some reason why he has been scurrying around so frantically ever since the storm, desperately assuring people that St Paul's is open for business. He is trying to make amends.'

'He is, but not for being in league with Cary.' Chaloner laughed suddenly. 'He spent the whole crisis fast asleep! He was mortified when Cartwright found him several hours later, and woke him up.'

'Well, the culprit is not Sancroft. Reliable sources tell me that he prefers the old cathedral to the one proposed by Wren. Besides, he is a good man, and St Paul's will do well with him at its helm. Assuming he ever returns, of course. The Mortality Bill was lower this week, but there were still more than fifty-five hundred plague deaths, and he will not come back unless it is safe.'

'So who did help Cary?' persisted Chaloner. 'There is no one left on our list.'

'It was probably another Mim,' shrugged Thurloe. 'In which case we shall never know his name. However, just in case it was someone else, I have set a trap.'

'What sort of trap?'

'I will tell you if it works. But come, old friend. We must pack, and depart from this poor, benighted city. I wonder if we shall ever see it again.'

The cathedral was very dark, particularly in the south transept, where the lamplight from nave and chancel did not reach. The man stood in front of Dean Cary's battered monument and wondered why his carefully laid plans had gone so horribly wrong. Once he had blocked the door to St Faith's, he had assumed that victory was his, but he had celebrated too soon. To have been thwarted at the very last second – he was sure it could not have been more – was the most bitter moment of his life.

With a heavy sigh, he raised his candle and peered inside the tomb – then recoiled in astonishment. The barrels of gunpowder were still there!

He stared at them in disbelief. They must have been forgotten in all the chaos following the storm – a mob had tried to rush the city gates, despite the warnings of

Henchman and Cartwright about the wrath of God; there had been flash floods; numerous skirmishes had broken out; and the Mims had used the opportunity to loot. As a consequence, the city had been in turmoil for days, so perhaps it was not very surprising that the gunpowder in the grave had been overlooked.

And it meant he had another chance to finish what he had started. He reached down and touched one of the kegs. It was damp from the rain, but he was familiar enough with ordnance to know that its contents would still be dry. All it needed was a fuse, and the crumbling cathedral would be gone for ever. Heart pounding with excitement, he looked around for some suitable kindling. He would light a fire inside the tomb, and then run for his life before the powder ignited.

'Mayor Lawrence,' came a voice from behind him, making him start in alarm. 'What are you doing here so late?'

It was Bing, who had taken to visiting the cathedral at odd times since the trouble. Lawrence stifled his irritation. He should have anticipated the violist's presence. Now he would have to come back another time and set the blast.

'Just looking at the place where my secretary will lie,' he replied, forcing a smile. 'Abigail and I will bury him here tomorrow.'

'Cary, Cary, Cary,' sang Bing, and loped away to make his report to Thurloe.

# Historical Note

Sir John Lawrence was actually a very brave man. Unlike most of his fellow aldermen, he did not leave London when the plague began to rage, but stayed at home (he lived just north of Cornhill with his wife Abigail and their nine daughters) and proceeded to work tirelessly, implementing the government's plague measures. He was Lord Mayor from November 1664 to November 1665, then went on to other prestigious posts. During the plague, he liaised with General George Monck, who was appointed to represent the government while the King and his Court enjoyed the safety of Oxford.

The plague measures, which did indeed include setting huge bonfires to purify the air, had only limited success, because neither the authorities nor the medical profession understood what they were dealing with. The fires raged for three days in early September, until a chance downpour put them out. One fire was at the west end of St Paul's.

The death rate rose alarmingly through a long and hot summer until its height in mid September. The 'remedies' and preventatives listed in *The Approved Plague*

*Physitian* include London Treacle, *sal mirabilis*, smoking, and chewing tobacco, and if all else failed, the author recommended 'a Godly and Penitent Prayer Unto Almighty God, for Our Preservation, and Deliverance Therefrom'.

The city was never locked down as suggested here – Samuel Pepys' diary tells us that he came and went at will. However, there was an attempt to reduce travel, and for a short time, only those with a Certificate of Health signed by a physician and a priest were allowed to leave. This scheme quickly proved to be impractical and was abandoned.

Poor St Paul's Cathedral was in a very sorry state by 1665. Part of the south transept had collapsed, its central tower was unstable, the nave walls were bowed, and it had suffered decades of neglect and abuse. It was patched up in the 1630s, when the quixotic Inigo Jones began to slap incongruous Italianate façades over the Gothic exterior. His peculiar west portico is shown on several contemporary drawings.

During this process, he demolished part of St Gregory's Church, much to the fury of its congregation. They complained to Parliament, and he was ordered to put it back up again. At the same time, the parishioners, with nowhere to bury their dead, began to dig themselves a crypt, which the Dean and Chapter feared might undermine the foundations of the cathedral. Digging stopped when a strip of land was donated for them to use as a cemetery.

The civil wars and a lack of funds stopped Jones from completing what he had started, and twenty years later, a new commission was appointed, which included Christopher Wren. His advice – to demolish the old cathedral and build one designed by him instead – was contentious, and feelings ran high on both sides. All the angst was for nothing in the end, of course, as St Paul's was destroyed in the Great Fire of 1666.

The Dean in 1665 was William Sancroft, later Archbishop of Canterbury. He fled to Tunbridge Wells when the plague erupted, and was kept informed of events by John Tillison, his Clerk of Works, and Stephen Bing, famed violist, music copyist and minor canon. Other canons in the 1660s include Benjamin Stone, Richard Owen and three Halls: William, John and Francis, although they may not have been related. Robert Kerchier died on 1 March 1645, but his stall remained vacant until Thomas Cartwright took it in 1665. It is not known if Canon Richard Henchman was brother to the more famous Humphrey, Bishop of London, but he was the cathedral's treasurer from 1663 until 1672.

Valentine Cary was Dean of St Paul's until 1621, after which he became Bishop of Exeter. He was buried in old St Paul's, and had three (legitimate) sons.

Other characters in *The Executioner of St Paul's* were also real. Matthew Rycroft was a churchwarden, who was entrusted with his parish's valuables during the plague, and handed them back intact when the danger was over. Sir Arnold Harbert lived in Creed Lane, while Matthew Harbert and George Antrobus lived east of St Paul's Churchyard (although not together). In 1666, Ralph Masley was living on Paul's Chain, Prayse Russell lived on Carter Lane, and Thomas Suger inhabited the intriguingly named Pissing Alley.

King's Head Court was a poor, mean place, home to Widow Ball, Widow Nay, Jasper Carew, and John and Robert Edwards. Joshua Kirton was Pepys's bookseller, and had a shop in St Paul's Churchyard. His brother William was Master of the Company of Stationers. I took the liberty of switching their first names, so as to avoid the confusion of too many Williams. Joshua Kirton's apprentice was a 'hunchback' named Randall. And there was indeed a loose band of criminals known as the Mims operating in London at this time.

Pepys frequented the Mitre Inn in London House Yard. Its owner William Paget built a 'Musick Hall' there, which was famous for its entertainment. John Hayes was the owner of the Turk's Head Coffee House, which was near the Mitre, while Outridge's Coffee House stood at the junction of Creed and Carter lanes.

John Thurloe, Cromwell's Secretary of State and Spymaster General, was not in London in early September 1665. He was at his home in Great Milton, Oxfordshire, celebrating the wedding of his wife's sister Ursula to the much younger John Upton. William Leybourn was the surveyor who produced a map of London after the Great Fire. He remained a bachelor all his life.

The seventeenth century saw the beginnings of the peculiarly British art of change ringing. The theory of 'cross-changes' was explained in *Tintinnologia* (1671), although bell-ringing societies had been in existence for at least four decades by then. Two early ringers were Robert Pemper and Edward Flower; ones active in post-Restoration England include Godfrey Wildbore, Thomas Denton, John Gaundy and Fabian Stedman. The practice still thrives today, and new recruits are always welcome. For more information about how to learn – and it's a lot of fun – visit the website of the Central Council of Church Bell Ringers at www.cccbr.org.uk.